ALSO BY ZANE KOTKER

Bodies in Motion

A Certain Man

WHITE RISING

WHITE RISING

a novel

Zane Kotker

ALFRED A. KNOPF NEW YORK 1981

THIS IS A BORZOI BOOK
PUBLISHED BY ALFRED A. KNOPF, INC.

 Published in the United States by Alfred A. Knopf, Inc., New York, and simultaneously in Canada by Random House of Canada Limited, Toronto. Distributed by Random House, Inc., New York.

Library of Congress Cataloging in Publication Data

Kotker, Zane. White rising.

1. King Philip's War, 1675–1676—Fiction. I. Title.
PS3561.0845W5 1981 813'.54 80–20011
ISBN 0–394–40776–8

Manufactured in the United States of America

FIRST EDITION

Typography and binding design by
VIRGINIA TAN

Map by David Lindroth

For David Kotker,

born in America

Author's Note

Most Americans know nothing of King Philip's War, a struggle which was to be re-enacted, with modifications, westward across the country for two hundred years. The war began in Plimouth Colony in the summer of 1675, though the momentum to fight had been growing for more than a generation. When men first sailed from England to make themselves a home in the new world, they were frightened of its indigenous farmers and fishers, and scornful, too. Nevertheless, some of the more religious of the settlers on the coast of what would be Massachusetts made friends with the local inhabitants and tried to be honest with them; alongside the pietists there were adventurers, and some of these also befriended the local people. Slowly, over fifty years, the various newcomers moved a few score miles inland and discovered that something was wrong. Though most of the earlier Englishmen had sailed across an ocean to "advance the Kingdom of our Lord Jesus Christ, and to enjoy the liberties of the gospel in purity and peace," the Englishmen were now "further dispersed upon the seacoasts and rivers than was first intended." And they were no longer quite so welcome.

Those who fought the Englishmen knew nothing of a year numbered 1,675. Theirs was a confederacy of tribes known as Wampanoag, which means "the land of the white rising"—that is, of the daybreak, the sunrise, the east. They called their leader *massa-soit*, which was not a name but a title that acknowledged its holder as the foremost of many leaders within the confederacy. The turkey-shooting Massasoit who is recalled today in elementary-school pageants at Thanksgiving time was a middle-aged man when the Englishmen set foot on his domains.

He welcomed them for rather pressing reasons of his own. His second son, whom the Englishmen dubbed Philip, and then King Philip, inherited a confederacy grown weak as a result of its contact with the English. Both courting and delaying the war that his father had forbidden, Philip found himself obliged to go among his people's old enemies to gather sufficient fighting men. When the war did erupt, in the thirteenth year of Philip's leadership, it took the lives of one out of ten of the English settlers: men, women and children. It took more than that from the daybreak people.

Though I began this novel with the hope of being accurate in all historical and psychological details, I found that goal impossible, perhaps even undesirable. Gradually, I gave way to the contradictory impulse of fiction in my attempt to retell a classic American story.

Acknowledgments

For help of various sorts, I wish to thank Joyce Berman; John Bowman; Andrew Cahoon; Ruth Crawley and Yvonne Peters of the Wampanoag Indian Museum in Mashpee, Massachusetts; Rosamond Dauer; James Deetz, formerly Acting Director of Plimouth Plantation; Robin Dizard; Arnold Eagle; Fran Gillespie; Lyman Gilmore; Charles and Cynthia Goff; Albert Goulding; Barbara Hail of the Haffenreffer Museum of Brown University; Nancy Hall; Jean C. Hickcox; Mildred House; Susan Jonas; Mike Kirby; Norman, David and Ariel Kotker; Robert Kotlowitz; Helmut Nichol, Curator of Arms and Armor at the Metropolitan Museum of Art; Hugh and Marilyn Nissenson; Johanna Plaut; Maurice Robbins of the Bronson Museum, Attleboro, Massachusetts; Michael Rosenthal; Neal Salisbury; Irving Shaffer; Alan Simpson; David Stemple; Carol Sturm; Shirley Tomkievicz; Milton Travers; Margaret Uroff; Pierre and Marion Vuillemier; Donald Weeks; Donna Whiteman; Donald Willard; and Ellen Wilson, Curator of Eastern Indians at the Haffenreffer Museum. My opinions are not necessarily those of any of the above, but their aid made research a joy and rewriting less lonely. Certain helpful institutions not mentioned above include: the American Museum of Natural History; the New-York Historical Society Library; the Museum of the American Indian, Heye Foundation; the Museum of Modern Art, Department of Film; the Northampton Historical Society; the Old Colony Museum, Taunton, Massachusetts; the Neilson Library at Smith College; and the MacDowell Colony. I would also mention Gloria Loomis and Bob Gottlieb, without whom I might still be wandering over the landscape to which I owe my first and final thanks.

Contents

A Note on Names

Wampanoag children were given names at birth but chose new names for themselves when they grew into men and women, or when great events prompted a change. Boys chose their adult names when at age fifteen they left the people and were led into an unfamiliar stretch of woods to spend the hardest months of the winter alone. The several names of Philip are found under Metacomet. Wampanoag names that do not appear on this list refer to other than people; that is, to locations or to tribes or confederacies. The tribe and its home were called by a single word, as with "Pokanocket," which is used either for the lands or the people. An asterisk indicates a completely fictional person.

Annawon: Great-man of Squannock and war captain of the Wampanoag.

Corbitant: Great-man of Mattapoiset and Pocasset; father (probably) of Weetamoo and of Metacomet's wife.

Hobomok: The trickster-like god of the hunter, to whom the wise-man turns for aid in illness or war, or whenever the natural course of events seems to demand alteration; the older of two gods I have called brothers, a generous god but unreliable.

*Johettit: The older of two brothers whose father left Pokanocket to live among Englishmen in Rehoboth; the name means "I will fight." (A Wampanoag did apply to live at Rehoboth, but records don't show if he was received.)

Kiehtan: The younger of the two brotherlike gods; the giver of seeds; the reliable god of order or fate; the unchangeable. (Kiehtan and Hobomok were two prime gods, though there were many others.)

*Kuttiomp: A friend and counselor of Metacomet.

Massasoit: The man called this by Englishmen called himself Ousamequin, which means "yellow feather." Greatest-man of the Wampanoag and father of Wamsutta and Metacomet.

Matoonas: Great-man of Pakachoog (near Worcester, Massachusetts), a member of the Nipmuck confederacy.

Metacomet: This seems to be the prime name of the man called Philip. The name Pometacom is very close to it, varying only in suffix and prefix. Metacomet is probably the name the boy gave himself: in documents he signed as a child, his name appears as Tasomacon. He was later nicknamed Wakwases–the crooked one and Wakwasesowannet–the crooked one of the southwest or southland—both names carry the meaning of "fox."

*Mishquock: A friend and counselor of Metacomet.

Naonanto: Greatest-man of the Nahiganset—or Narragansett, as the Englishmen would say. The people of this confederacy lived west of the bay called by their name today and were early sought out by French traders; Canonchet was another of his names.

Neimpauog: Metacomet's son (though his actual name is unknown).

*Nomatuck: Mishquock's son.

*Otan-nick: Younger brother of Johettit; the name means "a man of the town."

Petananuet: A praying man of Pocasset who married the widow Weetamoo.

Philip: See Metacomet.

Sassamon: A Massachuset; disciple of John Eliot; secretary to Massasoit and his sons.

Sunconewhew: Metacomet's younger brother; as did several other Wampanoag, Sunconewhew attended the "Indian" college at Harvard.

Tuspaquin: Great-man of Assawampset; husband of Metacomet's sister.

Unkompoin: Younger brother of Massasoit.

Wamsutta: Older brother of Metacomet; he was given the name Alexander by the Englishmen, who considered the names Alexander and Philip to be sufficiently pagan for bestowal on leaders refusing to be Christianized.

*Weskautaug: Wise-man of Pokanocket.

Weetamoo: Daughter of Corbitant; wife of Wamsutta, Petananuet and others; great-woman of Pocasset and sister to Metacomet's wife.

Great-man and great-woman: I have chosen the phrase "great-man" to translate "sachem" because it's without the connotations that "sachem" or "chief" bear. At this time in Wampanoag history, a great-man did pass his position on to his sons, though this was a fairly recent development. If a great-man had no sons, he could give the position to his wife or daughters.

Wise-man: I have chosen this phrase because it doesn't bring with it the connotations inherent in "medicine man" or "pawaw"; also to balance great-man, a balancing which reflects one of the functions expected of a wise-man.

The English names are virtually all historical, except for the members of the Peck, Strong and Hoskins families, and a few others. With the Wampanoag material, there was so little recorded that a novelist could feel justified in inventing characters. With the English material, it is quite different. Yet I have taken even more liberties here, producing a Noah Newman alien to the one recorded in history and a Preserved Abell out of whole and different cloth from the shroud in which I might have read his features.

WHITE RISING

"My father fed them when they were forlorn, a handful; they flourished and increased and got possession of a great part of his territory; my brother was seized and thrown into illness. With me, they disarmed my people, and took their land. I am determined that I will not live until I have no country." Philip spoke these words.

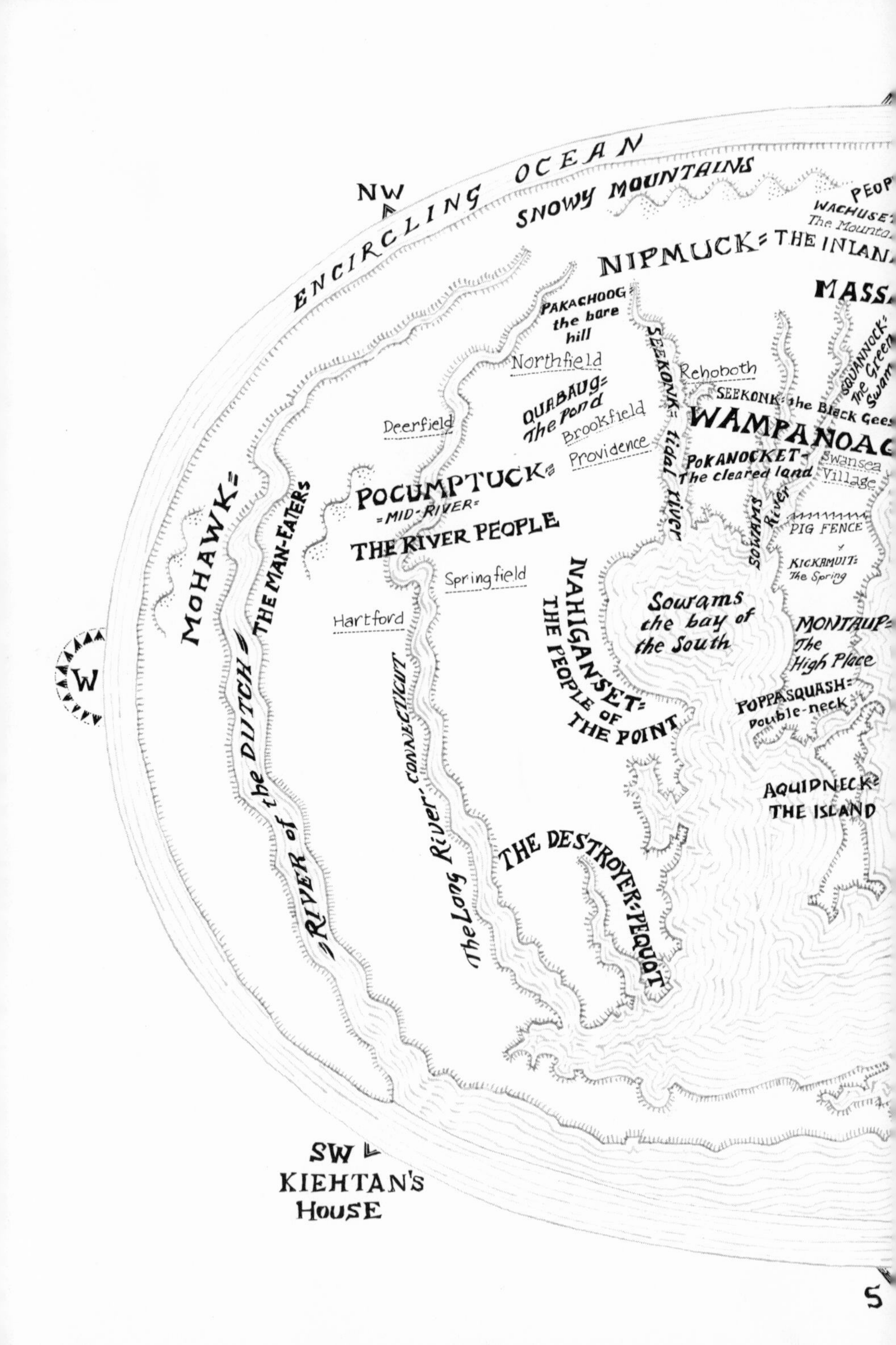

ENCIRCLING OCEAN
SNOWY MOUNTAINS
NW
W
SW
KIEHTAN'S HOUSE
S
NIPMUCK = THE INLAN
WACHUSET
PAKACHOOG = the bare hill
Northfield
SEEKONK = tidal river
Rehoboth
SEEKONK = the Black Gees
SQUANNOCK = the Green Swam
WAMPANOAG
QUABAUG = The Pond
Brookfield
Providence
Deerfield
POKANOCKET = The cleared land
Swansea Village
POCUMPTUCK = = MID-RIVER = THE RIVER PEOPLE
MOHAWK = THE MAN-EATERS
PIG FENCE
SOWAMS River
KICKAMUIT = The Spring
Springfield
NAHIGANSET = THE PEOPLE OF THE POINT
Sowams the bay of the South
Hartford
MONTAUP = The High Place
RIVER of the DUTCH
The Long River = CONNECTICUT
POPPASQUASH = Double-neck
AQUIDNECK = THE ISLAND
THE DESTROYER = PEQUOT

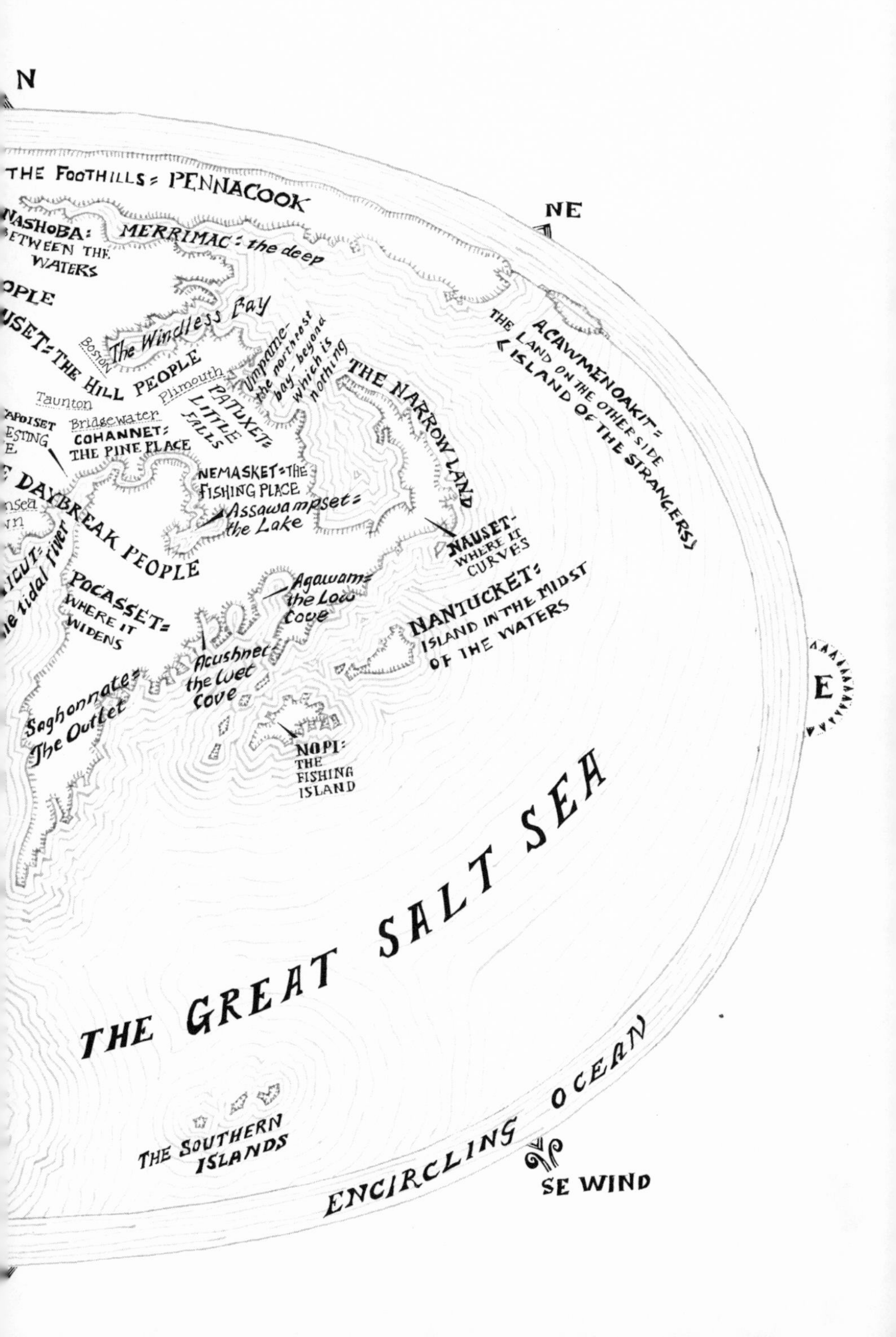
N
THE FOOTHILLS = PENNACOOK
NASHOBA: BETWEEN THE WATERS
MERRIMAC: the deep
NE
The Windless Bay
Boston
THE HILL PEOPLE
Plimouth
PATUXET = LITTLE FALLS
Umpame - the northeast bay - beyond which is nothing
THE NARROW LAND
ACAWMENOAKIT = THE LAND ON THE OTHER SIDE (ISLAND OF THE STRANGERS)
Taunton
Bridgewater
COHANNET: THE PINE PLACE
NEMASKET = THE FISHING PLACE
Assawampset = the Lake
DAYBREAK PEOPLE
NAUSET - WHERE IT CURVES
POCASSET = WHERE IT WIDENS
Agawam = the Low Cove
NANTUCKET = ISLAND IN THE MIDST OF THE WATERS
Acushnet the Wet Cove
E
Saghonnate = The Outlet
NOPI: THE FISHING ISLAND
THE GREAT SALT SEA
THE SOUTHERN ISLANDS
ENCIRCLING OCEAN
SE WIND

 I

SEED-TIME AND SUMMER

"You will never see his like again among the Indians; from anger he was soon reclaimed; easy to be reconciled toward those who had offended him; his reason was such that he could receive advice from mean men; and he governed his people better with few blows than others did with many. Truly loving where he loved, he has ofttimes restrained the malice of the Indians against the English . . . he is the most faithful friend the English have." These words were spoken of the old man whom the Englishmen called Massasoit. In Pokanocket, where the names of the dead are never said out loud, this one is now called the great-man who befriended the strangers. He died in the fortieth winter of the coming of the strangers and his sons stood in his place after him, the elder for a short time only: then came the second son.

1

She was there again. He saw the black circle of her eye, inside the brown circle, as it appeared to widen and narrow, widen and narrow. He looked at the pinkness coming into the light skin of her cheeks, the way it comes into the skin of English-women. As usual, he couldn't see the color of her hair, which was hidden by the black hood of the cloak. The closer he looked at her, the farther she moved from him, growing smaller. From here he could see how the dark hood fell to her shoulders and how her shoulders curved down to her arms and how the right arm was held forward, the sleeve dropping open at the wrist. Her palm was up and flat out and on it sat the small, perfect fox. He took a step toward her and she was gone. Gone. Good. He turned with relief and saw the snow, its whiteness in the moonlight. He had been born in winter, and knew its secrets. Winter would protect and shelter him. Above his head, so cold now on the snow, he saw the trees standing tall and mute. They held out their branches and welcomed him, naked as he was. The white eyes of the gods glinted from every branch and they hailed him. Again, the brother gods came to him, bringing the two names. They were tall, both of them, and looked like twins, though, as usual, he couldn't see them so clearly as he did the woman; they were more like presences at his sides, right and left. "Here," said one, "this name is for peace." "And this," the other said, "this name is for war." He opened his mouth to say "I want both." But they didn't hear him, and only leaned down, their long arms dangling, to clothe him in the two names. He was safe again, from the woman.

In the summer woods he opened his eyes. The world did not appear. He raised his head but there was no sign of daybreak.

Mist blew against his face. Beyond the pines the tidal river flapped like a great heart beating. Nearer, he heard the sounds of hundreds of men breathing as they slept. But he didn't know who lay beside him. He must be more careful. He had flung himself down carelessly, the death dance beating in the soles of his feet.

The three would die today.

Was that an eye? Something glowed in the darkness to his right. He raised his good hand and moved it through the space that separated him from whatever was glowing. It didn't blink. Then he remembered: silver. A silver coin had been tied into the hair of one of the two brothers who had come to him on horseback from the town out on the plain. Their father had been of the people but had long ago cut his hair and gone to live among Englishmen and plant wheat. The sons were returning: "We have come to fight in your war."

His war!

The bitter river flapped against its banks. He sat up. He could make out the shapes of trees, but nothing of color. It might start today, his war. At daybreak, when the three men would be hanged in Plimouth. If any of them spoke his name as the ropes slid around their necks, the war could begin. By sunset the soldiers would be here. Jerked by the neck on ropes, that's what Englishmen did with those who had murdered. Betrayers of the people they split into four parts and took the head to ram onto a pole.

"For the murderer, I use the club," he had explained in the rum houses, sitting in the big chair his friends always gave him. His friends, their green eyes wide, leaned forward to hear him. "A murderer kneels at my feet and opens his mouth to sing. I raise my club and sink it fast down through the hard bones into the softness of the brains. If the murderer does not cry out, the people cheer. Now, for a traitor I use the long knife. I make a shallow cut here, at the wrist, and pull the skin down and peel it over the fingertips. He sings. If he does not, the people come laughing with their torches to burn him. But," he had added last time, fingering the frill at the wrist of his English shirt, "no man has yet betrayed me." That trip to the rum house had been when the ice was on the rivers. When it broke, the purpled body of John Sassamon washed up on the shore at Assawampset.

It must be near daybreak. He stood. He made his way through sleeping forms toward the cedar path, his feet familiar with the way, even in darkness. From the ground came the soft, sluggish call of the brown dove.

John Sassamon. The round, wide faces of the people of the hill appeared behind his eyes. The wide-faced Sassamon had cut his hair short and learned to speak Englishmen's words as fast as they spoke them. And Sassamon had learned to take the words out of the air and flatten them into signs for the eye. Sassamon called himself John and sang to the Englishman's god. Sassamon came down from his own people and spoke of the Englishman's god among the people of the lake. Sassamon had betrayed the people over and over. Sassamon had whispered of the war to Englishmen.

It was right that Sassamon be killed.

So he had sent the three men to the lake as his long knife, telling them to make it appear to be an accident. But when Sassamon's body washed up, bruised and empty of water, the Englishmen at Plimouth had found witnesses and taken the three men off and boarded them up in a house and judged them.

Judged them! They were his to judge!

He reached the start of the uphill path.

Someone was watching him. He turned his head slowly: half the world lies behind a man's neck.

A man's form stepped out of the darkness: "I'll climb to the high place with you."

It was Weskautaug, the wise-man.

"Why should I be climbing Montaup?"

Neither could quite see the other.

"To speak to the three, to guide their feet. You caused them to die. You sent them to kill the preacher."

The great-man laughed. "Many think I sent them!" Tell nothing, leave no signs on the path.

As they made their way up the cedar path, the high whistle of sparrows floated toward them.

"Suppose I did send them." The great-man walked in front. "Suppose they found the traitor sitting on the ice beside his fishing hole. Suppose my careless nephew hit him on the head. Suppose my counselor pressed the breath from his neck and my counselor's son pushed him into the cold water. Would it be improper for me to cast out a traitor?"

"You should have asked for agreement." The wise-man's voice had complaint in it.

"That isn't necessary on matters of betrayal."

"Not my agreement! You should have talked with your counselors. Or are you like Josiah Winslow at Plimouth, who carries a bag of laws and asks no man for agreement?"

The cedar path would soon divide and one branch of it steepen.

"Agreement about what, then? About an accident?" The great-man's voice came again from the darkness. "Suppose the traitor wasn't murdered? After all, a hat and a gun and a basket of fish were found beside his fishing hole. It was an accident!"

Behind him the wise-man said nothing.

The great-man went on. "Come, be glad that a wise-man who taught of the Englishman's god is dead! Those who listened to . . . the traitor, the drowned man, may now listen to you. Yes, the people of the lake, as well as we of the cleared land, may listen to you now." Here he stopped himself from promising anything. He'd come too close to the old anger that lay between the two men.

Behind him Weskautaug's breath came faster. "You killed the traitor to slow the war! It brought Plimouth's nose close to us and that made the people of the point leave us, a thousand men! Some say you only pretend to want war. That you love Englishmen!" Weskautaug paused, and went on. "And we know who it was you called to us long ago when your brother grew sick and died."

That was part of the old anger.

"My brother was poisoned!" The great-man tried to twist the argument aside.

"You called Johneliot."

"It's two words. John Eliot." The great-man slowed the pace and let silence grow.

A swallow swooped toward them and away.

"Tell me, then, where the dreamer walked." Weskautaug withdrew himself to matters in which a wise-man has authority. "Where did he travel, your dreamer? The dreamer of the son who comes lately to war?"

"Let me examine it." The great-man ignored the other's addition of "to war" to his name. Metacomet–the son who comes lately: that was the name he had called himself, so far. He began, instead, to speak, very slowly, is if struggling to remember. "I shut my eyes. I saw in front of my feet . . . that there were two paths . . . stretching forward, exactly alike. On each path I saw far ahead of me . . . the backs of the old ones walking. 'Ho! Old men!' I called out to them . . . to ask the way, to know the real path . . . from the shadow path. But none turned to show me his face. None heard me. They do not hear . . . those of our generation." He savored the last words, words which referred to his secret name, as yet unspoken, but chosen in a pair with Metacomet long ago. And he leaned toward the wise-man, as if to encourage him to believe this false recitation.

"But I told you to send the dreamer to Plimouth!" Again the wise-man complained. "To shut the three men's mouths."

"He was searching for . . . the path." They were approaching the place where the path they were following split, and upward, near the top of the hill, there was a sense of the coming light.

"The dreamer was to plug the three throats with silver coins. So they won't talk. So the Englishmen won't come for you!"

"If the three speak and Plimouth sends its soldiers, we will stand." Metacomet's voice no longer halted.

"I can silence them for you."

"What happens happens." Metacomet could not make out the other man's face when he stopped on the path and turned to look. "Leave this to me and busy yourself bringing back to us all those who cut their hair and eat cows' flesh."

"Not pig?"

The wryness of the wise-man's voice made Metacomet laugh. "You should try it!"

"I'm going now." The presence at Metacomet's back drew farther to the right, along the path that circled the lower slope of Montaup. Metacomet walked slowly until he could no longer hear Weskautaug. Then he started rapidly up the hill. It must not be Weskautaug who silenced the three men.

Metacomet passed the cedar grove where gray-haired John Eliot had stood, speaking to the people of the cleared land. There had been wisdom in calling John Eliot, though the Englishman's words sounding through the grove had pleased many: "There are not many gods, but one. He is Father, Son, and Holy Spirit. He that is Father made the land and the river, beautifully and well, five thousand years ago, my friends, and more. He made the first man, Adam, to rule over this lower world. But Adam disobeyed him. So we die. Then He that is Son became a second Adam, and obeyed perfectly, to show us how. So we live. He that is a dreamer enters each of us, to make sure we rise straight up to judgment on the last day." The tall men and women of Pokanocket had leaned too quietly toward the smaller man in the soft light under the cedars. But three is not one and Metacomet had found out what he wanted to know, when he had invited John Eliot. He had found out what John Eliot feared most: it was numbers.

He climbed higher, past the hollow where his mother had taught him to speak to the old ones. Then he came out from under the trees and onto the edge of the great bare space that covered the top of the hill.

"*Hoo! Koo koo koo koo.*" Metacomet made the sound of the brown dove, once too often.

A lookout leaned from a tree not far off and called back to him: "There's nothing moving." The lookout spoke as if he were one of Annawon's men, from the green swamp.

"Expect the runner from Plimouth at noon." As Metacomet walked across the cool quartz, bits of ash from last night's torches blew against his legs. Here were the foot holes where he had stood thirteen summers ago, hailed to power after his brother's death by the thousand warriors of the daybreak people. Now the net of the daybreak people was broken and he had only a few hundred fighting men. His father had had thirty towns; he had fewer than fifteen. He must bind a new people from those to the north and west who did not yet cut their hair. He'd tried it, with the people of the western point, but they'd left him as soon as John Sassamon's body washed up and the Englishmen called their witnesses.

"*Yo hah weh hee!*" he sang at the top of the hill, for he was sure that Weskautaug was listening. Facing east, he saw that a white curve of light was gathered over the dark lump of Weetamoo's hill on the other side of the tidal river. Behind that hill stretched the daybreak people's string of salt marshes and coves, all the way out past the wet cove and the low cove to the narrow land, where so many of his father's lost towns were. Out there at the narrow land's easternmost tip was where the day's sun stood up out of the ocean. It turned Nauset's brooks a glimmering blue. Out there his own mother woke among her brothers, men who planted rye so they could make the Englishmen's drink and see the one god. From there the white rising spread itself slowly over rocks and water to bring light back to all the bays and coves of Wampanoag, both salt and sweet. Back even to Weetamoo's hill where the loud-spoken woman who had been his brother's wife slept, where her three hundred warriors slept, shunning the dance he had called when the judges met at Plimouth.

"*It dazzled my eyes, the river.*" Turning, he sang to the

second of the eight points of the world, loud as he could. Southeast lay the misty outlet–Saghonnate, the outlet which led to the salt sea. Over there across the outlet slept three hundred and fifty more men who should be dancing with him. But their small, shrunken great-woman wanted only peace and to drink rum with her new neighbor, an Englishman. "Have you no rum?" she had complained in her odd voice to Metacomet at his daughter's funeral. "When I dance at home, my neighbor Benjaminchurch brings rum for us all." He had not even corrected her pronunciation. Six hundred and fifty men kept from him by two immovable women. And then, there was his sister's fifty at the lake.

"*White in the morning whiteness, shimmering.*" He turned again. Southward in the gray light was the dark sweep of the island–Aquidneck, once his father's. In a rum house there Metacomet had been turned away: "Not you, boy!" Southwest and west lay the great bay. It glittered dully like the flat blades of knives. On its farthest shores and overland to the southwest slept the ruined Pequot, who crouched in Englishmen's barns and covered their mouths with their hands, as women do. These had fought Englishmen. These had lost everything. Westward across the bay, on the nearer shore, the shore that he could see, slept the thousand warriors lost to him. "Not now," Naonanto had said, fingering a coin. "No dancing now. John Leverett of Boston will be watching me too sharply, because of a drowned man." Trade, that was all that ever stirred the Nahiganset. "We will grow rich together learning metal work," Metacomet had promised these men once. "But we already know pewter." The men of the point held up buttons from their molds in reply.

"*The oaks and the ashes bend.*" Northwest and far off lived the once-wealthy people of the river, who now scratched at Englishmen's fields. When he'd first traveled to them, he'd used his brother's words: "The Englishmen have a hundred towns, but men from each of our towns can be hidden inside theirs on a single daybreak. We will fire their houses all at once, at one dawn, and they will run for their ships and leave us." The men of the river looked at their feet. West of them at the edge of the world lived the Mohawk, who would not even send canoes to Metacomet to hear him speak.

"*A new people cries,* . . ." Northward were the inland people, living on low hills by ponds and fresh-water brooks. These he warned of John Eliot, who already brought them spinning wheels. Seven hundred and fifty fighting men among the inland people, if he could get them. If he had another summer to travel, to talk. Nearer toward the north, where the neck joined the mainland and he could see a bit, lay what was once the cleared land. His own! Yet not his own. In the glint of the pre-dawn light he could make out some slanted roofs past the pig fence. Why had the Englishmen come here? In the rum houses his English friends gave him many answers. A skim of brightness came over their eyes when they did it and they shifted their weight on the ground, as if they wanted to stand more heavily or be as tall as he. To the left, at the greatest extent of his vision, he could make out the dark line of the four-sided fence that ran around the short, soft grass at the center of Rehoboth. So much space they needed for a town! Rehoboth was a giant squash, choking its neighbors.

"*I am* . . ." Northeast lay the path to Plimouth. If they jerked the ropes at sunrise, it would be now. Beyond, over water, were the hill people crouching on their knees around Boston, and far off the Pennacook, who ran into woods at the sound of the word "war."

". . . *born.*" Eastward again and Metacomet finished his song as bright yellowness shot up over Weetamoo's hill, like feathers opening in a bird's tail. Before the sound of his song vanished from the air, he ran southwest across the rocks and down over the top of the hill. He must silence the three men at Plimouth himself. In each handful of generations a great-man is born who is wise as well as great, one who knows the eye of darkness as well as the eye of daylight. This is dangerous for the people and can destroy them, but sometimes it saves them. If he could silence the three men, it would be a sign to him that he was to be such a saver of the people. He must try, by words.

He ran farther down the slope and faced southwest to the still-dark horizon there. At its rim the long path of the old ones reached the bridge and crossed into the other world. He crouched. He opened his mouth. By words are all things formed. He spoke aloud to the three, but softly: "Huu, my counselor, his son, my nephew, when your souls break their ties and set out for the path, do not fear. You will find the ridge that is narrow as a blade. Upon it you will have the strength and balance of young men. Where the path widens into swamp and quicksand, keep to its center. When it runs through stickers and blackberry thorns, go more slowly. Dash across the bridge and you will not be scorched by the fire. But when you climb the hills of the other land, you may no more rely on strength and balance. Then you must have words. Say this when you come in sight of the woman who keeps the animals: 'Grandmother, I have not killed too many of your deer, I have not killed too many of your bear.' When her dog growls, say, 'Grandmother, the relatives I left behind me, they are not yet ready to walk the long path.' Only when you scale the cliff to Kiehtan's house, the place of order, cool with breezes from the doors that are left open to those who die for the people, only then will you cease to need words. There you will be received with joy. There you will be greeted with song!" He paused and stood abruptly, sweating: "If you have not already betrayed me with the breath your own grandmothers shook into you! If you do not already sit at Plimouth wrapped in red blankets against the heat, singing Lord Jesus!"

Midmorning and the women were bending over the ankle-high corn, digging up the guns. The usual breeze from the southwest swayed taller, thinner trees at the top of the hill. Not the hickories, not the giant white oaks. Metacomet had taken steam with his two uncles and sat now by pots of paint in the shade of his house at the base of the hill. His generation had never painted for war, only for ball games, or to dance. Across his wife's field, smoke rose from the many houses of his own village Kickamuit–at the spring. Dark shapes moved against the light houses, and boys ran, dogs following after them. Women shuffled from fire to fire, busy with the food it took to feed the visiting dancers. The smoke rose from the houses slowly, easily, as things do in daylight when movement is more expected and a man doesn't whirl at the least shadow. The great-man must know the eye of daylight: his father's voice came to him, though not to Metacomet had such advice been given. Such was for Metacomet's older brother: the great-man must see far ahead, my son, as Kiehtan the orderly sees, Kiehtan who brought us seeds that we may not hunger in winter.

The eye of darkness is for the wise-man only, or usually so.

A wild yipping came from nearby and Metacomet's son ran into view, swinging a small white dog by the tail. The boy's round thighs were those of a runner and the sun glistened on his buttocks.

"Hear him singing! He's practicing to die!"

"We don't expect that of a dog." Metacomet reached for one of the pots.

His wife came away from her fire and the chickens followed her, running at her feet. She called to a woman in the field and pointed at a yellowed stalk which no one had yet dug up.

"Will you eat?" His wife came to him.

"No. Are the women ready to go to the swamp to hide?"

"Every village has word. At midafternoon, I told them." She sat on her heels, the chickens circling her and making their sharp, insistent sounds. She was young, her hair shone. Behind her, across the tidal river, the hill of Weetamoo sat smug and silent as ever.

"Good. Don't you go to the swamp. When you leave the fires, go to Weetamoo again. Tell your sister to be here at twilight with all her men. We will need them to stand at the pig fence."

"What shall I say this time?" She did not raise her eyes.

"Tell her if she doesn't come, I'll know she prefers to suck at the English breast." He dipped the fingers of his good hand into the grease pot.

"That's what I said to her yesterday." His wife raised her eyes; talk of her older sister emboldened her.

Angry, he spoke more softly: "Tell her I have a sister, too. Tell her my sister is already sooting her face for her son who died by the rope. My sister is already bringing her fifty warriors to me. Hear her feet? My sister is already dancing toward me from Assawampset."

If only it were the truth.

His wife said nothing.

"And tell your sister to send away that husband of hers. I'll give her a new one, a man of the blood. Her children shall be great-men among us again."

"But she has Petananuet's child within!"

"That is not the truth!"

His wife lowered her face and the chickens pecked harder at the ground by her feet.

He had already sent Weetamoo a brass kettle. Gifts would not bring her. "Tell her that if she doesn't come to me by twilight, my men will burn the English trading house near her. Then she'll see how much the Englishmen love her." He took his glistening fingers from the bowl.

"I do you service." His wife rose from her heels and the chickens followed her back to her fires.

When she was gone, the boy smeared a handful of strawberries against his chest. "I'm painting for war! I will fight!" His new teeth were big in his small face.

"Not unless the people are trapped." Metacomet rubbed grease slowly into his chest.

"But I will see the snake! I will become a great warrior that no bullets can kill!"

Metacomet hadn't seen the snake. The fox had come to him when he went into the winter woods to see what would protect him as a man and to hear by what name he would be called. A small, perfect fox. Much better than the wolf. But in the hand of a woman? A woman! She of the animals; she who was the doorway to the darkness. Those who see the woman may learn the eye of darkness, all the changing shapes of Hobomok, the deceiver. He had told no one. He didn't want to learn such things. He wanted to be like other men, not set aside. Her skin was almost as light as an Englishwoman's, and she was so much younger than he had expected.

Flies were landing on the boy's belly.

"Here." Metacomet shared the bowl of grease with him. "Maybe you'll see the star."

"I'll see the snake!"

To Metacomet the pig grease smelled more like something English than raccoon did. Even so, he'd never go to a rum house greased. Preserved Abell at Rehoboth would stare at his glistening, while the other men talked of what glass to hold to the eye while you looked at stars, or how to cut curves into wagon wheels. Hugh Cole in Swansea would pretend he didn't notice and go on explaining how to cure a fever. Thomas Leonard in Taunton at the eastern edge of the plain might laugh out loud. That would be better. He trusted that man.

"Your uncle's coming soon," Metacomet said, looking at the trees on Montaup. The midmorning breeze from the southwest was shifting westward.

"He's an Englishman!" The boy Neimpauog jumped up and smiled, showing his big teeth, the way Englishmen did.

Metacomet laughed and caught the boy by the ankle. "If war begins, you will hide with the women. Always be sure you have space to run. Don't get caught. If you're alive, the people is alive." He let go and the boy ran off.

Metacomet pulled the pot of red toward himself. He was sleepy.

"My brother." Sunconewhew stood above him, casting a shadow on the pots of paint. On the younger man's chest a line of yellow lightning zigzagged from the navel to the chin and went up along to his nose, dividing into two yellow brows that circled his eyes. Still, the patterns of the English shirts Sunconewhew usually wore were clear to be seen on his skin, where it had darkened in the sun and where it had not.

"What's on the road?"

"Nothing." Sunconewhew folded his long legs to sit. "Oxen going to Rehoboth, that's all." He spoke fast, having had John Sassamon as his teacher.

John Sassamon destroys softly, like water on rock.

A Pequot slave woman came for Sunconewhew's bowl. It was a pewter bowl.

"My men broke into the new cider after the dancing last night," Sunconewhew said.

"I heard."

"The dancing gets them too excited. And it's going on too long. It's the longest dance we ever had."

"We need the men here, until we know."

The woman brought the bowl, filled with steaming fish. She took Sunconewhew's cup. His cup was made of tin.

"I can't be sure of the young men. They're impatient. The wise-man keeps telling them to start the war." Sunconewhew began to eat.

"You're their leader." Metacomet dipped his fingers into the red paint. Sunconewhew also had charge of the twenty men who had come to the dance from various scattered places. Counting them, they had a hundred men from the cleared land, from the neck.

The woman brought Sunconewhew's cup, filled with water.

Metacomet ran a bumpy line from his shoulder downward, over the scars he had made when his daughter died, over those for his older brother Wamsutta. "If the soldiers come to poison me—"

"They won't poison you!" Sunconewhew interrupted just like an Englishman. "They didn't poison . . ."

Metacomet looked up to see Sunconewhew's lips form the start of Wamsutta's name, but then he seemed to remember not to speak the name of a dead man. The simplest things Sunconewhew forgot!

". . . our brother," Sunconewhew ended his thought. "Why should they poison him when they could have taken his head and hung it on a pole for all of us to see?"

"Is that what they taught you at the college in Boston?"

"No." Sunconewhew tapped his skull. "That I taught myself. And the college isn't in Boston. It's in the town called Cambridge."

Metacomet wiped his hand free of paint. His brother was proud, had named himself after the hawk.

"What did the uncles say?" Sunconewhew leaned toward him.

Metacomet thought of the steam house and the uncles sitting beside him. One was their dead father's brother. "Unkompoin says that to fight is to die. But he was speaking only as a younger brother does."

They were both silent, each remembering the sound of such a cautioning voice in their own throats.

Running to the steam house, Metacomet had seen that both his uncles were so old that the skin of their knees was wrinkled. So it was with the few who remembered war. The other uncle, Annawon, had been husband to their aunt and had led all their father's battles, all the battles that the old men told of. "Annawon says if the Englishmen are seen on the road, he will stand at the pig fence with his fifty men. He wants fifty more men, the men from the wet cove, to hide in the woods behind him. The fifty from the low cove should go to the landing place and get the canoes ready for us. I'll take our hundred men up the tidal river and we will appear behind the Englishmen at the fence." Metacomet stopped. Annawon had no plan for the three hundred of Pocasset because he didn't expect them to arrive.

"What did he say about the guns?" Sunconewhew finished eating and put his bowl down. They needed ten more guns.

"He reminded me how well bows work in the rain and how silently at night."

They both laughed. Laughter was not enough.

"Will you shave me?" Metacomet put his head on his knees.

Sunconewhew picked up the shells.

Iootash, to stand fast. In the dark steam house Annawon's deep voice had spoken the single word in such a way that it seemed to rise and fill the men.

Metacomet felt a pinch on the side of his head. His wife shaved him better than this.

"Rest my brother. The Englishmen won't seize you today. This is when they cut their hay."

Metacomet turned his head on his knees. "If only we still had the Nahiganset! Perhaps I should go to Mohawk again."

"Mohawk! Those savages! Mohawk stoops and labors like a woman to please Englishmen. If you go to them, they'll grab you and boil you and eat your face last, like some sweet English pudding. And if they don't? If the man-eaters should listen to you? All our other friends would flee! Rest. Rest. You will bind the new people. They are already formed in the womb. You are their father, rest."

The elder brother was glad to let drowsiness overcome him. The breeze was shifting slowly in its daily circle; by noon it would blow directly west over the top of the hill. He had been the younger brother for so long himself. He had walked on Montaup where all eight breezes collide. "Their coming together makes a hole. It is the door through which the old ones step out from their world into ours," his mother said, showing him exactly where to stand, and explaining it all in her soft Nauset voice. "Listen to them. They are the people Pokanocket. Your body is theirs, grown out of the old ones planted in the earth." He listened. They spoke. "Son," they said the first time, "Pokanocket longs to put on shirts and ride horses and shoot guns. Why do you let them?" "I?" he had replied, without opening his mouth. "It is not I who will be great-man. It is Wamsutta, my brother. He will assign the women their positions in the cornfield. He will tell where each man may fish along the streams." His mother was pleased that he had heard the old ones. "You have the ear of darkness, if not the eye."

"Lie down now. I will finish painting you."

Sunconewhew spoke and then blew on the shells to clean them.

Metacomet ran his fingers along the sides of his head. Close enough. Again, he obeyed his brother and this time stretched out on the ground. He closed his eyes. Everything was quiet and soft. His hand was on a tree. He was wearing his beautiful coat, cut in the English style but beaded by his sister with all the animals and plants of the world, male and female. He let the dreamer go, to walk through the thickets that stretch before sleep. Then suddenly, he was standing outside the wooden house at Plimouth where the three men were kept. In the pocket of his coat were three silver coins. His left hand was stiff and immobile in the pocket. He couldn't move its fingers to grasp any of the coins. His long hair was soft against the collar of his coat. Three men were led out. Hoods were placed over their heads. He stood silently and content, among Englishmen. He did nothing to stop the placement of the ropes around their necks. He opened his eyes: there were pine needles on the ground.

"What is this?" Sunconewhew's voice was behind him. Metacomet felt the pressing of the soft, wide brush against the right side of his back. Then a narrower, stiffer brush against his right shoulder blade. One line, another crossing it, a circle around them; powder, pollen, soft in the circle.

"The crossed lines of the world?"

"Yes." Sunconewhew pressed a dot between two lines. "That's Boston." Another dot. "This one over here is Cambridge, where Harvard College is."

"Yes, yes." Metacomet grew impatient with this brother who knew more of Englishmen than he. He shut his eyes again. He saw himself standing at his daughter's burial. Then, coming down from the burial hill, he was with Naonanto and almost two thousand men of both people drilled with guns beside his cornfields. Pocasset was still with him, and Saghonnate. Until Taunton. He saw himself standing at the god's house in Taunton, shortly after. He and his seventy men from the cleared land had painted and taken their seventy guns up the path beside the tidal river and gone into the god's house to talk. "Philip, my sachem, why are so many of Narragansett gathered with so many of Wampanoag on the Indian neck? Why are you drilling with guns? Do you plan war together?" "No, my governor, they only came for my daughter's funeral." "But Philip, my sachem, what men drill with guns at a funeral?" The Englishmen in their wide black hats chattered on and caught him in a trap of words: "You do plan war together." Then he and each of his seventy men had been made to place their guns at the door of the god's house and leave them behind. Without them they walked home like boys. Only John Leverett of Boston had not laughed at him.

He saw himself standing in Boston wearing his beaded coat for the first time. The pebbles over the dusty roads were noisy under the feet of his stallion. Tall, yellow-haired Englishwomen stared at him, women who had never greased, whose thighs were soft. The tailor marveled at what had been beaded onto the coat and said it must now be worth one hundred pounds. "This time I want two ruffled shirts, such as those John Leverett wears." The tailor measured him outside in the fading light. The light touched the sails moving slowly from island to island in the windless bay, all these islands had once sent tribute corn to his father. When the first shirt was ready, he put it on and climbed high up into the market house. At the top of the stairs sat John Leverett, in his wig and with his big mustaches. Perhaps John Leverett wanted to go against Plimouth with the daybreak people? Boston was much bigger than Plimouth. John Leverett should be able to take tribute easily from Josiah Winslow at Plimouth. But no, John Leverett did not desire to go to war against Plimouth. What John Leverett wanted was to push

Metacomet farther from the cleared land on the plain and deeper into the woods on the neck.

"And this, what's this?"

Metacomet felt two lines crossing on his left shoulder blade but one line was longer. "It's the Englishmen's sign! Their god's sign! Take it off."

Sunconewhew laughed and lengthened the other three lines to match. "I thought you were sleeping! Sit up."

He sat, and Sunconewhew held his chin and turned his face to one side: a circle around the eye, pigment to fill it in.

"Where's my bride?" Sunconewhew began on the other eye. "Naonanto's delaying. The girl must be old enough now."

The sunlight was warm on Metacomet's eyelids. "You'll have to wait until he's ready to give her. You must marry the woman he gives you first, to mix the blood of Nahiganset with ours, to form the new people. But then you may marry others. I was wrong to do it the Englishman's way. A great-man needs many wives."

The painting stopped.

Metacomet opened his eyes and saw a look pass across Sunconewhew's face, a look that Metacomet remembered well from the inside of his own face.

"But I am not to be a great-man," Sunconewhew said.

"Nor was I."

Metacomet spread his arms and motioned Sunconewhew to paint his chest. The younger brother did not speak as he colored the left side of Metacomet's chest red and the right side white. Nor as he sprinkled yellow pollen in great swirls over the paint. He was done, and motioned Metacomet up.

Sunconewhew looked pleased at his work. "No Englishman at the pig fence would even know it was you." Then he remembered. "But, of course, they're not coming! They're cutting hay."

Metacomet stood to his full height and looked down his painted body. "They would like to see me now at Harvard College!"

He dropped his arms, for far off near the river he heard the hollering he'd been leaning toward all morning.

"Ho! Pokan . . . ocket! Hear me!"

"It's the runner!" They hurried through the cornfield to the houses of the village at the spring. Men from the sleeping pines were running, too, and others from the wading place. They collected at the spring. Women came from the fires.

The winded messenger stopped at the spring. Women held out water, but he would not drink.

"Two are . . . dead."

A wail went up among the women.

The great-man and his brother moved closer to the messenger.

"One lives . . . the youngest one. When he was swung up, the rope broke. He fell . . . to the ground. 'I did not kill anyone . . . on the ice. . . . I watched . . . my father kill and . . . the son of Tuspaquin of the lake kill . . . but I did not kill.' "

The great-man stood bright with paint before his warriors. "What else did he say?"

"That they were sent . . . to kill."

"Who sent them?"

"You." The messenger reached for the water, and the eyes of the people turned from the messenger to the painted man on whom the sun shone.

He had not silenced the three. He was not to save the people by becoming as wise-men are. Only the eye of daylight was his.

"I did so." Metacomet said to his people, turning slowly to see each man and sending his voice out over all of them. "Once the great-man who befriended the strangers sent his long knife to Plimouth and asked the Englishmen to kill a traitor for him, but they did not. I sent these three as my long knife to kill a traitor and they did so. It is proper. Go. Paint. Prepare. Soldiers will be at the pig fence by sunset. They'll try to take our guns again. They want to make us women. We are men!"

The young men cheered and banged their guns against the ground. The old men stood with their hands crossed over their chests. The men in their prime raised their guns in the air and called out the great-man's childhood name, remembering the games of war they had played together.

It was begun.

2

Tasomacon–he who will make war. The birth name given to him by the old wise-man was gone from the outside of the great-man's skin, but it remained somewhere within. The men don't tell you that before you winter. The great-man who had given himself two names and who would soon speak the second name aloud walked about to see the hundreds of freshly painted men take their places. He stood a long time at the canoe landing, searching over the tidal river for sight of Weetamoo's canoes on the far bank. There was only the green radiance of foliage and the blue sheen of water. He ran along the river path. At his village Kickamuit women were stripping the mats from the houses and packing to go to the swamp. He ran along the path that went up the center of the neck, the pewter star rising and falling on his chest. He came to the wall of the pound, and when he was level with its gate, he could see the great gray hog that lay inside, dry and flaking in the sun. Four shillings, whenever the Englishmen came to claim it. The spit came warm into his mouth. He did like pig so much.

We must not fight the strangers.

We would lose everything.

He ran past stragglers of the wet cove still painting themselves in the woods, and emerged into an open area filled with the shining bodies of Annawon's men. The men were shooting off stones and bits of metal, to make a lot of noise.

"We're men today!" Annawon's men greeted him with a shout. Their voices all bore the accent of the green swamp.

"We'll bleed the first blood, then we'll win, for sure!"

"We'll stand." He called back to them. To his left rose the burial hill. In the far side of it his father sat with empty eyes fixed westward on the great bay where the canoes of the Nahiganset might try to cross. Metacomet made his way to the low fence his brother Wamsutta had persuaded the Englishmen to build in order to keep Rehoboth's pigs from coming onto the neck to dig up clams. Now the neck had its own pigs and Rehoboth had bred up the new town, Swansea, which reached to the fence. There Metacomet arrived. Beyond the rails he could see the new house Hezekiah Willett was building for his bride. He turned back to face his own land. The red sun stood just over the burial hill and the shadow of the hill was long on the flat field where the men made their noise.

"There is no word from your brother at the road." The old captain Annawon came toward him. This second uncle was a broad man and, like most of the old men, sure in what he did.

"Nor from Weetamoo at the landing." Metacomet gave his own report.

"A little longer." Annawon motioned toward the sun. On his gun were bits of braided hair. All the hair was black.

"That's all!" Annawon called out when the last light faded. The occasional firing ended. Then the men leaned their guns against the trees and set to lighting small fires. Some sang. Some began the gambling by which they would amuse themselves in the absence of dancing.

"The women aren't safe in our swamp." In the dusk Metacomet still leaned against the fence. "They're trapped out here on the neck."

"I'll send some men to guard them." The old captain's voice was comforting and steady.

"Send some men across the river, too, to burn the trading house near Weetamoo." Metacomet stood clear of the fence.

A guard was approaching them, with a tall man behind him. The tall man was wearing leggings and an English shirt.

"Great-man, I bring you what arrived at the canoe landing." The guard stepped aside and revealed the other man. It was Petananuet, Weetamoo's husband.

"Ho, friend!" Metacomet hurried from the fence. "Do you bring me your wife's men?"

"No, I am alone." Petananuet stood solidly on wide-spaced legs.

"Are you come to dance?" Metacomet motioned toward the dark top of the hill. Careful, he must be more careful.

"No. My wife sends me. She begs you to stop bringing the war. You will destroy us all."

Metacomet stood next to his visitor. "I do not listen to women. But, of course, it is different with you."

"Every man listens to his great-woman. Mine begs you not to burn our trading house as your wife said you would."

"And why shouldn't I burn it?" Metacomet reached out and straightened the collar on Petananuet's shirt. From close up, it looked as if Petananuet had tried to smooth away the dots cut into his cheek in the pattern of a turtle. "Surely your Englishmen would not suspect that you 'Indians' burnt it, would they?"

Petananuet turned the collar back. "And my wife begs you not to shout and sing at the fence. Swansea will complain of it to Josiah Winslow."

"But Pokanocket has always sung itself to sleep!" Metacomet put his arm around the other man's shoulder and left the fence, walking him among Annawon's men and their fires. "Quiet songs, they make a man sleepy. Peaceful songs. Tell your wife how quietly we sing. Tell Weetamoo she was a good wife to my brother. She is always welcome here, though she herself sometimes sang too loud, and danced too long."

"You don't deceive me. You're making war."

Metacomet dropped his arm.

"And when your war is over," Petananuet said, "I'll be here to creep out and bury your bones, as men buried the bones of their neighbors after the yellow sickness."

Metacomet led Petananuet in a wide circle around the

gambling men, making the most impressive use of their numbers. "My friend," he began, distracting the other from a section at the edge of the woods where there were no men. "Do you know the story of the boy who had many older brothers? They got angry at him because he said their father loved him best. They put him in a pit in the swamp and left him to the wolves. But the little brother got out and found his way south to the cleared land where men plant corn. He grew rich and had extra corn stored in bins. One day late in the winter, his older brothers came south. The fish were not yet out in the north and the brothers were starving. The little brother saw them coming. He gave orders to open all his bins. And he fed them. Now, my friend, I am that little brother. One day Englishmen will come to me, starving, as they came to my father."

Petananuet stopped walking and folded his arms.

"What is it that keeps you from me?" Metacomet stood still, too.

"The little brother is Joseph, an Englishman. His God got him out of that hole. His God will lead the Englishmen in war. And his God will give the Englishmen victory."

Suddenly, Metacomet pointed down toward the dark ground at their feet. "A snake at your foot, my brother!"

Petananuet did not even look down.

"Step on him! Put him under your heel! If the Englishmen's god can cause them to win, then he is Hobomok and it is Hobomok alone the Englishmen serve!"

"I pick him up," Petananuet said calmly. "He licks my wounds."

The great-man who knows Englishmen's stories spoke very softly to the man who could pray: "When the earth trembles with the marching of soldiers, you will stand openmouthed and staring in your fields. The cords of your harvest bag will make marks between your breasts!"

The guard was summoned to take Petananuet back to the landing.

"Burn the trading house tonight," Metacomet said once

more to his captain, and as the weeding moon brightened, he lent his voice to the songs of the green swamp, swelling the sound and sending it as far as he could into Swansea.

It was a good night for fishing. All the Nahiganset would be out on the water. Metacomet left the fence for the canoe landing. There he found the men who had come from the distant low cove singing the soft songs of the narrow land, songs that his mother's brothers had taught him as a boy. He went into the woods behind the landing, where his own men were. He searched the groups of men from the neck who were crouched by the fires. He was seeking a shorter man with the mark of the wolf cut in his cheek.

"Come fishing," he said when he spotted Kuttiomp rolling dice by a fire.

Shrewd Kuttiomp squinted at the dice, claimed the prizes he had already won, and stood. Kuttiomp knew the hearts of men, and because of this he always won at gambling.

They chose a handful of others, gathered pine torches and took a canoe from the landing. They pushed off and Metacomet scanned Weetamoo's hill across the river for signs of fire at the trading house but saw nothing that was not usual. When they neared the tip of the neck, her hill was behind them to the left and the damp fields of Saghonnate rose to the left ahead. To the right, Metacomet made out the narrow channel that lay between the neck and the island–Aquidneck. Turning into the channel, the men could hear the watery hiss that came from the whirlpool where Hobomok lived. "Shh!" They kept their faces from that wild swirl and dug through the current with all their strength.

Then they were safely into the channel. "Slow!" Metacomet called out. The Englishmen's ferry ran back and forth from the island to a landing on the neck. Even on their own neck, the people weren't free of Englishmen. Some of them might be watching now, from the landing to the right. He put down his paddle and took his English matches from his bag, holding the bag clumsily; the knobby fingers of his bad hand worked poorly after the paddling. The men lit their torches and held them over the side, as if they were fishermen out to lure sturgeon.

"Sing! Sing!" Metacomet began a fishing song and the men sang as they pushed along the length of the channel and entered the great, wide bay. The smoky shine of the weeding moon made a line all the way across the bay, and on the far side Metacomet could see the small, distant lights of Nahiganset's fishermen. The paddlers sang until they crossed the bright water of the moon and then one by one they leaned over and pushed the torches into the water.

Quickly and soundlessly they paddled through the dark center of the bay that had so long separated them from their old enemy. Now he would mix his brother's blood with Nahiganset's. It was good to paddle. He remembered the night he'd pushed through the water with his bolder friend Mishquock, all the way from Nauset to Nantucket. They'd been in a rush to kill a man of Nantucket who had carelessly spoken aloud the name of the great-man who befriended the strangers. Metacomet was never so eager to get to Naonanto, so he had chosen his slower, shrewder friend tonight.

Bits of song rose over the water from the fishermen on the far shore. When they neared the outermost of the point's fishing canoes, they could hear the men of Nahiganset calling softly to each other: "Ho! The southland is here!"

Canoes came toward them. The slight and nimble men of Nahiganset reached out and grabbed their single canoe and brought them to the inlet.

"Bring Naonanto to me." Metacomet declined to go to the large town on the point. He sat beside a fire with Kuttiomp to wait.

"I'll be the mouth. You be the eyes. He's too quick for one man."

Kuttiomp nodded and opened his tobacco bag. The fire did

not catch the full colors of either man's paint, but it showed the mark of the wolf on each man's cheek.

There was movement on the path and Naonanto was coming toward the glow of the fire.

"My friend!" The great-man stood and licked his fingers, finding them sweaty from the paddle.

"Southland, my friend!" Obligingly, Naonanto sucked at his own fingertips, though the two had not been born of the same people nor nursed of the same women.

"Your paint, I'm afraid it's spoiled from the water." The slighter, smaller man was free of any paint and his hair was long and braided.

Metacomet took hold of one braid and held it toward the light of the fire. A piece of cloth was twisted in with the hair. "Blue?" This was the way Englishmen greeted one another, with sharpness.

"Blue."

"Boston is visiting you? Bringing you gifts?" Metacomet let go of the braid and it swung toward the fire and away.

Naonanto stretched higher, toward the other man's ear. "Do not distrust me, southland. Do not distrust me, little brother of the bay. I took my thousand men from your dance, but I don't leave your war." Naonanto settled back on the soles of his feet and reached for the powder horn that hung around his neck. "Here." He took off his powder horn. "This is my promise." He handed it toward Metacomet. "It's good powder, too. I got it from Frenchmen."

Metacomet hung the powder horn around his own neck. He had nothing to give. He reached into his bag of shot and found his fingers closing around one of his two perfect bullets. He handed one bullet to Naonanto: "It's now that I need you."

The Nahiganset took the bullet and squatted down to the fire. He touched the *P* marked on it, and ran his finger quickly along the grooving. "Good design. From one of my lead molds? When we're one people, we'll put you to work!"

Metacomet drew back. "We won't give you any tribute!"

"Southland! Southland!" Naonanto jumped up and touched him lightly on the shoulder, laughing.

"We're to be brothers, equal." Metacomet stood solid and tall.

"Yes, but I'll be the older brother." Naonanto rubbed the bullet between his hands and did not even try to look taller. "I've got a thousand men. How many is it you have now?"

Metacomet didn't answer. "Come." He turned toward the bay and walked a few steps nearer the water.

Naonanto followed him.

"Look at Sowams," Metacomet said. "The great bay of the southland. Our fathers fought across it. You and I live at peace on either side of it. We should be one people. Send my brother his bride."

Naonanto laughed again. "We call that our bay, the bay of Nahiganset."

"It is half of each!" Kuttiomp shouted from the fire.

They all laughed.

"My friend," Metacomet went on. "Do you see my women over there?" He pointed toward Poppasquash swamp, where a few dull fires glowed. "The Englishmen are marching toward us and my women and children are trapped in our swamp. Hide them for me and we'll be able to move freely off our neck to fight."

"No. I can hide no one. Not even Saghonnate."

"Saghonnate? Oh, yes, Saghonnate." Metacomet managed to cover his surprise.

"She asked me." Naonanto touched the cloth in his braid. "Three hundred and fifty men and all those women and children? I refused. Boston already stares at me through spyglasses. The town called Providence sends John Leverett daily reports of when I void my bowels."

Metacomet circled the bay with his hand and said, "Kiehtan shaped it as one land—"

Naonanto interrupted, as did all those who knew Englishmen too well: "I'm told the one god made it!"

He would not stop his teasing.

"No." Metacomet dropped his hand. "The one god made their island and that's all he made. Take my women," he said quietly, "or I will forget your name."

"Watch this." Naonanto pulled back and flung his arm high and forward. Far off they heard the plop of something in the water. "I think I hit Poppasquash with your bullet. I have such a good arm!"

The perfect bullet!

Metacomet's eyes looked over the dark, distant water, though there was nothing to see. He would kill Naonanto.

"A hundred," Naonanto was saying. "I'll take a hundred. No more."

"I will send them." Metacomet walked away without turning to Naonanto. He got into the canoe with Kuttiomp at his side. Going home, they paddled more slowly and after a while Metacomet began to breathe easily. Perhaps Naonanto was not telling the truth. Perhaps the Saghonnate had never asked for refuge. Or perhaps Naonanto was telling the truth, but would keep on refusing the great-woman a hiding place. And perhaps Naonanto had thrown a stone into the water and not the bullet. Everything was all right: the new people was simply growing in the womb, like twins who struggle to be born, the one ahead of the other.

The farther they got from the point, the more peaceful the night seemed. Naonanto would take a hundred of the women and children and that was good. They pulled to the shore at Poppasquash and sent a man to tell the women in the swamp to be ready to cross the bay to Naonanto's at midmorning. They made their way back through the channel and passed the cove where Kuttiomp's summer village stood. There were dark shapes on the big rock in the middle of Kuttiomp's cove: cormorants. At the landing they pulled in the canoe and the other men went separate ways.

"Let's go fishing." Metacomet drew Kuttiomp aside.

"We just did!"

"No, let's. At your cove."

"On the night before war? It's not proper." Kuttiomp touched the bag where he kept his dice.

"It's proper if we don't use anything but our hands. We'll go for birds."

Kuttiomp shrugged and they walked south.

"Is he already hiding the Saghonnate?"

"No," Kuttiomp said. "But he'd rather hide all of the south than fight. He's waiting to see what happens. And who's winning. He'll join only a side that's way ahead. Unless he's attacked."

They cut cattails and struggled to light them with the matches.

At the cove, it seemed strange no one was sleeping beside a fishing line or wading out with a net. They dropped the bags from their belts and then their small cloths. With the lights held behind their backs, they started in. The warm water was limping like an old man. The tide was so low they made it all the way to the rocks without getting wet above their knees. When they were close enough, they called out "Ho! Ho!" and thrust the torches forward toward the black shapes huddled on the rocks. Sleepy eyes reflected the sudden shine of too much light but the foolish birds did not move. The men reached for the snaky necks of the cormorants and struck the feathered heads on the rock, tucking the broken necks around their belts.

"Peace would be good." Kuttiomp turned toward the shore.

Metacomet's throat filled with sorrow. "That's what our fathers said."

"It's what you came to me to hear, isn't it?" Kuttiomp dropped his light and sank into the water. Metacomet followed and swam all the way to the glittering sand where Sassamon had taught him his letters. "Here, this is A, it begins Adam." "And my name, how does my name begin?" "With this," Sassamon had said, beginning the long line of the *P*. The saltwater ran off Metacomet's greased body. Bending for their small cloths on the sand, the two men adjusted the bags on their belts and carried the birds by the necks. They made their way along the river path to the sleeping pines and hung the birds in the trees. They lay down and Metacomet was glad to know who lay beside him.

Surely tomorrow the Englishmen would come.

Father, I have begun the war.

Something with wings beat its way from over the high place and hovered at the skin by Metacomet's ear. There was a humming sound and the voice of his father came to him, bringing the words that come before all things and the time that is behind us.

"I painted in red and wore the white bone beads the first time I took the northeast path to see Awanagus–the stranger, whom I would befriend." The old man's words drifted with the snow that dropped through the smoke hole and vanished in the heat of the fire.

The boy Tasomacon kept his head low and out of the smoke. He had most of the old man's words stored safely behind his tongue, and he knew he could bid them forward easily; he listened now for the places where he was least sure, for the places where his brother, who was to be great-man, might falter one winter in the telling and nod for aid.

"Since I was the age of Tasomacon here, I listened to the old men speaking of the bearded ones who came once across the salt sea in 'a great bird with white wings.' A bird? Foolish, you say in your hearts. But any man can look backward and know what is and is not true. Who but Kiehtan can see it looking forward? My grandfather and the men of the island pushed off in their canoes and went out to the ship, where the bearded men helped them climb up. The bearded men gave our fathers bells to sound and the glasses you can see your own face in, and delicious meat. Wonderful things! It was salt on the meat. We

know that now. 'When do you plant?' my grandfather asked through his hands. 'By the moon,' the bearded men answered through theirs. 'And by the rising of the stars.' 'It is the same with us,' my grandfather said. Oh, it was good when we lived on our island in the bay."

Those on the sleeping platforms quieted to the high voice which always began the long, looping story with joy. Tasomacon lay naked on the furs of the boys' bed, beside his brother Wamsutta, who was grown.

"But the bearded men did not return to us until I was a man and married, not until my first wife's son had fifteen summers and was old enough to winter alone did the sails come again to our island. When they came, we ran to our canoes and rushed out to meet them. But when we tried to climb up, the bearded men loosed thunder and lightning upon us and we fell into the water. What kind of men could these be? I sent to inquire among the thirty towns that my grandfather first gathered and was told by my great-men on the coast and by those out on the narrow land that the bearded men were bad. They stole men and took them across the salt."

From her place on the women's bed, Tasomacon's shy mother raised seven fingers, one for each of the seven men stolen from her people Nauset out on the narrow land that curved like a half-moon into the sea.

The old man drew on his pipe and a glow lit the stone face of the wolf that crouched on its bowl. "A ship broke on the rocks near Nauset and, in return for the stealing, our people there killed seven bearded men. But this only woke the god of the strangers and he became angry and sent us the sickness that turns men yellow. At our towns near the falls on the coast, not one man survived it. The people from our fishing towns on the tidal river had to bury the bones. At the towns of the pine place, everyone died. There was no neighbor near enough to bury those thousands of bones. Yes, the bones of Cohannet lay upon the land, picked white by wolves: I saw them there.

"We of the cleared land died, too, two of every three of us.

I buried my first wife and her son, he who had seen the five-pointed star when he wintered and who would have led all the daybreak people with a clear, far-seeing eye. We were sick. The Nahiganset remained well and strong while we grew weak and yellow. Soon they came upon us in hundreds of canoes. They had fire sticks from ships with sails that had come to the bay on their side, but not to us. They put us from our island in the bay and demanded corn and pots and skins and made themselves our lords."

Shame showed on the face in the wavering air behind the flames: "The daybreak people paying tribute to the people of the point! I had to find a new path. I must know more of these bearded men who could make fire sticks. A path appeared. Him whom we now call the Tongue had been among those stolen by bearded men from a town near the falls. . . ."

Squanto. His real name must not be spoken on air, lest it make a channel for the soul's return. Tasomacon looked behind him but saw only the back of his brother.

"He was one day brought back home by a bearded trader who wanted skins as his reward. I gave the trader free passage among my thirty towns to ask for skins, and when he was gone the Tongue told me all there was to know of the island of the strangers. It is two moons over the salt to a dark land where the winter is long and where the two-legged people who walk are more numerous than the one-legged who only stand and cleave the ground with roots. The bearded are called Yengeese-men and they plant and fish but seldom hunt. They trap their game and keep it in pens where each kind grows fat and breeds, so that the young are born waiting to be eaten. Wonderful things! And they ride around on the backs of big dogs. Their houses cover the land, even the bridges. On one bridge are set poles to hold the heads of men who steal or kill. Their women, though, are weak. They stay indoors and give birth to too many children. Their greatest-man is called Kinjames, he has but one wife!"

On the big bed Tasomacon's aunts put up their hands to

cover their mouths and looked slyly from the short-toothed old speaker toward each other.

"The strangers asked the Tongue such things as 'How good is the land in Pokanocket?' 'How numerous the fish?' 'Is there metal that shines?' They were curious to know us. Yengeesemen are curious and very strong. Not in their bodies; they do not run or swim. But in their things. Wonderful things! It was not thunder and lightning, it was a fire stick, a hot mouth with which they had driven us from their ship; with which the Nahiganset had driven us from our island."

Tasomacon spread his perfect fingers on the fur: he longed to hold one of those metal mouths that shot out fire.

"Dare I befriend such bearded men? The Tongue was eager for me to do so, but I was wary. Then some new bearded men came to the narrow land and walked about at Nauset during the cold moon. They stole seed corn from a storage bin, a bad sign. During the midwinter moon, they took their ship to the northeast bay and sat themselves down at one of the towns near the little falls left empty by the sickness. With metal teeth they bit into trees and began to set up houses. I told my men of the fishing town Nemasket to watch them and soon Nemasket sent me runners every day. Soon we knew that the strangers were fifty men and as many women and children. They did not steal or murder. They carried metal knives and what they wore covered both their arms. When they sent the fire from their sticks, birds fell out of the sky. 'Yengeesemen,' I advised Nemasket. 'In their home island they ride on big dogs.' I was content and in the thirteenth moon when we leave our winter houses and go to catch fish, I sent the Tongue ahead to the northeast bay to announce my coming and I told my men to paint, for I would rise above our lords, the Nahiganset. I painted in red with white circles around my eyes and hung my white bone beads from my neck. On my left arm I laid the skin of a wildcat shot through the eye, perfect and unmarked. I took up my bow. My brother Unkompoin walked beside me when we went over the top of the hill at their town, sixty of us, the sixty left after the sickness, and a few more of Nemasket. We waited there, as is proper. Two bearded men with fire sticks came over the brook and when Nemasket saw them, they ran home. You know Nemasket!"

All of Pokanocket that was in the big house laughed.

"A young man with a fine, curious face and black eyes came over the brook, carrying a good copper chain. It had a green stone in it. This was Edwardwinslow, my good friend whose sons must be Pokanocket's friends, always, always. He saw my many warriors and he said to me that Kinjames wanted me for a friend and he put out his hand, though I did nothing with it, not knowing then. I and twenty put down our bows and crossed the brook with Edwardwinslow and we went up to the town they were building, to one of the square houses. I sat down on a green mat and the Tongue was brought to sit beside me. Then came the sound of the bright lips into which the ship traders blow on the bay when they call out the Nahiganset to give the things to them that they do not give to us. The great-man of the strangers came into the house, I licked my fingers but he smacked his hairy lips against my hand, instead. So I did the same to his hand. 'This is what they do in the land on the other side,' the Tongue whispered to me. They brought me the drink that makes you sweat. I felt dizzy and found it hard to see, and though I waited for the good feeling of the sweathouse, it never came. That was regrettable because the bearded great-man wanted to please me, and why not? I had sixty men and he had far fewer than fifty, I could see that for myself. I held my head straight against the dizziness and said that my enemies across the bay had been given fire sticks by bearded men. The great-man told me he was neither a trader nor a man from a town called France and so could give me none. But he promised to send me his own men with their fire sticks, if war should come to me again.

"It was enough. I told him that no town of the daybreak people would ever make war on him. I asked my counselors if they agreed and each said yes, we must not fight the strangers.

So I gave everyone tobacco. The bearded men showed us seeds, but none they had brought over the water matched any of ours. So I told them I would send them our women with some seed corn. At the end, their great-man took me back to the brook and smacked his lips against my hand and I did the same to his hand. The Tongue remained in the town of the strangers. We slept beyond the empty cornfields of the town near the falls, where our women were waiting for us. In the morning, I sent for some of the Yengeesemen to come among us under the trees and I gave them what tobacco and groundnuts I had left. I did not want to appear poor. Their teeth were very white. They know soft foods."

Tasomacon's plump, long-haired sister sat on the girls' bed. The sight of her new breasts made his lips twitch. She pulled her long, black hair over her eyes.

"No more would Nahiganset be our lord! I came home past the lake where the great-man at Assawampset gave me the first fish and asked me for a daughter to marry to his son. At the resting place I stopped and sat with the great-man of Mattapoiset, who promised me a daughter for my son. Neither he nor I had any children then, but we looked ahead, as great-men must. Never had the net that binds the white-rising people been so strong. This Corbitant of the lands of Mattapoiset and Pocasset looked even farther ahead than I. He feared lest the strangers turn their fire sticks upon us. 'No,' I told him, 'they want only skins. Tell your men to trap.' When I got home to the shad pond on the plain, the geese were darkening the sky. I sent the news of our new friend Kinjames eastward to the tip of the narrow land and north to the people of the hill and to the inland people, from whom my mother came. 'Tell them the southland is strong and well again; send wives!'

"That summer the bearded men came to me from the north-east bay and brought me corn to repay what they had stolen at Nauset. And they brought me my red coat. 'I am Kinjames man,' I told them at my summer house. 'This is Kinjames Bay, *do not let those men from the town called France bring fire sticks to my enemy. Tell them this is Kinjames Bay!' "*

Tasomacon's brother took in breath so quickly that Tasomacon knew he was not asleep. So easily had the bay been lost! His brother always grew hot at the thought of it.

"The Nahiganset stole me as I walked about in the woods and they bound me in cords. 'The Yengeesemen will come for me,' I told them. 'They will kill you and set me free.' Nonetheless, I readied myself to die and made my hands and feet as stone. Oh, my friends, the Yengeesemen did come, carrying all their fire sticks, and Edwardwinslow himself untied the cords that held me."

Outside the winter house beyond the plain, the wolves began their howling songs I want! I am! *Tasomacon feared the long damp hair on their deep chests. They were old men like his father, who never fought except when they were close together. He feared their restless pacing; all wolves were one, nervously walking, nervously answering each other's song.*

"The Tongue grew rich and drew many of my people to him at a new town he built near the little falls. They began to take him skins. When I complained, the Tongue told me he would raise the yellow sickness from under the ground where the Yengeesemen kept it and turn it against me and mine. Quickly, I sent my long knife to the bearded men. I told them to kill this traitor for me. It was proper. But they sent me back no head, no hands. So I did what a great-man must do when the eye of daylight fails. I turned to the darkness. I spoke with my wise-man. And in the third winter of the strangers, the Tongue died and was buried on his back, facing the sky, as the strangers prefer. Notice, my sons, I had shown no anger. Anger should stay on its own path, or it does damage. When you must strike, do so suddenly, like the snake. Surprise is the beginning of all great enterprise. Follow your enemy without a noise. Drink nothing and see that you thirst until he falls at your feet. Then you will bend and scoop up his blood in your hands! Then you will drink!"

Tasomacon nodded obediently at the old, chicken-fed face across the fire; his brother Wamsutta kept himself turned away on the furs.

"More strangers came, sitting down beside the deep and windless bay of the hill people. A great-man of the hill whispered to me, saying that Yengeesemen die easily without their fire sticks. They even twist their faces and cry out like children. Since the bearded men had not killed the Tongue for me, I agreed to go to war against them. I advised my thirty towns to paint. But I fell sick. I bled from the nose. My younger brother prepared to put on the belt of the people as soon as I should die. Then Edwardwinslow appeared at my door. He had with him chickens and I ate and did not die. Twice he had saved me from death. What else could I do? I told him of the hill people's plan for war. He and the bearded men sailed to the hill people and killed many. The hill stopped paying me tribute and began to pay it to the strangers. The one god sent a second sickness to the hill, a sickness that took the skin off men's backs as they turned themselves on their mats. On the narrow land my great-men who had painted for war ran to their swamps to hide. Their people began to sing to the one god and to pay their tribute to the bearded men.

"When I danced at the wedding feast of Governorbradford, the Yengeesemen gave me a black hat to wear and asked me for a boy to send across the sea to be raised on their island. 'To grow up like Kinjames, with only one wife?' I laughed at them. I returned to my new wives and planted Wamsutta in his mother's womb, to be the greatest-man of the people of the land white-rising, though its coves no longer reached eastward to where the storms of the salt sea break on the rocks."

On the big bed, Wamsutta's mother raised herself to preen, and lifted her breasts to squeeze them, pressing the nipples with her fingertips until they stood straight out.

"My son was born and grew. My daughter was born and grew. When my son went to winter, the bearded men from the windless bay turned their fire sticks against Pequot–the destroyer, whom we have never loved, and it is true, but the Englishmen burned all the Pequot houses black and killed even the youngest of the children, for no reason. Oh, it is easy to see clearly behind you. I ran northward with eighteen beaver skins. I asked Johnwinthrop on the windless bay if he meant next to knock our heads and burn our houses. 'No, no.' The hair was black around his lips and he raised his upper lip to talk, the way they do.

"When I got back, my son Wamsutta was home from wintering. He had seen the wildcat, which means war, and he had named himself Wamsutta, for the war. This troubled me and I took him to the northeast bay to inquire if we were still friends there. 'Yes, yes, we are friends.' Governorbradford brought the cloth on which he said our friendship was caught and fastened. He brought me a stick with which to repaint my promises. But I remembered my promises, each word that I had spoken! 'This is the face of my son who will be the first of all the great-men of the daybreak people,' I told him. 'Give him a name such as Yengeesemen have!' 'Alexander,' Governorbradford told me. 'It is the name of a warrior who knew not the Lord Jesus. And if he ever has a brother, let that one be called Philip.' I thanked him and showed my son Alexander the huge hot mouths of metal that sit by the bearded men's houses, ready to spit fire even across the sea. 'Beware,' I said to Alexander, 'the cost of war between unequal warriors is high. That is how we lost our island, being sick while Nahiganset was strong.'

"You, Tasomacon, were born and named against my heart for war, by my wise-man. But you, my son, must not make war. For we must never fight the strangers. They would take all we have and kill us with their sicknesses. When you are counselor to your brother and have made yourself into a strong cord ready to be pulled against his rashness, you will do best to remind Alexander not of the wildcat he saw in the snow but of the eager, clumsy bear who slips on rocks and is easily seized by men and ridden into the water by those who laugh at him."

The wolves sang, together and alone; Tasomacon kept his face turned toward the old man's and Wamsutta kept his turned away.

"My mother's people called me north. A man of the hill people who had not died in the second sickness wished to speak to my mother's people of the one god. Her people wanted me to listen for them, as I had knowledge of the bearded men. 'Brothers,' the man said, 'the one god warns us to follow his laws unless we wish to die. His first law is to rest one day in every seven.'

" 'Only one day?' I called out, because the man had left a silence. But he continued: 'Brothers, his second law is that we honor our fathers.' Again he left a silence and I called: 'And who does not?' Without answering me, he said, 'The strangers of the windless bay are to be a father to us, we are to be the children.' With that I finally saw clearly and I knew that from that place on the path I had chosen, I could proceed no farther.

"My son who does not sleep," the old man's voice became a whisper meant only for his second son. "The strangers wanted to come inland and I gave them the towns of the pine place, which were still empty from the sickness. You see what they do at Cohannet. They forbid the people to fish at their own weirs. They clear so much land that the game leaves. They bring the land they clear close around them, like a house. They rip open soil that is so hard it should be left to the beaks of birds. And, there is the metal. It is of Hobomok: like all the elder brother does, it goes against the way of things. My son, I suspect their one god is like Hobomok; he changes things to give the Yengeesemen what they desire. But he has no equal. That is not orderly. The people stumble, who have but one eye. And in the trading house? There is no order there!

"During the first winter of the trading house, a man could take a beaver skin and be given the year of beads in return, three hundred and sixty beads, more beads than the richest great-man ever wore. With that many beads, an ordinary man could get scissors and needles and knives. So many beaver were taken that it got harder than it usually is to catch them. Our men tried to take otter to the trading house. Now, two otter skins have always been equal to one beaver. And for the first winter we took two otter, a man could get the year of beads. But the next winter it required four. When the man was surprised to get nothing for his two otter, the Yengeesemen would take the otter and give him a few needles. Soon the man would return with two more otter. But the trader would take those skins to pay for the needles. Soon our men got no beads at all for their skins. They got the drink, instead, which opens the eye of darkness too wide, which lets our men see the face of the strangers' god. I find my men dead and stiff in the woods.

"Worse, I have some men now who want to leave me and go to live among Yengeesemen. They want to work every day and be like women who dig in the fields!" No joy was ever left in the old man's face when he reached this place in the story. "And the pine place was not enough. The bearded men miss the sea. They wanted to live near the tidal river Seekonk and sail their ships on our bay." The whisper grew sharper. "This spring when ice breaks, we will fish at our shad pond on the plain, because the men of the new town called Rehoboth will allow us to. Nevertheless," and here the voice strengthened, "it is good to have the strangers on the plain; they sit between us and the land path to the old enemy, though the Yengeesemen insist we practice peace with Nahiganset. How long can a man admire himself who no longer ducks and dodges in war? We must fight. But not against the strangers, my son. We must never fight the strangers, we would lose everything."

Tasomacon was the only listener by the time the old man hissed to a stop. It was so quiet that the wolves seemed to be howling their scattered songs right up against the dirt embankment of the house. Then the songs peeled off to a single call and were gone. It was wolves that had eaten the dead after the first sickness and let their spirits loose upon the land to shriek and curse their anger and their shame.

At daybreak in the sleeping pines, the great-man Metacomet woke and ran to the pig fence. There was no sign of Englishmen.

The women at the swamp climbed into the canoes that came for them and crossed the bay. Returning, the men in the canoes crossed the path of a lone swimmer on the tidal river–Titicut. They helped him out and listened as the squat, young Saghonnate told why he had sneaked off from his great-woman. She had asked the Nahiganset for shelter. Naonanto refused her and so she'd gone to her English neighbor and asked him to take her hand and walk beside her to Plimouth if war began. At Plimouth she would give her men to Josiah Winslow and they would turn all their guns against the daybreak people.

Word of the Saghonnate betrayal reached the pig fence.

"I have forgotten her name," Metacomet told Annawon, and made him wake the men who had gone to burn the trading house near Weetamoo on Pocasset. Both great-women must not abandon him for Englishmen.

"Did it burn?"

"The roof of it only."

"That's good enough." Weetamoo, at least, would be forced to come now.

At the pig fence, it was exactly like the day before. Annawon's men shot off stones. They sang. They shouted. On the other side of the fence, there was the sound of hammering at Hezekiah Willett's new house. Far off on the road there was a blue wagon with red wheels, but it did not approach the neck. And twilight came without Weetamoo's canoes appearing at the landing.

The sun dropped behind the hill, to slip sizzling into the

ocean west of Mohawk. Hugh Cole would laugh. "The earth is round as a ball, my friend, or we'd never have got here!"

The next morning, too, was the same: no Englishmen. Annawon remained at the fence and Metacomet took the steam alone with his uncle Unkompoin. When the steam was high and each man felt as if he had no skin to separate himself from the world around him, Metacomet spoke. "The great-woman of Saghonnate will not join us. Forget her name."

"She prefers peace." Unkompoin sounded approving of her.

"The great-woman of Pocasset does not join us."

"She will live."

"My own sister doesn't come from Assawampset."

"She mourns her son."

"Our own people are broken. I must bind a new people."

"The Nahiganset cannot be trusted!"

"Let's not speak of them now. Let's consider the inland people."

"The Nipmuck cannot be trusted!"

"And why not? Your brother's mother was from among them."

The old man said nothing to that.

Impatiently, Metacomet prepared a pipe for both of them and passed it to the older man. "We must have the Nipmuck, and, with them, speed is important. I'm running a footrace there, against John Eliot. Already my grandmother's town has become like one of those among the Massachuset. Soon Quabaug, too, will be filled with men who sweep out Englishmen's barns and who plant trees in Englishmen's orchards. They'll sell brooms, they'll make barrels. The women will wear wigs and cough. They'll want walls in their houses. They'll build houses that don't move. An Englishman will come to sit in judgment over them. They will have to pay out so many shillings if they get drunk, or so many if they go near an Englishman's house after twilight, or if they grease themselves. The men of Quabaug will be slaves to the Englishmen, treading eels for them in every stream. Yes, John Eliot will tell them how they can be slaves, even after their deaths. How they can tread eels for Englishmen even at the rim of the world!" Metacomet paused, to give his uncle a space to speak.

The slender old man spoke slowly: "When he came here, Johneliot told us there are no slaves in death. We shall all rise, slave and free."

"My uncle!" The steam was cooling and Metacomet put away his pipe without further words. Then each man sang his song, the two songs blending and each song tying the man whose it was to his own memory, that of it which was already known and that of it which was yet to come. "*Yo hah weh hee.*" Metacomet raised his head in darkness. "*It dazzled my eyes, the river; white in the morning whiteness shimmering. The oaks and the ashes bend: a new people cries, I am born!*" This was where Sassamon had always shut his lips in the steam house, for Sassamon had lost his own song and could only call out "*Lord Jesus! Lord Jesus!*" or keep silent. When the songs were done, the two men stood into a stoop and ran from the low, dark house into the shock of light and the fluidity of air. In the water, Unkompoin struck out with far-flung hands as Englishmen do when they swim. Why didn't the Englishmen come? There was only one way to find out. And it was not necessary to become a wise-men to do it. Metacomet sank deep into the river and swam noiselessly through the cold central current until he felt the pebbles of the home shore. He rose, cold and shining and separate in his own skin as the fox, who hunts alone, who looks for what the wolf ignores and who knows many and smaller secrets.

Metacomet walked among the men eating by the fires at Kickamuit, where his wife and a few remaining women cooked.

"I'm here." His quicker, bolder friend, Mishquock, stood to

greet him. On this handsome man's chest was painted the snake of Hobomok.

"Does it work against bullets?" Metacomet pointed at the snake whose head was up to strike.

"We'll see!" Mishquock laughed and shrugged. Beside him, his son laughed, too.

"I need a man who looks as if he prays."

Mishquock turned to the next fire and moved toward two young men. "Here are the two brothers from Rehoboth."

"Wait." Metacomet stopped him. One of the brothers looked up: he had the eyes of a man who promises too much. And the whites of his eyes were marked with red lines. The other brother looked up: something silver glinted in the hair he had left at the top of his head. The silver coin. These two might be useful in judging the movements of the Englishmen, but not yet: they were not yet his own.

"Not them," Metacomet said. "Their heads are already shaved."

Mishquock turned back to the first fire. "There's the one who swam from Saghonnate."

Inside the matted house that stood alone beyond the cornfield, Metacomet opened a square English chest. He pulled out a black hat and a pair of English trousers for the Saghonnate, whose name was Will.

"You'll need a shirt." Metacomet chose one of Suncone-whew's shirts, as his own were too fancy.

The Saghonnate worked the buttons easily.

"Your great-woman is going to Plimouth?"

The Saghonnate took a breath and spoke in the voice of his great-woman, a voice that was like shellfish walking on stone: "Naonanto will not receive us. He greases his body with silver. We may trust only Englishmen. Benjaminchurch will take us to Plimouth."

Metacomet closed the lid with a bang. "With that voice you

could challenge her, my friend. You could make yourself great-man of Saghonnate. I'd give you a woman of the blood to marry. How many men would come to you?"

"Me? I'm known for my fishing!"

The man was too young. But he would do for the day.

At the horse grove, Metacomet smoothed the nose of his black stallion. "Here you go!" He swung his son up onto the stallion.

Mishquock's son jumped onto the rump of the brown mare and Mishquock settled himself in front of the boy. Will mounted the colt, wearing his trousers and shirt and hat. A fourth and last horse watched: it was the spotted horse the brothers had ridden over from Rehoboth. Plimouth would sooner sell him guns than horses. The stallion had been a gift from the governor when he'd first asked to buy a horse; the mare they'd stolen; and the colt was born of the two.

Metacomet tied a broken gun into the net and swung himself up in front of Neimpauog.

Mishquock kicked the mare and was off first, making a noisy way out of the grove and onto the path that ran up the middle of the neck.

Pigs squealed and scattered in the woods.

"Hey, pigsuck! Go guzzle clams!" Metacomet shouted down at his pigs. How rapidly the path was widening. Englishmen in boots made their way along here from their ferry landing. They brought wheeled carts out here from Swansea and Rehoboth when they wanted to buy extra corn. The path was even getting dusty. He could do what they did in Boston, lay pebbles over the dust to keep it down. Boston! Kickamuit!

When they passed the pound, he could see over the wall a gray horse sharing the space inside with the hog. The men who'd found the horse yesterday had drawn him the letter burned into her ear: *R*. She was from Rehoboth. They came within the sound of Annawon's men and then cleared the woods and rode through the flatland toward the fence. The old captain stretched his neck to catch a word or sign. On the mare, Mishquock waved the guards to hurry away from the gate.

"I'm going to the forge!" Metacomet called to Annawon. Then faster and faster, high on the insides of his thighs and up: they jumped the pig fence into Swansea.

Not his own land. Not his, not anymore. He had sold it when his son was born. Green salt grass, blue water on either side. For him it was a pig fence. For Swansea, an Indian fence. The black stench of Englishmen's fields came into his nose. The paint tightened on his skin. The men of Swansea had never seen him in anything but a shirt.

The sound of hammering grew louder and louder. At the new house a light-haired man came to the doorway. Hezekiah Willett began to wave, slowly and then excitedly, as his eye passed from the first horseman to the second.

"Ho! My friend!" Metacomet waved back. Behind him, Neimpauog waved and shouted, too. On the far side of the new house, a black man stood watching. Then they were past this house.

In the next field there wasn't any house. Nothing but a blue wagon with red wheels that stood as if abandoned forever. In the salt grass, cows twitched their tails. Josiah Winslow of Plimouth owned this field, though he seldom visited it. He let his son Job farm it for him.

Trees of the first swamp ahead: Mishquock took the high path through it. Black water stood in the pools at the base of the trees. When they came out of the swamp, Metacomet could see the cluster of twenty reed-roofed houses that was Swansea's outlying village. Smoke rose from each squared-off smoke hole. It was midday and the Englishmen had to eat at their appointed times! Would they wave a painted man through? Metacomet sat higher on the horse. No one came to the door of the first house. It was the house of a fat man who had dared ride onto the neck at the funeral of his daughter. The fat man had refused to take off his hat to Metacomet. Only to his god did he take off his hat, the fat man said. Drunk, Metacomet had knocked the hat off the man's head.

At the second house a long-nosed man of less than thirty summers stood in the door. As the horsemen drew near, Job Winslow made a slight wave with his hand. Metacomet responded with something equally slight. It was proper. This man's father had tricked Pokanocket out of seventy guns but his grandfather was Edwardwinslow, who had saved the life of Metacomet's father twice. The great-man of all the daybreak people filled himself with air as he rode past: tell your father I am strong, his soldiers cannot take me.

Girls in the gardens by the other houses stopped work to watch the passage. At the last house appeared a young man whom Metacomet did not recognize: even this small village was growing too fast. He passed that house and let the air out of his mouth. Swansea was a cow. No one arms to hunt a cow, no one paints. The woman of the animals would spit on a cow, submissive to its master. Who could eat cow? But a pig, now a pig was born to be eaten.

"The men of Swansea don't love us," the boy called, close to Metacomet's back.

"Their old ones loved us." The movement of the horse carried Metacomet ahead of his own voice.

Stones of the English burying place.

Road to the trading house his father hated.

Fields. How wide they were!

"This was the cleared land where your uncle who was poisoned gave the women their fields." He could feel the boy's head turn and he slowed the horse a bit.

Behind them, Will slowed the colt.

The second swamp. Dark, smelling of dampness. When they came out of it onto the fields again, the river Sowams to their left had narrowed and split into two parts, each part slowing into the curlings of a snake. Northward, ahead of them, the old east-west path of the people crossed the road. When they reached it, Metacomet turned his face west to look over the bridge. Beyond the bridge was the big, walled house of the preacher whom Hugh Cole admired so much. Quickly, he turned his face east. At the end of that path, on Mattapoiset, stood the much larger group of houses that was the main part of Swansea. Hugh Cole's rum house was over there, on what had been Metacomet's wife's land. He had sold it to Hugh Cole in the second summer of his leadership, shortly after he married. For fifteen pounds of silver, which he sent north to the French, for guns. Far in the distance straight ahead appeared the dark lines of the Englishmen's high, five-rail fence that kept the horses belonging to Rehoboth from wandering into Swansea. Mishquock had reached it and was opening the gate. Mishquock passed through, and then Metacomet, who left it wide for Will.

They came out onto the wet, windy plain that was the bottom of the world, as Montaup was the top. A naked place, a low center where winds collected in a wide, flat way. A little farther and they saw cows licking at the water of the shad pond.

"That's where we fished," Metacomet said to his son. His face felt warm.

Sowams trickled to a brook and Metacomet veered east away from it and toward a third swamp. Will was riding well behind them now.

"Call out," he said to Neimpauog, when they were under the trees. *Pa-zung!* The boy gave the wet, worried bark of the green frog.

The reply came, and a guard stood out, calling to others under the trees, "It's the crooked one!"

"I'm going to get a gun fixed,'" Metacomet called and did not slow himself. He heeled the stallion toward the road and when they reached it, he stopped.

"Listen," he spoke into the sudden quiet. Westward, toward Rehoboth, Neimpauog thought he heard the heavy feet of oxen. Eastward, toward Taunton and Plimouth, there was nothing. No soldiers' boots.

Movement behind Metacomet, and he turned.

"My brother!" Sunconewhew stepped into the road.

"I'm going to see Thomas Leonard." Metacomet leaned down from the stallion. "To find out why they don't come."

"I'll expect you back this way." Sunconewhew's yellow eyebrows pulled together.

"No, I won't return this way."

Already it was too long that the three of them stayed so close together in the road, an easy target. The blood of the people could be lost at one blow. Unkompoin's daughter would be closest to the blood, a timid woman without forethought. Metacomet kicked the flanks of the stallion and swung off the road into the wood to the north, beginning a great arc from the plain into the speckled light beneath the trees. Here lay his father's various winter valleys. It was hard riding here because the Englishwomen never cleared the brush. He'd sold these woods in the tenth summer of his leadership, to pay the fine of a hundred silver pounds that Plimouth had set upon him in the god's house: guilty of planning war. Since then, he'd sold no more land. Nor would he.

"See that?" he called over his shoulder. "That path goes north to where I wintered."

"I will see the snake!" Neimpauog's jaws moved against his father's back.

They rode a long distance.

If his sister came to join him in the war, she might take this path. Her face would be blackened now, for her son.

"Cranberries!" Neimpauog took an arm from around his father's belly to point at the low, dark bushes. The terrain roughened here. Remnants of the old deer hedge slowed the stallion. Metacomet could see deer running into the trap, confused at the shouts from the hedge, and he could see himself, a boy among the boys standing with women beyond the hedge, calling out. How faint the trail marks had become on the trees! They weren't his to deepen now. Ahead were the poles of his hunting lodge, waiting for him. All the land was waiting for him.

They reached the silted pond and Metacomet urged the horse to go around it, past a waterwheel. The smell of fire was in the air, and the sound of men singing.

"My father, smoke is coming out of the ground!"

"It is in order. They make coals in those mounds. Coals give the hottest fire. It's so hot that the iron melts. You should feel how hot it is in the forge! That's why they sing, to keep cool." Metacomet circled behind the forge and rode around the big house with the many glassed-over windows and came under trees again. There they found Mishquock, dismounting.

As they got down, Will arrived on the colt. Metacomet took the flintlock from his net and showed it to Will. "The jaws, here, that hold the flint, they're out of line, crooked. Give it to the gray-haired man inside, to James Leonard."

"And say I am a humble 'Indian' of Saghonnate." Will swept off the hat and bowed, his short hair falling forward. "Who prays Lord Jesus every day and tells who made the world that I want to go to heaven when I die and that I never, never eat lice or touch the vulvas of girls who are virgins!"

They all laughed.

"And give him this." Metacomet handed Will the second bullet marked with a *P*. This one he wouldn't lose. He could trust Thomas Leonard.

Will took the bullet and walked off on his heels, to show how awkwardly an Englishman manages in his stiff-topped shoes. He disappeared among the trees behind the forge.

The men took their guns from their shoulders and sat to wait. Gray squirrels ran lightly up into the trees, froze as if they were dead and then ran on again.

"That's the house where I burned my hand," Metacomet said to his son as he filled the English pipe with tobacco. "That's where the green and silver pistol was; *pis-tol,* I picked it up. . . ." He made a sound like the cocking of a pistol and showed how he had held the barrel with his left hand and pulled the trigger with his right. Then he dropped the imaginary gun and lurched over to the side, clutching his left hand to him. It was not thunder and lightning, it was a gun. "Thomas Leonard caught hold of me; he was my friend."

Neimpauog had heard the story of the pistol many times. He looked worried now, so near the house, the forge. "Why do you have so many English friends, when they don't love us?"

Metacomet sat up and reached for his matches. "Hugh Cole loves us. I am always welcomed in his rum house. He showed me how King Charles writes his name. And the boy I knew in Rehoboth, the one who gave me the two bullets, he loved us. Ste-phen, that was his name. He found me while I was wintering and he took me to his barn and let me sit on his horse. He gave me milk to drink. He showed me his sister. She had yellow hair." Metacomet struck an English match. The girl had reached out her hand to touch him; she was not afraid to touch him. You can trust a man who shows you his sister.

"Bury me with some of those matches," Mishquock said, leaning forward to the flame.

Mishquock rushed toward things without caution. So had he rushed through the water to Nantucket, to kill the man who had spoken aloud the name of the great-man who befriended the strangers. At Nantucket, Metacomet had accepted silver, instead, from the man's friends. Mishquock had been angry. But the silver bought guns. A man needs balance.

Metacomet shook the flame off the match.

"I showed my son where my old trapping lines began. We passed the place on the way." Mishquock leaned against the tree and the snake that was painted on his belly widened as he took in smoke.

"Yes, the white pine, to the fork of the brook." Metacomet drew in smoke. "Until you asked my brother to change your location!"

"Why did you do that?" Mishquock's son spoke up. He was almost old enough to winter and needed to know everything.

"I didn't like my trapping neighbor," Mishquock explained

to his son. "Sometimes I found my traps had been loosened by a man's hand." Mishquock was happy to tell things to his son.

"Who was the thief?"

"It was someone who talks like this." Mishquock began to whine like a wise-man singing. "Once there were two brothers born on a night cold enough to crack rock. The younger one taught us to clear the land. The older one could change his size and shape and sing the whales—"

"Stop! That's not yours to tell!" Metacomet broke into another man's words, but here it was proper. "And telling stories when the snakes are above ground?"

"Those aren't Weskautaug's exact words. . . ." Mishquock stopped talking and grabbed for his gun. In the distance an Englishman was running out of the forge; he jumped onto a horse and rode off.

"Is it safe?"

"He's riding to the rum house to get Thomas Leonard."

Mishquock let go of the gun.

"Is only Kiehtan, the younger brother, good, then? And is it because he taught us to clear the land? Because he brought us the seeds?" Metacomet's son was far from wintering but he was a great-man's son and must understand what men said, though he kicked at pine needles to disguise his interest.

"Oh, no." Metacomet drew in smoke again. "Hobomok is good, too. It was he who showed us how to hunt, long ago, before we planted."

"But Hobomok deceives. He is a thief." The younger boy's voice was high.

"How else could he hunt?" Idly, Metacomet began to pick up pine twigs. "He must change the way things appear, to fool the game. Tell me, what do you see now of Hobomok?"

"The waterwheel. It snatches us up and drowns us."

"Only if you get too near! It's good, too. It changes corn to meal faster than a hundred women. It cuts wood quicker than fifty men. What else?" Metacomet looked at Mishquock's son, to encourage him, too.

"The forge?"

"Yes. It melts iron and changes it into guns, into plows. Thomas Leonard has promised to show me how. A plow opens as much earth as a hundred women would, scratching at their fields with shells."

"But, my father." Neimpauog's high voice was impatient. "Is not Kiehtan angry when we change the world? And the windmill will bite us!"

"Stay away from it." Metacomet's hand was filled with the twigs he had been gathering. "Hobomok's iron comes from the earth . . . which is Kiehtan's." His voice went on, but he didn't know what he wanted to say. Male and female, plant and animal, night and day . . . the order of the world is in its pairs. So we understand things. Yet when he had argued it with Hugh Cole, the Englishman said no, the oppositeness of things is not the secret of the world. It is the points between things that matter, measuring them, numbers. And the numbers all add up to one. Metacomet tossed the twigs into the air.

"Boys, how many?" He covered the fallen twigs with his hand.

"Ah . . . thirteen?" Nomatuck spoke first, being older.

"Thirteen!" Neimpauog followed.

"No. Fourteen. Keep your eyes open. It's better to deceive than it is to be deceived. My son, I named you Neimpauog for the thunder, so you would know Kiehtan's voice, but don't be deaf to Hobomok. They are equal. Are you going after birds?"

The boys took their slingshots from their belts and started out.

"Stay nearby."

When they were alone, Mishquock leaned closer to Metacomet. "This young man by the fire, Johettit of Rehoboth, the one with the red eyes, I wanted you to know him. He speaks against you. He says you love Englishmen and he gives rides on his spotted horse to any young men who listen. The young men begin to follow him and your brother can't win them back. They call your brother an Englishman without a horse."

Metacomet moved forward. "Does this Johettit challenge me?"

"No! He only wants to get the war going. But Weskautaug encourages him in this and the young men begin to gather around the two of them."

"Hah!" Will jumped in front of them.

They straightened up.

"It's hot in there! Only a black man could stand it. I ran off before they could grab me and send me to the southern islands to trade me for one!"

Metacomet put his pipe away and took the gun from Will. It smelled of forge fire and Englishmen's sweat. The metal jaws were warm and straight. If only his people could shape iron! They would be as strong as Nahiganset, strong as Englishmen. They could have peace.

Using his ruined left hand carefully, Metacomet tilted coarse powder into the gun's barrel. He wrapped a slug and jammed it down the mouth of the gun, shoving it farther with the rod. He cocked the gun and aimed toward the pond and fired. The slug went skidding over the water.

From the woods on the other side of the pond there came, surprisingly, an answering shot.

The boys ran back into the grove.

Metacomet handed the gun to Mishquock and he motioned Neimpauog to follow him. "Do what I say, now, when we meet Thomas Leonard. Englishmen expect obedience from their boys."

They ran halfway around the pond.

In the clearing, a green-eyed man moved toward them.

"I can see why you didn't come to me at the tavern, my friend!" Thomas Leonard reached out and touched Metacomet's shoulders where they were the brightest with paint. He laughed.

"You smell of beer!" Metacomet touched his friend's shoulders, too.

"I left my wife alone to serve at the tavern, so I can't stay long. But who is this?"

"This is my son. I wanted you to see him. Would you know him anywhere?" Metacomet ran a finger along the boy's nose, across the pattern on his cheek. "Hold still, now."

Neimpauog stood like a frozen squirrel.

"Would you know my son if you found him by your forge one night?" Metacomet dropped his hand. "If you saw him among prisoners marching to Plimouth? If you noticed him at Newport, where they sell the slaves?"

The green-eyed man looked at Metacomet long and silently. "I would know your son anywhere, my friend. Yes, I would." Then he flattened his palm outward from the bridge of Neimpauog's nose. Neimpauog didn't move. "This is where my boy would come."

"I know your boy." Metacomet completed the silent exchange of promises. "I saw him at the rum house during the moon when ice leaves the rivers."

"Will there be trouble, then?" Thomas Leonard pressed his black hair back and the skin on his forehead marked itself with lines.

"Yes. When the soldiers come for me. When will they come?"

"Oh, is that it?" The green eyes widened and the forehead smoothed as Thomas Leonard smiled. "No, no, Plimouth won't be sending any soldiers out to you, my friend. Not now that the hangings are done. They're just glad you didn't start shooting during the trial. They want to forget Sassamon now that they've done right by him. They want to get their hay in! It's time, you know. But you're worrying them with that dancing you did and all the singing by the fence. Quit that and everything will be fine."

"My name was spoken at the hangings! The young man said it was I who told the three to kill–"

"But it's the three of them who actually killed Sassamon.

That's what the jury found and that's what matters. The murder is all paid for."

"The young man who is still alive?"

"They'll hang him again, soon enough. This time the rope won't break."

"They won't come for me?"

"What does Plimouth want with your skin, my friend? They've got enough heads to hang on their poles. They like you right where you are!"

Metacomet's gaze wavered.

"Will there be trouble?" Again lines appeared in the skin above Thomas Leonard's green eyes.

"If you hear of any, go to Aquidneck. It is safe there."

Thomas Leonard laughed again. "I can't do that, my friend. I'm the major here at Taunton!"

A smile came to Metacomet's lips as he remembered that. So, they would fight as equals, if war came. It was good.

"You'll want this back." Thomas Leonard stretched out his hand in the English manner and Metacomet took it. The heavy, perfect bullet passed into his palm.

They parted. Metacomet nodded to release the still-straightened Neimpauog, and they ran around the pond and back to the others.

"Come," he said to Mishquock and Will as they gathered up their things. "We'll ride through Rehoboth, too." He had a curiosity now to see more of his friends.

They mounted and rode west. The stretches of sky above the pines darkened to a deep blue. Behind them the weeding moon rose white and almost round in the low branches. They passed the cranberries.

Suddenly, Metacomet spoke to his son: "A black fox is very rare. It's of the blood of great-men," he said, but nothing more. The boy tightened his arms around Metacomet's belly. They reached the path to Metacomet's wintering.

. . .

His burned hand could no longer hold the bow, and his father insisted he take a gun. The old wise-man had refused to allow it. Tasomacon must be as others. Sitting up in the snow, Tasomacon held the spear in his good hand, ready against wolves. He was afraid to shut his eyes and let the dreamer go. When he did sleep, he saw himself in a canoe, spinning in flood waters. His hand on the side of the canoe was whole again. The snow fell and his traps sustained him. He ate all he could, afraid to fast.

Delaying, he explored, and discovered the red-haired boy out trapping. By the door of Stephen's barn, the girl stood in a dark cloak, like a blackbird. Her eyes were a pale blue and she put her hand out to him, as Englishwomen do, but he had not touched it. You never know when Englishwomen are unclean.

Alone, he returned to his shelter. During the moon that melts the snow, he fasted. What he saw was clear and whole, not as other boys often see. Not the shadow of wide ears or the front leg of the fox but the whole animal. He was glad not to have it be the wolf. He noticed then the color, the blackness of the perfect fox. Only after a while did he see the palm, the enormous hand. The fox became a tiny thing, in that hand. To what body was the hand attached? His heart refused to look upward from the wrist, or along the shoulder, but his eyes obeyed. At the face his breath stopped. Huu, the shudder! He must not see the woman. Yet, there she was. Younger than she should be. Her cheeks reddened as does an Englishwoman's pale skin, but her eyes were very dark. They glowed and seemed to pulsate as she looked down at him.

More frightened than before, he put off listening for his new name. The last snows came. He could wait no longer. He crouched in his shelter. Carefully, he stripped Tasomacon from the soles of his feet. From his legs, his male parts, his belly, his arms. From his misshapen fingers. With no other name but Tasomacon would this hand be whole. From his eyelids, from the roof of his mouth.

He was alone. Without any name.

The fear came.

He thrust his head out of the shelter, clumsy for breath. The cold was sharp but comforting, being something other than his naked self. He looked up. The one-legged, mute people were smiling upon him. The pale snow moon was shining in their branches and a whiteness of feathers was falling on their dark, outspread arms. The mute people had no names, no words at all, yet they were not afraid. Then the gods gathered in the branches and each one hailed him, all their white eyes glinting. He laid his head on his hand in the snow and the brother gods came to him until, standing on each side, they clothed him in the two names: Metacomet–the son who comes lately, and Pometacom–the generation that rises.

When the last snows melted, his slender uncle came to lead him out. It was to Thomas Willett's big house on the tidal river Seekonk that they went. The men of Rehoboth were drinking rum and eating pig to celebrate the birth of the light-haired Hezekiah Willett. His father came to him covered with the smell of roasted pig, and was pleased with the name. "Yes, you are, indeed, a son born late to me! And what did you see? The wolf? The star?"

"No, my father."

The old wise-man who was nearby leaned close.

"I saw the black fox."

"That is good, my son. The black fox is rare and of the blood of great-men."

"And nothing else?" The old wise-man touched him.

"A perfect sitting fox."

In the next season, the wise-man's son had wintered and returned as Weskautaug–the voice; the wise-man's son had seen the woman of the animals and set himself aside to learn the wisdom of the darkness. Not since that winter had any other boy of Pokanocket seen the woman, though two had seen the book of the Englishmen's god, with all its letters shining.

"When will I marry, my father? Now that I am Metacomet?" He had stood close to his father in Thomas Willett's crowded house, away from the old wise-man.

"Your bride has scarcely learned to speak, my son! When she is grown, she will bring us all the lands of Mattapoiset." Metacomet had contented himself with girls, sometimes even in Boston where he went to the women's house he had heard of from the men of Massachuset. The Englishwomen had hairy legs, but he liked to touch the clear skin of their breasts and watch the color come into them, though he wondered, always, if they were clean of blood, despite their promises. "Pometacom–the generation rising will avenge you," he whispered much later over Wamsutta's grave, but spoke the second name aloud to no one else.

In the thick summer twilight, the horsemen turned out of the woods and south onto the Englishmen's road. The great plain stretched low and wide before them and in the last light Rehoboth's four-sided wall of posts cast long shadows eastward. The posts were so high that even from the horse Metacomet couldn't see over them to the town's great lawn of grass. Once he had run on the soft grass with Englishmen, all rushing out of Preserved Abell's rum house on a spring night. He had been the fastest. Now, as they approached a pointed corner of the wall, Metacomet could see through the gate there that the greenness of the grass was darkening to gray; even the white sheep on the grass were turning gray. As the three horses neared the corner, shouting came from the houses on the road ringing the fence. Would someone bang the drum at the rum house and summon soldiers to shoot at these wild, painted men riding by? The greatman who loves Englishmen filled his chest with air and readied himself to yell or scream, if it should seem correct.

At the corner, Mishquock kicked the mare to the right-hand side and took the dusty road that ran round the common, past gardens and houses. The shouting had become a great silence.

People stood silently at the doors of their houses, not waving, not running. Smoke rose noiselessly from the chimneys, to show those who waited how to spread their terrible quiet.

No drums at all.

Metacomet let the air out of his mouth; he would be silent, too. It was proper. The hooves of the horses clattered and pounded louder. Rushing past Preserved Abell's rum house, he scanned the faces of the men gathered outside to watch. He saw no one he knew. The horse was going too fast and the light was too dim. It had been so long since he was inside the rum house! What a clock does, when to press cider apples: he could hear them talking. Friends, see how my head is shaved? See how my shoulders shine with oil? It is for you I have become a wild man!

The colt's uneven gait closed up behind them and Neimpauog's fingers grasped each other tighter in front of Metacomet's belly.

Still no drums.

At the second corner, they turned left. More houses and then the barn of the red-haired boy. If the horseman turned his painted face to look for the yellow-haired sister now, to snatch her up to him on his horse, would she struggle to flee him, her heart beating wildly under his thumbs?

Drums! They were coming!

Faster and they reached the third corner and then turned right, away from the wall, and were past the limits of the town, veering toward open land. He caught the sound of other horses' hooves behind the colt, but when the three of them heeled to the old path across the plain and home, the sound ceased.

They rode straight for the neck. It was not important, the drums. The men of Rehoboth loved him, knew him. The drums were for show. Just as his ride was. Preserved Abell would be laughing now in the rum house, with the others. He himself would go back to the rum house soon, wearing his best shirt. No soldiers were coming. The summer would grow to its lightest and the corn ripen and he would learn metal. They jumped the pig fence into Kickamuit, and the salt air of the sea came into his nose like peace.

4

He left the stallion in the grove and walked in the light of the moon through the emptied village at the spring and across the cornfield to his own house. Inside, he found his wife on the bed. He lay beside her, remembering when she first came to him, her body, where the legs divided, warm. She had not known what to say to him afterward and so she had repeated her formal greeting: "I am the daughter of Corbitant, your bride; I bring you all the lands of Mattapoiset." He had wanted to laugh. Now he ran his hand along her buttocks and the thighs, which opened to him. He went into her and she moved with him, but when it was over, there was fear in her voice.

"I took her the blanket today and she pushed me away!"

He quieted her gently with the fingers of his left hand on her mouth; she was the only one he touched with this hand.

"You needn't go to her anymore. The Englishmen aren't coming." He shut his eyes.

He lay in a circling canoe, his left hand whole upon the wood of it. Flood waters carried him to an unfamiliar place. The waters ahead of him divided. There were two rivers. Which way should he go? He saw a canoe far off and decided to follow it, to familiar places. Then he noticed that the canoe was drifting, being empty of any paddlers to give it direction. Or was it two canoes, and were they both empty?

The next noon, when Sunconewhew arrived from the road, Metacomet took his brother into the separateness of the house.

"This came." He held out the letter that had been delivered by Englishmen shortly before.

Sunconewhew unrolled the letter and held it toward the light by the south door. He read out loud: "To King Philip at Mount Hope Neck, from Governor Josiah Winslow at Marshfield in Plimouth Patent, my greetings. Rest easily, now that justice has been done. We look forward to peace and to restored amity between ourselves and you, for your brother and your father before you were our friends. We wish you good health and send you our solicitations on this fourteenth day of June, in the year of Our Lord, Sixteen Hundred and Seventy-five." Sunconewhew looked up.

"It's good!" Metacomet was pleased. "Very good. It gives me the summer and the winter to get ready for a real war. We'll end the dance. We'll send the men home, and I'll travel north again. I'll find a thousand men—"

"May I start wearing shirts again?"

"You interrupt as much as an Englishman!" Metacomet took the letter from his brother's hand and opened the English chest. "It is no surprise that you are called an Englishman without a horse."

Sunconewhew's body became still. "I meant to speak to you about the young men. This Johettit—"

"See? I'm interrupting. Send me this Johettit's younger brother. Who knows a man better than his younger brother does?" Metacomet dropped the letter into the chest. "Come, get your ink. We will write to Josiah Winslow."

Sunconewhew took what was needed without looking at his brother; the pride of the black hawk was gone from his face.

"Now, help me remember my English words." Metacomet walked toward the north door. "What words did Josiah Winslow make me put my mark to at the god's house, after he took away my seventy guns?"

Sunconewhew returned to the south door and sat on his heels. In a cool voice he recited: "Whereas my father, my brother and myself have formerly submitted ourselves and our people to the kings of England and to the Colony of New Plimouth and whereas by my indiscretion and the naughtiness of my own heart that put me upon rebellion, and nothing of any provocation from the English . . ."

By the other door, Metacomet put up his hand. "That's enough." It still made him angry. "And what were my words when I refused to go to Plimouth? The words I sent when I got home from John Leverett's in Boston? When Josiah Winslow called me to Plimouth yet again?"

Sunconewhew dipped the pen into the ink and said as smoothly: "A governor is but a subject to the king. I shall treat only with my brother King Charles of England. When he comes, then call me. I shall be ready." Sunconewhew took the pen from the ink and held it to start.

"See? You can remember every word! There's no need for reading and writing." Metacomet seemed to have forgotten his irritation. "Now, give me the words you came upon in the big book at Plimouth. The words the traitor wrote there before I sent him out of Pokanocket forever."

Again Sunconewhew brought forth words: "This is to certify that I, Philip Pokanocket, am of sound mind and body and do hereby dispose of all my lands at my death to one John Sassa—"

"Enough! Half a dead man is as dangerous as a whole one!" Metacomet left the doorway. "Tell me, you who know Englishmen so well that you forget your own people, why don't Englishmen care about the words they speak out loud? It's only when they've grabbed some word out of the air and twisted it along a cloth that they consider it to be true. If it's written, even a lie of theirs is true." Triumphant, he sat down on the bed.

Sunconewhew held the feather point in the air and spoke as gently and as steadily as the southwest wind, exactly as a man should speak: "It is the same, my brother, as when a man says that a thousand fighting men from the north are joining him, if they are not. Now, what do you want to say to Josiah Winslow?"

Metacomet covered his surprise with his best voice: "To Governor Josiah Winslow at Plimouth Plantation, from King Philip at Pokanocket, garden of the southland, I send you greetings. We have been concerned of late with dancing for the weeding moon, many of us, and have neglected to send you our wishes for your good health. . . ."

In the three generations since the daybreak people had been one people with one great-man foremost among the towns, they had not chosen a single wise-man to be foremost. Metacomet's grandfather had said it was simple to choose a greatest-man, for it was he with the most fighting men. But the choice of a wisest-man is more difficult: this must be someone whose reputation alone persuades all others to him. His father had been very concerned that the daybreak people lacked a wisest-man, for if a small people like Pokanocket cannot keep its balance without both a great-man and a wise-man to lead it, how can a larger people? Yet the wise-men whose reputations grew in that generation were only those who knew something of the one god, and Metacomet's father was determined never to let another preacher speak to the daybreak people. Nauset's thighs were already stuck on Englishmen's pews and the men of Nopi and Nantucket were building houses in which to sing Lord Jesus. Metacomet had his own reasons for not choosing a wisest-man. One was that Weskautaug's powers were not remarkable, though they were growing. The other reason he would have to let go now. It was clear that he himself was not meant to become both wise-man and great-man. Still, he didn't want Weskautaug. Better to leave it open. At noon on the day after he received the letter, Metacomet climbed the steep wesern side of Montaup–the high place to the cave where Weskautaug stayed in summer. The bag of Kiehtan's seeds tied to his belt bounced and slid against his thigh as he went up. He stood in front of the cave.

"Ho!" he called out; perhaps Weskautaug wasn't inside, or wouldn't come to the opening. The wise-man didn't like it that the dancing was stopped. Nor had he liked it long ago when Metacomet had called John Eliot. Weskautaug wanted war, and soon; the number of his followers shrank summer after summer.

Then Weskautaug was standing outside the cave's entrance, with a staff in his hand. It had been a long while since Metacomet had seen Weskautaug in daylight. They had danced together and led the people together, night after night from the time the judging began to the time of the hangings, and yet he had not seen the wise-man's face by daylight in that span. The face didn't look exactly itself. One of Weskautaug's eyelids drooped lower than the other, yet it always did that.

The wise-man gave no greeting but said directly: "Couldn't you plug the third one's throat? Were your fingers stuck? Couldn't you move them?"

Tasomacon the boy woke inside of Metacomet.

"I brought the seed bag," Metacomet said, struggling to keep his own deep voice over the high voice of the child. His fingers were clumsy as he untied the bag.

"I have never told you how curious I was to hear that you saw the fox when you wintered," Weskautaug said. "Why not the snake? Then you could have fought with us. Or the wolf, why not the wolf? You could have bound us tighter. But the fox? Crooked and clever, but not large enough, not strong enough for this war."

Metacomet worked at the lacings. "The black fox is of the blood of great-men."

"Hah! The wolf is of the people."

"We must bind a new people." Metacomet handed him the bag full of the first seeds. "Call Kiehtan."

Weskautaug's eyes suddenly lidded themselves and then

were open again. It was as if he had not blinked at all, as if the gaze of the owl were in his face.

"What for?" Weskautaug reached out and took the seed bag.

The two tall men stood about half a body's length apart. The eyes of Weskautaug rested on Metacomet's lips as he talked.

"Ask Kiehtan if he sees war this summer. The Englishmen don't want to fight now. And we can't win now. Another summer and we could win. The dancers should hear Kiehtan's voice and then they'll go home peacefully and come back when we need them."

Weskautaug did not alter his gaze. "It may take some time to reach Kiehtan's ear. He's fat and sleepy this time of year. And sometimes he doesn't hear. He'd rather rest in his fields, with his wealth piled around him. Yes, why not the wolf? Was it because of your hand?"

To escape that gaze, Metacomet lowered his own eyes and saw that the near fullness of the weeding moon was painted on the other man's chest. "Kiehtan will hear you."

Weskautaug's voice seemed to float: "If he doesn't, I'll call Hobomok."

"No!" Metacomet felt the black presence of unexpected things darting, of hail during the hilling moon, of the sudden rumbling that the earth makes. He kept his eyes on the painted moon. "No. Hobomok cannot be rebound, once he is loosed." He didn't realize that he was speaking in the high, soft accent of his mother's people Nauset.

"Exactly, my friend."

Metacomet raised his eyes to the other man's face and watched again as the eyes lidded themselves while they remained open, or so it seemed.

"Get me a virgin," Weskautaug said. "Kiehtan will admire me so much more if I can lie beside a virgin without touching her! Get me Kuttiomp's daughter."

Metacomet nodded.

Weskautaug's shadow swooped over Metacomet's foot as the wise-man moved back into the cave. Metacomet would have jumped if he weren't holding himself so rigidly.

Three days was what it usually took to reach Kiehtan. Metacomet prepared baskets of beads and coins to take north on his summer travels. He put in pewter spoons and plates of tin. Soon the women would be home again. There would be time for many things.

The younger of the two brothers of Rehoboth finally arrived at his house. This man's face was long, like all those of Pokanocket. Unlike Pokanocket's, it was filled with the pockmarks of Englishmen's diseases. His name was Otan-nick–a man of the town.

"Tell me, my friend," Metacomet began. "What did you see when you wintered?" He looked at Otan-nick's face carefully to see if it had the look of a wise-man's: as if there were no words stored behind the tongue nor any paths opening before the eyes, but only cries and screams of *now!* of *here!*

"Great-man, my lord." The silver in Otan-nick's hair gleamed as he spoke. "I did not winter."

Waves like an earthquake. Not to winter!

"And your brother?"

"Nor did Johettit."

Metacomet could not speak now of streams in which Otan-nick might fish or of fields a bride of his might plant. Or of the eye of darkness. He motioned the young man off, calling as he left: "Tomorrow noon."

At midafternoon, a messenger came running to the house where Metacomet was still sorting goods to take north.

"Englishmen at the ferry landing! They want to talk with you. This is what they said, 'If King Philip, sachem of Pokanocket, will be kind enough to receive us.' "

"Take them to the cedar grove. It will be cooler there."

When the messenger had gone, Metacomet sent his wife to find what women remained on the neck to help prepare food. He sent for his slender uncle to sit beside him and he opened the English chest. Under the shirts he found the beaded belts of the people. He took out the smallest and tied it around his head: its two clubs marked the union of Pokanocket and Assawampset. He took out the next in size and hung it over his chest: like the pewter star it covered, its white beaded star was for the cleared land, for Pokanocket itself. He let the largest belt remain folded in the chest: on it were beaded all the plants and animals of the whole daybreak people. It was too hot to wear that. He went out toward the cedar grove, positioning men to stand among the nearby trees with their guns out of sight.

"So, they begin to come to us." He spoke to Unkompoin, who stood waiting in the grove with the strand of wolf's teeth around his neck.

Then the Englishmen arrived, four men and one boy.

Metacomet shook hands with each of the men and motioned them to sit.

"*Awanagus-antowosh?*" The boy interpreter was hardly older than Neimpauog. His blue eyes kept returning to the trees where the knives of the guards showed in their belts.

"No, boy. *Een-antowash.*" Let the Englishmen struggle in his language, let them give him respect.

The boy began slowly in the language of Pokanocket. "We have come to talk with you, King Philip, my great-man. . . ."

Where had the boy learned these words? From some runaway servant, perhaps. A man who gave Englishmen work in exchange for food. Or from a woman of the daybreak people who had left her husband and gone to live as a sweeper in an Englishman's house in Newport. Or perhaps from a slave who had managed to limp away.

"Talk? I have heard too much talk." Metacomet, too, spoke slowly in his own language, for it was only a boy. "Too much talk from men who came here because their island was covered with houses and all its trees were gone."

Silently the women offered water and chestnuts with strawberry cakes, and fresh clams in their shells. As the boy slowly changed the words into English, Metacomet turned from him to the man who was called John Easton.

This man was of the same age as Wamsutta would have been. He was well dressed, with shoes that were high under the heel. His fingernails had been cut level across.

"There can never be too much talk." John Easton gave back English words, slowly, to the boy. "Talk replaces war."

Laboriously, the boy changed them.

Patiently, Metacomet waited.

Easton's eyes were on him. Surely John Easton of Aquidneck must know that Philip of Pokanocket could speak English? Very good shirt John Easton had. Wide, dark hat. When the boy had finished, Metacomet said quickly in English, "Take off your hat."

John Easton reached for his hat, without surprise. "Not because you are king," he said. "But because you are friend. Because your father welcomed mine."

"Never mind, leave it on."

The flies were landing on the man's face and bare brow.

"Go ahead, put it back on."

Easton obeyed the English words with a loosening of his lips that was not quite a smile.

Metacomet returned to his own language: "What an Englishman says he will do in talk is not what he does." He looked at the fresh grease on his forearms while the boy translated. "What Pokanocket says in talk never matters to Englishmen. They only listen to us if something is written or if it is spoken by those among us who pray to the one god." The flies were drawn to the ungreased skin of Easton's face. "If twenty of us who do not pray say that a man was not pushed under the ice and only one of Nemasket who does pray says that man was certainly pushed under the ice, which man does the Englishman believe?" As he waited, Metacomet watched John Easton open the shell of his clam and swallow the contents. The three Englishmen with John Easton did not open their clams.

John Easton did not even prepare to interrupt until the boy was done. Then he said, "Your father and mine were friends, Philip, my great-man." And he ate another clam while the boy began to change the words for the great-man, who had already heard them. "Now your father, whose name may not be spoken, has died and mine is dying; let us be friends in their places. I am acting as governor of Rhode Island in place of my father. The English are worried, Philip, my friend, my great-man, I do you service. They are worried because there are so many strange Indians—"

Easton interrupted the boy to tell him to return the word to what he had originally said: people.

So, John Easton, too, knew both languages!

"People," the boy repeated, "gathered on the neck and because you fire off your guns at the pig fence and dance and shoot after dark and you ride, painted, through the towns. And you have sent some women off to Nahiganset in canoes. Do you plan war?"

The three Englishmen looked at the great-man, but John Easton was opening another clam.

Metacomet took a chance and addressed not the boy but John Easton, slowly, in the language of Pokanocket: "War! War costs too much. Has Pokanocket ever wanted war? Did my father offer war to yours?" He saw that John Easton's eyes moved up from his clam and met his, and he knew that he could speak a bit faster. "No, my father gave yours an island to live upon. Have you come only to tell me what to do? You know and your father knows that the neck is my place. Outside my land, I follow Englishmen's rules. Do not own a horse. Do not own a boat bigger than a canoe. Do not approach an English town on the seventh day. Do not go to an English gunsmith. Nor own a gun, nor powder, nor shot, nor even one of those longer knives. I obey their rules, do they obey mine? Their cows come into my corn, and when I return the cow to satisfy their rules, they demand the cornfield from me as well. Inside my fence I do not obey. And tell me, what gives Englishmen the power to set their laws over me at all?"

John Easton leaned forward and replied slowly but directly in the words of Pokanocket: "Philip, my friend, I know your grievances. I am not blind to your affairs. We Englishmen of Rhode Island have our own reasons to dislike the laws of the Englishmen of Plimouth and of Boston, as much as you do. But draw yourself back from the heat of war. I have come to offer a new kind of talk, talk that can turn war to peace. You must find a great-man whom you trust and we of Rhode Island and of Plimouth and Boston will find an Englishman we all trust, if such is possible! The two of them, your man and our man, will talk for each of us and decide what is fair to be done next between us. This will keep the peace. What do you think of it?" The governor swatted a fly, but, as a courtesy, attempted to disguise the movement of his hand.

A man to admire, this John Easton! Metacomet smiled, showing his teeth. The three Englishmen with the governor looked uncomfortable at not being able to understand the talk, but Metacomet continued in his own language: "I like it! I will talk now!" He stroked his greased head, feeling relief. At last an Englishman who wanted to talk, not write down words.

"No, no, my friend, my great-man." John Easton returned to English words, but indicated by a nod of the head that he did it only so that the three men with him need no longer writhe and squint. "No, my friend, you must get a great-man from a town that is far away. Someone who does not know the past between us. And so must we Englishmen. I am thinking of Governor Andros, who lives along the river of the Dutch. He might speak for us. That would be better for you than if we got Englishmen from the towns along the Connecticut, for if you do go to war, my friend, the Connecticut towns will come against you, too. Governor John Winthrop at Hartford, the old man's son, will join Leverett and Winslow to destroy you. But this Edmund Andros is fair and you would like him. He knew old Mr. Willett from the Seekonk, your father's friend. Now, you find someone who is also fair and bring him out to the neck. Await a word from me. I and my friends must go home now. It is growing late. Will you do it?"

"I will do it! I like it! You come to me again. I will be ready with a great-man from the north. Yes, I will be ready. And, boy, do tell the gentleman, my friend, that before his next trip, I suggest greasing against the flies." He restrained his face from laughing as he stood for the parting.

John Easton rose stiffly from the ground and put out his hand. Metacomet took it.

"Do you know Thomas Leonard?" the great-man asked in a confidential tone.

"I know there are some Leonards over at the forge in Taunton, but I don't know any of them, I'm sorry to say." John Easton took off his hat then, and waved it as he walked away.

When they were gone, Unkompoin said, "It is as if Edwardwinslow has come again to see your father."

The full moon rising over Weetamoo's hill ran a wet path shining across Titicut. Metacomet walked on the sand. Matoonas of Pakachoog, he was too old. Muttuamp of Quabaug? He'd left that town and built a fort in a swamp nearby, to which he made welcome all of the inland people who did not pray to the one god; but Muttuamp had so many fighting men, more than half of all the men of the inland people. Muttuamp might demand tribute from Metacomet in exchange for this favor of talking to Englishmen. The one-eyed uncle of Nashoba way up near Merrimac–the deep? Possibly. The slant-headed nephew of Nashoba, whose cheekbones widened and whose forehead sloped in too fast? He was rash, like Wamsutta, like his sister's son who was hanged. No, none of the Nipmuck would do. The best one would be the great-man of Pocumptuck–the river, the young man of the river people who wore the white tuft of the sea gull in his ear. This man's people had known wealth; they remembered plenty. And the Pocumptuck hadn't a lot of fighting men, two hundred and fifty at the most. This man, he was the one. Kuttiomp could travel north to get him and bring him to Pokanocket.

Metacomet turned on the sand, his toes widening. The foxes of the evening barked. He searched the cornfield for their narrow knowing faces, their wide ears. That other sound?

Drums. From Montaup.

"He has spoken!" Someone was running toward him, calling. It was Mishquock.

"So soon? It's less than a day!"

"Weskautaug sent you this and I didn't like the look of him." Mishquock handed him the seed bag.

Kiehtan had spoken into the ear of the wise-man; that was the voice Metacomet longed to hear aloud in his own ear.

"Come with me." In his house Metacomet pulled the belt of the world over his shoulders and arranged it so that the ends reached evenly to each knee. "It's in order," he said. "We'll send the men home now."

They walked out; the sound of the drums that Weskautaug's father had made, like those of Rehoboth, came continuously as the two stepped under the cedars. As they moved up the hill, the sound of whistles joined the drums. As they stepped out from under the trees into the cool evening wind, the whistling stopped and the drums quickened.

"Be careful," Mishquock whispered, nodding toward Weskautaug, who swayed in the flickering light of torches. "He's walking in a funny way."

It was not like Mishquock to be cautious.

"How?" Metacomet saw only that the wise-man had tied a skirt around his chest, just below the white moon painted there.

"Oddly, oddly." Mishquock was hurrying now, through the outer ring of dancers, made thin by the absence of so many women and children.

"Great-man, I do you service." The soft voice of a child saluted him.

Metacomet saw a girl's slight body, walking as if she had no knowledge of men. Breasts like plums, her eyelids turned up at the edges. She looked exactly like Kuttiomp's wife as a young girl. He saw his lips against those breasts, where no milk was. "You have already done us all a great service, my daughter. You made Kiehtan speak sooner than we expected!"

When they got to the middle ring, they came first to Mishquock's group. These men had cut the sign of the turtle into their cheeks. Faces turned to greet Metacomet. One man had painted a black five-pointed star on his chest. He was red-eyed: Johettit. Metacomet kept on walking, but raised his hand to greet this man whom the young men followed. Johettit turned away, as if he had not seen Metacomet.

Metacomet reached the men of the wolf, where he belonged.

"Look through here." Kuttiomp came up to him, handing him a reed.

Squinting through it, Metacomet saw Weskautaug's face closely. It seemed rounder than usual, swollen, the way a woman's is when she is unclean. He handed the reed back to Kuttiomp.

In the inmost circle, the old men were kneeling, their torches inclined toward Weskautaug. The wise-man swayed back and forth, repeating in his wavering voice the words for the two hanged men. That was as it should be.

> *"You did well, warriors.*
> *In the southwest you will not hunger."*

The wise-man marked the song he was singing by hitting his staff against the quartz beneath his feet.

> *"You start at the rear of a long file, warriors,*
> *but when you reach the house of the grandmother*

there will be only a few walking ahead of you;
hundreds will be coming behind you.
At her oval lodge the grandmother's dog
opens his mouth to you.
She gives you food that shuts your eyes;
She of the animals.
When you wake, you will climb easily
up the ladder worn slippery by many feet.
You will climb to the lodges above.
There your grandparents will run out to meet you!
They will take you on their laps.
You will be like a baby to them.
You will hear the voice of Kiehtan.
Some see his face.
A few hear his voice.
It is gentle, even a child need not fear it.
So, go quietly, warriors.
Do not look back.
Tell the woman we are not ready to follow you
on the long path."

Kuttiomp's shoulder touched his, yet Metacomet could not see what was improper. Everything was as it should be. Now Weskautaug held the bag of bones over his head and shook it: the bones that Hobomok had given the people, bits of bone from each animal we may eat.

In response Metacomet rose from his heels and held up the seed bag and shook it over his own head and then moved forward to begin the dance of the two-headed snake. Metacomet walked over the quartz and his great-men and his captains fell in behind him, in their order, and all their warriors.

Metacomet led the line of the people in and out through the drummers and the whistlers. He stopped on the right beat to stamp the ground, *he-uh, he-uh.* Then, at the center of the quartz rocks, he stopped. He turned and waited.

The two-headed snake began to move in the other direction, led by Weskautaug. Everything was as it should be. With its two eyes, the people of the daybreak looked into the darkness and the light. Back and forth, the people went following first the wise-man and then the great-man. So it should be. The weeding moon rose higher over the hill. Metacomet's feet and legs grew numb as the dance drew him taller and thinner against the rock, risen above the earth by the hammering of his feet against it, strong as the metal of the strangers. He would be strong, the people would be strong; strong, they would not be forced to fight, but would regain respect and their own judgment.

He-uh, hah-way. While Weskautaug was leading the circle, it stopped abruptly and Metacomet nearly fell into the man in front of him.

The drums became silent.

Weskautaug would tell now what Kiehtan had said. He would speak of peace and the long dance would end.

Slowly, a terrible noise grew up in the silence. It was a howl that brought the stubble up on the back of Metacomet's neck and glued his feet into place. A scream filled the air until Metacomet leaned toward it, fearing he would vomit, for the noise wished to be inside him and needed room made for its entry.

In the center of the flat rock, Weskautaug passed back and forth, his face twisting in the yowl that issued from his mouth. And his steps sank into the ground deeper and deeper, as if it were mud beneath him and not stone; yes, his legs sank into stone, up to the knee.

Then he stopped making the noise.

In the new silence, a mist formed about Weskautaug. He raised to his lips the long stone tube of his father and his voice doubled and deepened as he spoke through it to them.

> *"I the wise-one have sent out the dreamer.*
> *He has found the dead left to rot."*

What was this? This was not usual!

"He has crept inside,
crept into the mouths,
crept down through the gullets. . . ."

Light drumming began.

The muscles of Metacomet's feet and legs moved against his will, though he did not allow his feet to move.

"He the great-one, see-er of the clear image,
has followed the dreamer
and this is what he saw:
blood of the cow!
blood of the bull!
blood of the hog!"

Metacomet's feet formed one with the rock and his vision narrowed so that he was able to see Weskautaug only at the center of his eyes. Weskautaug handed his staff away and raised two empty hands. Between the hands a vibration began. Something glowed there. A white thing appeared. It was small, at first. It grew larger, becoming what? A skull. The skull of a cow. Weskautaug held the skull high in his hand:

"Who sees a cow?
Who sees? Who sees?"

The light drumming ceased. The skull grew larger. Weskautaug sang:

"You want to hear Kiehtan?
You want to hear his humming?
Ask him, I ask him now:
shall we go against them?
Shall we fight the strangers?"

Weskautaug's face was blurred by the mist and there came a whisper, deep and stonelike, hissing and slithering from below the dancers' feet: y e s s s s s s s s.

That was not the voice of Kiehtan. Something was wrong with Metacomet's ears, his eyes. He must see real things, the things men touch, and he turned his head and saw the few women and children frozen in the postures of the dance outside the circle.

"You do not hear, hear, hear?"

Weskautaug's voice was incredulous, mocking, and suddenly the wise-man began the dance of the two-headed snake again, before Metacomet was ready. The great-man stumbled into line. This time, Weskautaug chose the pattern where the two leaders pass each other on the rocks at the center. Metacomet forced his legs to move, and when the two men passed, Weskautaug whispered to him. But Weskautaug was too tall. Metacomet's own eyes came only to the tip of Weskautaug's nose. And he did not hear what Weskautaug had whispered. He leaned closer.

"The third one named you."

Metacomet wasn't sure if those were the words Weskautaug had spoken.

Weskautaug leaned toward him again: "It was to begin the war."

"Who says to begin?" Metacomet's voice seemed to come from a place apart from himself.

Kiehtan the lips of Weskautaug said, but the sound that issued from them was *Hobomok*.

"Who says to begin?" he asked it over.

Kiehtan said the shape of the lips, moving with the torches. But the sound that reached his ears was *Hobomok*.

"Who says?" Metacomet's voice was dry and it caught along the walls of his throat.

But then he could not see the lips of Weskautaug, for his

own eyes were level only with the white moon painted on the other man's chest. His ears heard only the echo *Hobomok*. He turned from the center then, blinking, facing the old men. He could see easily over the tops of their heads. With them he was the right height. He swallowed and sang with the others. He kept himself side to side with Weskautaug, afraid either to face him or to turn his back to him. The wavering whine began again, next to Metacomet.

"What did Kiehtan say?"

This time the men ringing the two leaders began to answer. "War! Kiehtan said war!" Their faces were eager.

Metacomet's mouth formed no words.

Surprisingly, Weskautaug began the circling again. He led the line back and forth toward each of the eight points of the world. When he doubled around quickly on the rocks, he caught Metacomet with his eyes and the great-man felt his stomach lurch: on Weskautaug's face was the snout of the wolf.

"What did Kiehtan say, say, say?"

This time Metacomet's hands beat the ground as the whole ring of men, young and old, flung itself down and began to call out the song for war.

5

"Kiehtan spoke for war, but he did not say how much of a war." The next day Unkompoin stood first in the council of Pokanocket, being eldest. "I say a small war only, and only if soldiers come to the pig fence to take our guns away. If we fight, we will lose our land. We will lose the bones of our dead who sit in the hill. Here we were born and here our grandmothers dipped us into the tidal river and greased us black and wrapped us in beaver skins. Here we sat strapped in our cradles, with our knees bent and bound tight, looking across these fields. Here we ate fish and strawberries and at the fall of the leaf we went north to the woods to chase the deer through our hedges. In winter we built our houses in valleys where the wind does not reach and we ate the fish and the meat we had dried over our summer fires. We swallowed bread from the cornmeal left from these fields and we chewed roots from the woods that we had burned and cared for. Spring came and the shad and the salmon filled the streams with their white shining. Herring hung pierced through their noses on our longest sticks. . . ."

As his slender uncle worked his way through the words that he had promised to deliver, Metacomet looked at the eighty men of Pokanocket gathered in the cedar grove. Not quite eighty, his brother still had a handful on the Taunton road. The pig fence and the landing were being watched by the men of the green swamp and by those of the two distant coves. He had forbidden Weskautaug to attend the council, sending a runner to the cave on Montaup. "Tell him this: there was once a man who could sing whales into the cove. He sang one in, a large, spouting whale. But this man's brother could sing in minnows. And he did. One and another and another, until there were hundreds of minnows in the cove and together they ate that whale." Otan-nick of Rehoboth was standing alone. It was the first time he or his brother had been asked to stand among the men of the land.

Unkompoin finished speaking and sat down. Another old man, this one from Kuttiomp's village, rose: "Why fight? Kiehtan did not say to start a fight, did he? Blood of the cow, he said. Blood of the pig. That would be easy enough to provide him. Why fight with Englishmen? They give us knives and coins and we grow numerous for the first time since the yellow sickness. We could kill a cow or a pig, but nothing more."

Johettit of Rehoboth was standing on the opposite side of

the grove from Otan-nick. Around Johettit were many young men.

All the old men spoke for peace. Slowly the voicing of opinion made its way down to the men in their prime. Mishquock stood, the snake gone from his chest and replaced by fresh white dots. He, too, spoke the words Metacomet had given him: "Kiehtan saw war ahead, but he didn't say when. I see it, too. I see that one day we'll cross the pig fence. We'll fight and be men in the eyes of our sons. We'll empty the Englishmen's towns. But not now. We must not begin in haste." A sound of breathing came from men who were not accustomed to such slowing words from Mishquock. "Only when our guns come. Only when we have enough men." Mishquock sat down.

A man from a village on the slope of the swamp stood quickly: "We can't wait. We've lost all our land except what we've got out here on the neck! We're already trapped out here. Are we afraid to leave a few planted fields and go into the woods? Then we're already Englishmen! As boys we learned how to move about the woods in summer or winter, living on roots and bark. Why wait any longer? Let's go into the woods. Let's fight now!"

Some cheered, though it was improper. Most of the noise came from the small group around Johettit. Metacomet kept his eye on them.

It was Kuttiomp's turn and the short man stood: "Kiehtan saw war but he didn't say what we must do first. Before we push the Englishmen from their forge, we first ought to know how to pour iron. Before we catch the horses they leave behind, we ought to know how to shoe their feet. Before we burn their towns, we ought to know their words so that we can speak to the traders in the bays. We can't risk everything by starting now. When the leaves—"

"Let's fight now!" Suddenly, Johettit stood, swaying. "I have seen a picture of the war before my eyes. . . ."

Drunk? Metacomet signaled Mishquock to push Johettit.

The young men near him rose from their heels and closed around the speaker.

"You speak out of order!" Metacomet said, eyeing the men in their prime who would help Mishquock if he signaled. "You'll speak when your turn comes."

Johettit's friends stood more easily then and let Mishquock through. They knew Pokanocket's rules. Mishquock grabbed hold of Johettit's arms from behind and held him as Metacomet spoke.

"Son of Rehoboth, you have heard Englishmen interrupting but here we wait our turn."

Johettit gave him a look of hatred.

"*Ho-uh! Ho-uh!*" From the pig fence came two shrill calls.

No one moved.

"Let him go." Metacomet motioned Johettit free.

The clamor on the path became guards and four Englishmen. At the grove, the guards thrust the Englishmen forward and placed four muskets at Metacomet's feet.

"These Englishmen were on our side of the fence!" The guards looked pleased with themselves.

The Englishmen stood close to each other, talking fast. One was light-haired.

"Greetings to you, Hezekiah Willett. And to you, William Sabin of Rehoboth." Metacomet said, in English. "And to you, Seth Read, is it? And to you, sir?"

"Peck. Clement Peck." A man past the prime, but hearty.

"Clement Peck." It had a familiar sound, but the man's face wasn't one he knew from the rum house. "You have come to look for the gray horse? And to ask the damage her iron-bottomed feet did to our fields? How kind of you. She is yours, of course, at the usual rate. Twelve shillings for straying."

Metacomet saw Johettit ease his knife out of his belt and he raised a hand to signal Mishquock.

"Great-man, my friend," Hezekiah Willett began rapidly. "I was working in my field when they came by to ask me to talk for them about the horse. That's all they came over for. They don't want trouble."

"Now we strike!" Johettit called hoarsely, and swayed forward with his knife up.

His friends reached for their knives.

Mishquock got the knife from Johettit.

Metacomet put up his hand to Johettit: "I speak for Pokanocket, not you."

"Too slowly!" Johettit's face swung up as Mishquock caught him by the elbows again. "You speak too slowly and you don't listen to your men!"

"I always hear my friends. This man Hezekiah Willett is one of them." Metacomet changed to the words of Pokanocket: "Put away your knives. This is the son of my father's friend. Are we Englishmen, that we forget our friends?"

The men around Johettit returned their knives to their belts.

"I thank you for your kindness," he continued in his own language, so that Johettit's admirers could understand. Hezekiah Willett translated for the Englishmen: "Thank you for coming down to judge the losses to our corn caused by your gray horse. These men of mine will take you to the fields where you may do your judging. I trust you will not underestimate the damage."

The faces of the other three Englishmen looked pleased and they ceased to stand so close together. Metacomet sent them off, with the guards carrying their guns.

"Go ahead," Metacomet said. The men began again to speak in turn.

Finally, Johettit's turn came and he stood unhampered.

"You've waited too long!" He tried to control his swaying and his slurred words. "We're no better than the chickens you eat out here. I could have stayed in Rehoboth! You wait while Englishmen spit on my father. You don't even want to go to war. Kiehtan said fight. Let's fight!"

"Now! Now!" The young men beside him stamped on the ground.

More young men joined the cheer and some of the men in their prime began to shout with them.

"I haven't spoken yet!" Metacomet called out over the sound. "A governor of Rhode Island came to me to befriend us. The Englishmen want to help us make peace. The Englishmen came to do us service. We can have justice and our own judging. We can wait . . . until we are ready to fight, until we can win."

"No! Fight now!" The guns beat on the ground, the stamping came twice as loud as before.

"We've been asked to talk—"

"Blood of the cow!" This time the ground throbbed with the guns beaten against it. Unkompoin moved closer to Metacomet and Kuttiomp came near.

"In three days," the great-man brought his voice over the noise of his people. "In three days, when the Englishmen stop work in their fields to go into the god's house, you eager ones may ride up to the farms on the neck and shoot at cows, if that's what you want. Cows, nothing more. I will talk with the Englishmen myself. I will delay the war. You shoot cows."

The men heard only the word "cows" and raised their guns to salute him.

In the sleeping pines, by the low fires Metacomet walked, unwilling to leave his men. The gambling was quieter than usual, but the complaint extended from fire to fire. "We should dance tonight!"

"No dancing." He walked on. Mishquock had gone to the cave to sit beside Weskautaug, to make sure the drums did not sound. Kuttiomp was sitting beside Johettit. When the young man woke and was sober, he and Kuttiomp would ride to the long river to find the great-man who wore the tuft of the sea gull in his ear. They would bring him back to talk to this Edmund Andros.

The face looking up from the fire was Otan-nick's.

"Come." Metacomet motioned the young man off his heels and into the dimness under the pines. When he was sure no one else could hear, Metacomet said, "Your brother is going north for a few days. He'll come back. You are a man who stands apart. Tell me, would you desire to learn the eye of darkness?"

Otan-nick moved to avoid something on the path.

"Our wise-man has no sons." Metacomet suggested where the learning could lead.

Otan-nick shrugged.

"You might become the wise-man of Pokanocket." Metacomet made it clear.

At last Otan-nick spoke: "My father told us you were one of those great-men who become wise as well."

"I am not! I couldn't. . . ." Metacomet stopped. "I'm not that kind at all."

"If I did it, would I also be wisest-man of the daybreak people?"

"What?"

"After Weskautaug."

"He'll never be that!"

"Why not?"

"He's a little man."

"I don't want to do it, then." The pockmarked face closed itself. "I'd rather learn leather."

They walked back to the gambling fire and Metacomet saw the English boys. They were strapped to the ground, their arms wide above their heads and their legs staked wide at the ankles. They were Hugh Cole's two boys, the youngest ones.

"Spies!" His men worked fast at the cords.

"Untie them!"

"What?"

"Untie them!"

"But they crossed over at the wading place into our woods!"

"I invited them. Untie them."

Angrily, the guards undid the knots.

The boys stood, wobbly and quiet. Metacomet rushed his English as fast as he knew how: "Go home by way of the neck, boys. Tell Hezekiah Willett there will be trouble soon. He and his friends should go to Aquidneck. John Easton on Aquidneck is a good man. Then go home. Your part of Swansea is safe enough. Give my good wishes to your father and don't come out here again. I can't save you twice." He touched their shoulders. Both had brown hair and each looked like a copy of the other. Many children, one mother, the Englishman's way. The boys were breathing heavily, they had no wind. They took off their hats to him in thanks.

"These boys are going home to their father," he told the guards, who belted their knives with disappointment. "Pokanocket does not betray its friends."

We have our own laws.

The young men didn't wait for three days. Johettit's friends woke to find him gone north and that noon they took three horses from the grove, all but the black stallion. They rode them over the pig fence and found Hezekiah Willett's house empty. They went on, howling and hooting, to the cluster of reed-roofed houses. These were empty, too, except for a few men. They set fire to the reeds on top of two houses and then they shot their guns over the fields. With the smell of bloodied cows in their nostrils, they rode back to the neck to boast. How they ran from house to house, how they hauled out blankets! Kettles! Knives!

The next day, in the woods beside the Taunton road, Sunconewhew watched as the English soldiers marched through. Each carried a gun: none was without. Guards in the swamps watched the English soldiers cross the plain, turn west at the bridge and go into the preacher's walled house and shut the door. Later, Sunconewhew did not breathe as seventeen more soldiers came along the road, each riding a horse. Guards in the swamps on the plain watched them turn east, take the path to Swansea town on Mattapoiset and join the townspeople gathered inside Hugh Cole's rum house and shut the door.

So, Mattapoiset!

The next noon the young men rode off to see what they could find in the empty houses on Mattapoiset neck.

Metacomet sent Mishquock running for the stallion to catch up with the young men. "Go after them and keep them steady. They mustn't shed any blood. John Easton will be here soon." He wished it were Kuttiomp he was sending, a steadier man. But Kuttiomp was gone north. "Hurry up, and no blood!"

Metacomet ran to the spring in the empty village. The spring at Kickamuit bubbled up over the sand. At Nauset beach he had played among his mother's people on the shortest night of summer. He had ridden on the shoulders of a cousin into waves that deepened around them, playing horses at war. The water shifted and darkened and his cousin vanished from beneath him.

He sat by the spring, facing his wife's own cornfield and their single, distant house. When the hilling moon came and the corn was up to the knee, would the women be home to hill it? And when the corn was to the waist, where would they be? And shucked and shelled and ready to bury for winter? Would the men be over in Nahiganset, too? Their warriors' fingers mucky with clay? Turned into women who work at pots! Who would burn the brush in autumn? He turned from the cornfield. On the tidal river he saw what wasn't there. He saw the pale sun of winter on gray water and empty marshes turning the color of copper, birds diving. His ears heard what wasn't there. The wind beating on the sides of Montaup. He knew that English soldiers would sink their heels into the soft earth of this cornfield. They would be carrying cocked guns.

This was the eye of darkness; he must look no farther.

Finally, he heard the howl of runners on the river path from Mattapoiset.

Six were running together and a seventh was being carried

by them; the eighth was leading the horses. They crossed the sands to the spring.

"*Ho-ah, he-ah!*" They were running, red and full of joy. Who were these strange naked painted men approaching him?

He saw the blood that dribbled into the dust from the man they carried.

"They have drawn our blood first! We'll win!" The voices were exultant.

They lay the wounded man on the sand. Metacomet saw the white dots on the bloody chest.

My friend.

Mishquock's face was turned away. His hand was held close to the mucky chest. Metacomet reached out his own hand.

"We pounded at a door in Mattapoiset, to get our axes ground. They ground them fast, you bet!"

"We shot a cow, it bled from the eye and fell down, it's front legs were sliding out. . . ."

"A boy saw us and his father told him to shoot. . . ."

"Silence on their wide fields . . . asking for rum . . . the English boy . . ."

Metacomet's hand reached Mishquock's face and turned it toward him. In the eyes was a narrow slit of light. It widened now, with the face toward Metacomet. Mishquock tried to raise his fingers sticky with the blood, but he couldn't lift them off his chest.

Metacomet nodded to him: yes, the first blood. It's yours. We will win.

Mishquock's lips opened as if he wanted to start a word. He couldn't and the lips closed, pressed together like a baby's when it sucks. Then the light in his eyes narrowed and was gone.

Metacomet let go of Mishquock's head and it rolled back to where it had been turned. Metacomet crawled to the spring and pressed both his hands into the water and covered his face with mud. He wept.

"We remember war, after all, my nephew!" Smiling, Annawon held up the sixth head: yellow hair, not a face the great-man knew. He kept two of the heads and passed the other four back to Annawon. In Annawon's basket were a number of hands and feet that the great-man did not bother to examine.

"Hang it all on poles by the pig fence."

"It was clever, my nephew," the old man said as he gathered up the basket. "Clever, how you began the war without appearing to. It was like your father, when he let himself be caught by the Nahiganset to see if the Englishmen would save him with guns."

Heaviness came to the great-man's head; this he had not seen before in his father's story. But if a man may have two names; why shouldn't a man's story have a front side and a back? He hesitated no longer. He wrapped the two heads. He sent them westward by canoe to Naonanto with this message: "Hear my name. I am Pometacom. Burn the town called Providence and see how Englishmen die."

He put some of the Englishmen's clothes into baskets and gave them to runners. "Go north. Tell the Nipmuck I am the generation that rises. Those who join me will be clothed. Those who don't will be stripped, as I shall strip Boston."

To other runners he gave a hen and a rooster, in separate baskets. "Go north to Pocumptuck–the river. Halt Kuttiomp and Johettit and send them home. Tell the Pocumptuck that I am at war. Let these two in the baskets scratch at Englishmen's fields. Pocumptuck should join me. We'll push the strangers from all the towns along their river."

To Weskautaug he sent salt: the wise-man had caused him to move from where he was stuck on the path. He waited for the weeding moon to wither and die; for darkness.

. . .

When Johettit returned, Pometacom made him a captain at once. He sent him to hide beside the walled house near the bridge. New soldiers came, from Boston.

"What is he like? This new captain from Boston?" Pometacom motioned Johettit into his house. His wife and the Pequot slave woman were finally stripping the mats from this house, too. When dark came, they would all leave the neck for Pocasset.

"He is bold, my king! He came right out the door and into the woods after us!" Johettit's black star was gone and his chest painted red right up to and under his chin.

"What for?"

"He's an Englishman! Englishmen don't dodge in and out behind trees. They stand in a field and fire their guns all at once."

"Does Annawon know?"

Johettit laughed. "He knows now!"

"What's his name?"

"Mosely. He wears a wig. When your men saw him take it off, they thought he had two heads."

"Watch for the soldier Benjamin Church from Saghonnate. He's not foolish enough to wear a wig, nor would he stand in a field to fight."

Johettit touched the great-man on the shoulders as he left. Pometacom pulled away. "Be at the landing by sunset," he said. "But first take a few men up to the neck. Go into the houses there one last time and find the god's book. Rip it apart. Throw it on the road. Our god speaks out loud to us! And from now on, whenever you kill an Englishman, do this first. Throw back your head and call out, 'Lord Jesus, deliver him from my hand!' Then watch to see what happens. Nothing!"

As Johettit left, the women pulled the last mats off the top of the house. Pometacom opened the English chest and took out the three belts of the people and dressed himself in them.

Sunconewhew appeared where the south door had been. "My brother!"

"Quickly, what did Naonanto say?"

"He's happy to have the heads." The yellow line zigzagged up Sunconewhew's chest, but his greased shoulders looked as naked of a shirt as ever.

"Did you see any of Saghonnate?"

"Yes. One or two."

"So! They are all there!" Benjamin Church must have been too busy to take the great-woman of Saghonnate to Plimouth. Better she had gone to Plimouth. This way she might turn Naonanto's men against the daybreak.

Sunconewhew stepped into the house.

"Pack up your books." Metacomet held open the chest. "The women are afraid to touch them."

Sunconewhew knelt and took out the books. Sunconewhew had fear hanging about his neck and the pride of the black hawk was entirely gone.

Pometacom reached into the bottom of the chest to take out his beaded coat. He shut the lid.

"You won't be marrying any Nahiganset woman!" Pometacom put his arms through the two sleeves. "But you'll wear a brighter coat than this. The coat of the new people of the whole land."

A drop of rain fell on the lid of the wooden chest.

Sunconewhew rolled his books into a mat. "Will Weetamoo receive us?"

"Perhaps. Perhaps not. There's no knowing what Kiehtan knows. We ride with him, as on a current."

"How can we leave the neck? They'll take our land! It's written that way." Sunconewhew tied the mat.

"What's written isn't always true. Kiehtan spoke. He didn't press his words flat for our eyes. What he spoke was true. We're at war."

Rain began a steady pattern on the chest.

. . .

At sunset, his sister came.

She hadn't sooted for the death of her son!

She stood before him at the canoe landing where everyone but the men of the green swamp was loading canoes. Her hair was matted and dusty, her eyes empty of light. But they found him, those eyes, and fastened him and pierced him: "My brother, your war forced me from my home. These are the last words I will speak to you. You sold my husband's land, you let the ropes squeeze the life from my son. . . ." Her empty hand moved against her thigh in the gesture of spinning and she stopped her words.

"Josiah Winslow killed him."

"You killed him, to begin your war, to get my men back." Then, like an Englishwoman, she pulled a black cloth across her face, across her lips.

His sister sat across the fire, wrapped in darkness.

She leaned against another woman and was led along the path to the water.

Before Pometacom stood his sister's husband, Tuspaquin, the great-man of the lake. His whole body was sooted black, except for two circles of skin showing around his eyes.

"I bring you fifty fighting men." Tuspaquin stepped forward. "Assawampset will dance. Assawampset will fight."

"I grieve for you." Pometacom rubbed Tuspaquin's shoulders. "We will avenge your son."

The net of the daybreak mended itself.

Pometacom stood in the foremost canoe. The people were quiet and all he could hear was the water slapping against the canoes or against the sand of the shore. The twenty canoes of Pokanocket were ready, and on shore Weskautaug stood in the rearmost, waiting to give Pometacom the signal. The ten canoes of Assawampset were ready, paddlers clinging to the branches near shore to hold them close. The ten canoes of the wet cove and those of the low cove were ready. Only the ten of the green swamp were still loading, as Annawon had only now arrived from the pig fence. Pometacom saw in the darkness what was not there: Mosely's men running from Swansea, through the woods and into cornfields, to be greeted by squealing pigs and whining dogs. From the rearmost canoe Weskautaug called out that all was ready.

"Leave the dogs!" Pometacom shouted as the four-legged ones splashed in the water, trying to get into the canoes.

Thunder sounded in the distance.

"We need no dogs for this hunting! Push off! Push off! No singing when we land!" He need not have told them. The people moved together as one: the wolf is smarter than the dog; he turns to his own kind in danger.

"So, I am at war, great-man, my brother-in-law! I thank you for your love and care!" Weetamoo's jewelry glinted by the fire.

Her servants closed the doors to her house at the edge of the swamp. Pometacom and his wife and son waited inside to be greeted, but Weetamoo did not stand. She did not move toward them. Nor invite them to take off their leggings to dry them. The rain beat down on Weetamoo's mats above their heads as they stood, waiting.

"You've been at war since your husband, my brother, was poisoned." Pometacom felt the beaded coat wet and heavy on his shoulders.

Still Weetamoo did not stand.

"The Englishmen aren't your friends. Did they believe it wasn't you who burned their trading house?"

A look like spitting crossed the great-woman's face.

Pometacom began to take off his coat, without being invited to.

"They may not know who burned their trading house,"

Weetamoo said in her bold, full voice. "But I do. We of Pocasset know the crooked one. We know the fox, too well."

"Thank you for your greeting. It's wise of you, my sister-in-law, to take in your sister and her people. What woman would want it said of her that she refused her sister life?" He guided his wife forward and, at last, Weetamoo stood to make the formal greeting.

He had forgotten how tall she was. And her belly was slightly rounded; she did have Petananuet's child!

Weetamoo stood separate again. "You, who are no brother to me, you have taken my life. My husband was my life and he is gone. When the noses of your canoes were seen on the water, my husband told me to turn you back. When your canoes struck the sand and were pulled up, Petananuet walked away from me. He will find another woman. My life is gone. Now I give you my lands. Here, great-man, snakes and vines in a swamp! They are yours!" Weetamoo, the fierce, became a shadow, swaying.

"Come, my sister, rest." He gave the beaded coat to his wife and took Weetamoo to him, holding her. "I am a brother to you. I will find you a new husband." Into her ear he whispered, "You are Pocasset. I am Pokanocket."

Now he had six hundred warriors.

"We are men," he pulled her tighter.

Through the notches on his gun, Pometacom sighted on the face of an Englishman stamping through the brush at the outer edge of Weetamoo's swamp. He and the people were trapped inside, so it was proper that he fight. He squinted to see the face. It was not Thomas Leonard. Nor Hugh Cole. It was no one he knew. The man got caught in the thick vines, stumbled and fell. A second Englishman came from behind and started to fall over him.

"They're blind men!" Kuttiomp whispered at Pometacom's left.

"They don't see in the dark the way we do." Pometacom looked out of the swamp to the bare green poles in the twilight. He had set new house poles at the edge of the swamp next to Weetamoo's, only to abandon them for the thickest part of the swamp when the Englishmen came near.

The second Englishman stood up and Pometacom pressed the butt of his gun tighter against his cheek. He moved his weight forward onto his toes. A man was about the size of a doe. This one was black-haired, red-cheeked and not one he knew. Too soon to fire. Let more of them come into the darkness of the swamp. He waited; the branches tied at his shoulder cut into his flesh.

"Come, Englishmen. Let us fight! *Johettitea!*" Ahead to the left, Sunconewhew's soft, wheedling voice mocked the Englishmen and drew them one by one into the swamp, farther in under the dark trees and among the tangling vines. There was no sound from Annawon, who held the center ahead. Or from Johettit, who took the right.

The Englishmen's wooden fingers beat on their drum *over here*. The Englishmen's brass lips sang out *here I am*. Why didn't they hide themselves?

"Hear that?" at his right Otan-nick whispered. "The drum is telling the soldiers what to do. And that? The trumpet says where."

Didn't they plan it out ahead? Didn't they move as one? Pometacom lined his sights on a third Englishman, one who was carrying a heavy metal stick. Behind this was a fourth, coming so closely it was almost as if to get protection. A boy, hardly old enough to winter. The boy peered tentatively through the foliage. The man in front of him managed to move forward through the brush about a body's length. The boy stood to one side of the opening and stuck a pole into the mud. The pole was attached to his wrist. The pole went deeper into the mud than the boy expected. He held a match to the gun.

A matchlock! Deer could run from Seekonk to Cohannet before those guns went off! A flash appeared in the outer pan of the gun, but no bullet flew out the muzzle end. A look of panic covered the boy's face.

"*Iootash!*" Annawon's deep voice suddenly called out. Stand fast!

Pometacom sighted again on the Englishman in front of the boy and hardened his finger against the trigger. "Tell the grandmother . . ." But before he pulled, white smoke came from Sunconewhew's men and the Englishman's chest reddened while his legs slid into the mud. The boy's frightened face got caught in Pometacom's sights but dropped out of view. In its place appeared a new face: a short-haired old man who was no Englishman. Nipmuck? Saghonnate? No, Massachuset. Betraying the people.

Pometacom ran a few steps forward in the ooze. Otan-nick and Kuttiomp moved beside him, close as leggings. Pometacom leaned ahead and sighted on the round face of the Massachuset, and the gun shook against his cheek. The face of the old man separated into many parts. Heaviness, blackness inside Pometacom's head, an echoing inside his chest. He ran forward, but it was as if he himself were located behind his own body. Then the two of him connected and he was full of air that had to be screamed out. He yelled as he ran, a noise not only his own but one that joined the howls of his men around him.

He stopped and spit a bullet into deerskin and rammed it down into the gun. The English boy was still alive; he had abandoned his gun and was tying a rope to the leg of the first Englishman, the fallen one, who was now dead. Obscuring smoke collected around the opening but the Englishmen kept on coming in under the trees. Their bullets came from bags that never emptied. The dead man's leg got caught in vines when the boy tried to drag him out. A brown-haired Englishman got in over the vines, planted his gun-rest and fired, without aiming, right into the nearest bush.

"They have powder to waste!" Kuttiomp's bullet smashed into that Englishman's arm.

Pometacom fired at the next Englishman, a bearded man in

the prime of life, and the man arched backward so that his head was out of sight but the opening in his chest grew larger and larger as he fell. Now would Tasomacon make war! Now would Metacomet chase Englishmen! Now would Pometacom bite at thighs and crush through bone with the jaws of the wolf! He ran toward the drums and stopped.

He was too close. The great-man must leave space to flee, even when the people are trapped. He loaded his gun again. It was good to stand, at least, and not flee. If Thomas Leonard came through the trees, he would call to him before he shot.

In a little while the smoke and the increasing darkness filled the opening at the edge of the swamp. Gradually, the Englishmen ceased to enter and the shooting stopped.

It could not be true. In the darkness Pometacom ran to the highland where the dead lay. The wailing had begun and his wife and the other women left were already beating the ground with branches. Weskautaug stood on a fallen tree, with his eyes shut, singing. Pometacom broke through the circle of women and looked at the four bodies lying on mats. Not be. An old man from the village on Poppasquash hill. Not. A young man from the cove village. But the third had a yellow line of lightning running from the belly over the chest and up along the center of the neck. Be. That is as far as the zigzag went. Sunconewhew's head was not there: his brother's head was not attached to his brother's body.

"Dig his hole as deep as you can, line it with wood, mat it with many thicknesses. He is of the blood of great-men." Pometacom stood beside what was left of his brother's body. The ground he stood on was soft. It would not support a roof. In his fingers he could feel the copper chain with the green stone that he'd put into their father's grave, the red coat he'd hung on the tree nearby. He felt the gun he'd placed in the ground beside Wamsutta's body. He would save Sunconewhew's gun. He needed it. And Sunconewhew would laugh at him for burying it. He would put Sunconewhew's books into the earth, instead.

"Don't wait for dawn. Dig the holes now." Pometacom did not leave the body. Thousands of the daybreak people had sat all night on the burial hill at Kickamuit in a snow-bearing wind, waiting for dawn before they dug his father's grave. His sister had wanted the ancient, gray-haired man to be buried in an Englishman's box, stretched straight out! A thousand had sung for Wamsutta, slowly and heavily as the leaves of the trees fell about them on the ground. Now, in a swamp on Pocasset, a single wise-man and a few women sang for Sunconewhew. The headless body must be bound tight, with the hands over the knees, as an infant sits in its cradle. The mats must be sewn twice and the earth piled firmly and weighted down by logs. Sunconewhew would not rest easily, not without his gun and with only part of his body under ground. The Englishmen must have taken the head for their poles at Plimouth.

"Wait," Pometacom said aloud to his wife. "Set my brother poles for a roof, even if they sink. And get a good skin to cover them." Later, he would have his wife hang Sunconewhew's English shirts in the trees, for the air to take. His brother would not be comfortable on the long path without his shirts.

He turned then, to go back to his men. Do not speak to me, my brother, nor linger; on the path you will keep your balance, only do not look back. We are not yet ready to follow after you.

The faint singing of the mourners reached the men sitting by shelters on a platform in the swamp where Pometacom spoke: "We fought well today. And we don't fight alone. A runner has told us that my brother-in-law, who crept from here by darkness, has pushed the Englishmen from the town called Middleborough near his lake. He holds Nemasket, too, and one of the lost towns is ours again. The great-man of our wet cove, who also left by darkness, has sent a runner to tell us he has burned the town called Dartmouth, near him. The bearded ones ran off! The daybreak people is one again. And now the inland people of the north are beginning to join us. Some of you know that the old wildcat Matoonas pounced upon the town near Pakachoog, called Mendon. He tore Mendon to pieces! For the first time the inland people and the daybreak people are fighting together. We are becoming a new people, my friends, the people of the whole land. Our sons will winter in the farthest woods of Nipmuck. Our daughters will marry westward in Nahiganset. For I do suspect that the orange light we saw in the sky over the Seekonk was above the town called Providence. I do believe our friend Naonanto has burned that town." Here he paused.

The frogs whistled in the silence.

Annawon stood. "My nephew, I would bet that Naonanto, our friend, as you call him, lit no fire at the town called Providence. He has received the Saghonnate and I would bet he has taken the coat with the silver laces that his visitors from Boston held out to him. I would bet he has drawn his name on Boston's letter and given up war forever."

"My uncle, it was four ancient great-men of Nahiganset who set their marks on Boston's letter, not our friend. Our friend is in the prime of life and is the foremost among all Nahiganset's great-men. Our friend wants war. He takes the Saghonnate only to keep them from Plimouth. If he doesn't want war, why should he have sent me word that he is willing to take the women of Pocasset so we can go north?" Pometacom saw movement in the eyes of those who watched him, but their faces remained turned toward him, not toward Annawon.

"So he can sell them to Englishmen at two coats apiece," Annawon said.

"He promised me he would give Boston nothing of ours, not the least bit of fingernail from any woman we sent him!"

"It could be a trap. Lobster to catch bass." But Annawon sat down.

"My friends." Pometacom spoke to all the men. "When Naonanto sees we are winning, he will join us. Now I took you off the neck and I will take you out of this swamp. We'll go north at the dark of the hilling moon. You'll love the swamp near Quabaug! Aren't the roasted snakes tasty?"

Laughter. No more disagreement. All men stepped where Pometacom stepped; they almost held their left hands stiffly now, so eager were they to follow after him who did not hesitate. Perfectly the people, he was perfectly alone. And, for the first time, he was no man's brother.

Wailing of mourners, bark of the fox.

A fox has no shadow in the swamp. "Listen well, and tell this to your women. When the hilling moon dies and we have three dark nights before the moon of squash and beans, we will slip out on the northern path. We'll cross Titicut on rafts. The old men have already started to gather wood for the rafts. After we cross the water, we'll crawl on our bellies over the plain. Beyond Rehoboth we'll cross the Seekonk on our rafts and then run into the northwestern woods. When leaves fall, we'll push the Englishmen from the long river in the northland, and when the leaves are thick again, we'll push the Englishmen out of Boston. When it's time to plant, we'll come back to the southland and push out from here any who don't wish to serve us and then we'll plant. Sing softly, men, and sleep. The women will sit beside the dead."

A few of their songs rose and blended with the sound of the distant wailing. Pometacom put his hand over his eyes and felt on his fingers the dryness of his sooted face. How could they cross the plain unnoticed? Or get back to Kickamuit, on which a stone fort was being built? The sound of its building, of metal hitting stone, reached him in the swamp with each noon wind. Two hundred of the Nahiganset had already walked to Plimouth to give themselves to Josiah Winslow, led there by forty men of Saghonnate. And some of the great-men of the Nipmuck had put their marks on a letter to Boston, promising never to fight Englishmen. None of it turned Pometacom back, or slowed Pometacom down. There was only one path now on which to walk. His feet fell straight upon it, and he ran.

"*Yo hah weh hee: a new people cries, I am born!*" With his knife Pometacom began new cuttings in his arm, near those for his daughter. See, my brother, I bleed.

He stood and seared the gashes clean with fire. Father, I have killed your son.

He raised the arm no longer bleeding: "*Low in the southwest a black hawk circles and there is lightning over the land.*"

II

ANNO DOMINI

1676

"And Isaac's servants digged in the valley, and found there a well of springing water. And the herdmen of Gerar did strive with Isaac's herdmen, saying, The water is ours: and he called the name of the well Esek; because they strove with him. And they digged another well, and strove for that also: and he called the name of it Sitnah. And he removed from thence, and digged another well; and for that they strove not: and he called the name of it Rehoboth; and he said, For now the Lord hath made room for us, and we shall be fruitful in the land." Genesis 26:19–22.

7

The ground hardened in Rehoboth's common and the snows fell early and high over slanted roofs. With the snow, the reports of Indians burning the frontier towns out west on the Connecticut ceased. There was new talk.

"King Philip's coming down from the Connecticut. The Narragansetts are opening their wigwams to him for the winter. Don't you see, girl? That makes it legal." Isaak Strong bent to unlace his boots.

"What legal?" Witty said, having noticed only that Isaak was sober. The boys were asleep in their corner of the upstairs room where she and Isaak, too, lived like children.

"To declare war! The Narragansetts promised Boston they wouldn't give Philip any help. Now that they are, Plimouth says it's a defensive war and we've got every right to go in after him."

She watched him pull off the first boot.

"And Boston says if we catch Philip down in Narragansett country, we can each have a hundred acres of land, everyone that enlists. Robbie Benson's going. He wants to get a hundred acres out on Mount Hope. He says the Indian neck's got the best oysters." Isaak got the second boot off. "Now, I figure we could get a hundred acres on the neck, too. We could sell it for, maybe, thirty pounds, put that with our twenty and be out of here, for the Connecticut plantations!" He moved his arms as if to get more space in the small room. "We'd be free, girl. Cleared right out of Plimouth Patent."

"You seemed fond of Plimouth's legal opinions a minute ago." She stood up and shut the door to the room. Her father, too, spoke of freedom as the law on one hand and as its absence on the other. For her, freedom had more to do with whether she had her eyes shut or open.

Isaak's black hair fell in triangles over his forehead as he pulled at the stockings she'd knitted.

"Isaak, you wouldn't go in the October call-up. You were going to take five pounds and buy yourself off. Who'd be head of household for your mother?" She sat beside him on the bed and began to unbutton her dress.

"The fighting was in the north then, girl. We're lucky we never made it to Northfield!"

Luck: she didn't object, as her mother would, detailing the endless reach of God's hand. It wasn't God's hand or luck that had kept them from Northfield, where they'd be dead now, anyway, stripped naked and left to rot by the Connecticut. It was the fifty pounds they hadn't managed to save by the time Northfield opened.

"The war's down here this time, girl. And if we don't wipe them out while they're slowed by the cold, we'll have ourselves a swarm of two-legged grasshoppers come spring, jumping all over the land. This time, we've got to do it." He slapped her knee and crawled to his side of the bed. "And afterwards, we'll have our land."

She pulled the nightdress over her head. She could count on the fact that most of his plans didn't work out. "Stop hauling water like some squaw," he'd say, and then go off without drawing enough for the day. She lay down beside him and pulled the covers to her chin. Maybe there was such a thing as luck.

Downstairs the next morning, Mama Strong gave her son the last of her wool money.

"*Humn*," she said, nodding at Witty, the flesh under her neck jiggling. "Now don't start out toward the inn till you've got your powder and your bullets."

"I got to have a jacket, too." Isaak smiled for them, the only two women on whom the smile no longer worked.

He came back at noon for his dinner but he didn't return at twilight. After supper Mama Strong went to sleep on the big bed downstairs. The serving girl went to sleep in the hallway upstairs. Witty sat up in the big chair by the fire in the house that Mama Strong kept by refusing to remarry. The house and the hundred acres would go to Isaak, if she ever did. And some to Purchase. Isaak's younger brother sat up with Witty now, his blue eyes resting on her throat. Mama Strong slept at a decent distance. Witty covered her throat with her hand: this was the chair where she'd held Maie in September, wrapped like a huge baby in a blanket. Her hot face, her thin hands, her stillness. Up out of bed to sort out her box of shells, neat for death. "Look at me, Maie. Keep your eyes open. Smile at me, see? I'm smiling. You smile." But the corners of Maie's narrow mouth had not moved and her eyes had shut. "I can't play with you any longer, Mama. I'm tired." "God tests us," Witty's mother said, implying He'd had something more like punishment in mind. But it wasn't Witty's fault. Nor Maie's. Witty was sure of it. She took her hand away from her throat. Purchase had gone to sleep. Isaak got home very late and couldn't open the latch by himself.

Purchase helped her get Isaak up the stairs and then he left them together.

"You're drunk." She got Isaak's new jacket off. His shirt smelled of beer.

"Hundreds of us, girl! More than on market day, and every one drunk as a lord. Oh, I tell you, we boys were running the town tonight!" He stumbled getting his pants off, but he didn't fall. "It's big, the new inn. We couldn't have fit into Abell's. And not one of us is getting fined, either. There's too many. The constables were looking the other way. Oh, I can't get out of going now, girl. I'd have to take a paddling and think what that would do to me!" He strutted his hard, muscular body before her and fell crookedly onto the bed.

She covered him from the cold and lay down beside him; the smell of beer was in the cracks of his neck. "Isaak." She began to say goodbye.

"Whatever we can pick up is ours, Witty. I'm going to get some of their slippers with the beads for you."

"Oh, go to sleep!" She lay still and narrow.

"And you know what else?" He turned toward her now and whispered.

"What?"

"You can buy a little boy of theirs for just six old coats. Then you turn around and sell the boy to the slavers at Newport or Taunton for three pounds. Three pounds, girl!"

"You wouldn't!"

"And it only takes two coats to get a girl. You can sell a girl for two pounds."

"Isaak!"

"And sometimes," he whispered directly into her ear, "you don't even give the buggers any coats. You just grab the girls . . . like this!" But he had drunk too much to say a real goodbye. He slept.

In the morning, he greased his boots a second time to keep out the water of the swamps. As he left for the makeshift rafts at the wharf on the cove, a light snow was beginning to fall.

In January when the snow was up to the windows, Witty received a letter from Governor Winslow's secretary. In February when the bay froze over and it was too cold to breathe, Robbie Benson got free of duty in the north and brought her Isaak's gun. The serving girl opened the door to Robbie. Mama Strong came running through the snow from the sheep pen, where the pregnant awes were busy after grain. Purchase came up from the woodlot at the brook, where he'd been cutting; he was head of household now. Witty sat in the big chair and rested the gun across her knees. She took hold of Caleb's small hand. Ephraim stood like a man at her side and the baby ran about near the hearth. Poor baby . . . no, don't shut your eyes, don't wander off. "Go slow, Robbie," she said. "Start from the beginning."

Mama Strong picked up her knitting.

Purchase crouched beside the hearth.

"The beginning?" Robbie was a short, sturdy man and now he cleared his throat: this was a formal act such as other men had carried out. "When we first went over Seekonk, we didn't find any sign of the Narragansett. They'd cut the ferry ropes and we had to row hard against the wind. Couldn't find anyone at all. The captain, he's a tough man, Mosely, he finally caught one Indian in a barn, but he couldn't get him to talk. So he wrapped a cord around his head. Pulled it tighter and tighter, see? The eyes, they were starting to come out of the head. . . ." Robbie saw that the boys were staring at him and he hurried on.

"Pretty soon that Indian said he'd show us where Philip had come down to hide. He said it was in a big swamp that belonged to his sachem and that we'd never get into it. Naonanto's town, he called it. Saturday we started to follow this Indian. On our way we burned some wigwams and the boys caught a couple of Indian children. We got to the point at dusk and slept in the open. It was snowing hard. We were up and marching before dawn and I can tell you, it was a whole lot warmer marching. Fifteen miles inland along a ridge. Isaak was merry during most of it. 'Beats haying,' he said. I remember that. 'Beats shearing.' We hiked till afternoon without fire or food, except what we chewed as we walked along. Massachusetts was marching in front of us carrying those French guns, the ones with the knives on them?"

From the hearth Isaak's brother nodded at Robbie.

"We must have passed five swamps and then we got to the edge of a new one. The Indian said this was where we'd find Philip. The Massachusetts boys saw some Indians under the trees and went in after them. There was some firing up ahead and then we were running in. The ground was frozen solid as ice and snow was coming down fast and heavy, even under the trees. There was brush caught into the ice and you could hardly keep up on your feet. We came to a high sort of island way inside the swamp. There was a palisade of poles around it and they'd even plastered themselves a hedge of logs outside the palisade. No place to get in! But the Indian finally got us to the pathway in. It was one dead tree to balance on! All set up so they could pick off their attackers nice and easy, one at a time. We began to see what we were in for."

He stopped and looked at the faces of the boys. He cleared his throat. "Your father was a brave man, boys."

"Did he get hurt?" Ephraim's voice was private, scarcely a boy's, though he was only eleven.

"It was quick. I don't think he felt it much."

"Keep on from where you were, Rob." Witty wanted the story to happen as it had happened to Isaak, or as close to that as she could get. She shut her eyes, thinking of Isaak jumping over the gully at her father's house when they were young.

"Do what she wants," Purchase said. He was in charge.

Mama Strong's knitting needles stopped clicking.

Witty opened her eyes. They were watching her. "Yes," she said. "Keep on." She nodded at Robbie. With so many deaths, it was hard to know what was real.

"The officers gnawed it about a bit. Do we fight on the Sabbath, and so forth. You know them. But soon enough we started across the log. And as soon as we set foot on it, our men began falling. Even the captains. The captains didn't dare spare themselves from crossing the log. They knew none of us would have set foot on it if they didn't go first. Isaak was behind me, I think. He was a good shot, you know. He probably got inside. It took two hours to go over the log and maybe a thousand got in. There were a thousand Indians waiting for us inside and firing back at us and each and every one of them's a good shot. Every last Jack Nigger of them. Then somebody saw Philip. He had his bodyguard around him. They never leave his side, you know. We all began to scream 'Give us Philip! Give us Philip!' I never did see him myself. I'd have known him, too, with that bad hand of his, and that air he has, of watching. It was a big place, Naonanto's town. A lot bigger than Rehoboth. Maybe five hundred wigwams. The squaws had been cooking dinner, you could smell the meat boiling. We were so hungry, too. We tried shooting into the wigwams, but it turned out that they were lined inside with tubs of seed corn so that the bullets just ripped in and stopped, very neat. The squaws and the kids were perfectly safe inside those houses. The snow was swirling all around outside and the gun smoke was heavy. You couldn't see much. It was getting dark, too. Three hours we must have fought. And the bucks were picking us off, some of them sitting up in the trees outside the wall. They threw everything at us: arrows, axes, stones. It got too dark to see much of anything. 'Burn them!' the officers finally called out. So we poured our powder on the first row of wigwams and set it off. The wind was high and pretty soon the women were sizzling like meat in those wigwams." He stopped and eyed the women to see if he told too much.

"Go ahead," Mama Strong said.

Purchase shifted his position on the hearth.

Witty squeezed Caleb's hand.

"There was one girl of theirs catching on fire. I can smell her now. I wanted to help her and I thought I might shoot her to make it easier. But I needed my bullet. I wish I'd done it now. At night I sometimes think of her twisting in the flames. She wasn't more than fourteen, I'd guess. Well, we burned five acres of those wigwams, and every soul in them. It got quieter. We caught an old woman outside the walls and she told us there were a thousand fresh warriors of Philip's right behind us in the woods. And we'd heard of another thousand of his waiting about a mile past the swamp. We had to get out, even without catching Philip. Our men who'd got hurt, their wounds were swelling and stiffening. So we picked them up and got going. The sun was on its way down, not that you could tell there ever was a sun behind those snow clouds and under those trees. Once we got outside the swamp, we were sorry we'd left it. The snow was blowing at our eyes like knives and there were eight hundred of us to carry the two hundred hurt ones. Four to a man, see? I didn't get Isaak. But I did see him, then. He was four or five ahead of me. It was a buckshot wound in the face, I'd judge. Smashed into the jawbone, maybe into the bone behind the ear. He died as they carried him. I know because they buried him right beside the path a few minutes after he died. Soon as they could dig a little, not very, I mean . . ."

"Did he say anything?"

"He couldn't talk anymore. His jaw."

Ephraim looked down.

"Then what happened?" Witty asked it automatically, almost politely, although the story was over.

"I had to keep on walking and carrying the one we had. My toes froze and I didn't dare blink for fear my eyelids would stick together. The water from my eyes was running down my cheeks and freezing there. We got back to Smith's long after midnight. They cut off our shoes and gave us rum, but they hadn't any new shoes or stockings. The captain was raging. So was Josiah Winslow in his fancy clothes, two hundred pounds a year we pay him! Before we knew it, all the Narragansetts were gone. They up and headed north to the back country along the Connecticut. Philip went along with them. Or maybe not. Maybe the Narragansetts went north alone to join Philip up there. Yes, sir, some of the men began to say that Philip had never even been down here in that swamp! And it's a fact that nobody who knows him from Abell's had actually seen him. So we boys had to set off into the woods to catch up with who knows what ahead of us. Without any food from Josiah Winslow, without anything to drink. The Indians were eating fine, you can bet your . . . Sure, we found what was left of half of Rhode Island's horses and cows, hundreds of carcasses along the path. The Indians ate every step of the way, I can tell you. We'd have deserted right there in the woods but for the eight pounds Plimouth would have fined us. I got out in Boston. Never forget that day!"

Witty folded her hands over the gun. "What are you going to do now?"

Robbie stood up. "I'm putting in a veteran's claim for land. We're going to get a whole township, us veterans. There's two hundred acres over by the lake at Assawampset up for the taking right now and there'll be more. That's a drop in the bucket, next to the seven thousand acres out on Mount Hope Neck. They can't put it up until a full year passes, and it'll take a couple years more to clear the claims, but when we get the neck, we'll start a new township of sixty holders. Wonderful oysters, Witty. Sally and I are going to wait for Mount Hope. You ought to claim, too. It's widows' rights, they say. Even women can get some land!"

"You can stay here until you get married again," Mama Strong said, casting off stitches. "We've only got one man left, but the boys can help Purchase and we'll make do."

On the first day of March the black-hatted men of the general court at Plimouth awarded Widow Witty Strong born Peck possession of the six ewes her mother-in-law had given her a few years back. The men gave her the ewes in recognition of her unusually good carriage and because she was left in the hard position of having three small boys to raise and no older boy to support her while she did it. Of the cows, she got her widow's third: four cows. Ephraim got his four and the younger boys each got two. Because she had the ewes, she didn't get either of the horses and Ephraim got the pair of them. As for the land, there wasn't any, of course. She got a third of the twenty pounds she'd saved out of her wool money, six pounds thirteen shillings and fourpence. Ephraim got the same. Caleb and the baby each got three pounds six and eightpence. She hadn't any rights in the house; if she did, she could have opened an inn. Mama Strong would never hear of an inn; she'd managed alone on sheep, and her sons. Purchase took Witty's elbow to lead her out of the stuffy room.

"You're lucky," he said as they sat to eat in the inn where they'd spent the night, she in a room of women and he in a room of men. "Six ewes and they'll be lambing soon."

"Yes." She smiled at him. His hands looked so much like Isaak's: long fingers, wide nails. Barley was three shillings sixpence per bushel and wheat was four and six. Fear came into her throat. She could take the boys and go to Boston and look for work as a housekeeper. But who would welcome her, with three children? Rehoboth was full of widows. If she wanted to remarry, she'd have to go west, to buy in at a frontier town. With six pounds thirteen? "Yes. Six ewes and twice as many lambs, I'll do fine."

"A man in my room last night told me Philip stole twenty Englishwomen from Lancaster." Purchase had the same smile as Isaak. "King Philip and his ladies!"

She couldn't get used to how they called him king.

Out in the light, she and Purchase went to unhitch the horses. Witty could see the gray stretch of the ocean below. Far, far out beyond all that water was England, and the Dutch Republic, Spain. Her parents had come across the water, her mother only a girl Maie's age. Her mother'd been so glad to leave Leyden, where the brick houses were too close and the fat-faced Dutch children with their upturned noses and their silk dresses had scorned her. When the ship reached landfall out on the Cape, her mother stood on the deck in a heavy wind and stared at the yellow grass of the headland, afraid for the first time. Getting into the small boats, she watched for dark heads to rise fast above the dry grass and for painted men with handmade bows and clubs to run onto the beach. But there were only gulls, their calls wheeling past her through layers of air. Standing on the steady ground, she'd felt dizzy. And the grown-ups were so quiet, remembering the tales the Virginians told of wild men. Beyond the headland stretched the green of pines. Whose land was it? It was a wide land. But how far back did it go? And who owned it? Wild men screeching gibberish and throwing sticks? She helped with the washing of the clothes and hung wet things on the bushes nearest the sand. Would the men be naked, or would they be wearing leaves like Adam? When she'd stood on the sand to thank God for having brought them safely to shore in His hand, she'd noticed that the grown-ups had their eyes open, too. But still there was no movement, only the wind and the birds, and the sea washing over the beach grasses.

"Let's get going!" Purchase helped her mount Cloudy, his hand a steady place to put her own.

Her father had been twenty-one, the same age as Purchase. But her father had landed at Boston. It was good, the feel of a man's hand.

"Look at that!" Purchase whistled when they turned a corner.

Witty wasn't sure what it was. She squinted at the post on their right and made out that the thing on top was a head. Smaller than you'd think.

"It's his brother, King Philip's brother," the guard at the gate explained to Purchase, eyeing the sea as if it were a comfort. "And you can bet he's coming back to get it, too!"

How unlike a king Philip was: Tasomacon. She had seen him close up. He'd been standing very straight. And he didn't talk much. Maybe that is like a king. If only her own brother, Stephen, were here. But Stephen was underground a long time now, bundled up in his shroud.

Purchase rode on his mare in front of her. It was good to ride behind him, good to have a man to be the other half of, if only for a day, and even if she'd known him since he was Caleb's age. If she called his name softly? Walked into the woods slowly? No, she was half again his age. But if she married again, she wanted the man to be tall, like Purchase. Like Isaak. She knew where Isaak was now, all the time. God was making him wait for her, keeping him sober. They passed the fort house outside Plimouth, the place where the woman and a baby had been strangled the day before. Their man had been away from the house too long.

They reached the Titicut and took the ferry over the river to Taunton, the horses shy above water. Then they passed onto the great plain and found that yesterday's rain had washed away more snow. Water ran in new gullies and stood in ditches that edged the fields. The flow and drip of it was the only sound, that and the hooves of their horses on the muddy road. And, sometimes, the calls of birds. As they approached Rehoboth, it was quiet, too. Not many men out cutting wood or sowing peas. Philip might be breathing in the woods at the edge of the plain, watching. The men stayed near their barns and houses, helping the goats to kid. Spring was coming, but so was Philip. With the western towns burned last fall and the northern towns going under this spring, Rehoboth was becoming a frontier town again, just as it had been when her parents settled it.

Mama Strong opened the door. "*Humn*, children, he's nearby." People seemed to speak of him with a capital *H* as if he were the Devil himself.

Mama Strong had ordered a raft for her sheep: "As soon as the lambs are born, I'm going to Aquidneck. You'll stay here, Purchase, and take care of things. Witty, take Hannah with you and do what you like."

But you can't stay here. Not alone in the house with Purchase.

Witty got Purchase to drag her sheepfold across town through the common, to her father's house. Her father would never leave Rehoboth. Not for some Indian scare that would never take place. Nor would she. Besides, she knew Philip. Well, her brother had. And Philip saved his friends. Everybody said so. He had saved Swansea. Saved the Cole boys. Twenty women from Lancaster for his own bed, indeed! You can't believe everything you hear.

"I bet you can marry Joseph Hoskins, girl," her father said when she got home. "He's got a good holding and his wife will never last through March, from the looks of her."

8

"When will we eat it?"

"Tonight. For the new year." Witty worked quickly in her mother's house, familiar with the bowls and pots that were better than her own or Mama Strong's. Conception Day tomorrow, Saturday, March 25th. Sixteen hundred and seventy-six years ago tonight, Mary was combing out her dark hair over there in Galilee, waiting for the spirit of God to enter her. How? Keep combing your hair, girl. You'll find out.

"I want some for my birthday." Caleb, her middle boy, leaned farther toward the cake.

"I'll save you some." His birthday wasn't until Thursday. After Maie, he was the child most like herself.

Beside Witty, her mother shaped bread into loaves, her palms white with flour: "I know Will's safe up in the north and Purchase and Submit's in good hands over at the Hoskins' but I do wonder what your sister's doing."

"Raising the dead."

Emily Peck blinked her pale eyes and did not reply, keeping peace between her daughters.

It was true that when Maie died, Eunice had marched up from Swansea in her odd black Baptist clothes to speak to Maie. Eunice had muttered her words over a stiff white face that was already set in the proper expression for being introduced to elders. Sprinkling of holy water: rise. You are forgiven.

For what? A lot of children had died late in the summer. There must have been something in the air, in the wells.

Witty refrained from saying anything about Baptist women and how they ran their men. That was one sure way to get her mother talking against Eunice. A woman's desire shall be subject to her husband, dear; Adam was first formed; do not usurp authority. Neither of Emily Peck's daughters had married well; that is, neither had married the godly.

"Now, I hope you're going to choose farming, boy." Clement's voice came across the room to the women. He was talking at Ephraim. "I remember when I first saw men working the land. It was up at my uncle's place in the country. Lodovicus Peck, not a gentleman, mind you, but every so often a Jack would put off his hat to the old man and make a leg."

At Witty's elbow, Caleb whispered. "Is he going to tell about the ear?"

"I don't think so." Her father's story had always seemed so ordained, coming somewhere between "Let there be light" and "And there was." Ordained in its good ending, its fruitfulness. Her father had only listened to the preachers for amusement, at first. He'd stood in the courtyards of London, happy to be out of the stink of the felt shop and eating his meager packet of luncheon as slow as he could. Then he'd seen the king's men slice off the ears of one of the preachers. The ax had nicked the man's neck but left one ear dangling. The preacher reached up and pulled off his own ear. That alone convinced Clement Peck of the new gospel.

"I never could have gotten any land over there," her father went on to Ephraim. "So I signed up with the saints, though I'm not the kind of man that always wins the battle of the heart. First I finished out my seven years in the felt shop. Then I signed up for seven more on a farm over here. Oh, but the men I came over with in '35 were the most liberal and forward-thinking in all England. Not like the fellows coming now, money's all they care about. Hingham smelled so sweet, full of cedar as it was then. I hadn't been there long before the men my age went off to fight the Pequots. Everybody talked about it but my master wouldn't send me. I was a grown man, worth three boys to him. The years went by and I began to sneak off at noontime, when we were supposed to be resting, to hire out for an hour's building on the cart road. I needed more than what I'd be due at the end of my seven years if I wanted to marry a certain Emily Cushman of Scituate. Her parents didn't want her marrying a bonded man. She did, though. Didn't you, Emily?"

"I did, Clement." Emily hadn't married the godly either, which was one reason she'd been so keen on getting her daughters to do it.

"And when I got out of bondage that time, I got out of the Bay Patent, too, clear away from all its magistrates. I came west to the frontier right here under your feet. Boston always had to rush around putting up its towers in a day. Plimouth is worse, but how could I know Rehoboth would get snapped up by the Plimouth men? I wanted something slower, myself, something like the Dutch cities where the law is stronger than the clerics and men can think what they please in their own homes. If I were you, I'd take myself way west to the Connecticut. Black soil thick as a snowfall, and free. Of course, there's the other thing. Out there, you'd be too busy cutting trees to bother with much else. Now me, I meant to breed myself some squashes over here. I meant to keep a record of them, all the generations of the squash. Think what we can do here! We've already got the best of everything from home! Canals. Forges. Dutch windmills. British wheels ticking over our streams. Your generation's going to have some fun. What'll it be, boy? Ships that sail under water? Wagons that fly in the air? Spyglasses to see the planets with? Or the little bugs in the water? If you stay in Rehoboth here and farm, you'll have some time for that sort of thing. You'll reap the harvest we sowed. But the Connecticut, that's where I'd go, nonetheless. Now your grandmother, she'd have to wait to hear where the Almighty intended to send her before she'd join on."

Emily was ready: "His hand maintains any that follow Him."

"His hand and a few flintlocks!"

It was the same to Witty as when they'd debated over her head and Stephen's. "Those Plimouth people," her father would say, addressing himself, as usual, to Stephen. "Always the Lord's hand pushing things overboard or into the fire, never the wind, eh? Never their neighbors' fingers!" And when Stephen laughed, Witty's mother would look up worriedly, quick to see if Witty's eyes had been clouded by doubt.

Now Witty sneezed when the flour filled the air.

"Christ save!" her father called from the big chair.

"Clement!" On the single issue of blasphemy, Emily Peck would usurp authority.

"Oh, come on, Emily. My parents said it."

"And we didn't come here to breed squashes, either." Resolutely, Emily picked up one loaf of bread and then the other. She walked easily, attributing her good health to the fact that she had married an adventurer. She had to stay alive to win him over. What had hovered above the sky at Leyden, over the narrow brick houses of the godly, over the shoulders of those who patiently taught themselves the crafts they would need in the new land, had given Emily Cushman the assurance that she could speak out on this issue. Now she moved deliberately toward the oven with the two loaves, setting one foot before the other. But it scarcely mattered toward what destination Emily Peck traveled, since all her roads were simply lines in God's hand.

So Witty was home, caught again between two choices.

"But I don't like farming, Grandpa. I want to be a pewterer." Ephraim's voice had grown smaller since they'd come here.

The next day was Saturday and the new year came in with it, bringing one hundred fresh soldiers from Boston. They stopped for beer at the inn on the Boston road and then arrived, past twilight, at the homes where they were to be fed and bedded. Witty opened the door to a sixteen-year-old named Duncan; his red hair gave him an earnest look, and he was tired.

"Came from Boston, then?" Emily did not attend the boy's reply but directed that they move out from the front room, where they'd stayed the winter for warmth. Tonight they would eat their supper in the small room to the back of the house. It was spring: official as the moment that her father raised the wooden window of the barn. Clement arrived from his orchard, where he'd ventured to prune his apple trees, though there were rumors that Philip's Indians were in the woods close by the Seekonk.

"Bless this food, oh Lord, and town. Give us the heart to keep calm and remind the young how much more difficult it is to build than to destroy." Clement sat down in the big chair at the end of the table.

Ephraim took up with the soldier, only five years his senior: "This is where King Philip started, in Rehoboth, right here." Ephraim's black hair was no longer quite so soft and glossy as it once had been.

"Oh, thank you, but I don't care for milk." Duncan refused the buttermilk and accepted beer. "Right here, is it? This is where he rode last summer, hollering and shooting at cows with his broken hand?"

"That was in Swansea," Clement corrected. "The town south of here. Baptists."

"This is where he crept through in July, out of Pocasset swamp," Ephraim continued, only to be interrupted by the serving girl.

"Just like the muskrat, to which he is related!" Hannah's cheeks were red with the high color of the Scots.

"Crept out of Pocasset to burn Dartmouth and every one of its Quakers, serves them right!" Ephraim repeated the tale told by his father.

"Ephraim!" Witty corrected him with the one word; hers was the voice of reason, as was her father's. Philip could not be everywhere at once. And Quakers did no one any harm. "You, Hannah?" The girl was her charge until Mama Strong came back. She was the daughter of a Taunton malter who used too much of his own product. "You can pass the buttermilk."

"I know what he did in the Bay Patent," the boy soldier went on. "He rolled the shrouds right off of dead people after he burned Brookfield last summer. And in the fall, while Springfield was burning, he sat on that black horse of his, laughing. Screaming!"

"Philip is a reasonable man." Clement silenced the talk. "Like his father before him. His brother Alexander was the crazy one."

Sunday, Duncan got up and, with Ephraim to wave goodbye, he marched off with the others toward the Seekonk, to see if there were, indeed, a large bunch of Mount Hopes nearby. As it was told later in the town, two lame old Indians called for help from the edge of the woods by the river, and when the soldiers went in under the trees, they were quickly surrounded by hundreds of Indians. They fought all Sunday afternoon, standing back to back until there were no backs upright to lean against. A single scout from Rehoboth ran home, and some Rehoboth men rowed over the Seekonk out of sight downriver and ran into Providence for help. But the Baptists over there were still thick into their Sunday prayers. By the time they finished, the hundred soldiers were dead, except for one who had broken his leg and hidden in the crevice that tripped him. The patrol from Rehoboth found him at twilight.

The wounded man didn't know for sure if it was Philip they'd been fighting. Or even if it was Mount Hope Indians. "Who can tell them apart, Sergeant? We had those Cape Cod Indians of yours painted up yellow so's we wouldn't shoot them. I couldn't have told Jack from Jed. But I can tell you this. The buggers took some of our boys off and tied them to trees. Dancing, taunting them, see? Just like it was Our Lord. And, as with Him, I can tell you, it was just the beginning." The men of Rehoboth pried the fellow out of the crevice and then they turned in the Sabbath twilight to catch the yellow eyes of the wolves that were waiting under the trees with their long red tongues hanging out of their mouths. The men left the bodies and ran home to their houses and to their women and to their new, half-finished meetinghouse on the green inside the palisade.

That night Witty sat with the boys in her own pew, hers and Isaak's and Mama Strong's. She sat between Purchase and Hannah, among the town's sixty householders, and their women and children, for a special humbling. Young Pastor Newman raised his hand over them: "Oh Lord, Our Father, because of our lapses, Thou hast armed the savages to be a whip to us, that we may bend our stubborn knee before Thee. We are carnal; we lie and steal; we set prices too high; we think upon another man's woman. Smash our terrible pride! Grind our ferocious will! Then leash, oh God, these dogs of war, and draw them off from us. Cause us to know Thy true name, here in the wilderness that Thou hast made to bloom. Doubters, bow your heads in the face of Providence, as your fathers before you did. Relieve us of the unbelief that has swept over this second generation, we whose fathers showed us the way in the wilderness but whose own feet have now strayed from that straight way. Ah, God is good! This is the latest proof of His hand, that He watches! Yet He is ever ready to guide us back to the path and to put out any fire that threatens us, if only we will soften our hearts. Surely He will snatch us from harm in the nick of time!"

On Monday morning a rider from Plimouth reached the green.

"He didn't even get off the horse," Clement said to the women back at the house. "We all stood there and he read out that Plimouth was sending us word to abandon Rehoboth. 'Move back to the coast,' he told us. Where's he think we've got to go to?"

"We could go up to my sister's in Scituate." Emily stood by the hearth.

"No. Philip won't destroy his friends. We're staying. Most of the other men are, too. I'm going out to dig the pit."

Sound of a spoon popping over the bricks of the hearth. Witty helped her mother pack up Duncan's belongings to be sent back to the army house in Boston. Then they started gathering their own things by the door, things to be buried in the pit.

"He's never got here before," the older woman said.

"He's not coming now." Witty went to her basket near the hearth. She watched the baby pop the spoon along. She had to stop calling him baby, he was four. He seemed to be using the spoon to make gunshot in a war of his own. Suddenly he dropped the spoon and tenderly lifted a small twig of a fallen soldier up on his own flat palm and carried it straight to heaven on the bench, as God had carried his father, Isaak.

She took a faded infant's dress out of her basket. It did seem that Philip had always been coming and never gotten here. He hadn't arrived in '62, when he was supposed to be coming to avenge his brother's death and when Witty was meeting Isaak in the Rose Meadow. Nor in '67, when he was thought to be bringing the French right along with him and when she'd been pregnant with Maie and nursing Ephraim. Nor in '69, when he was said to have befriended the Narragansetts and the next thing she knew, she was pregnant with Caleb; if Philip was ever really coming, it would surely have been in '71, when Waitstill was conceived. Philip had wanted his guns back then. So, you see, Philip was never coming. Her father was right. You can't believe everything.

She headed toward the door, pressing the infant's dress into her pocket where she had already secured the small lace cap.

"You're not going out, are you, dear?"

"If we're going to the green, I've got to get my sheep over!" Witty was out the door.

"Now, dear, I didn't mean you shouldn't bury the dress!" Her mother called after her from the doorway.

Meaning don't bury it, Witty knew. She crossed the mud of the barnyard. Meaning come and tell me soon that you are a good girl, that you have obeyed even my unspoken commands —oh, especially those.

The horses by the barn pressed their ears back to stare her past the winter-shrunken haycocks, black with damp. They were alarmed by yesterday's wailing and by the distant smell of the dead at the river. She had been foolish to come back to the house of her parents. A grown woman made into a child again, half size, as short as you get when you kneel in prayer.

"You getting the sheep?" Her father looked up from the pit.

"Yes. Don't let Ephraim go with the warders." She headed past the pit to the willow. At just this angle the March sun of all her earlier years had slanted into her bones. And isn't this where she had been standing when she first met Philip? Yes, the very place! If only he were here now, she would bargain for her life, the boys', the town's. This was exactly where she'd been standing when her brother Stephen had come out of the barn leading Daisy, with the Indian boy astride. "Talk slowly now, Witty. He doesn't speak English very well."

The Indian boy had slid down from the horse and stood looking at her. He was wearing soft shoes and leggings and an English jacket. He kept one hand behind him. He was taller than Stephen, with a long face.

"Go on, go on." Stephen had urged him closer. "It's my sister Wit-ty."

She had put out her hand in common greeting, but the Indian hadn't taken it. When she lowered her hand, her fingers brushed against his jacket and she drew her hand back, startled.

"Taso-macon," her brother said.

"Taso-macon," she repeated carefully.

His eyes held hers; his were dark and heavily lidded.

"He's been living alone all winter in the woods." Stephen was proud of his friend.

She nodded her head. The Indian boy nodded his. The seconds seemed to spread out and enclose her. She brushed back the hood of her dark cloak and with her thumbs she pushed her long yellow hair over her shoulders.

Then he was gone, almost as if he had not been there at all, gone across the lot and running along the gully.

"Look what he gave me this time," Stephen said. It was a

white stone. "See, you can look straight through it. Put it up to your eyes. He says it's lightning turned cold."

Stephen had forgotten to bully her. She held the stone to her eye.

"Mr. Willett says they live alone for a whole winter, then they're men. Papa would never let me try! Isn't he thin-looking, though? And did you see his hand?"

Later that day, she had found the blood, her first. She believed it had come when she touched him.

She didn't see the Indian boy again, though Stephen did. "When he saw me by the falls in the plain, he waved me over to where they were standing. I went right out on the rocks with them. They laugh a lot when you're alone with them." That was the spring that Stephen died, the first of many.

Past the willow and Witty was down into the gully, out of sight of the house. She pressed a quick hole in the earth with the heel of her shoe, knelt and spread Maie's little dress on the ground. From her pocket she took the ancient white lace infant's cap: Maie's, hers, even her mother's, from Somerset in England. She rolled it and the dress neatly together and pushed them into the hole and smoothed the earth back over them. The Indians had taken all of Isaak. They would not get her last bit of Maie.

She stood, breathing fast. People said she hadn't been well since Maie died. Isaak. It was nothing. It would pass. It was only that she didn't expect much anymore, much that was good. And that the things her mother was convinced of began to make sense. The world might truly be nothing. God everything. Her father might be wrong. The holy light that seemed to engulf Emily Peck's head was beginning to graze the back of her own now and then. It made the world luminescent at sudden turnings and convinced her, if only temporarily, that it was but the things of the spirit that mattered.

She ran along the gully under the line of birches her father had planted the spring they left Hingham to come out here. Witty remembered nothing of Hingham; Rehoboth was her home, as much as it was these trees'. She looked up as she ran along the gully: bare branches, beginnings of buds. Don't go under the trees, children, Philip will get you. No, Philip's my friend. If he comes, I'll run out to meet him. But what if he doesn't recognize me? Or if I don't him? When she'd seen him coming out of Abell's several springs ago, he hadn't looked at all as she remembered. The gully grew shallower and rose higher and she was out of it, into the March wind.

The barn and the house were behind her now and straight ahead was the drop-off. Below her the salt meadow stretched far away to the line of trees that hid the mill river and the cove and the Seekonk, whose tide she could hear. Temporary creeks and one real brook crossed the meadow like streaks of light. When she was a girl, this meadow had been her favorite place. If you looked at the sky, you could see for sure that God was holding everything in his hand and that with a small squeeze He could make sunshine come out around His fingers and trail in long ribbons down to the meadow. She looked across to the trees hiding the Seekonk: on the other side of the river and southward Isaak lay buried in his army jacket.

A sharp noise. She jumped.

It was against the law to fire at anything but a wolf now, or an Indian. Could it be an Indian gun? Far off; out of range?

She walked slowly, steadily, to possess the land. It was the way Isaak had walked. The way her father walked. The way she'd walked in Stephen's boots after he died, when her father finally took her in the fishing boat. "Ho, Rosie! Ho, Patrick! Ho, Samson and Hollow!" Her nose shut at the stench of her sheep. The black part of the ewes' faces rested on white, woolly backs: here was one gigantic animal in four parts. Two more waddled up to gawk and comment, like townspeople.

"Ho! Willow!" She thrust her fingers, nails still caked with dirt from the gully, into Willow's soft coat to feel for signs of trouble. When she touched the scar left near Willow's nipple from last year's shearing, the ewe stuck out a quivering pink tongue narrow as a snake, and gave a desperate call. Who would shear this year? She could ask Purchase. . . . His eyes at her throat.

"Ho, girl. Steady, girl."

These sheep are from the hills, Witty. *Humn.* Mama Strong liked to explain those things that cannot be said with *humn.* They aren't down-bred and placid. You've got to satisfy them, not too soon and not too late, just like a child, *humn.*

If she got the hundred acres on the neck that she'd put in for, maybe she could ask Purchase to plow for her. In exchange for knitting? That might do. A hired man was twelve pounds a year. But the new law made it clear no one could live without a head of household, lest the prayers lapse. Purchase at prayer seemed hardly worth the legislation.

"Here, Tick!" Witty felt through Tick's wool; hers was the softest. In a few weeks it would be in her left hand, like bits of cloud between thumb and forefinger. Her right hand would pull it taut by the wheel. By tautness are things tamed. The lambs nudged at her knees, urgent for pap. Six ewes, thirteen lambs: her wealth had indeed doubled. But the wolves were after her lambs all the time.

"So, little ones," she whispered. "You are mine. Be careful now. Philip's coming. He doesn't like lambs. He's a wolf."

She could do it, too. So long as only sheep were listening.

By the railing, she gave two short whistles for Timmy and he came pounding from the horse meadow, whining and eager. Her high, brief whistle stopped him short. You've got to take the puppyness right out of them, *humn*, fast as you can. What if Purchase got married? Brought another woman into the house? There'd be no room for her. She whistled Timmy to his proper station at the rear and led off with the sheep following her. She avoided the mud of the gully and walked alongside the horse pasture, heading for the front of the lot. The horses followed her on their side of the railing.

"Hey, Daisy! Hey, Ben!" She soothed the worried horses as best she could. She passed plum trees that were shivery and faded; she passed raspberry bushes still pressed to the ground from the weight of vanished snow. By the back of the barn, she noticed that the first green shoots were up. Spring was coming. The new year was truly beginning. Isaak's grave and Maie's, they were graves of the old year. Things would begin again now. There was air and breath, male and female: but there were also little animals found dead and stiff, their fur moving in the breezes. Never mind. It was all fine. Rot and sunshine, the world was fine.

Hoo! Koo koo koo koo.

The brown dove seemed to be answering her thoughts, and she spread her fingers to the sunlight. Forgive me, Isaak. I was busy. And you always had an eye for . . . I will plant for you. Things will grow. The children.

Philip's eyes, long ago when he stood by the willow, had been the color of oak leaves under snow. That was how she would recognize him, by that color. The old people spoke so differently of the Indians. Her mother used to come upon Indians in the woods, suddenly and unobtrusively there. Before anyone had the faintest notion they were about! Witty had always wanted to find them so. They would signal her to come near. They would pick her up and carry her to the seashore and stroke her belly and comfort her.

To her left the door of the house opened.

"Are you all right, dear?"

"I'm fine, Mama."

The door shut.

Her father wasn't at the pit anymore. The spinning wheel lay on its side in the hole. She reached the road. The lead ewe stumbled.

"Oh, Rosie, my Rosie!"

The creaking of a wagon had frightened her.

"Goodbye, Widow Strong! Fare well! Well!" neighbors called out to her as they passed with a laden wagon.

"Are you going to Aquidneck?" she called up to them, touching Rosie to calm her.

"Sure are! Only a fool would stay here!"

"Henry!"

"Sorry. Pardon. Hope it goes well with you."

"And you!" She waved. "Tell Mama Strong I'm expecting her back by shearing time."

"We're going down to Indian neck!" one of the neighbor children walking beside the wagon shouted to her. "Going to ride the ferry!"

Witty passed the empty house of the town's Indian, old Sam. He'd run off to hide last summer when the trouble started and had never come back. She reached the southeast gate of the common. The warders opened it for her. Inside, there were hundreds of cows standing about on the yellowed grass.

"Is Submit, my brother, here?" she said to the first boy.

"He went out to the river, ma'am."

Lately, people called her ma'am.

The gate shut.

She couldn't see Purchase, either, though she looked among the men leading their cows in. He'd promised to bring her cows. Ephraim was to help him.

"Come on, Timmy!" She led the dog and the sheep toward the center of the green. They passed the new house the town had built for Noah Newman. Its fresh thatch was like gold. She passed the small meetinghouse, and the stocks. Becky Peters' face, long ago, as Witty stood holding her mother's hand; the saliva dripped out of the mouth like vomit when they brought the glowing iron to her forehead. Men had gone to Dedham to get the branding iron: its *D* looked more like a bow and arrow than any other town's. "That's what happens when you do wrong," her mother had said, "with an Indian." Witty passed the larger, half-built meeting house where they'd gathered last night. The voices of the town did not yet fill the new meetinghouse. They lingered along in the benches of the old meetinghouse: singing, praising, cursing. If she were to vanish from among her townspeople, they would not speak well of her. She wasn't at all like her mother. Whatever happened to Widow

Strong? No, I mean the young one, Witty. Oh, she went to live with her father. No, she fell into the river, down by the falls on the plain, where the Indians used to fish. The black geese fly over her to nest. No, no. She talks to herself and does not remarry. Witty? She set off one day through the forsythia and on. Just put one foot in front of the other across the great plain of Rehoboth, biggest stretch of flatland in all of Plimouth Patent. Her children call for her. We ourselves have stopped searching. This plain is ninety miles square, some say one hundred. We said eighty to the old sachem when he sold it to us. Maybe she went to live with the Indians. She always liked them, you know. Her brother knew Philip.

Widow Strong, gone? Maybe she cut south and climbed through the five-rail fence and plowed through miles of Baptists to the neck. Her sister, sputtering prophecies with the Baptists, every minute dunking themselves in water, splashing it all over themselves, sprinkling it on their minister that hasn't one jot of education. Never stepped on the sacred ground of Cambridge, old England, not for a second. Speak right out of the heart they do, Baptists. Don't have any heads. Yes, sir, God speaks daily into each and every ear down there, common as birdsong. Her sister could tell you, a queer one in queer clothes always trying to get Witty to settle down there beside her. Cheap it is, too, over to Swansea. Those Irishers can't afford much. They're just like the Indians, anyway. Same aptitude for painting themselves up, same fondness for drink. Only twenty pounds to buy in at Swansea, in the third rank. And that's all Witty Strong's got. Except she doesn't even have that anymore. No, that Witty would plow clean through any Baptists and keep on heading south onto Mount Hope neck. Montaup, the Indians call it. You never can tell what they'll call a thing. There she'd find Philip, drunk as a pig on red tomatoes. She likes her men drunk. Or she'll live alone out there. She always wanted to live free in some thicket, an Adam, without words.

Witty Strong? She's stubborn as a man. And that is worse in a woman than a long, thin nose. She's probably slinking along the Seekonk, north past where it bends among the Nipmuck. Look for her in wigwams, second wife to some dark lord, slave in his smoky hole.

She wouldn't dare.

Try the Rose Meadow or look in the salt grass, high as her shoulders. We have stopped searching for her. We didn't like her much, anyway. Uppity. Stubborn. Talks like a man. Now that I think of it, she can't have gotten too far. Try over in the green. See? The small building? No, not that one. That's going to be our new meetinghouse! Fancy, with a tower and a bell. And not that house with the fence. That's young Pastor Newman's. He had fat knees when he was a boy. Fine, isn't it? It's got an orchard. Yes, that one, the small meetinghouse, the one we outgrew. She used to crouch under the pew there and try to go straight up to God till one day she got a bit off the ground and scared herself good. She always lacked the grace her mother has.

She's probably not anywhere you'd expect. Not by the bridge here where the sheep stand worriedly staring into the pond. Nor by the wall of the graveyard, which is as close as she can get to her brother or her daughter, whose hair is tied for the last time in lavender ribbons sent from England. Her eye's on three stones that are so far off she must make out the marks from memory: S. P. 14/2/55. That's her brother Stephen. C. S. 4/3/71. That's her dead baby. M. S. 17/7/75. Oh, that's . . . that's her daughter Maie, taken in the summer, in the season of the dying children. If only her husband, Isaak, were here, they would all be together, see? Then she could keep her eyes on them at once and feel peaceful and not always be darting about in her head to find them in their separate resting places. Oh, come, rise up to me, my girl!

Back inside her father's house, Witty was both warmed and trapped. Her mother talked as they readied the table for the noon meal. "It's our fault. We were brought here and set down on this shore to teach them. But what did we do? Gave them the apple, same as Eve. Fermented. So if they drink themselves silly, we've got only ourselves to thank."

Witty nodded. As she passed the hearth, she touched the soft black hair of the boy still playing at spoons. The noise of the spoons stopped.

"I'm hungry!" He pulled at her skirt with his fat fingers.

"I named you Waitstill to make you patient. Be patient and we'll eat soon." She tugged at the neck of his coat and went for cornmeal. The door opened and Hannah came in. Where had she been? Ephraim dragged in after her, carrying that gun of Isaak's.

"Mama, I've got a plan. The men are down at the cove strapping up some rafts, and they say we could take the sheep on one of them and go—"

"Put that gun down, will you? And, Hannah, you can finish setting the table. We're not going to Aquidneck."

"Mama, what's wrong with you?" The willfulness Ephraim had shown as a child was developing into the will of a man.

"Ephraim, we're staying right here. Look, I'm putting up molasses pudding. You want to be here when it comes out of the oven, don't you?"

Try harder. Win them with kindness, not the whip. The boy who came to her shoulder if they stood close together finally put the gun against the wall and she felt better.

"The men do say you can get a raft cheap," Hannah began.

"Nonsense. Ephraim, did you get the horses to the green?"

"Yes."

"Good, go call Caleb for dinner."

The boy didn't move.

Emily Peck lowered her eyes toward the salt pork she was turning, making it clear that she didn't believe the Strong boys behaved well.

"Go."

To Witty's relief, Ephraim went.

Her mother said nothing.

Witty could not go on staying here. At Mama Strong's there was more air. She bent low into the flour barrel. The yellow grain lay way down at the bottom. She'd last been at the mill just before the big wheel froze up. It was in the mill that she'd heard too clearly the sound of the water running, of the wheel turning. And overhead there'd been massive beams that seemed aware of her. Birds were flying up in the rafters, and at her feet rats were moving about, their little eyes too full of knowledge. The other women were talking of the children that were dying. "We get what we deserve. I prayed for my Mary and she rallied." The odd light, the luminescence, had begun about Witty's shoulders. Men were laughing, looking at her skirt. What was wrong? She straightened up. "Give me fair weight!" Laughter. Here at her mother's, the dark molasses spread itself through the yellow corn: Maie's favorite pudding. In the Dutch cities they cut glass so you could look through it and see close up the small, wiggling creatures that grew up out of the meal. And the structure inside a leaf. There are forces we can't see at all.

"Mama, will they hurt me?" Caleb was home, pushed through the door by his older brother. "Ephraim says they'll cut off my hands."

"They won't hurt you, Caleb." Witty leaned to set the pudding into the back of the oven, a nice low heat.

"Mama, I saw Uncle Submit on the Green. Can I go warding with him later?"

"Certainly not, Ephraim. You have to wait five more years for that."

Ephraim twisted up his face and lunged at Caleb. "Philip's going to get you! He'll cut off your hands! He'll make you crawl on stumps when he cuts off your feet."

"Stop it, boys!" It was exactly what Stephen had told her before he met the Indian boy. "Sit down, boys."

"I don't have a gun, Mama." Caleb's pale forehead wrinkled into the lines she knew he would have as an old man; his blue eyes were the color of her own.

"You're not supposed to. You're only six."

"I'll be seven on Thursday!"

Caleb's alarm alerted Wait, who grabbed at the fabric of her skirt and pressed it to his face. "Will I die, like Papa?"

"No."

"We won't hold dinner any longer for Grandpa." Emily Peck stood at one side of the table and when she spoke the boys quieted. "He ought to be out sowing peas! We thank You, Lord, for all You give us, good and bad. Food, the new year, the whip of war, the garden of the wilderness to which You brought us, in Your hand, opening it to set us safely down so that we might teach the wild men Your Name. Amen." She sat down. "Don't know but what we moved out of the bedchamber too soon. It's cold here."

Witty began to stand, to change places.

"No, no, dear. You keep the warmth."

To do for others. Witty sat. A mother's lessons were never unlearned. Emily Peck approaches heaven, wearing her apron. Mama Strong, on the other hand, always took the best seat for herself.

"Duncan hates buttermilk." Waitstill slopped his milk away in imitation of the soldier. "Duncan would rather drink beer."

"Yes, Duncan hated milk." Witty emphasized the past tense of the verb. Her fingers rested on the place in the table where she had once tried to carve her name: WITE.

"Where's Uncle Purchase?" Caleb always asked for Purchase, who so resembled Isaak.

"Warding." Witty picked up her spoon.

The door swung open but was stopped before it banged.

"There he is!"

"It's Grandpa!"

There was a man in the room. Clement Peck stood his gun against the wall, and shoulders realigned toward him.

"So, boy, pretty soon we fight the Indians, eh?" He stopped to rub the back of Wait's neck.

"Yes, Grandpa!"

Clement sat in the big chair at the head of the table and addressed himself to the women. "They're outside the north pasture. They've picked off a few horses. I hope they don't make a poor man out of my friend Hoskins!"

"How many horses did they get?" Emily set salt pork before her husband.

"A couple. Ours are safe in the green."

So were Cloudy and Peter. Witty ate. Hoskins' wife had died mid-March.

"Grandpa, why aren't we going to Aquidneck with the others?" Ephraim began on his grandfather.

"Aquidneck! For a fellow who wants to be a wheelwright, or what is it? A pewterer? You ought to know, at least, that we farmers are late plowing. It's this week or not at all." Clement put his hand to his eyes, made a short prayer and began to eat.

"But they'll kill us!" Ephraim's black eyebrows drew together.

"Whatever for? The Mount Hopes aren't stupid, boy. Philip knows he doesn't have to waste his bullets on the likes of us. All he's got to do is kill a few horses and burn a few barns and our neighbors will be kind enough to run off with their tails between their legs." Clement stopped talking to eat. No other voice replaced his.

"Why, all a person has to do, lately," Clement went on when he was ready, "is scream 'Philip' and some people load up their wagons and leave town. If the Mount Hopes can get free mills, cows and land by shouting, why should they bother killing? Are you going to let a few hundred of them scare fifty grown men out of everything they own?"

"But they've killed a lot of people, Grandpa! They take off your clothes and then they cut—"

"Nonsense. When I was your age, everybody was dying of the plague. Now that was something." Clement worked at his food again.

After a while Clement raised his finger in the air. "Listen."

Far off the high, faint *lud-a-lud-a-lud-a-lud-a* of a turkey.

"That turkey's got two legs and you know what between them, or else I've got wings."

"Clement!"

"Now, listen everybody. We'll go to the preacher's as soon as we're ready. But we needn't hurry. Slow and easy."

Wait began to wail.

"What's the matter, boy?"

"Mama Strong said I could go to Aquidneck!" He began to hit Witty, who grabbed his hands.

"Now, listen here, Wait." Clement leaned toward the boy. "What happens when you let a big dog know you're scared?"

"A dog?" Wait's face whitened.

With the second boy silenced, Clement gave another general command. "Eat your food, the Mount Hope boys don't have anything to eat and the girls here will be taking your plates away before you're done."

Witty stared at Ephraim's jaws as the boy chewed the last of his salt pork. At Groton in the Bay Patent, the Indians had caught a child and fed him to the pigs while the parents were forced to watch. That couldn't have been Philip. He couldn't be everywhere. But what if it wasn't Philip in the woods today? Witty let go of Wait's hands.

"Why can't we go to Aquidneck?" Caleb, not yet silenced by Clement, moved closer to Witty.

"Grandpa just told you why! They'll take all our things. They could take Hollow and the other sheep. And your cows and the horses. Even Timmy. They'd burn the barley left in the barn. Then what would we eat?"

"Fish. I like the fried kind, with the crust."

"And where would we live?"

"In the woods."

She smiled at the blank, uncomprehending hair.

Then Purchase was coming in the door. Witty set Caleb aside and stood, motioning down Hannah, who also stood.

"They're getting closer." Purchase pulled off his cap.

"We're going over to the green." Clement stood and headed toward the mantel. "You see Submit today?"

"Yes, sir." Purchase stopped before Witty, who took his cap from his hand. She felt her face grow warm and wondered if she was blushing.

"I got your cows in," he said to her. Then he sat and stretched his hands behind his neck. Witty picked up his plate, her own hands moving stiffly, attempting grace.

"Submit was there when we buried Captain Pierce this morning." Purchase spoke toward Clement.

"Buried him?" Emily stood up from the bench. "What I heard was that you boys all ran upriver, dug a hole, pushed a dozen bodies into it and ran back."

"No, ma'am. Mr. Newman came and we prayed, proper and all."

"Not, I trust, to his usual length." Clement returned to the table and set his bandolier on it with a jingle.

"Stay clear of Grandpa, Wait. You'll get powder on your clothes." Witty set a mug of beer before Purchase.

"You don't use paper, Mr. Peck?"

"See for yourself!" Clement unscrewed the little caps on the powder cans and began to fill them.

"But you're the one who always likes the latest thing!" Purchase moved aside as Witty set his plate down.

"Now, that depends. If it were only fashion I was after, I'd have gone to Spain, wouldn't I? Italy." Clement enjoyed the talk of another man.

"I want to be a farmer, Grandpa!" Caleb called out.

"Well, bless your heart, of course you do!" Clement turned and smiled.

"Could He dry up the bay?" Caleb went on.

"What's that?"

"Could God dry up the bay and we could walk to Aquidneck?"

"Course He could, boy!" Clement looked to his canisters.

"It's not likely, though. The great miracles are over. God doesn't talk to us men directly anymore. And why should He? We've got His words written down in common speech, clear as day. We don't need some high and mighty priest with Romish quotes to tell us what it means. It means what it says, boy. And what it says is that it's our turn to do the work. God made the garden, but we've got to finish up creation. Not wait around for flashes of light like so many Quakers in a cornfield. Not that I'm against a man doing what he wants in his own barnyard, because I'm not. But God wants us up and doing for ourselves! Look at the things we can do nowadays!"

"He'll dry up the bay if He decides to, dear," Emily said to Caleb.

"Shh!" Clement held a finger up again. "That turkey's getting nearer."

Caleb examined his hand on the wooden cup. "What will they do with my fingers, Mama?"

"Finish up, we're going to the green." Witty took hold of the broom and began to sweep.

Clement put his arms through the straps of the bandolier. "What's the sergeant saying today? I hope he's sober."

"We're not to hide in Newman's house. We're to go out beyond the palisade and shoot them. Whoever shoots Philip will get—"

"Now that sounds like Preserved Abell! A reasonable man would tell us to hole up and hide our seed corn. We got to be plowing by Friday."

"There's a thousand of them."

Clement moved toward his gun. "Philip can't have a thousand men! He must have lost a thousand men by now. And what he's got left must be starving."

"When they get hungry, they eat their leggings," Caleb called out. "They even eat their babies."

"Oh, that's silly, dear." Emily blushed. "They're really nice to their babies."

"Bring what else you've got for the pit." Clement opened the door. "Ephraim, come help me shovel it over." Then he was gone.

Witty swept beside the table. There was mud on Caleb's boots; they were Maie's old boots. A hand on her elbow. She straightened up.

"Witty," Purchase said. "If you want to go, I'll take care of your animals. Just take the boys on one of those rafts and go stay with Mama."

Everyone in the room was watching, weren't they?

"Run along. I'm staying here."

Purchase let go of her elbow. Then he, too, was gone. Witty began to sprinkle sand on the floor.

"Is she all right, Mrs. Peck?" Hannah's voice was a whisper.

"Witty! What are you sanding for now? Go up and get the bedding, dear."

Witty stood the broom in the corner and ran up the steep stairs. She must keep her mind on things. She dragged the boys' feather beds to the stairs and shoved them down to Hannah, who gathered them to take to the wagon. The window in the little western room upstairs was banging and she went in and leaned out to catch the shutter.

"Get on, Daisy! Get on, Ben!" Outside, her father was leading the horses across the barnyard to the wagon. Their dark backs glistened in the sunlight. The horses paid no attention to the dogs that jumped and sniffed at their feet, inferior beasts, third-rankers at Swansea, Irishers. Ephraim walked out of the barn with Isaak's jaunty step. It was too quiet. Sound was collecting, as before thunder. The boys were sliding at puck on the frozen brook far off on the salt meadow. Ephraim was raising a long stick, Caleb was skidding to a stop. Maie was screaming with laughter in the snow by the brook. Witty banged the shutter and fastened it. A month at home and she was already seeing things that weren't there. *Humn.* Perhaps she should have gone to Aquidneck. Incorruptible, indeed. Stephen could have helped and where was he? Up, out of the grave, the sheet unwinding. Incorruptible are the godly. Stephen must have experienced considerable decay by now.

"What's Witty doing now?" Her father's voice came from outside. "Get her down here!"

She gathered up her bedding and Hannah's and ran down the stairs. She handed it to Hannah and filled her apron with thorny apples and tucked the edge of it over her waistband: pregnant with apples. She grabbed up her own basket and went out.

The dogs were whining, their tails low. The pit was shoveled over and a dark circle of earth marked it. Hannah held Wait by the hand. Clement was passing the reins to Ephraim. Caleb stood by the willow. The wind was strengthening. There was rain behind it.

"Give me that!" Her father threw her basket up on the piled wagon and then went behind it to where he had left his gun and shot bag.

"I want to ride!" Wait let go of Hannah's hand and climbed up onto the wagon.

Witty tucked the apples tighter. They were all waiting for Emily.

Caleb came from the willow to take Witty's hand.

"Hold on tight up there!" Witty called to Wait on the wagon.

Then Emily came running toward them from the back of the house. "I saw one! In the horse meadow."

They walked stiffly to the front of the lot. Witty stumbled on a root and nearly pulled Caleb down.

"*Mecanteasssquohqueshsuccomme!*" The shout came from the horse meadow.

Witty straightened up and began to run jerkily, dragging Caleb along. Some of the apples slipped out of her apron. At the road, the trotting horses passed them. Wait was hanging on to the wagon and Ephraim pulled the reins taut. Far down the road, the gate swung open for someone else, someone who had reached safety. Witty turned and saw her father walking backward in the road, his gun up and in both hands, but not against his check. She saw her father's house, the birches with their pale buds, nothing else.

Then they were all inside the palisade and the gate was shutting behind them.

"*Johettiteacoweasass!*" The hiss came from just outside the palisade.

They ran across the yellow grass for Newman's house. My name is Wit-ty, Ste-phen's sis-ter. Unh, they would have said, chopping.

Sunlight came in through the three big windows of the new house on the green and shone softly on the oiled wood of its walls. It would have looked so peaceful if only people weren't carrying buckets of water to set beside the windows. Men were cleaning their guns and joking. Witty spread her bedding near the front of the sitting room and Wait sat on it immediately.

"Sleep." She touched his head. "You're a tired boy." He rubbed the edge of the quilt between thumb and fingers.

Witty looked around the room. This was her first visit inside the house Rehoboth had built for her old schoolmate. The new pastor patches up our wounds, the older women said, but the old pastor went after the plague itself and worldliness is its name. Not in this luxurious room could the ascetic old pastor have sat up by night to pen his alphabetical list of each word in the Bible, catching angels in the corners of his eyeglasses. His son Noah was another matter.

"You stay here, Wait." Witty knew that Ephraim was avoiding her because she'd refused to let him join his two young uncles warding. Caleb was running fruitlessly about looking for children his own age. She couldn't put off joining the women in the back room any longer and she picked up her basket and walked past the huge, three-hearthed chimney into the small room behind it. Older women, mostly. She would have to watch her tongue.

"Wolves crying outside Medfield the whole night before the savages came. They only attack at sunrise, and hello to you, Witty Strong. . . ." It was Mrs. Pitman, with whom Witty had learned housekeeping: seven years in the house at the base of the hill.

Witty nodded a small reply and chose a place on the cold side of the table. The older women stood on the hearth side. Witty unpacked her contribution to the table: rum. Too much rum. She could open an inn right here. The Strongs like a drink, from time to time. She untucked the hem of her apron from the waistband and rolled what was left of the thorny apples onto the table. I am delivered. She would make the salve later. First food, then medicine: this is how women make war. Out the window behind her could be seen the top of her father's house, and all of a sudden Witty remembered that she'd left the pudding over there in the oven.

"Stood there and howled, the way they do, the whole pack of them raising one foot and then another," Mrs. Pitman was going on. "A sign straight from God. Medfield should have spent the night in prayer searching their own hearts. That's where the Devil is, in the human heart. Not under the ground. Not wearing a crown. Squelched him, stomped him, thrown him out of their hearts and those wolves would have vanished in the night."

The godly women like her mother and Mrs. Pitman always put the blame on themselves. Herbs hung from the beams over Witty's head. Dried, dead; I am the resurrection and the life. Her mother: it is not the world that endures, dear. Her father: get up early and aim between the eyes. Mama Strong: *humn.* She caught the eyes of the serving girl Hannah and then those of pasty-faced Susan Hoskins, let go from service in her sixth year at housekeeping to nurse a dying mother. Susan blushed.

Witty looked away. Did the whole town expect Witty Strong to marry Joseph Hoskins?

"Are you all alone now with the boys, Widow Strong?" Susan said as soon as Mrs. Pitman had finished her summation upon the lacks of the women of Medfield.

"There's three of us dead, Susan, if that's what you mean. And four still living. It's about equal."

Susan lowered her head.

Emily Peck gave Witty a critical look.

Witty chided herself.

"Pardon." The word came not from Witty but from a short, dark-faced woman sweeping ashes. It was Pequot Molly from Abell's Inn and she stood holding her broom awkwardly to indicate some need. Witty stepped aside, allowing the slave woman to sweep under her feet. Molly didn't have a husband anymore either, though once she'd been married to a black man chosen off a slave ship at Newport. The Pequot men she would have married were all dead. Or sold on the block. Alone now, Molly still lived in Preserved Abell's household, hearing what prayers the sergeant spoke between kegs. Witty stamped her feet to warm them. For the first time, she thought of Philip's wife. Had he one? Two?

"Wolves aren't the only sign. What about that poor child born over in Bridgewater, with the lolling tongue and slanted eyes? That was the Almighty making His remark! And all the children dying here last summer? Becky, there's a girl! Give me a hand." Mrs. Pitman called upon a woman with a grossly wrinkled face.

Age had all but buried the white *D* on the forehead of Becky Peters, who scurried forth and bent to push Mrs. Pitman's pie into the oven. With her mistress, Mrs. Newman, and the children gone to the island, the servant Becky was queen of the hearth. Study now the ways of a servant, girl. Witty could join Philip and his wife and they could all hire out as servants together.

"If God wants to help us so much, He could easily send some more smallpox to the Indians." Susan Hoskins hid the beginning of a smile.

Mrs. Pitman's round face was gray as a stone. "He doesn't want it to be that simple for us! That's why He's brought this whole war about. He wants us to look inside our own hearts, Susan, long and hard."

"We shouldn't wish them sick or dead, dear." Emily Peck looked up from the table. "We were brought here to teach them and they were gentle when we first came, like children." She raised her apron to the corner of her lips.

There was something in Emily's manner that compelled the others to hush themselves. She ran the corner of the apron through her fingers. "The women used to bring me berries. Poor things. They worked so hard. They couldn't understand why I didn't work in the fields. Little baskets of blackberries they brought and stood there, smiling, with those wide eyes of theirs. The men were shyer. They walked in that way of theirs. You know how they walk. When they dressed in their own way, they were wonderfully . . . wonderfully handsome." Emily stopped abruptly.

"My mother said . . ."

"They all died in a fever, turned them yellow as daisies. . . ."

The voices wove together to provide the things left unspoken. Witty saw that her mother's face was still focused elsewhere and for the first time was curious about her.

"They're Jews, anyway," Hannah said. "The lost tribe."

"They're not Jews." Witty repeated what she'd heard from Isaak and Robbie Benson. "They're Tartars, from China."

"From China, dear?" Mrs. Pitman said. "Now, how could they get here from China when nobody else can, hard as they try?"

Laughter.

"If the Mount Hopes aren't Jews, then why do they separate their women every month, just like the Hebrews in the Bible?"

"To give the girls out on the neck a rest!"

"Do you know it's their women who make water standing up? The men sit down."

Laughter. Always laughter.

Witty kept her head down and searched for the handful of almonds she had brought. Yes, she could go to Boston and hire out as a maid, providing she sent Ephraim from home early. Six pounds a year she could get. Buy some of those forbidden curls: ah, not with braided hair, dear, nor gold or pearls, but with good works. Very well, then, straight hair. Widow seeks husband. Six ewes of her own, sits down to make water. Almonds, smell of almonds and the midwife reaching into her to bring out the dead child. It's a girl. Was a girl. The prayers beginning. Cecilia Strong, she'd whispered into that dead ear, I baptize you without benefit of clergy. You shan't flit about nameless in the woods. Ox piss is good as holy water, girl. That's why we left old England. There is no miracle beside the word.

"Like a bunch of monkeys, if you ask me, sitting bare-bottomed on the ice . . ."

"I'm afraid you may be right this time, Susan." Mrs. Pitman's mouth was opening again. "Perhaps they are animals. But if they're human, they're surely children, the way Emily says, the wild kind, too. Untaught, like children who think you can't see them because they've got their hands over their eyes. Animals or children, both of them have to be trained."

"Mama?" Ephraim came searching for Witty among the women. He halted their conversation by the grace of his age which, being between that of boy and man, confused their responses and paralyzed their throats.

"The warders are going to lay logs against the house, may I—?"

"Yes. Go ahead." Witty let him go. Better outdoors with the men.

Then Wait came, sleepily holding his coat close. She took him to the pantry where the slop jars were. He was finicky and slow. As she waited beside him, Caleb darted past her toward the back door. Then the latch was open and the door swung to the outside.

"Caleb!" She ran to catch the door. He was already a good distance outside, a skinny boy moving under the bare branches of scraggly apple trees. "Stop! Caleb, you come back!"

She pulled the door shut behind her and ran out, looking each way. Warders were walking along the earthwork platform inside the palisade. The sky's single cloud slid over the sun. She called Caleb's name as loud as she could, but the wind pushed the sound back into her own ears, a small, tinny sound. She ran on, farther from the house, scanning the orchard for enemy shapes.

The smell of burning came to her from far off and she heard the scream of a horse.

A light touch on her arm.

No! She jumped.

It was only a drop of rain.

When she caught him, she could barely breathe. Caleb wasn't out of breath at all, nor did he flinch when she whacked him.

"What . . . are . . . you . . . doing?" She pulled him around.

"Nothing! I've been good!"

"You . . . didn't . . . come back!"

"I want Him to see me." He pulled his arm out of her grasp. His eyes were sullen in the narrow face.

"What?" She turned him by the shoulder and started him back.

"How could He see me when I was inside the house? And save me?"

Witty understood. "But you weren't good! You didn't obey! You didn't even honor your father and mother." She felt another drop of rain and pushed him into a run beside her, holding his hand tightly.

"I don't have a father anymore!"

"Well, you can honor me twice."

"I want to go to Aquidneck!" He started to break away

again, but she wouldn't let go. Ahead, she could make out the lean body of Purchase piling logs against the side of the house. As they neared the back of the house, they heard a dog bark.

"It's Timmy!" Both called at once. They turned to see if he was in the orchard, but he wasn't.

Inside the house, everything seemed so dim and stuffy. In the back room Witty pointed Caleb to a bench. "Now sit there by the fire and don't get up until I tell you to." Men told women what to do. Women told children.

"There she is! Widow Strong? Will you come and help us?" Susan Hoskins was calling to her from the sitting room.

"Stay here," she repeated to Caleb.

At the threshold of the sitting room she saw that she would have to pass near the round shoulders of a man she knew even from the back was her father's friend Joseph Hoskins. She pinned up the strands of hair that had come loose while she was running.

"We've got to make it thick enough to slow the bullets." Susan relayed the instructions.

Witty stretched to hold the bedding up over the beautiful glass of the window. Hannah was on the other side. Susan pounded a small peg through the bedding and the material nearly jerked out of Witty's hand. A shame to mar such smooth, sweet paneling, but it scarcely mattered if only the soul endures.

"Mrs. Pitman's got it all wrong, don't you think?" Susan whispered to Witty and Hannah, keeping her voice low but sharp against the deeper voices inside and against the thumping of logs that were being rolled to the outside of the house. "Babies with lolling tongues are what you get when a woman and a wolf . . ."

Again the bedding was jerked in Witty's hand and she got a glance through the glass at Purchase shoving a log forward. She watched how he moved. Then she realized that Hannah was watching Purchase, too. The bedding was up and light came through its colored pattern darkly.

"Hey!"

"We need light!"

Witty and Susan and Hannah went to bring the men lamps.

Then they began at the second window.

The piling of logs had moved to the other side of the house by the time they got to the third window. The women could hear what the men in the room were saying. Witty looked down onto the top of Joseph Hoskins' head, at a bald spot round and neat as a slice of lemon.

"The sergeant bothers me." The jingle of a bandolier.

"Me too. We ought to have that Mosely from Boston." The rasping of a ramrod.

"Too fancy! He wears a wig. You can give me Benjamin Church from over on Pocasset. He's got a brain. And he's a reasonable man. Joseph, there's something I want to talk over with you."

"What's that?"

"You . . . you start your plowing?"

"Can't say I did, Clement. With . . . the funeral."

Outside, a shot!

Inside, everything stopped.

A second shot . . .

Outside, the sounds of running, of footsteps, of men throwing themselves against the front door and of the door opening.

"Watch out! Watch out!"

The door slammed shut and a bullet struck it, shaking the house. Everybody began shouting.

"Ephraim? Is Ephraim Strong inside?" It was her own voice over the melee.

"He's here, Witty." Her brother Submit answered her.

He's all right, Isaak.

Purchase came toward her, hands out, calling. Then he

passed her and she heard what he was saying: "Hannah! Hannah!"

"You boys get the seed corn buried?"

"We had to stop digging, Mr. Peck."

"Stop digging?"

"Sergeant said to leave the corn, Papa." Though Emily had named her last son to demonstrate God's weal to Clement, the demonstration was in name only.

"Leave the corn? You boys go right back out there and bring the corn in!" Clement headed for the door.

"I'll go, Papa." Submit stood with his hand on the door. "But I'm waiting till the shooting's over."

Then Susan Hoskins was standing with her hand on Submit's arm. First Purchase and Hannah. Now Submit and Susan. Matches were being made all over. All the young people . . . It was time for Witty Strong, widow, to open her eyes. And to think she'd even imagined anything with Purchase, all that night in Plimouth! She could run and hide her shame in the sea where the Mount Hope women bathed, buttocks up, as they vanished into the dark ocean. They shall rise neither male nor female when they wake in Christ. She could find the Indians, needy as herself; she could hide in the woods with them.

"Bring the lamps over here!" the older men called out from a corner of the sitting room. They were prying up the beautifully sanded floorboards. The boards cracked as they were raised and Witty could see the dirt of the Seekonk plain beneath them. She went for lamps. By the time Submit got back with the first bag of corn, the hole was two feet deep and looked just like a child's grave. Witty stumbled handing over the lamp, and Joseph Hoskins reached up to steady her with a hand.

"Easy there, girl," he said, his fingers closing around her arm.

. . .

Out the window of the back room, Witty could see that the light was fading from the sky. The cows were beginning to settle down under the few trees planted on the common. Even from this distance, she could see that they were their usual selves, chewing, moving their heads from side to side, staring with their round, dark eyes. Not so usual were the blue and red wagons strewn about near the house. Bits of yellow thatch lay on the damp ground. Upstairs the men were stripping it from the roof. "Wait and see if it rains first!" Noah Newman had called from under the roof where he was writing down what might be the record of the town's last day. He didn't want to dampen the exposed furniture. "No," the men said. "They'll have their fire here at dawn." The men's boots were up there, scraping.

Witty turned back to the small room where the women were putting supper on the table, though bits of dust and thatch fell through the cracks in the ceiling and drifted toward the food. Witty pressed cut-up apples through a loosely woven cloth.

"Hold tight now," she said to Wait. "This is the last." It was good to be near the smell of food, the whole house stank so. The drifting dust got into her nose and dried her into an old woman. A little leaven leaveneth the whole lump, but even the thought of Purchase was impossible now; she was embarrassed to think of him at all.

Above their heads came three sharp raps of the drummer.

The triple roll meant two things, *help us* or *save yourself*. Whichever might be more practical at the moment. Every language has its limitations.

"That'll never float over Seekonk!"

"It won't even get to Swansea!"

"Where is he?" Wait looked up over his head for the drummer, careful to keep his fingers tight around the bowl.

"Upstairs. He's probably got his head poked right out through where the thatch should be. Are you ready now?" She pressed the pulpy apples through the cloth.

Wait's hands were white on the bowl.

Witty took the cloth off and poured the apple juice into the pot of pig fat. Heal burns, without a scar: *humn*. She stirred the mixture, leaning over it to protect it from the dust sifting through the ceiling.

"Hey! It's got into my pudding!"

She saw her own pudding then, browned and crusted in the oven at her mother's. She saw Maie's cap in the gully, cold and dirty. She saw Philip in the woods, dirt caked on his English jacket. How old was he now? Thirty-six? Thirty-eight? Surely not forty, not bald. There were a dozen Mount Hopes living in the woods out toward Taunton. Some had left the war in the north and walked down from the Connecticut River during the snows. They were seldom seen, though a sick one was found in the Taunton mill searching for grain on the floor. The town's own Indian, Sam, might have gone there. He'd left in June because he was scared the town might turn against him, and besides he couldn't get his harvest in without his sons, who had gone to join Philip on the neck. She thought of the gully at her father's and wondered if Philip was camped there.

She didn't have to marry Hoskins. Nor should she think about it here in the stink of so many bodies. Surely by Friday this would all be over and her father would be plowing. Mama Strong would be coming home. Perhaps she wasn't being dried or ground to dust. Perhaps she was being squeezed out of a small, dark stinking place, being born. The spirit can grow suddenly large, exploding like kernels of corn. On Friday she would think about what to do.

"Watch out, Wait! The lamp!" His hair grazed the edge of the flame.

Above their heads the three sharp raps of the drum, louder.

Noah Newman raised his hand over the table set in his house for what might be the town's final supper: "Guide us tonight, oh Lord, and be with us tomorrow among the savages Thou hast sent to chastise us. Amen." He pulled back his big chair and raised his glass for a less formal word: "Boys, there's a rumor that soldiers may be coming from Connecticut to help us. But they won't be here by morning. We've got no one to help us except the Lord. And isn't He enough? What else do we need? He was sufficient to the prophets on the pillories! Sufficient to Paul of Tarsus! He will be our captain!"

Cheers and glasses up.

Roll of the drum overhead.

"What's that for? There aren't any Baptists going to come over from Swansea to help us!"

"I bet Swansea's already dragging out their benches to watch us burn!"

"And the Quakers on the island are climbing trees so they can see it better!"

"Plimouth's what ought to hear that drum! They started this whole thing, putting those Indians on trial. Our King Philip doesn't like anything but the bent knee."

"Come on, it was Boston that started it. They wanted to sink their plows in Narragansett country, just like anyone else."

The men's voices carried the length of the table. Unlike the women, the men didn't pretend the war was their fault. They seemed to pass the blame like a hot potato, heaving it at anyone more powerful than themselves: Boston, Plimouth, the king. Or dropping it on anyone less powerful: Baptists, Indians, women, Rhode Island.

Witty spoke to Caleb: "Try the barley cake. I made it."

"I'm not hungry." Caleb rested his head on her lap.

Woe to them that are with child, and to them that give suck in those days. The stars shall fall from the sky. The Son of man shall come on a cloud. Across the table, Emily Peck nodded her assent that the boy be allowed to droop. These might be the last days.

"It was King Philip the Haughty who started it!" a warder called from the floor, where the young crouched to eat.

"It's not our fault. That's clear enough. The king's law says you can settle where there's no Christians and that's all we did."

"When you come down to it, the Indians are plain lucky to have us, we brought them the law!"

"Unfenced land is public land—" Clement Peck spoke somewhat more slowly than the others and this gave a sense of consideration to his words, but he was interrupted by Hoskins.

"What do they need land for? All the buggers do, pardon me, Mr. Newman," Hoskins said, using the "mister" as a diminutive. "All they do is hunt and fish."

"Hey, Joseph! Your field's right on top of a Mount Hope field and you know it." Clement cleared his throat and went on more slowly, "Still, the field wasn't fenced in, so it was legal."

Newman attempted to resolve the debate. "The way I see it, it's the same as what Thomas More said. When your town's full, you've got a right to move into the next one." The pastor had to stand midway between the men and the women, like Emily Peck's grandfather in England, who had believed that if he neglected his prayers entire cities would crumble.

Witty saw her mother pick up the corner of her apron and run it absently through her fingers as she had earlier. Then Emily Peck leaned over the table toward the men: "Mr. Newman, fenced or unfenced, legal or illegal, the fact is we have the fields that were theirs. Now, the kingdom ought to be for everybody, oughtn't it?"

Mr. Newman did not appear to hear Emily, and restricted his next remarks to his end of the table, though his slight smile toward Clement may have been in reference to her. "We bought this whole plain, and properly, too. Eight miles inland by seven down the river and every inch paid for. It was before my time, though. What was it? Three thousand beads?"

Emily sat back.

Witty brushed at her own skirt. The men were lying. Her mother was right. And she herself might even get one of the Indian fields at Mount Hope.

"It was ten strands." Hoskins leaned over the table toward Newman. "I was there, Pastor. The old sachem, see, he reaches right into our basket. He pulls out every strand in the basket.

Then he chooses the ten best, very carefully, very slowly. Then he looks up and says, 'No coat? No-oo co-wit?' " Hoskins let go with a peel of giggles that brought a fine spray of food out of his mouth.

Witty looked away.

"Well, it's ours. And tomorrow we got to hold tight to it."

"You bet we do, Clement."

"But the sergeant says we should spread out. . . ."

There was noise at the pantry door and big, bearded Preserved Abell moved into the room, causing the faces turned toward Newman to reposition toward him.

"The devils have gone and made themselves right at home in our barns!" Sergeant Abell moved toward the hearth to warm himself.

Witty stood with the women to clear the table and bring on puddings.

"They're sitting out there, eating those horses they spent the afternoon roasting. This gun here, boys? I shot it twice at a foxskin tied to a stick. You got to watch out for that. Philip, he's clever. But not so clever as he always thought he was." Abell moved his arms as he talked and this cast whirling shadows on the far wall. Beside him, the old Pequot, Molly, worked at the hearth.

"They'll be hollering and dancing soon enough," the big man went on. "Then they'll sleep. Tomorrow's a different story. We'll get our asses burned if we don't get out there and fight. It's Philip we're after. Plimouth's sure to pay a big price to the man that catches him. And the rest of them will crawl off like snakes if we get Philip. Now, there's lots of them out there. Nothing to be scared of, though . . ."

"You tell us, Sergeant!" a warder called, recognizing the entry to a favorite pantomine the men from Abell's knew well.

"Oh, I think these good people know." Abell delayed, glancing at the pastor.

"Tell them, Sergeant!"

"There's only three kinds of Indians, you see." Abell gave

in with no further urging. "There's kings"—he effected a low bow—"like our esteemed Philip."

"Huzzah for the king!"

"There's praying ones"—Abell folded his hands and did not look in Newman's direction—"like our esteemed Sam."

Cheers again.

"And then there's my Molly!" He cupped his hands under imaginary breasts of his own and minced about. "Course, I don't recommend any of you get into a fight with my Molly! She's a big one!"

Laughter.

At the hearth, Molly did not even turn to watch them laugh.

Witty's eye rested on the long-handled bread shovel. She would not be joining any Indians in the woods. Or going out with them as servants. They'd all be sold as slaves. She was on her own.

After this moment of glory, the sergeant consented to eat. As he sat down to the table, Clement Peck spoke for the older men: "Sergeant, we've got something to say. We don't need an offensive here tomorrow. We don't need to go beyond the palisade and kill those poor devils. All we've got to do is catch Philip—"

"Hang him!"

"Draw and quarter him!"

"Catch him and the others will fall into line."

"Oh, you got to catch the Narragansett fellow, too!"

"Yes, all the leaders. Mosely'll catch them, or Benjamin Church. I didn't mean we're going to catch Philip ourselves personally tomorrow, despite what the sergeant says. What we've got to do is keep our town in as good shape as we can. That's the long and short of it. They'll burn our houses. There isn't much we can do about that. But we've got our seed corn in here now and we've got things buried outside the wall. We've got our animals in here. All we've to do is keep hold of that and I—"

"Come on, Mr. Peck! We're going out to catch Philip tomorrow!"

"You don't want the Mount Hopes back on the neck, do you, Clement? Planting?"

"Catch Philip and set him planting in your own field, Clement."

"Put them all in our fields. Let them plow!" a warder called out.

"Are you crazy?" This was Hoskins. "We'll have to sell every one of those bucks straight out of here. They'd never settle down to work with their own fields so nearby!"

"Buy ourselves some niggers with the money!" another warder called.

"Their women we'll keep."

"You bet we will!"

"Got to sell every last man. Make sure they don't gang up—"

"There's no Indian wouldn't drop his hoe and pick up a gun if—"

"You think they're not ganged up now? What makes you so sure there's not another bunch of them sitting around Swansea right now? Or outside Plimouth?"

"They could strike at all three towns tomorrow. Wipe us out." The talk grew slower.

"We could be hugging the coast, praying for boats. . . ." The men's voices trailed off.

"They'd take back the town, our fields. . . ."

"Philip'd count his silver in the meetinghouse."

"Don't think he'd have any mercy."

"We'd be as bad off as our fathers."

"Worse. They had the old sachem."

Oooh wah! hu-oo. Outside, the single beginning wail of a wolf.

The men standing behind the bedding at the windows slipped their flintlocks onto full cock.

Caleb Strong threw up.

Witty rinsed his face with a cloth. "You'll feel better now," she said. She carried him to the bedding on the floor of the front room and laid him down. "Everything will be all right." She was as bad as the men, telling lies. The field she got at Mount Hope could be Philip's own.

Wait followed, tugging at her skirt. "Mama, is Papa coming back tonight?"

"No, I've told you. God picked Papa up and took him to heaven. He's invisible now, he's in the spirit. Lie down. Here."

Caleb drew the quilt over his face.

Noah Newman was standing by the Bible table, preparing for the evening prayers by polishing the old pastor's glasses. "Ladies," he called out. "I hope you've remembered to bring over any lemons you might have. We could be under siege here for weeks, like Romans trapped among the barbarians, when they ventured too far north!"

Outside, two wolves wailed together.

Witty's hand shook as she pulled the quilt from Caleb's face. His open eyes stared up at her and he looked as if he were already dead.

"If God be on our side, who can be against us?" Newman began. "Paul tells us, as he told the believers in Rome, 'We are the children of God. If we be the children, we are also heirs, even the heirs of God, and heirs annexed with Christ.' So if we die with Christ, we will rise with Christ." Noah Newman read from the book on the table almost above where Witty sat beside the two boys. He shifted his weight on his feet and the toe of his muddy, crusted boot came nearer to the bottom of her dress.

"They that are in the flesh cannot please God. Paul said, 'They that are in the flesh value the things of the flesh; but they that are after the Spirit the things of the Spirit. For the wisdom of the flesh is death; but the wisdom of the Spirit is life and peace. Now you are not in the flesh, but in the Spirit, because the Spirit of God dwells in you.' "

There was mud on the knees of the pastor's pants, too, thickening the fabric of them. Witty wondered if his knees were as fat as they'd been at reading school.

"We are saved by hope: but hope for things we see is not hope: for 'how can a man hope for that which he sees?' And later in this same epistle Paul told the Romans, 'None of us lives in himself, neither does any die to himself. For whether we live, we live unto the Lord; and whether we die, we die unto the Lord: whether we live therefore, or die, we are the Lord's.' "

He shut the book.

"But, Rehoboth, are we living in the spirit? Or, as much as we can? For every man is two men: him carnal of the flesh, an old Adam, wild and dark, and him of the light who cleaves to the Lord Jesus and hopes to rise. The war goes daily on within the country of the self, and if we do not always find the new Adam victorious, when the daily darkness comes, we must nonetheless balance our spiritual accounts, and vow to try harder on the next day. Every man is the head of his own state, suppressor of rebellion within and chief of war. And so I charge each man of you to think whether you have governed yourselves well this passing day. If so, think whether you have also led your wives toward salvation and strengthened them in their courage and kept them from the troubling idleness that Eve encountered in her garden plot."

Witty felt a sneeze coming on and tightened her lips: it hurt her ears to sneeze silently.

"And, you of the gentler sex, have you each subjected yourselves singly and separately to the will of your husband and served God through him? Struggling to understand to your fullest what your husband has described to you of the subtlest demands of the faith? And, servants, have you followed your masters' biddings with fidelity and pleasure, walking the second mile, and serving the Lord thereby? Lastly, little children, hear me. In the dark night comes Satan, Prince of the World, who yearns to take you toward the things of his domain, riches, and land, and mighty flocks. But life is short and the end sudden.

Look Satan in the eye and bid him pass by: if you can do that, children, you will see him wither into shade before you.

"The fight outside at our doors, friends, is nothing to the fight within our separate hearts, for only in the inner battle come we near the danger of dying to Our Lord. Stand fast! As Paul urged the Ephesians. Clothe yourselves in the breastplate of righteousness and take up the shield of faith, and then what? Then, stand! Or God will further peel the rod of affliction to you. Yet, peace, rest, my friends; Rehoboth is surely a fertile field. To God we will yield." Newman raised his face and shut his eyes. "We will be sown, oh Lord, Our Father. Only do not sow us entirely with thorns. Let a remnant remain in Rehoboth, the fruitful land, to call forth Thy Name, anew."

When they sang the psalm, their low and singular voices blended slowly into one voice and even Newman's vanished therein.

Caleb was whispering his own prayer, but once done, began again:

"*Almight God, protect me now,*
Your angels hold at bay.
And let me live through the dark night
and wake to praise the day."

He started a third time:

"*Almight God, protect me now—*"

"Why are you saying it again?" Witty interrupted him.

"Oh, Mama, I haven't said it right yet! Listen: 'Al*might* God, pro*tect* me *now*!' Did you hear that? The *God* wasn't loud enough to balance out the *now*." He began to sob, rubbing at his mouth with his hands. "He won't hear me if it isn't right."

She sat up and held him to her, her hand on the yellow hair. She rocked back and forth. "The words are printed on your heart, Caleb. You're a good boy, a good boy."

Gradually he stopped crying. She should have thought to give him beer at suppertime. It was all her fault. She should have gone to Aquidneck with the other women.

She lay awake a long time, waiting for Ephraim to come from the window where he was standing guard with Submit.

"Ephraim?"

"Are you awake, Mama?"

"Tomorrow you can do whatever you need to. You don't have to ask my permission for anything." She rolled up on her elbows.

"I know, Mama. That's what I did this afternoon." He lay down.

"And you don't have to be a farmer, either. Next week we'll see about the pewterer. You may have to go out early, though, before you're thirteen. We'll all live at Mama Strong's until we get our land."

"The Taunton pewterer's the best." He leaned on his elbows beside her. "Mama, you know the oak tree in the north pasture? Near the woods?"

"I think so, yes." She lay under the covers, her chin on the bones of her hand.

"Well, I've been thinking, if they get in tomorrow and take you and the boys captive . . . well, they might take me, too. They might think I was still a child. They'd send us to different masters, though. And if you and I could escape our masters on the same night and meet at the oak, maybe I could take care of you. And the boys. I'm a good shot."

She couldn't answer.

"The night before Whitsuntide."

Her throat hurt: "Papa would be proud of you."

He turned his face away.

"*Succommee! Mecanteass!*" The shouts were nearby, right outside the window.

All talking in the house ceased.

Distant laughter followed and drumming began from somewhere beyond the palisade. It sounded as if thousands of Indians were gathered by the pond, right next to Mama Strong's.

Her head on her arm, her arm cold. Be still and know that I am God. He will bend you till you bow, dear, so long He labors over you! Stand fast, girl! Philip was by the gully. She reached out and touched the arm of his jacket. He smiled at her and nodded. She moved her yellow hair over her shoulders. Then he was running across the field, down into the gully. Come back and I will give you half the land. Isaak's head lay in the mud, the wounded side down. She turned his face up; she couldn't tell where the bullet had struck, couldn't find the bone of Isaak's ear. The things of the flesh do not endure, but rust, as iron does. A man finds his soul in tending to his business. We don't expect large miracles in these times, girl. The smallest evidence of His order is enough; His gears set into the whirling snow. Gears of His eyes, and standing in that gaze. I named her Witty so she'd use them, Emily. He is Submit to show you what God wants.

Hoo! Koo koo koo koo. Faintly. From the northwest. By the base of the hill.

"What should we do?" A voice from near the window sounded matter-of-fact.

"Nothing. They're too scared of ghosts to do much at night."

Laughter from the northeast, closer. Witty stiffened.

"Ever seen a man who's been scalped?"

"Worse. And they always do it."

Oooh wah! hu-oo. A third wolf. Then a fourth. From the northwest and the north. Howls that sang on the air like sobs and vanished in a thin, high wail.

Laughter, from the southwest.

A single wolf again, nearer, the other wolves joining in. As if at a wedding feast, to sing.

"Pray for rain."

"*Keen squaw! Keen squaw!*"

"*Kuttannawshesh!*"

"Come out and fight us or be known as women!" Pastor Newman translated aloud from where he stood at the east window holding the bedding up against a sliver of dark blue sky.

Something struck the side of the house, spattering of thumps.

"They're here, Mama!" Ephraim's voice near her ear.

Ephraim was touching Caleb, his gun in his hand. "Come on, Caleb, get up and help me load the gun!"

Witty sat up.

"They're over the fence!" a man's voice at the south window reported.

Bullets struck the south side of the house two or three at a time. Men shoved their guns right through the glass of the windows to fire back, shattering, splintering.

Wait pushed up under Witty's arm. There was a sound like rushing water.

"Hold your fire down there!" The sergeant's voice came from the floor above. "We've got men out on the palisade. They'll fire a double shot if they're in trouble. Don't shoot until you hear that!"

Boots overhead.

"Stand up!" She put Wait on his feet and struggled to stand on her own stiffened legs. "Get your shoes on!" She stepped into her own.

Wait sat on the bedding and cried.

"Come on! Come on!" She stuffed his feet into the shoes.

"We're holding at the palisade!" The voice from overhead. "They're going off. They're piling hay at Pecks'!"

Witty ran with Wait to the back room.

"There it goes!"

Again the sound of rushing water. Witty pulled the bedding back from the window and saw a flash of orange outside, above the palisade.

Her father's house: black smoke collected about the flames. Her father was standing behind her. She handed him the edge of the bedding.

"I'm sorry, Papa."

Then the house next to theirs went up.

Suddenly the day had form. The Indians would burn all the houses. Not until that was done would they jump the palisade and bang at the walls of Newman's.

"Mama!" Wait's voice was a sob.

"Don't cry anymore. Everybody has to help now. You can do your part. Go around and look for sparks. We don't want any fire inside the house, Wait. Stamp on them with your shoes. See?" She acted it out for him.

He stamped and was off, his eyes busy on the floorboards.

Her father was gone from the window. Her mother stood in his place, tears giving a glister to her eyes.

"I had all my babies there but two," Emily said. "Even the ones that died."

"Let's have a bit of breakfast, girls!" a male voice called out.

Cakes over the fire: bread. Emily and Witty moved to prepare it. The ordinary day edged forward. All we wanted, oh Lord, was the ordinary day.

Witty took small breaths in the third room of the first floor of that enormous house. The room was a bedchamber on the opposite side of the house from the sitting room, very grand.

"Bring her in here!" Witty called from beside the bed. Mrs. Pitman had fainted from lack of air. Witty finished stacking the small supply of linen by the various jars of salve and ointment.

"Drink." Witty held a wet cloth to Mrs. Pitman's lips. Small noises, wrinkled throat, round stone-colored face. The old lips sucked a bit of moisture from the cloth. Witty refolded the cloth to wipe Mrs. Pitman's face.

"How are you?"

"I'm fine, dear, just fine. I didn't sleep at all, though, that's the trouble. Do you think that I'm sometimes too firm as a mistress? Was I with you?" Mrs. Pitman's eyes looked dark and sunken in their sockets.

"You were always cheerful, as I recall." Witty laid her palm on Mrs. Pitman's forehead and found it cool. "Perhaps the war doesn't have that much to do with you and me. Maybe the Mount Hopes just want to go home to plant."

"And those fool Baptists in Swansea would let them right in, too!"

The burning reached Abell's inn.

"Ready?" Witty wrapped her hand in cloth, and together she and Hannah lifted the pot of boiling water off the fire. Slowly they worked their way through the bedchamber toward the polished stairs in the front hall. Looking up, they saw the tip of a saw moving in and out through the smooth boards of Newman's ceiling.

"Watch out!" The steaming water slopped onto Witty's ankles, but the two women kept on toward the corner.

Upstairs, Witty could see through the roof frame that was bare of thatch. A shaggy orange light flickered westward in the sky. She and Hannah set the water by the men who were sawing through the floor.

Witty stood up, straight through the eaves. She was outside, free! A swarm of dark forms were throwing hay over the northwest gate.

"Hey! This is water. You were supposed to bring oil."

"We're saving the oil for the wounds."

. . .

Downstairs in the back room, women were preparing biscuits for a midday meal.

"Witty." An old man put his arm around her shoulders and breathed an old man's breath into her face. "If something happens to me, take your mother to her people in Scituate. And you're all settled, girl. Hoskins says he'll do it." Clement's smudged hands grabbed at the biscuits and he was off again.

Witty reached for the long iron bread shovel and bent to the hearth; she shoved it into the coals. The fire was low and she did not add a log. She stood up and reached a hand inside the oven in the wall. It was warm, but not hot.

Grain has little similarity to the bare seed. If she died, she would see through the glass better, face to face. She wouldn't see Maie's face covered with dirt and yellow hair. Nor Isaak's jaw gone. Nor Stephen peeling off his shroud. She would see them in some other form. We shall not all sleep. We shall change. Sown corruptible, we shall be raised incorruptible. Sown in weakness, we shall be raised in power. Sown in a natural body, raised spiritual. It wouldn't even matter if she died.

But with the boys, it was different.

"Waitstill, I may lift you up quick sometime and put you in the oven. I'd put the door on, too, to hide you. Don't be afraid if I do. Lie still inside. Don't make a sound. When there's no more noise, come out."

"I don't want to go in there!"

"Waitstill! You come back here!"

The men were calling out: "What's that noise?"

"Hey! What's that noise? From the southwest?"

"It's the mill."

"It's the millstone, I bet you! They're cracking it, like they did up north in Springfield!"

"It'll be all right. You can start over again." Purchase was standing beside Witty, his voice hoarse and his long fingers streaked with grime. "Mama's got her ewes on the island. She'll let you breed them."

Witty nodded. The one thing she'd possessed was gone. The northwest gate place had cooled enough to let hooves pass. They were all gone now from the common: the horses, the cows and the sheep.

"The fires must be up to the northeast gate now, to the pond, probably to our house." Purchase stopped.

"Purchase, take Caleb, if . . . you have to. He wants to be a farmer. Send Ephraim to a trade."

A double shot rang out from the palisade and Purchase ran to the window.

"They're over! They're over! The whole lot of them!" the sergeant called, rushing down the stairs. The warders began to run in from the palisade. The dogs came with them, scratching, whining, barking. Timmy wasn't among them.

"It's Philip out there!"

"I saw him, too!"

"He's got his black horse out there!"

"Did you see Philip?" Witty pulled at Submit's arm. "Did you see him?"

"No. I think I saw one of Indian Sam's sons, that's all I could make out."

"Tawhitch weasasean?"

"They're asking why we're afraid," Newman whispered by the north-facing window of the bedchamber.

A hail of bullets began to strike the house. The piled logs started to slide down. Splintering of wood. Falling. Things falling. Bursting into flame. The bed ticking at the window. Roaring, hot, dark.

Witty hurled water from a bucket. Flames were eating the little air left in the room. Burned feathers were falling everywhere. No air to breathe, her throat gulping, her shoulders heaving. She ripped off her apron and dipped it in another bucket and wrung it out.

She pressed the apron into Caleb's hands. "Hold it close . . . to your nose! Share it . . . with Wait!" Through the window hole black smoke was rising and spinning away. The blue wheels of a wagon were right outside the window and beside it Witty could see two heads. One darted out of sight. On the ground lay something she could only slowly make out: the rump of a cow.

"Get away!"

She went back to the hearth. She pushed the boys in near the low fire under the chimney. "There's . . . air in the hole up there! Up, look up!" She shouted at them, huddling next to each other with the apron to their mouths and noses.

At the hole called ear there was too much noise. Whine of bullets, coming toward her. Explosion of new fire, driving other bullets away from her. And burning. The whistling of approaching fire that heretics learn, fire that eats.

"Help me! Help me!" A man stumbled from a window toward her, his hair ablaze. She grabbed a quilt and threw it over his head. He began to sweat and stutter in her arms.

"Over here, come over." She pulled him toward a bench. She got him to lie down.

"Miss? Miss? Is it dark? Is it dark here? Am I blind?"

"Turn this way." She took the quilt off and pressed his head toward her. "Do you see the hearth fire?"

But he kept his cheek flat on the bench and would not move and did not answer her. Outside, the noise surged toward them and away, like the ocean. She reached for salve and spread it on the scorched flesh of the head. The eyes looked all right, but the man—or boy, as she saw now—said nothing. It was the wagon-maker's apprentice. It could be Submit. Ephraim. She hadn't seen Ephraim for some time now.

A bullet crashed and whined through the room and splintered into the wall above her. Caleb and Wait sat in near to the failing fire and were all right. Witty pulled the bread shovel from the coals. She stood in front of the boys with her hand wrapped in her skirt to hold the shovel. She stood for what seemed a long time and then gradually she realized that the new shots were all being fired from inside the house, moving away from her. And the house wasn't shaking anymore. The Indians weren't firing back at the house. It grew quiet, and clean cold air began to come in at the window holes.

"Why did they stop?"

"Beats me." The sergeant sat in the pastor's chair at the long table.

"We killed plenty."

"Aw, we hardly shot any!"

Joseph Hoskins was walking toward Witty, his round belly leading his short frame.

"I'm a poor man, Witty Peck . . . Strong." He stuck his thumbs into his belt and leaned away. "And you're a poor widow, clear as I can see. There's no one finer than your father, and if you're looking to marry, I'm the first that wants to hear about it."

His gums were red: the first sign of scurvy.

"Why, Mr. Hoskins!" She could not imagine kissing those cracked lips.

"I'm an old man. Fifty-eight in June, and you're a young woman." Though he was potbellied, he did stand well on his feet.

"I'm not so young, sir." She smiled. "But it seems a bit heady to talk like this until we're sure it's over."

"I only waited till I knew if I was rich or poor." He moved his fingers from the belt and grinned at her. "I'm poor. But I been poor before."

She had lost everything, but the more she lost, the lighter

and stronger she felt. Nobody else had any more than she, not even Hoskins, if she got her land.

"We'll see." She reached to feel if her hair was pinned up. "I've got three boys, you know, though my oldest is going out soon."

"I'm a father eight times, myself."

"After it's over, we'll see." She smiled again.

"Take your time, girl!" He made a motion that would have been the tipping of a hat, if he'd been wearing one.

It was reasonable, but something told her she wouldn't have to do it.

Ephraim's hair was damp with sweat and plastered to his head. Caleb was getting a bit of real color into his pale face. Wait was asleep on a bench, his heels a good distance from the newly built fire.

"If they don't come back soon, boys, it'll be dark and we'll be safe for the night."

"Drunk is what they are."

"No, they're not. They're just smart. Why should they risk anything now?" Clement Peck pressed his palms down on the top of the table. "They've got us laid out flat back into the plain we sprang out of. Not a hoof nor a seedling in sight. Not a roof. Not a bin. Every man jack of us is poor, a pauper." Emily sat at the table beside him.

"Where did they go, then?"

"To sleep it off. They'll move on to Providence or Swansea tomorrow."

"It's over, then? You think it's over?"

"This part's been over for some time!" Clement began to move his palm back and forth over the boards of the table. "We're into the next part. Ours who went to Aquidneck won't be coming back this year! Town's got nothing but six bushels of seed corn under a floor and whatever it can dig out of its pits.

You hear any cows out there, boys? You hear any horses? We've lost it all. Our children will have gray hair before they get as far as we were. We're set back, far back."

"Swansea will sell us seed corn."

"What'll we buy it with? Bond service?" It was a new thing to hear bitterness in Clement Peck.

Emily laid her hand on his shoulder: "The Lord saw how much we loved the things of the world. Now we're rid of that, the rot. He'll care for us and feed us."

"No, girl. We just came too far west. They were stronger." Clement put his head into his hands. "We lost it all. We lost everything."

"We have our lives, Clement. You'll plant."

In the pantry the back door hung open. Witty watched it move to and fro in the northwest breeze that always came with the twilight. Things have unsuspected patterns that are not always visible to the eye. But the patterns endure. The material things do not. Some patterns you see with a glass, some are whispered in your ear. Oh, it looked surprisingly light outside, translucent, almost, through the doorway. Or perhaps her eyes had grown too accustomed to the dimness of the house? The orchard looked eerie, cinders blew about under the apple trees. The door banged open again: she could trust the odd light now, she could be free.

Her feet took her. Outside, she moved slowly like a rock rolling or like thunder preparing itself. Then her feet became light and she ran. It was like flying and she wanted to laugh. The common was empty of living sheep but strewn with the legs of dead ones and with flaking coals that were once wagons. The cinders blowing everywhere blew unobserved: God was not watching over this orchard. Yet her mother was right, the only power was his. This land Rehoboth was empty of Him only because He was still being installed. This grass did not host nor this orchard celebrate His Being only because He hadn't entirely got here yet. She circled left and ran southwest to the gate. She was strong, she would find her own way; but first she had to get Maie's cap.

"Where's Witty?"

"Where's Widow Strong?"

"Where's Mama?"

Her father's house was burned to the ground. Yesterday's pudding must be a crust of indistinguishable ashes in the blackened heap of timber. Odd, but she distinctly heard the bleating of a lamb ahead. A little farther now and she would reach the ashes of her father's barn. She breathed deeply in the sulfurous light. She had not felt so pleased with herself for such a long time. She was sure to get her widow's claim, she could feel it; and it wasn't far off, either. The smoke was settling in low clouds and there were no birds in the singed trees. The sheepfold was still smoking. Ahead, past the drop-off, the salt meadow was crisscrossed by its creeks, silver under the dark clouds. She turned to the gully.

"*Squaw*."

"*Squaw*."

The voices were whispers at first and she thought they might be memories. Then she saw the shapes rising by the scorched birches. Standing, coming toward her. Two of them. Very tall, both very tall. Smeared with grease and their eyes reddened. She opened her mouth. The taller one reached for her hair and raised his club. His eyes were dark and she did not know who it was. Then she was stunned by the fall of the club and saw two pictures that moved apart: both of the faces before her, four eyes turned silent as fire. Twice her brother walked into the woods. Waving goodbye. Waving goodbye. Twice her mother reached down to her as she was sleeping, to push back the corner of her cap. Her cap. Then enormous hands came and picked her up, high into the sky over the great plain of Rehoboth.

III

SEED-TIME AND SUMMER

"Before he struck, he made a small speech, directing it to Philip, and said, he had been a very great man, and had made many a man afraid of him, but so big as he was, he would now chop his ass for him." From the dictation of the English war captain Benjamin Church.

10

Over the top of a hill in the northland the newborn quarter of the fishing moon floated among thousands of stars in the great black belly of the sky. This was the hill the great-man of the river had given to Pometacom and here Pometacom sat in a house too small for winter, small enough to pack and run with. Not that he ran. Englishmen ran from him. Outside, he could hear the long river–Connecticut swelling to flood its banks in a rush toward the southland. Sowams, the southland, the name of it brought water to his mouth. He swallowed spit with his smoke and thought of fish. The men from the other houses on the hill must be eating shad now. They had all gone south or east at the full of the moon. Not to fish, though every mouth prepared itself for shad, but to burn. In the east, to burn the towns ringing Boston. In the south, who knew? He was left on his hill in the north with guards, old men, women and boys. There were two beside him and he nodded the younger one to begin. Neimpauog's voice filled the small house.

"Wakwah the fox they call you, he who rose against the bearded men in the fifty-fifth year of their coming into our bays and our brooks, of their taking our cleared land and our guns. By night and by water you led us safely from our home to Pocasset, where Weetamoo's houses stood within the cedar swamp. By night and by water you led us safely from that swamp to crawl across the cleared land into the western wood and you slowed those chasing after us by scattering your wealth along the path. With sorrow we ran from the southland and our dead, our old ones and the hills where they sat; we shall return to plant the cleared land in our time and raise new roofs of skin over the dead. Northward we came to where every bank and stream is strange, to where the fox would bind a new people." The boy coughed.

Pometacom watched his son to see if it was blood he coughed up, but it wasn't. Neimpauog went on: "With joy we came north looking for the inland people, who had begun to fight Englishmen. They were not in their towns. Quabaug was empty. We waded across the low, shining snake beside it, and poled the lusty narrow river to Muttuamp's fort. There we found them crouched and waiting: thousands of women and children of the Nipmuck. Soon there was a whooping from the hill nearby and into the swamp came the four great-men and all the warriors of the inland people. They had burned Brookfield and emptied it forever of Englishmen. They were playing ball with the head of an English boy.

"The four sat and the fox removed his beaded coat and took his long knife and split his coat in half, saying: 'Great-men of the inland people, I will clothe you. It is a long war and a time of cold may come to us, to the new people, the people of the whole land which is born by this cutting.' The fox split the coat sideways to make four parts and gave the right tail to Muttuamp, who has the most warriors, and the left to Matoonas, who has the fewest but who burned the English town near Pakachoog and so started the war in the north. The fox gave the sleeves to the two great-men of Nashoba, who are loved by the men of Nipmuck but who share only two hundred men between them. The right sleeve you gave to the one-eyed uncle and the left sleeve to the slant-headed nephew. 'We are now bound as one people,' you told them. 'Never say that Philip has wealth while his captains starve.' "

Philip. Philip? Had he called himself Philip? By the fire, the great-man kicked at the pitch pine and it flared up in bursts of blue and green. The slant-headed nephew had touched that left sleeve with such scorn. And it was not because the nephew was offended to have the sleeve from the broken hand as his portion.

The boy who was speaking paused, looked uneasily about the house at the sleeping women, at the older boy whose head was shaved on one side and who wore a blue feather in the hair on the other side. Beyond the house they could hear the mating calls of the foxes, so late were they into the winter. Still Neimpauog did not begin again.

The boy must have forgotten the next words. Pometacom gave them to him. "Wakwah the fox persuaded . . ."

Neimpauog took the words gratefully and, leaning his elbows on thighs thinned by hunger, resumed: "Wakwah the fox persuaded the four great-men of the inland people to go west with him to the long river and bind themselves with the people of Pocumptuck. There Wampanoag and Nipmuck and Pocumptuck played ball by the river that has no sand and then the three people went upriver together to empty the town called Northfield, the farthest town of Englishmen upriver. As one people, they ran into the meadows where the Englishmen . . ."

Pometacom saw the slant-headed nephew's face again. At Northfield, the nephew had led the new people into the open to fight, against Pometacom's instructions.

". . . were cutting corn and they sank their axes into Englishmen's heads and cut skin off the foreheads so that their bodies would be incomplete and the people of the whole land would have Englishmen for slaves in the other world. The rest of the Englishmen loaded their wagons and went out of Northfield forever. But the new people went separate ways, because . . . they still followed separate great-men. The northland had as many warriors as the southland and neither would follow the other. Nor would the inland people of the north even find for themselves a single great-man to be foremost among them." Neimpauog came to a stop.

Once again Pometacom gave the needed words. "Northfield was emptied . . ."

"No. I cannot. No more." There were dark circles under the boy's eyes.

"You spoke well, my son. Next time you will go further." The great-man's eyes were drawn to the older boy who wore the blue feather. "Would you like to go on, my son?"

"But you have never given me this story, my father!" the

dead Mishquock's boy objected. He'd kept his birth name, Nomatuck, the war being his only wintering.

"I give it to you now."

Nomatuck stretched his lips into a smile.

Neimpauog put his hands in front of his eyes.

"Northfield was emptied?" Nomatuck began, securing the beginning as his own.

"Northfield was emptied." Pometacom pulled his mantle closer over his shoulders. He was never warm anymore.

Nomatuck tilted his head back and began slowly: "Northfield was emptied of Englishmen and the great-man of the river who wears the tuft of sea-gull feather in his ear stood on his own hill and looked upon the town called Deerfield. He did not need the new people. He would empty it alone. So he ran down upon the Englishmen cutting corn in the gardens below and he killed cows and pigs. He loaded the backs of the Englishmen's horses with this flesh and went back up to his hill. He waited for the Englishmen to go away in their wagons. But the Englishmen did not go. When a single people acts alone, its hands are weak."

Pometacom nodded his pleasure at the recitation.

Neimpauog took his hands from his eyes and began to play with some red fringe on a fur.

The older boy continued: "Then the great-man of the river did beg the fox of the southland for aid and the people of the whole land came together again and painted in one color, to match the red leaves of the woods. The soldiers who stayed at the three towns mid-river marched north and cut down Deerfield's wheat. They loaded Deerfield's goods onto wagons and started back. They came through the woods where we lay as the fox had told us to, sending our breath toward the earth. Oxen dragged their wagons over the path and we could see sacks of wheat and feather beds bouncing in the carts. Then the whole people rose up and howled as an infant does on the first day. The Englishmen's blood made the red leaves brighter. The wheat fell like rain and the feathers like snow. We took the clothes off the dead Englishmen to hang up on poles at Deerfield, and when the living Englishmen still in that town saw the clothes, they did pack and go from their houses forever. Yet the people of the whole land continued to follow different great-men. The new people must be more than bound, the new people must be melted like iron, into one bar. The fox spoke of it with his wise-man." Nomatuck stopped to swallow and clear his throat of smokiness.

"Didn't you fight by the bloody brook, either?" Neimpauog looked up from the fringe to his father.

"Why would I? We weren't trapped."

"The great-men of the Nipmuck fight." Neimpauog lowered his face.

"They know no better."

"He of Nahiganset fights." Neimpauog gave his father an upward look, keeping his face down.

"Naonanto saw the snake." Pometacom pushed the mantle higher. It would be much easier if he would fight. The men of the north would hear him better. But there was the fox. And the woman's hand, her face in the black hood, the darkness of her eyes widening and narrowing, as if a heart beat in them. And not the snake. "Your new brother fought at the brook in the woods."

"I fought at the brook!" Nomatuck affirmed. "My father always fought. He saw the snake."

"Yes. Your father saw the snake, and even though it didn't keep the bullets from killing him, his blood gave us the war. His blood gave us the winning. His blood may soon give us the coast towns near Boston and the towns of Nahiganset in the southland. Since the snows melted, we have heard that his blood gave us the town called Groton near Nashoba and the town called Medfield nearer Boston, as well as the town called Lancaster, earlier. And his blood gave us the towns we emptied before the snows came: Brookfield and Northfield and Deerfield." Pometacom nodded now toward Nomatuck as he said: "And last of all, Springfield, at the roundness of the harvest moon."

Nomatuck heard the signal and went on. "At the roundness of the harvest moon the fox sent us downriver to the farthest town of Englishmen on the river people's land, to Springfield, large as Rehoboth. We burned and burned until smoke rose in columns and a delicious smell came from the house of many books. Upriver and downriver were cleared of Englishmen. There remained only the towns mid-river, but it was proper to rest and eat, for only a few dead leaves hung yellow from the lowest branches. None of the north's great-men wished to offer it, so the fox gave the three-day feast to the people of the whole land and we ate together. Still the inland people could not choose one man from among their four, so that we might name our greatest-man, one great-man for the whole people.

"When the underfur of the wolf was thickening and the white frost moon prepared to rise, the five hundred warriors of Muttuamp persuaded the others to go against the mid-river towns. Muttuamp desired caution: he set a fire to lure the Englishmen out of one town, but while the Nipmuck all lay on the path ready to shoot, they were jumped from behind by Englishmen. Half the world lies behind a man's head. Such simplicities the Nipmuck forget. The Nipmuck ran from that town as the men of Nemasket once ran from the hill outside Plimouth. They went . . . eastward in the snow-bearing wind. . . . Muttuamp's many warriors began to turn from him to the slant-headed nephew of Nashoba who . . . lacks caution. Who . . . it was . . ."

"That is enough, my son. You spoke well."

The adopted son sat back at full attention. Now he would swallow the forthcoming words. They belonged to him.

Neimpauog stopped playing with the fringe and laid his head down on the furs.

Pometacom leaned toward the fire. His shoulders were cold, even under the mantle. He went on with the story himself: "The people of the river climbed their crouched hills to winter in the narrow valleys westward. We stayed here and I sent some of the sicker women and the old people south, with a few men to guide them, to Naonanto's swamp to join our other women.

Snow crusted thick over the cornfields and ice came to the river. Eagles sat on the ice and the stones we skidded did not break through. It was the coldest winter in nine. When our men returned, we went westward, too, I and the forty warriors left to Pokanocket.

"We went toward Mohawk. We got powder from the Dutch and crossed the river of the Dutch on rafts. We waited outside a winter town of the Mohawk. But the man-eaters called out, 'It is the daybreak people come to kill us!' And they would not talk to me. We returned to our shelters. I gave shirts and hats and neckcloths to my men. They put them on and went west to hide under trees at the edge of Mohawk's lands. They shot at Mohawk's hunters. It did no good. We were recognized. 'It is the daybreak!' the man-eaters called and came running toward my men on their long, thick legs. They knew we were not Englishmen.

"My men ran back to me where I lay sick in the shelter. Every day we moved our shelters eastward. The man-eaters crept after us. They came into the valleys of the river people, which angered our friends. But then came our own heart finally! Naonanto walked among us with his men."

Neimpauog slept. Nomatuck's bright eyes tested the great-man and would not let him go.

"We went eastward on willow skis to meet Naonanto at the river and he told us first the sorrowful news, that many of the women we left with him were dead."

Nomatuck's mother.

The boy's bright gaze didn't waver.

"The Englishmen had come without warning upon Naonanto during a snowstorm. They ran into his swamp with knives tied to the fronts of their guns. They got across the log into his fort. He killed many of them, but lost two hundred of his men, and many others. And as it grew late in the day, he ran out of powder. He used arrows but the arrows did not pierce the thicknesses of the Englishmen's coats; nor did his axes reach past the knives tied to the front of the Englishmen's guns. The Englishmen spread powder on his houses and burned the women. Then Naonanto was ready for our war. Then he joined us.

"I gave him the powder we had from the Dutch. He sent his cousin to show the forgetful great-men of the Nipmuck how to creep into a town by dark. This cousin and the two great-men of Nashoba crept into the town called Lancaster together and broke into a walled house. They took away twenty English-women and, at last, the slant-headed nephew was pleased with the men from the south. Naonanto has six hundred warriors left of his thousand but that is the most of any great-man of the whole land. At the first thunder, we will name him foremost among us. The new people will be born whole: the daybreak will be its head; the river people its arms; the bickering inland people its legs, which run each way; and the people of the point its heart.

"Through the snow-melting moon we ate bark and roots and became as our fathers of old before Kiehtan brought us the seeds and when Hobomok and the hunters walked about alone. When the ice-breaking moon was full, Naonanto went south with all his men and half of ours, to burn the towns near his home. The slant-headed nephew went east with the Nipmuck men and the other half of ours, to burn the towns leading to Boston. There shall be no more fighting in the open: Naonanto has persuaded the Nipmuck of that. When the planting moon rises and the year starts fresh at the first moon, we will all meet at Wachusett–the mountain to hear the first thunder. Then we shall fish and rest, but we must not sit down for long. When the leaves thicken, we will rise and burn Boston and push out the Englishmen who brought the sickness that killed the hill people. And at the fall of the leaf we will cut our corn here in the northland and go home. We will . . . burn Plimouth and take to us all the land that is of the daybreak." Pometacom stopped and pushed a log farther into the fire. "That's all, my son. Sleep now. You have a bride to think of. Kuttiomp's daughter will be back from the southland with the seed corn soon."

Nomatuck lay under the fur. "I'll need the silver coins, for her father."

"I'll have them when I sell the Englishwomen that Naonanto's cousin brought us. We'll give the wedding here, when we fish." Pometacom leaned close to the fire and let the pitch pine soothe his aching eyes. Then he, too, stretched himself out.

There were silences in his story, as there had been in his father's. Weskautaug delayed in naming a wise-man to be foremost among various wise-men and so melt the new people into one piece of iron. The great-woman of Saghonnate, who had survived the fire in the snow at Naonanto's, had come north with Naonanto. But only to Quabaug, not to the river. Not to Pometacom nor to the people of the daybreak. And he was silent about the coat with silver laces Naonanto wore north. Annawon was right: Boston had given it to Naonanto in return for his promise not to fight. Pometacom moved his legs on the bed. The bed was made larger by his brother-in-law's absence.

His brother-in-law Tuspaquin was watching the slant-headed nephew for him and sending reports: "Here at the town called Groton, the ugly one digs up the dead. He cuts children apart before their parents' eyes and feeds them to pigs. The men of the inland follow him sometimes, and sometimes they don't. He cannot count all the men of Nipmuck his." Pometacom moved his face from the fire and stretched the mantle way over his head.

Slight, nimble Naonanto was now the older brother of the new people, or would be at the thunder.

"Will you go against my Englishmen's towns in the south?"

"Let me speak plainly, southland," Naonanto had said, fingering the laces of his coat. "You bring men together and cause them to dance as one, but I kill Englishmen."

"Wearing a coat from the Boston tailor?"

"Have the women ready to plant, southland. I go, straightaway."

With his eyes closed Pometacom saw the faces of his friends

in the rum houses at Rehoboth, at Swansea, at Taunton. Surely Naonanto would keep out of the cleared land. He saw the face of Mishquock dying in the sand, his lips pressed together. *Nom*, Mishquock had been trying to speak his son's name then. Pometacom would have adopted him anyway.

Outside the house, a guard coughed.

He needed guards, not against Englishmen but against the arms and legs of the new people. No one of the northland could be trusted. Muttuamp was dull-headed. Matoonas was feeble. The uncle and the nephew of Nashoba were mad dogs that foamed at the mouth. And the river people wanted peace. It was even whispered that the Pocumptuck planned to snatch the fox of the south and float him downriver. John Winthrop's son at Hartford had offered forty coats for him, alive.

Twenty, dead.

The men of the river were cold.

Surely his green-eyed friends were speaking of him in the rum houses of the southland.

Flee, my friends.

If he comes, I cannot save you. I am but a cord against his rashness.

Call of the foxes, louder and more sweet.

When the sun was well up, Pometacom made his way downhill over ground that was only now beginning to soften, so late did spring come to the northland. He had heard of this lateness, but had never seen it for himself. Beside him his uncle Unkompoin walked, smelling of the skunk oil that calmed the pain in his knees. Will of Saghonnate walked on the other side, without his usual cheer. Behind them were four tall guards; these were all of his left in the northland, except for the boys, and Otan-nick, who wrote his letters, and Weskautaug.

A single canoe was drawn up at the landing. In it sat a young man whom John Easton would have admired, had John Easton ever come with Edmund Andros to talk. The great-man of the river sat in the canoe and squinted up at Pometacom on the shore. Of course, the cleverness and courtesy of the river people didn't make them reliable.

"Ho, great-man!" Walking the last few steps, Pometacom spoke first to ease the heart of his ally who had seen his fields at Deerfield, Northfield and Springfield cleared and who now wanted only to forget the war and let it move eastward to Boston without him. But with the Mohawk sniffing again at the edges of his land, he couldn't do that. The fox is clever, sometimes in ways he doesn't see until they're upon him and past.

The great-man of the river returned the greeting from where he sat in the back of the canoe: "Southland, you're in better health! Get in. I'll show you the fishing places." The white tuft of the sea gull dangled from his ear.

No planting places? He had to get the planting places, too! From the shore, Pometacom motioned the great-man of the river and the other two men with him to move to the middle of the canoe. "My uncle and I will sit in the back."

The men in the canoe looked surprised, but they moved.

Will of Saghonnate stepped into the canoe and took the place left free in front. Pometacom and Unkompoin took the back. The four guards of Pokanocket gave the canoe a push and then lifted another canoe into the water and followed.

Perhaps the river people were afraid to give the daybreak planting fields, afraid they'd never leave. They paddled for the middle of the water, neared an island, swung right and downriver into the current.

The great-man of the river tossed his shaven head as if there were still hair to trail from it. "Here at the island the shad is very good, very good. We stand on the rocks with our spears and watch them."

Once on the water, Pometacom grew absent. He wanted to hear of the south and not the northland. He stared at the back of the other great-man's neck; it was young and full-fleshed. "Perhaps the fish watch us, too. What do you think, my friend? Do they look up and see us with our spears ready?"

"The fish cannot see into the air!"

"I know, I know." Pometacom sat straighter and moved the paddle to fit his left hand better. He must be more careful. He had to get the fields before Naonanto returned. Icy water splashed on the fingers of his left hand. The hand ached. He could not change hands paddling before the others did. "The great-man of yours who used to summer on my hill here told me I could plant in any of his fields. He's not coming back this summer, either."

"He's afraid of the Mohawk." The great-man of the river paddled with a patience that was suddenly missing from his voice. "When the Englishmen were here, we didn't fear Mohawk."

"When the people of the whole land are one, Mohawk will taste its own fear." Pometacom watched the plump neck for a reply; none came.

The paddling was wearying, even downstream. He'd lost his strength lying sick in the west where the wind rattled the ash trees and scared the last of the game away. At last Kiehtan had whispered in his ear, words too low, too slow to understand, yet he'd known from them that he would recover. And the voice was gentle. You cannot change what Kiehtan sees. It destroys a man to try. Only Hobomok may be cajoled. Kiehtan must be obeyed.

"So much mud!" Will called out from the front of the canoe.

Pometacom studied the banks of the river, wider and wider flats covered with a black mud crusted by wind and sun. The mud ran from the river up around and under trees, burying the brush and the bushes, reaching halfway toward the branches.

"So much mud!" Will called, louder and more cheerfully, and his voice spread in the emptiness.

They laughed.

It was good to shout.

The Englishmen were gone from the river here. And no more than one or two Mohawk could have gotten to the river unnoticed.

The great-man of the river pointed with his hand: "Where that stream comes out, it will be silver with shad!"

"Where are they now? It's already the fishing moon!"

"Too cold."

It would not be too cold in the southland. The moons were wrong here. Pometacom noticed sap like pink blood coming into the distant trees, where a little snow still lay thin and white beside the yellow grasses that stuck up here and there. The hardened mud nearby looked something like shore sand after rain and that, too, made Pometacom long for the southland. Sometimes it seemed to him that what happened in the northland didn't matter. They were approaching a small cliff with water dripping from it and the sound was pleasant. But did it matter, the cliff's being there? What could matter, or even take place, outside the southland? At home the sky would be blue over naked birches; scarlet buds would be coming out at the tips of the branches. Otters would be lying tantalizingly within reach, licking their stomachs. The wind would stir the branches of the trees: click, click, pleasantly clicking together. Low flatness, the whole world would be blue and green. Not high and yellow like this. Not cold.

"Those are good fields!" In front of Pometacom the great-man of the river raised a dripping paddle eastward and Pometacom understood those fields would be his, for his women.

"They'll bloom with the southland's corn, my friend!" He thanked the man of the river quickly, careful not to promise any of the corn as tribute. He leaned forward to examine the unfamiliar fields where he could now assign places to the few women left to Pokanocket. Pokanocket! This was hardly the cleared land. When he looked closely at the low muddy stretch between the riverbank and a distant bluff, he saw that the fields were not entirely unfamiliar, though. This was where he had visited during the corn moon to see the strewn and naked bodies of Englishmen, covered with flies; the buzzards flew low over them, their wing tips glowing in the sunlight. At home his people sometimes called the corn moon the moon of everlasting flies. At home the eels were crawling out of the mud and into the warming water. The cod raced from the shallow to the deep saltwater and the herring toward the fresh. The shad might be in the pond by Sowams river. He would turn his squirrel skins outward and be warm, if he were there.

"I will live by myself in that town!" In front of the canoe, Will pointed at a line of young elm trees that ran straight as twine along the bluff at Northfield.

"And leave your people?" one of Pocumptuck's paddlers said to Will.

"My great-woman refuses me." Will finally switched to the right side to paddle.

Pometacom changed hands with relief that clouded when he thought of the small, nutlike great-woman whose name he did not speak. He had let Will walk to Quabaug to rejoin her and his people Saghonnate, but she refused Will. Will was hers no more. Will had danced at Montaup.

Movement?

Pometacom's eyes were drawn to the bushes on the eastern shore. Probably birds. He eyed the second canoe over his shoulder. His four guards, too, were studying the shore. The warriors of the river could be crouched in those bushes, ready to push out and surround him in their light canoes.

Pometacom stared at the neck in front of him, waiting for a sign.

They paddled. Slowly the neck swiveled around and Pometacom saw a blackened face.

Brother, are you my murderer?

Then the face was gone. He saw only the neck again. Perhaps it was the sun turning the neck black, making it look like a face? Perhaps the neck hadn't swiveled at all? In the northland, what did it matter?

Aw-awk! Aw-awk!

The white-winged soaring of gulls came to Pometacom and he was steadied by the sight of birds over water.

"You have gulls so far inland?" Unkompoin's voice came from behind Pometacom narrowly as if through pain.

"We have many gulls downriver at my fields, Uncle. After the gulls come the shad. Then the salmon! Be silent, friends, the mountain." The great-man of the river turned his eyes downward into the water.

The three visitors followed his example. Pometacom looked into dark water, toward dark shapes within it. This was no trap. If someone killed him, it wouldn't be this well-mannered river people who wished for peace. It would be the brutal uncle or the slant-headed nephew of Nashoba. They were hungrier even than the river people. The Englishmen had cut down all the Nipmuck corn at harvest time. But by now the nephew should be filling his belly along the coast, eating horses and peas found in Englishmen's fields. And his own men were eating shad in the southland. Was something bad happening in the southland?

On the east bank where he dared not look, the mountain of Hobomok rose steep and pointed. It was full of cracks and crevices in and out of which would soon run hundreds of rattlesnakes. The world's thunder began in the caves of this mountain and the trembling of the earth started at this root. So said the river people. Weskautaug had corrected them, reporting that Hobomok lived in a whirlpool in the southland but all Weskautaug had gotten for his trouble was a refusal when he asked to climb the mountain by the river. Pometacom looked up at the gray round of sky above his head. The location of Hobomok's home might be argued, but it was clear to any man that Kiehtan's sky stretched over the whole land and all its people. Surely things were going well among his men in the southland.

"Honor to you!" the great-man of the river called out to end the silence, still careful to keep his eyes from the mountain.

They paddled a distance without speaking and rounded a curve. Pometacom could hear the sound of the falls, far off. His head swirled, light with hunger.

The great-man of the river spoke quickly, without turning his head: "Southland, I'm showing you where to fish, but if the war goes on, how can we fish? As soon as we gather at the falls, the Englishmen will circle us with guns."

"The men of the whole land will keep them away." Pometacom kept his voice slow.

"Not unless the Englishmen are pushed out of their forts mid-river."

"After Boston, my friend. We'll clear those towns after Boston."

The sound of the falls was increasing. Pometacom saw nothing ahead. The river must curve here.

"Even Naonanto couldn't take those towns! I was there with him when he first came north."

"Come, you got lots of horses at those towns. We ate." Pometacom leaned forward to hear the other man better.

"We expected your war to be done by now. You said one dawn. A few of us outside each of their towns, you said. Now it takes all of us to go against each of their towns. And Boston. Boston's all you people speak of, to please the inland people. And my women don't want to open the ground with shells anymore. They want metal."

"You'll have a forge! I promised you. When the men come back, they'll bring the molds."

"That will make the Englishmen at Deerfield very angry."

"There aren't any Englishmen at Deerfield!"

Then the great-man of the river took his paddle out of the water and turned around. "Southland," he said, "we want the Englishmen to come back to Deerfield. We want to work for them again. They gave us good things, strong things. And they kept the Mohawk away."

"Go join the cowards who left us our hill by the river!" As Pometacom shouted, his guard canoe drew up.

The man of the river shrugged and returned to his paddling, the movement of his back making it clear that he cared not at all what Pometacom said of him.

Pometacom motioned the guard canoe away. It was improper, his shouting. Anger was for the enemy, for women, for dogs. His companion was right in wanting the mid-river towns cleared. That had been his own plan: the river, Boston, then the south. It was not Naonanto's plan, though. "Take Boston," Naonanto said. "And then we'll see."

The great-man of the river kept on paddling, too silently.

The falls roared.

Would they turn the last curve into a trap? Forty canoes on the riverbank and the warriors of the river waiting to knot him with ropes? Slowly they moved past the curve. There were no canoes. Far ahead Pometacom could see the empty river pour itself forward into the sky.

"We are as brothers!" Pometacom shouted above the roar. He must make apology.

The man of the river didn't answer. Perhaps he hadn't heard the apology.

They paddled hard left for the bank. Rhythm of water. Movement on the bank? Pometacom turned to his guard canoe; there was no alarm shown on those faces, though the eyes were busy. They reached the bank and angled the canoes out of the water and stepped from them.

His guards came toward him.

Bushy.

Not much mud, though.

Loud. Loud. They could be pounced upon from behind and never even hear the approach. They walked singly to where the water fell over the edge. Here they circled left and began to climb down a steep hillside. The spray of the water wet Pometacom's face and made him colder still. Water dripped from his nose, and his eyes narrowed against the wind. They got to the bottom.

"The fish jump all the way up!" The great-man of the river seemed cheerful now.

Perhaps he remembered the promise of the forge.

They all turned and looked upward, some twelve or thirteen

times the height of a man. The gray water was spouting white foam and flowing over the rock cliff that swung out in a wide arc before them.

Remnants of branches were hanging from the far bank, and vines. They were all that was left of the bridges where the river's fishers had stood last spring.

"This is the best place. We always come up here to fish."

"I'm ready. When?"

"Another moon." The great-man of the river shrugged.

They swallowed. They laughed. The winter must end soon; none of them could endure it much longer.

Across the water Pometacom made out the fallen poles which had surrounded Pocumptuck's underground food pits. The Englishmen had broken in and taken some of the river's stored corn, too. And in the northland the shad came so late in the time of hunger.

"Over there." Pometacom pointed to the far shore, where there was a small stream. He spoke close to his friend's ear. "That's where we'll put the wheel and the forge, you'll see. We, too, have wonderful things! You'll plant again and store corn again, all along your river. You will no longer scratch at the fields of Englishmen! They are gone because Kiehtan wanted them to go. My friend, Kiehtan knows all that will happen in the whole land, southland and northland."

The great-man of the river nodded, but hesitantly.

Pometacom threw an arm around the other man's shoulders. "Your men will be content, my friend, when the fish come."

The man of the river smiled then, nodding more readily. His eyes appeared to be measuring the length of cordage needed for new fishing bridges. "All around here will be the white flowers of the shadbush," he said, breathing easily, as young men do. "When Naonanto returns to us from the southland, he will be pleased to see the salmon."

Pometacom took away his arm. It had not been easy to give the new people to Naonanto. It was necessary. He had done it. He remained the father of the people. Naonanto held the people together and showed them where the path lay. But they should still listen to their father's voice.

They turned and climbed back to the top of the falls, pulling themselves up by the vines and bushes. Above them a pale sun emerged to touch the river, and as they paddled upstream, a narrow mist rose over the water. *Tahkees. Co-ld.* It is the will of Kiehtan that Naonanto be the greatest-man. We cannot alter that will. The great-man wiped his nose with stiffening fingers.

It was hot and damp inside the small house. His wife kept the cherry bark steaming but it didn't do any good against Pometacom's painful throat. At least, the little house was full of people. When he'd lain sick in the west, there had been so much unknown space around him and scarcely any of the many voices one expects in winter.

"Hah! The baby is here!" He removed his mantle.

Weetamoo had brought the baby and its milking nurse. But not the Englishwoman that Weetamoo's new husband had taken from the town called Lancaster. That Englishwoman was a black-haired one whom Pometacom admired.

The milk nurse took her hand from the head of the infant girl, who turned wide, intent eyes upward to understand the large presence, the new sound. That done, the baby returned to her sucking.

"So! You know me today, do you? I am your uncle!" The baby reminded him of his own daughter, whom Kiehtan had taken. Pometacom removed his damp squirrel skins and handed them to his wife: "Hang this."

His wife's face had grown thinner from the winter. The baby was thin, too; worse than the last time he had seen her.

"My sisters!" Pometacom greeted his sister-in-law Weetamoo and his own silent, aging sister, who had not spoken to him since the evening when they had left the neck.

"So, you have received our fields?" Only Weetamoo's face had a glow of health to it.

His own sister did not reply to his greeting, but nodded from the women's bed where she sat sewing.

"They are good fields. Downriver, on the other bank, safe from Mohawk." Pometacom took off his leggings, wrung them into the fire and handed them to his wife. He lay down on his side of the house. Oh, warm. In the west the heat of his sickness had grown so large in his body that it could not be contained. It had no form, as does even the changing shape of fire or the quick explosion of a gun; and it certainly did not have a quiet, still form as did the round ball of the sun: burning him, beside the sea as he ran once at games, the sweat dripping off his legs. The heat of his sickness was greater than anything with form; it filled the world. It was the same with the cold that came afterward: though furs were wrapped around him, the cold crawled under his skin and sat inside him. A man can reach a place where he will surrender.

His left hand brushed against the stubble of his head. His wife must shave him soon. The necklaces of the women splayed over their breasts as they sat at their work. The pewter star was gone from his chest, given to Dutchmen for gunpowder. "Pewter?" Hugh Cole touched the star. "Not silver? Only pewter for the governor?" There were silver laces in Naonanto's coat.

"The spring is so late here. At home the black geese must have flown." His wife's voice sounded ragged and high from cough.

"It was cold in the southland, too." Weetamoo's voice was lower. "The bay froze over and there were icicles hanging from the bellies of Naonanto's dogs. Still, we went every tide for clams, though it was such a distance to the water. For my wedding, Naonanto's women stuffed clams into deer flesh." Weetamoo was sewing something silver into a band for Naonanto's cousin, her new husband.

So, all the men of the blood of Nahiganset wore silver now.

Tahkees. Co-ld. The great-man wished Weetamoo had brought her Englishwoman with her. He never spoke English now. He shut his eyes. *Tahkees.* "Get up and run, boys," his father called out on winter mornings. And Tasomacon pushed aside the mat of the big house with his two perfect hands and ran with the other boys racing great circles as they laughed, the snow falling in large flakes and melting on their bare arms. The round yellow sun, Nippaus, touched first the tops of the black-twigged trees and then the frozen skin on the top of the pond, so silent, so still. He did not shiver as he stepped onto the ice that cracked beneath him. He and the other boys all ran toward the center where the ice gave way entirely: he was the great-man's son and always the first boy in for the morning swim. Now when the ice cracked before his eyes, the body of Sassamon floated up, rising to show a purpled face he did not want to see, *pur-ple*. The eyes of it were empty, but the holes stared at him.

Pometacom squeezed his eyelids. Too often in the northland he saw things that weren't there. He had expected his seeing with the eye of darkness would stop here, and earlier, when he failed to silence the three hanged men. But it kept on; it was bad for the people. Perhaps someone close was causing him to do it. Not the river people. Someone he didn't suspect. For forty coats even a man of his own people might betray him. He should talk to Weskautaug, yet he didn't want the wise-man to know his fear.

"Without the horse to ride on, I wouldn't have reached Quabaug." Weetamoo was talking. "The baby was born that night and then we ate the horse. So I named her for a pony!"

Three women laughed! His sister was laughing, too. She must think him asleep. He made his breathing slower.

"I wish I had that horse to eat now. I'm tired of bark and cones. Of . . . all this." Weetamoo made a noise like laughter and weeping together.

"How can you complain? We're at war!" His wife corrected Weetamoo.

"We should go home. I don't want to plant in other women's fields. And who in the northland loves us?"

An older voice came in: "Plant. And tell the women of

Pocasset not to worry about herring. The old women of the river say the mud is sufficient."

His sister was talking! And she was faithful to him. Pleased, the great-man opened his eyes a crack to watch the women.

Weetamoo's copper earrings swayed as she shook her head. "Why not go home? Naonanto's gone home. Do you think he'll bother coming back to us?"

His sister stood up from the bed: "Go home, then! Or why not go straight to Boston? If you get there before the full of the moon, John Leverett will embrace you. He's waiting for you with blankets. Let him rub his mustaches against your face. Let him give you guns. You can come back and shoot us!"

His wife looked from one woman to the other: "You don't mean what you say, either of you!"

Weetamoo stopped sewing and pointed a finger at his sister. "She didn't paint herself when her son died! She wore a black cloth, instead. She's an Englishwoman and she thinks the one god is stronger than any other!"

"Quiet!" His wife raised her finger to her lips. "The preacher who slipped on the ice told her that. She'll forget all he said soon enough."

His sister ignored both younger women and approached the baby.

The nurse was settling new moss around the baby. Then she strapped the baby into a cradle and set it up against a basket. The baby looked into the fire and wailed. The nurse pinched her ear to make her stop.

His sister began to clap her hands softly in front of the baby.

"We'll plant here." His wife's voice was low. "We've got to have food for the winter."

Weetamoo punched her needle through the band. "Who could live through another winter here?"

"But Kiehtan wants this war and we're . . . winning it." His wife's voice faltered.

His sister began to sing as she clapped. The baby tried to

move her small strapped head to follow the swaying woman, but couldn't. Only the baby's eyes could move and they darted from side to side.

"The women of Saghonnate say Kiehtan's against the war." Weetamoo's lap flashed with the silver. "So do the women of Nahiganset."

His wife said nothing.

"The women of Nahiganset say you can't hear Kiehtan's voice unless you burn children for him. That's how they saved themselves from the yellow sickness."

His sister interrupted her own singing: "It has been clear from the start that Kiehtan disapproves of our war. When my brother readied for it, Kiehtan took his daughter. When it began, Kiehtan took my son. And now look at the children, they're all withered. We have to rest or the children will die. We've got to fish here. And plant here. Why hurry home, if the children die on the way?"

"Hobomok could help us. The women of Nahiganset say your wise-man could reach Hobomok for the whole people."

"Shh!" His wife looked toward the bed. "At home Weskautaug isn't honored. He took from other men's traps. I don't know why everyone up here seems so pleased with him."

His sister stopped singing again. "The baby isn't breathing well."

The baby's mouth made sucking movements as she slept. It was clear that she had gone in the dream to the breast, pink and round and tipped with a hardened nipple. But her nose and throat seemed to block much of the incoming air.

"She needs fat to eat." Weetamoo spoke with bitterness.

"Surely Naonanto's cousin brings you meat!"

"None. His meat goes to his first wife. Her children are very fat. I get nothing. I am, instead, given out like fat to every wishful great-man of Nahiganset who visits my lord. They are little men!" She dimissed them with a twist of her mouth. "It would be better for me if my new husband didn't return from the southland!"

"Do you still think of Petananuet? Your husband who prayed?"

"I am told he's living the winter with his sister in the Englishman's town near us at home. He hasn't taken any wife. When I go south, I shall look for him."

On the bed the great-man opened his eyes wide: "I will eat."

His sister stopped singing. Weetamoo busied her fingers with her needle. His wife put down her work and went to the fire.

"What is it to eat, my wife? Sturgeon? Pigs full of snouted clams?" He stretched himself.

"We still have some of the Englishmen's peas. The horse Naonanto brought us is eaten. But the wise-man sent a present." She bent to the coals to pull out a roasted horse liver.

The thought of poison came to the great-man. Foolish. Weskautaug would not kill him for twenty coats when he could get forty. Still the great-man had no hunger for horse liver. He had eaten too much horse. The horse ate him; its name was Awanagus. "Give it to one of our sons. I have the last of my tobacco."

His wife gave him a bowl of groundnuts and peas. Her fingers touched his shoulder. She moved to bring her breast near his face and then was gone. She was only recently returned from the house of unclean women and had missed him in the days away.

He would tease the women from their treacherous moods; after all, they were hungry, too. "Don't you women want to eat beside me?"

Two laughed; not his sister. Perhaps she didn't know what Weetamoo's black-haired Englishwoman had done, serving Weetamoo and her husband from the same bowl!

The great-man took a spoonful of the soup. The groundnuts were old and sticky. He remembered the one bite of deer flesh he had managed beyond the western mountains: it had filled his mouth with darkness and the blood of the wound and he spit it out.

"I return!" Outside the house, Neimpauog's childish voice was greeting the guards. Then the door was turned up and the short-haired boy stepped inside the house.

Thin, but almost nine summers old, almost safe from the sicknesses of children.

"There was nothing in my traps."

No rabbit, stringy but sweet as fish.

"Your mother has horse liver for you, my son. Maybe your new brother has found a bear. We'll dip its fat in some sap and watch your legs grow plump."

"If it snows again, I shall go for turkey."

"All by yourself? A turkey is bigger than you!"

"I am growing." Neimpauog took off his leggings and his skins and stood in his necklace and his belt. "See! I am growing. I am a man! It's time I wore a covering."

"Hoo! That little thing?" The great-man smiled at his wife.

"My father!" Neimpauog came threateningly toward him with his hand raised over his head.

"Yes! Yes!" The great-man threw his hands in front of his face, as if to defend himself. "You will have a covering, my son. You are big. Very big! You're the son of a great-man who bound a new people!"

Neimpauog drew back and stood tall before them. "I'll be like my new brother. I'll have a house of my own and a woman in it!"

"Oh, not yet!" They laughed at him. "Here, eat."

Blood oozed from Neimpauog's mouth as he ate the liver. Pometacom left some peas in his bowl, for otherwise there would be nothing but broth for the women.

"Where do you think our warriors are now, my father?"

Pometacom shifted his feet toward the warmth of the coals. "At the shad pond on Seekonk plain. Or eating the black geese in the woods by the sea."

"I will fight when I'm a man!"

"Yes, first you must winter." Pometacom lit his tobacco from the fire. "In wintering, it will be as it is now, full of hunger. Night will come and you will go to a shelter of poles, but it will not be home. Only when you sleep will you go home, my son, only when you dream. All the time now I go home, I dream my way home. Do you know the dreamer yet, my son? Do you travel in his shadow?"

"No, I'm afraid to step out after him."

"So was I. But you must learn to follow him before you winter. Otherwise the dreamer will kill you. He's the most dangerous of all enemies. Except, perhaps, the great-man of the Pennacook."

"The Pennacook? Because they don't fight beside us?"

"Because their great-man listened too closely to the stories of his father. His father told him never to fight the strangers. But . . . things change, my son. You're familiar with the way Hobomok changes his shape? Our fathers' stories, too, they . . . change, if you listen carefully. And Kiehtan himself changes, though we seldom think of him as doing so. How does Kiehtan, the unchanging, change?" He avoided Weetamoo's eyes. "He causes plants to grow, for one thing. I am not saying Kiehtan is stronger than Hobomok because he can do both things: they are equal."

"But Kiehtan is the unchanging! The seasons do not alter, my father."

"It is the fishing moon. We are not fishing."

Neimpauog laughed. They all laughed together. It was funny.

Pometacom drank in tobacco and swallowed it as far as he could, to fill his belly, to ease the pain in his throat and shoulders, to make him sleepy. Johettit had promised to bring him tobacco seeds from the southland. He would bury the tiny pellets in the mud under a tree out on the island. Kiehtan would cause the seeds to bloom in the north, as he did in the southland.

From outside came the indistinct voices of women moving in several directions.

"What is it?" The women in the house turned to each other.

"The women must be back with the corn!"

Pometacom stood and pulled up the door. Women were running from house to house and one was hurrying toward him. It was Kuttiomp's daughter, with a large basket in her head net.

He began to make out the words of the women.

"The cows on the cleared land are dead! The stones of the strangers are broken! The wagons are gone from Pokanocket!"

"I pray your favor, great-man!" Kuttiomp's daughter reached his house. Her eyes were eager. "Naonanto salutes you! He means to start north when his belly is full of shad!"

"Welcome, my daughter!" He let go of the door and it shut on more of the women's words: "Rehoboth is burned! Providence is burned!"

The women crowded around the girl to take the load of corn from her net and he made his way to the bed.

"Rehoboth? Is it emptied? Are they dead?" He sat down.

"A few houses are standing. The people are hiding in the ruins. The fever is among them and every day the buzzards fly lower." The girl bent as the women removed the net from her head.

"Why did you go there?"

"Naonanto burned the towns on his side of the bay so easily that he came up to the Seekonk and crossed above the town called Providence. We met him there and our men killed a hundred Englishmen in one day by the river! He took us to Rehoboth and we fought until half the powder was gone. Then he stopped us. He wanted powder so he could take us across Seekonk to burn Providence." The women took the basket from the girl's net.

"The dead?"

"Three men of Nahiganset. None of Wampanoag."

"Of Rehoboth?"

"Of Rehoboth? None that I know of. Only a silly woman who ran out!"

Ah, good.

"And Swansea?"

"Naonanto didn't go there. We could see their houses on the neck, though, when we went down for the corn. There weren't any Englishmen in those houses, except the yellow-haired man near the pig fence."

The women opened the basket.

Hezekiah Willett could go free.

"The big town, Swansea?"

"We didn't get to Mattapoiset. Annawon sent men over to look, though. They could see that only a few Englishmen were living there."

The women ran the hard yellow kernels over their fingers.

Those in Swansea could go free, too. Hugh Cole, all of them. He would ask for a small tribute, corn, no skins.

"And the neck?"

"The shad are in the water!" Kuttiomp's daughter unwound the braids from the top of her head. "And the leaves are budding. There are trees down from a bad storm we missed last summer. We could hear your pigs, squealing in the woods! And some of our dogs greeted us, but most of them have gone off with the wolves. The stone fort . . . by the spring at Kickamuit? It's finished. Englishmen live in it."

"And are they building square houses beside it?"

"No. Only the fort."

The women made noises over the corn. Even his sister looked excited.

"The men of Rehoboth, are they planting?"

"No, they stay shut up in the walled house or under piles of brush. They don't have any food."

"They have shad!"

The girl loosened her hair from its braids.

So the rum house in Rehoboth was gone. The great fireplace with drafts to take off the smoke, gone. His friends were no more there, happy to laugh with him. They sat under brush and shook their fists.

There was singing as the women gathered in his house.

The great-man stood up from the bed and put his good hand on the girl's black hair. "You are like the crow, my daughter, bringing us Kiehtan's seeds from the southwest, so we may plant and live."

The taste of roasted pig came into his mouth.

The wise-man's house was at the other edge of the settlement on the hill, its back side under trees where no other houses stood. Inside the house was the smell of elm bark simmering. Not so sweet as the cherry. The wise-man sat on a bed mending a fishnet and only his two wives looked up to the visitor. An unfamiliar servant crouched at the fire, steaming branches.

"Great-man, you come alone?" The elder wife spoke.

"My guards are waiting outside."

"There are groundnuts for you."

He slid the mantle from his shoulder, standing with the seed bag at his belt. He took the bowl the elder wife brought and sat on the bed beside the wise-man.

"You'll be ready for fishing before the shad are!"

"That is my expectation." Weskautaug looked much thinner and older than he had in the summer. The drooping eyelid hung lower over his eye. The sinews of his neck were sharper.

The wise-man's younger wife was stirring at the pot; she had the body of a woman who has borne no children. The older wife moved to the other side of the fire to smoke the tobacco Pometacom gave her. One of Weskautaug's daughters sat on the bed, running something through her teeth. The younger wife brought Pometacom his soup.

"Have you chosen a wise-man yet, from among those of the northland?" Pometacom took the hot bowl into his hands.

"I am still considering." Weskautaug's eyes darted up, as the owl's do.

"But it's almost time! Even here in the north the first thunder is heard near the birth of the planting moon."

The wise-man returned to his fishnet. "There isn't any wise-man up here I admire. Three of the Nipmuck are as dull-headed as you would expect of Nipmuck. The fourth is . . . odd. The wise-man of Pocumptuck is clever, but he doesn't know the old ways and won't touch a snake."

The groundnuts in the bowl were as sticky and old as anybody else's. Tall as he was, Weskautaug seemed a little man, unable to make things come to pass.

"A little man, see?" Weskautaug spoke the very words from inside Pometacom's ears and held up a perfect little man made out of the fishnet string. "I'll make a little man out of anyone who tries to slow the war. We should go quickly to Boston and then home to fight." He extended an end of the string. "Pull."

"You tire too easily! It will be a longer war than that, my friend." Pometacom balanced the bowl against his left hand. "Through the summer, to the fall of the leaf. We can't burn Boston any faster. And we've got to clear the mid-river towns before we leave the north." He reached for the string. "I've heard the wars of Awanagus in his own land go from summer to summer until men grow old and die." He pulled the string.

The little man unknotted himself and became a single strand of string. A simple trick. Any fisherman could do it. Pometacom resteadied his bowl with his right hand.

Weskautaug puffed himself up with air. "So my father undid the Tongue for your father!"

Foolishness.

"Come, Naonanto will be back soon. I want to tell him which wise-man you've chosen to dance beside him at Wachusett. We need a balance: the greatest-man from the south, the wisest-man from the north."

"One from the south, one from the north," Weskautaug repeated, like a singer. It seemed an affirmation.

The woman came and took the bowl from Pometacom.

"I'm going now." Pometacom stood so quickly that Weskautaug had to shift his weight to keep himself balanced on the bed. But on the mat at his feet the great-man saw that the string had reformed itself into three tiny men.

Three out of one. Was Weskautaug practicing against the Englishmen's god? Pometacom sat in his own house, knotting deer twine around the widening crack in the stock of a gun. The wooden parts he could fix, the metal he couldn't. The stock was cracking. The year was cracking, cracking open. The thirteenth moon was almost full, the first moon would soon be born. He wound evenly and tight. When Otan-nick arrived, the great-man said, "Have the Englishmen begun their new year?"

"They have, great-man, my lord. Several days ago." Otan-nick's fingers reached for the writing tools.

"What is its number?"

"One thousand six hundred seventy and six. That's how many years since the god came to show his face to the people." Otan-nick's own pockmarked face raised itself. "And during the old year, my lord, I killed no Englishmen! Though I left my home in Rehoboth to do so. And my brother has a third scalp, so I hear from the women. And it's the scalp of a woman!"

"He should have grabbed her and sold her for silver. But Johettit is the firstborn, like Adam's son. He kills." Pometacom wound twine; how smoothly he wound it.

"The second-born writes letters."

"And keeps chickens!"

They both laughed; each avoided the other's eyes.

"Do you learn much from the wise-man?"

"No. He finds me insufficient. I don't have the eye of darkness. Let me leave him." Otan-nick sharpened the quills in small, precise movements.

"Stay awhile longer." Pometacom pulled a piece of string

from his sleeve to lengthen the twine. "Does the wise-man ever ask you about the one god?"

"Yes. About his voice."

"And what do you tell him?"

"That the one god doesn't speak out loud."

"Does he speak to Weskautaug?"

"No!" Otan-nick laughed. "His words are all written down. He never talks."

Pometacom finished knotting the bit of hide. "Your town is gone. Was there word of your father from the women?"

"He's hiding in the woods near Taunton."

"I will spare him. He is the only one in the woods that I will spare."

Otan-nick looked neither pleased nor displeased.

"Tell me, did you ever go to drink rum at Preserved Abell's house?"

"No."

"Your father, did he?"

"They wouldn't let him in. An 'Indian.' "

"But they always welcomed me! They pulled out the big chair for me, they built up the fire!"

"You were a king. We were the least of them."

The great-man said nothing. One thousand six hundred seventy and six. The Englishmen thought the world itself grew older, just as a man does.

Otan-nick adjusted the writing materials: "I'm ready."

Otan-nick's long face was so clearly the face of Pokanocket. Behind it Pometacom saw a row of such faces, all moving their lips to speak: "We're ready," they said. "Ready. Why does Pokanocket long to cut its hair, to ride on horses? To lose itself among a larger people?"

Perhaps in the northland he was actually becoming like those who are both great and wise.

"I'm ready," Otan-nick repeated.

The great-man began: "To Governor John Leverett, who dwells at Boston, One Thousand Six Hundred Seventy and Six.

Know by this paper that the Indians you provoked to wrath will war many years, twenty-one years, if you will. Consider that we lose nothing but our lives, while you lose many fair houses and your fine cattle. As for the captive women, I will deliver them at an appointed place, before shad-time." As he spoke, two thin old men came in and sat by the fire.

". . . at the rate of twenty pounds silver each. But I will send no man to talk to you of peace. There is no peace!" He turned to the old men: "Twenty pounds, that's four times what we'd get if we sold them as slaves!

"Signed with his mark," he continued, turning back to Otan-nick. "By King Philip, dwelling along Connecticut." With the pen Otan-nick extended to him, the great-man wrote his mark large. First, the long horizontal line of the *P*, then the round circle rising over its left end like the sun at daybreak and then the two dots over its right end, such dots as King Charles always made beside his name.

"Are those your words to the town called Hartford?" The old man whose eyes were black-rimmed as the buzzard's spoke. It was Naonanto's uncle.

"No. These are my words to Boston. Boston is more important. In Hartford, the Englishmen are sick, even John Winthrop's son. No one creeps off to Hartford. But how many of our men have crept off to Boston to be loved by Englishmen?"

"Four of Nahiganset. Two of Pocumptuck."

"None yet of Wampanoag?"

The two old men sought each other's eyes.

"Tell me, uncles!"

"One," Unkompoin said. "Of Pokanocket, of the village Poppasquash."

"Track him."

His slender uncle nodded.

"Have him brought to me. With my long knife I will cut him. Those of mine who weaken and run off to Boston will die. To leave the people of the whole land is to betray them. I will stoop and lift his blood in my hand and drink and be satisfied."

Otan-nick rolled up the letter, his eyes on the great-man. Such quiet anger was talked about among the people.

"We have word from the town called Marlborough." The old man with the buzzard's eyes moved toward the fire. "The Nipmuck who went east burned the houses of Marlborough while the Englishmen were together at their god's house. But then the Nipmuck ran into the woods and ate cows' flesh until they fell over. While they slept, the Englishmen found them lying in the woods and shot them."

"Even for a few days the Nipmuck cannot be trusted. . . ." Tuspaquin must have left the Nipmuck for the trip he'd planned to spy out Plimouth.

A guard raised the door and, outside, they could hear the muffled sound of singing. "They're beginning at the great-woman's house."

"We're ready." Pometacom touched the seed bag at his belt. "Uncles, when Naonanto returns and we go to the mountain, you'll stay here and assign fishing places. I like the big falls best. Give planting places to the women and let them begin whenever my sister says to, she knows the women of the river. The time is wrong here, my friends! Men do not fish here until the planting moon! Women do not plant until the weeding moon. But you'll have a good time with the women, no? When we come back, we'll find you fat and glossy!" Pometacom stood, but when Otan-nick and the uncle of Nahiganset were gone, Unkompoin shut the door behind them to keep the great-man in the house.

"What is it?" Pometacom tilted his ear to the old man.

"The Englishmen have come back to Quabaug, to the town called Brookfield, to plant."

"When?"

"Before the birth of the fishing moon."

"Why did no one tell me?"

"No one dared."

"Are they back at Deerfield, too? At Northfield?"

"No."

"I don't kill my messengers!" Pometacom left the house.

The great-man of the river must have known the Englishmen were back at Brookfield when they were paddling on the river. Even as they stood at the falls and when they listened to Will shout over the water. The new people was scarcely born and the hands continually hid themselves from the eyes and covered the ears. Perhaps the son that the one god made out of himself did not recognize its father's face but struck and flailed at it.

The great-man's guards walked beside him to the houses of Pocasset farther downhill. One guard raised the door of Weetamoo's house and the great-man stepped inside.

> *"She waited, she waited,*
> *too long for war."*

Weskautaug was singing and the wise-man of Pocasset sat glumly on a mat by the bed and watched the master whose superior skill Weetamoo had requested. Many of Pocasset and Pokanocket were crowded onto the beds: there was no larger house here on the hill in which to gather. When Pometacom's wife saw him come in, she stood up and stepped forward to the center of the house.

In reply to Weskautaug, the people sang forgiveness for Weetamoo:

> *"Let her be released from punishment.*
> *Let her be; let her be."*

The baby girl lay on a mat near the fire and Weskautaug stood beside her. The baby's small cloth hung loosely between two emaciated legs.

When the song was done, the great-man's wife stepped forward and set a pot of water on the mat beside the baby. "Wise-man, I bring you the water."

The great-man stepped to the mat and deposited the seed bag. "Wise-man, I bring you the seed bag."

Weskautaug bent to take up the seed bag. He began to slap it against his palm. Pometacom left the center of the house and found a place among old men, the men in their prime being absent. Kuttiomp's daughter came through the door, ripening and beautiful. When she sat, Pometacom could feel the smoothness of her thigh under his hand, the warmth of her moved against his thumb and fingers; he smelled the smell of her. She was to be his new son's wife: he should not think of her. The war was, indeed, too long. He wanted many wives, such as his father had known, wives with eyes made bright from food. And he wanted a full belly for himself. To be warm. To shut his eyes. To rest. And his own people, faces familiar to him.

Weskautaug stopped singing and knelt beside the baby. He sniffed a circle around her navel. He stood again, clapping the seed bag lightly against his buttocks. Then he began to twirl. Pometacom watched as if he could see nothing from his own dark, lidded eyes. This was the northland and he wished for the southland's salmon and the pinkness of salmon flesh; he wished for women and the flapping of the tide. Nor did he think such as Weskautaug could save this child.

When sweat came out on his forehead, Weskautaug stopped twirling and bent over the baby. He scratched near her navel and she screamed. He sucked at the spot and spit into the bowl of water, a milkiness collecting there. Weskautaug was slow; it could take the night for this crafty brother, him of snake and birds, to find out if Kiehtan wanted the child. Anyone could see she would die. The wisest-man of the whole land had better be quicker than Weskautaug.

"Let me stay!" Angry English words came from a dark corner on the bed across the house. Weetamoo's black-haired Englishwoman was being put out to make room for more of the people.

Pometacom turned to see her, eager for her face.

"It's cold. *Tahkees!*" But she was pushed toward the door,

and when she stumbled before the men's bed, she stared up at him with eyes like the two perfect bullets given him by the boy of Rehoboth. Then she was gone.

All were silent now. Weskautaug was twisting his mouth and opening his eyes as wide as they could go. He stood on one leg and then the other; he spread his arms like the gills of a fish, like the wings of a bird. He pulled his lips into a little hole; he popped his eyes wide again. Oh, brother cunning, you'll tire yourself. A preacher only stands and speaks and the people's faces fill up with pockmarks. Weskautaug fell on the mat and lay still. There was blood on his forehead.

On the mat the baby kept breathing in her faulty way and slowly Weskautaug stood up and thrust his arms over her head. He dropped his arms and turned to Weetamoo. "Kiehtan wants her, great-woman." He tossed the seed bag back on the mat.

"No!" Weetamoo's black-streaked face appeared beside the wise-man's. "Try it again!" She struck the ground with her feet.

"It will do no good, great-woman. What Kiehtan wants comes to pass. Unless you seek Hobomok."

Weetamoo grew calm. She reached for a basket of peas and shoved them toward the wise-man. "Here. Go to Hobomok, then."

"That will do no good, great-woman. Hobomok is angry with you." He reached for the basket, anyway, and handed it to his servant. "She will not live."

"You are the wisest-man in the southland! You are well known among the daybreak people." She pulled her bracelets over her wrist and handed them to him. "The people of Pocasset have long honored you. Those of Nahiganset come to know you."

"I will do as you say, great-woman." He untied the bone bag from his belt. "But for this child's life, Hobomok will not stir himself to alter what Kiehtan sees. You delayed the start of the war. Hobomok wants none to hold back from this war. Not the warriors of Pocasset in the summer. Nor those of Pocumptuck at seed-time."

"My father would have won the war long ago! It's the great-men of Pokanocket who delayed the war, he who befriended the strangers and he who warns Englishmen!"

The people took in their breaths.

Pometacom raised his hand, palm up. "You are in grief."

Weskautaug nodded toward the great-man. "Your great-man pardons you. We will proceed." He called to someone outside to enter.

The people made noises with their mouths and moved higher on the beds. The wise-man of the river came stiffly through the door, with a small rattlesnake in his hands.

Weskautaug took it and knelt. He guided it around the infant's belly. The mottled snake curved itself tighter and the baby screamed. The snake only drew itself into a living belt.

This could take longer, until dawn; the wise-man sat on the mat to wait.

The great-man moved from the bed; he desired to go outside.

"Does the smoke bother your eyes, great-man, my brother? Should I have a draft over my smoke hole, as the Englishmen do?" Weetamoo turned to him.

"Kiehtan took my daughter," he said, touching her shoulder. "If he takes yours, too, they will each have a cousin to play with in the southwest. It's warm there."

He went outside. He would bury the baby on the far side of the hill, or on the island in the river where he meant to plant tobacco. Her grave would make the northland more their own. It, and the tobacco, and the corn. It could be a long time before they went home.

He drew back when he saw Weetamoo's black-haired, black-hooded Englishwoman huddled against the house, for what little warmth came out of it.

English came over his tongue: "Good evening, I am told you sew."

"Yes, I sew, Philip, my sachem." She was shivering.

"Make a small cloth for my son to cover himself. Make it of English cloth." He looked down at the pale skin under the dark hood of her cloak. There was something about her that seemed oddly familiar. Her eyes were dark.

"But I have no cloth! I have nothing!" There was pinkness, from the cold, in her skin.

"Make it from a piece of your own clothing and then you will have a shilling. I will give you a shilling for it."

She nodded.

"Cold," he said, looking for her hands. They were tucked into the cloak.

"*Tahkees,*" she said. She looked at him, instead of lowering her gaze as a woman ought. She shivered in jerks.

She must stay healthy or they wouldn't get the twenty pounds of silver for her.

"Go to my house," he said. "The servants will let you in."

She looked confused.

"Just for now, just to get warm. I will tell your mistress where you are." He gave her his hand to help her to her feet. Suddenly he spoke to her as if she were a friend, a sister. "You will not be a servant forever."

Her palm was surprisingly soft and fleshy. He wished to push the sleeve from her arm, to hold her body close to his, to let his nose enter the warmth of her neck.

She did not drop her gaze, even now.

A scream came to them from within the house.

He let go of her hand. There was a glow collecting over Weetamoo's house. He could see it clearly, a white mist struck with light. There is no force so great as Kiehtan's will; all things ride there, rest there, are held.

Inside, he saw, as he suspected, that the snake had fallen from the baby's belly and was slithering among the mats, making its way under the bed where the women sat screaming.

"It has no teeth," he reminded those who could hear him. But that did little to stop the screams.

"The Englishman's god can make even the dead live!" Weetamoo's shout turned to a wail.

The next night the great-man's wife spoke. Her voice was soft by the fire inside their own house. "Will you go again and look at the sky?"

Pometacom rose and went to the door, pushing the mat aside. A light snow had fallen. The cold hurt his nose and eyes. He looked up and saw that the stars glimmered like the eyes of a thousand children. He looked down and saw that the river was dark and that there was no glow over the island yet: the baby's soul had not left the grave in which her body sat. The wind was high and moved up over his hill like a king. One guard lay sleeping in a blanket. The other seemed alert enough for both.

Pometacom stepped farther out of the house and held the mat open behind him. He was startled to see on the new snow that two shadows of himself moved forward. One darker, one dimmer. "Wake your companion," he said sharply to the guard, and fled back into the house, letting the mat fall.

"The glow? No, I saw no glow. Your niece is still struggling to break the ties." He sat in the warmth and stroked his wife's blackened cheek and tried to stop the shiver coming over him.

"Kiehtan is angry." His wife began to cry. "Do you think the Englishman's god could bring the babies back? If our daughter and our niece knew his name?"

He held her and found that she was shaking. "Hush, now. The baby is struggling to break the ties. To find the path. She'll travel well. She'll be greeted by our daughter. They will sit upon the laps of the old ones to wait for us, for all of us. They will see the face of Kiehtan."

Her tears ran along his arm, over the scars there.

His wife slept. He covered her and lay upon the bed. Himself and two shadows. When he shut his eyes, he saw babies' bones strewn around him in the midst of blackness. He heard wailing and, recognizing it as real, stood and went to the door again. Outside, he saw a ball of orange flame down the hill from among the houses of Pocasset. The flame was rounder and brighter than the moon, and it cast more light. The fire rose to consume the house of sickness that Weetamoo was giving to Kiehtan. Quickly, Pometacom shut the mat and lay upon his furs.

"In the beginning," Sassamon had told him long ago on the shining sand at Kuttiomp's cove, "God set two lights in the sky, one for day and one for night. God made the earth himself, for he is not lazy like Kiehtan, who engaged laborers to do the work for him. And the one god has no brother. What we call Hobomok, the Englishmen call the Devil, and he is not a god with them. Sometimes he is a servant to the one god, that's all." When Pometacom passed into the country that never changes, he put his two perfect hands around Sassamon's neck, and, gasping, as if it were himself who could not breathe, the great-man thumbed the soft bones still and stopped the voice issuing from behind them. No, he said, the one god is like Hobomok. And I am not the brother who kills. I am the brother who takes his people to fields of corn, where the bins are full; and the people grow fat on chickens. Light with hunger, he whirled in the canoe. He held tight to both sides with each of his perfect hands. She came then to the bow of the boat, with the fox in her palm, but the sleeper forgot her face by morning.

The men were back! Pometacom walked rapidly down the hill. The sun shone softly on the river and a mist was rising over the green water.

Something was wrong! The women at the canoe landing began to wail and strike the ground. Were so many dead?

Pometacom began to run, searching the canoes below for signs of his own men, but there were only those of Nahiganset. In the crowd at the base of the hill, the buzzard-eyed old man of Nahiganset stood mute. A short, slight warrior was talking. It was Naonanto's cousin: "They surprised my cousin who wears a silver coat. . . ."

Not calling him by name? Pometacom stopped at the edge of the gathering.

". . . My cousin was sitting near a brook, laughing, and telling over again how he burned Rehoboth and Providence, how he lured a hundred Englishmen under trees with only two limping men. The fox could have done no better, my cousin said. Then he heard a noise. He jumped up. He ran to the brook. His silver coat fell from his shoulders. He ran faster and slipped on the rocks. Water got into his gun. So he stood waiting, as a man should. An English boy was sent to him in the brook, a boy who knows our words. 'Boy,' he said, 'You are too young. Tell them to send me a man.' The Englishman took my cousin westward, toward the mouth of the long river. We have watchers outside the square house where he sits."

The wailing increased.

A clear voice came from the edge of the crowd: "And at Hartford?"

"At Hartford?" The slight warrior turned in Pometacom's direction.

"They'll send his head upriver."

The slight man drew back. The buzzard-eyed man let a sound come from his mouth. Pometacom stepped into the crowd: "Who speaks now for Nahiganset?"

"I." The uncle's voice was broken. "I and my nephew. My nephew knows my heart."

"Will you stay at war?"

"We debate it." A closed look came over the old man's face.

"Grieved and in bitterness I am." Pometacom walked through the crowd to the old uncle and rubbed his shoulders. "I loved your nephew. He was a brother to me in the southland and in the north." He turned to Naonanto's cousin: "And you? Do you stay at war?"

The slight man rested his hands on the gun barrel before

him. "First, I will speak for my uncle. He won't fight. Nor his warriors, who are two hundred men. I and the rest of Nahiganset, we will fight beside you. For where has Nahiganset to set its house poles? Pocumptuck can make peace with the town called Hartford and set poles and rest and fish. Nipmuck can threaten Boston and then make peace and set poles and rest and fish. But Boston is already plowing my land. We will fight. With the north, with you or alone."

"We will go eastward to Wachusett, straightaway. It is a hard path we walk, my friend, thorns and briars, without your cousin, whom the northland loved."

"I have stepped out on that path, southland. My cousin waits at the end of it to greet me." The young man's eyes looked dead, without light.

"Your uncle's men won't walk to Boston, will they?"

"No, my friend! They are only hungry and winded. Their whole heart is for fishing and planting. They will not betray you, but only stay here, along Connecticut. Or go north to the Frenchmen."

"I loved your cousin." Pometacom touched the young man's shoulders. "He is gone forever."

"I have lost a hundred and more in the south. You shall be the greatest-man of the new people."

In his ears Pometacom heard the cheers of almost two thousand hailing him. But at the river's edge there was only the wailing of women.

12

Gulls flew over the green water. The rest of the warriors began to arrive and canoes ferried them steadily to the hill. From these men, Pometacom would double his guard. He looked for his shrewd friend Kuttiomp and did not see him. From him would come the most useful report of what had happened in the south. The returning men walked with more strength than when they'd left: shad. He watched the current in the river meeting the wind which came, surprisingly, from the south. Naonanto's head was surely moving north by sail, toward Hartford, blown by this wind, this breath of kings. An ancient man stepped off at the landing.

"My nephew!" Annawon embraced him. "In the fifty-sixth winter of their coming, the strangers have been pushed from the cleared land."

"We will be known as those who fought the strangers!"

The old man pulled him closer and whispered: "I'm told the slant-headed nephew wants to sit down after Boston, as soon as the fish come into the streams. He says he will not go against the mid-river towns."

"He doesn't speak for the whole people!" Pometacom drew back.

"Who does? Without the men of our friend in the silver coat, we have fewer than the northland."

"Half of Nahiganset comes to me."

"Good. Good. We lost some in the south, but that should give us more than the nephew." Annawon's eyes turned to the hundreds of men at the river's edge, more of Nahiganset and Pocumptuck than of their own. "But we should leave for the mountain quickly."

Johettit was running toward him. "Here it is!"

He handed Pometacom a small bag. Inside were the thousands of tiny seeds. "Are they from my own planting place near the tidal river?"

"From there. I had to go with the women, by the moon!"

"I hear you like to be with women. You like their hair."

"You heard?" Johettit was pleased. "I'll show it to you later."

"We could have sold her for twenty pieces of silver."

From the landing, Kuttiomp hurried past, without a look.

What did it mean?

The molds from the iron forge lay heavy in the canoes and brought them almost down to water level. So lay he, upon the people of the whole land.

They crossed the river in Pocumptuck's canoes, waving to their old men and to their women and children staying to plant. On the far side of Connecticut they traveled in a twisting pattern, to confuse Englishmen or Mohawk, whose guards might be watching. Inside the line, all was orderly. The broad captain Annawon led the daybreak people with the thirty warriors left from the green swamp's fifty. After a space came the men of the cleared land. Pometacom walked at the front and Weskautaug at the rear; Weskautaug had promised to give Pometacom the name of the one man he had chosen from the wise-men of the north as soon as they camped that evening. "I want him to be from the north, of Nipmuck," Pometacom had urged. "Perhaps the odd one, if the others are dull-headed." After another space came all of Pocasset, with Weetamoo in front, leading the two hundred fighting men that she had left. The men of Assawampset–the lake and those of the two eastern coves were absent, being on their way to the mountain from the coast, with his brother-in-law Tuspaquin. After another space came three hundred men led by Naonanto's dead-eyed cousin; the coins that Weetamoo had sewn on bands were dangling from his knees. Weetamoo had been glad to hear her husband would be walking behind her. After Nahiganset came another space and then about twenty of the short-haired people of Massachuset walked together in their hats and shirts and neck cloths. Behind them came the people of the river, a hundred of the warriors only. The older men of the river, and some in their prime, had refused to go any farther into war. Counting the absent men of the lake and of the two coves, that gave Pometacom more than seven hundred and fifty warriors. Even if the nephew of

Nashoba had gotten all of the inland to follow him, there were surely not seven hundred and fifty fighting men left among them. There were still uncounted the men of Saghonnate and their sullen great-woman. Pometacom must persuade her to himself, or at least keep her from giving her allegiance to Nashoba and the northland.

Toward the end of the first day, Pometacom turned the line over to another man to lead and stood at the side of the path until Kuttiomp passed. He pulled at the arm of his friend. They had not yet sat to talk. "Come." The great-man pointed to the soft moss along the spine of the hill. They dropped out of the line and made themselves comfortable sitting.

As they filled their pipes with the bits of tobacco left at the bottom of their bags, they watched Pokanocket pass before them. Kickamuit village was walking, one by one: there had been twenty fighting men of Kickamuit, though now there were seven. Eight. Nine. The great-man's adopted son was the last of them. Nomatuck raised his hand in a surprised salute, and licked his fingers.

Pometacom licked his. "A good husband your daughter is getting, my friend."

It was pleasant to talk after the long silence of walking.

"And your new son is getting a good wife." Kuttiomp spoke almost inaudibly; these were unknown woods.

"I don't have all the silver coins yet. I will get them at Wachusett when we sell back the captives." Pometacom noticed that the wolf on Kuttiomp's cheek had changed in shape over the winter, following the tightness of those whose teeth have grown short.

"Yes." Kuttiomp's eyes still avoided his.

"We will have their wedding at the big falls when we get back from Wachusett. Before we go against mid-river."

"Fish!" Kuttiomp said the single word with longing.

The warriors of Kuttiomp's cove village were passing: there had been twenty. Six, seven, eight. They were thin, sick-looking.

"Do you miss your cove, my friend? Your cormorants? You gave me no report when you returned."

Kuttiomp took his pipe from his mouth to answer, but instead was distracted. He pointed at the approaching band of warriors, those who had come to Pokanocket from various places. "Look there!"

Johettit was waving something at Pometacom and looking pleased again: it was a lock of brown hair.

"He got it at Rehoboth, a woman's," Kuttiomp explained.

"I heard."

There had been twenty of these scattered warriors; now there should be six, but someone new was gone from this group. Will of Saghonnate? "Do you see Will? Where is Will?"

Kuttiomp said something the great-man did not hear, and neither spoke as the women of the cleared land came along. Not many, only the young and strong, and those of the great-man's family. Kuttiomp's wife was gone, among the winter's dead. Bundled with house poles, Pometacom's black stallion was being led by his sister, who was more eager than usual, impatient to meet Tuspaquin at Wachusett. The horse's belly was so thin it scarcely broke the twigs at the side of the path. This was the only horse of Pokanocket that had not been eaten. The Englishwomen and their children walked behind the stallion. They stooped awkwardly under their bundles, carrying them poorly. A yellow-haired child stared at Pometacom as they passed. The Englishwomen did not look at him, their faces toward the path at their feet. The child's cheeks were bright red, as if painted. His wife smiled when she saw him. Kuttiomp's daughter greeted them with the same surprised look Nomatuck had given them. His son Neimpauog walked as far back from the women as he could get, a small bit of English cloth hanging between his leggings to cover his nakedness.

"Where is Will of Saghonnate, my friend?" the great-man repeated when the women and children were gone.

"Gone to Boston. To give himself to Englishmen."

The great-man spit out smoke. "He will be tracked. Killed."

He scanned the remaining warriors of Poppasquash village that were passing before them now. The runaway from Poppasquash had not been found. Three, four, only five. Again a new face missing.

"Did another man of Poppasquash go to Boston?"

"No, my friend. He went south. Home." Kuttiomp moved nearer to Pometacom. "It was very beautiful at home, my friend. Very warm. You should have smelled the sweetness of the trees in the air. The small islands are become separate lands, each with its own king. I bet that you would find the man of Poppasquash camping on one of them."

"No man can live alone." The great-man emptied the bowl of his pipe. His hand trembled.

The warriors of the hill village were stepping along the path now. Once ten, they were four. The warriors of the bayside village followed. Once eighteen, now six. But the missing ones from the bayside were not all dead or vanished. Some were simply old and had stayed on Connecticut to mend the nets. Still, he had left from the cleared land only the thirty-seven fighting men.

Pometacom cleaned out his pipe. "Do you, too, wish to end the war? To make peace after Boston? Were you, too, cold during the winter? Have you, too, a need for coats? Twenty? Forty?"

"I will never betray you, my friend." Kuttiomp laid his head upon his knees. "I have no wish to see your head on a pole at Plimouth. When we wintered, we learned to live on roots and bark and to spit out the poisonous. We learned to endure the cold. But there is a hunger that wintering did not prepare us for, the hunger of spring."

"A man will endure that, too, if it is necessary for the people." Metacomet who remembers peace wished to lay his head upon his knees and rest. Instead, Pometacom examined the tail of Pokanocket's line that was approaching. The wise-man was no longer there! The wise-man's servant walked last in line!

The great-man stood abruptly. "Where is the wise-man?"

"I do you service, King Philip, my lord." The servant spoke in English.

"What is your name?"

"I am only a servant. I have no name."

"Your people, then?"

"Mohawk. The Massachuset caught me when I was a child and sold me to Englishmen in the town near Nashoba."

"Where is your master?"

"He's gone on ahead. He said if you should ask for him, to give you this." The Mohawk handed him a narrow roll of bark.

The great-man's hands shook again as he opened the bark. Inside it was a little man made of sticks. As he touched the figure, one of its arms fell off.

"It is himself, he said, if you need him."

"And where has he gone?" The great-man held the bark uneasily.

"To the mountain, by a shorter route. He has to arrange with the inland people about the dance. He has much to do, my lord."

"Did he send me a man's name?"

"No, my lord. Nothing more."

"Go along," he said to the servant. "My friend will walk with you." He motioned Kuttiomp to join the servant at the end of the line.

"But you are without any guard!" Kuttiomp was reluctant.

"It is safe. I will follow you to camp before the Pocasset come into sight along the path. Go."

The great-man ran off the path. There were no oaks here. He looked for a hickory. The force gathering around him was so great that he felt as if he were already bound to the enemy's pole, already powerless to move anything but his eyes and mouth. The darkness was all around him but he could not turn his head to see behind himself, or to the sides. The terror engulfed him and he could not move at all. All that he saw might suddenly change and swerve, turn at a tilt and he would only be able to open his mouth and sing. He would not wail; his wail had become his song and only his song could free him. He put down the bark and his mouth worked as he scratched at the ground, pushing away damp leaves; his eyes blinked.

He crossed two lines in the earth and tossed the last bits of his tobacco onto them. He picked up the twigs of the little man, and threw them on top of the tobacco. He made a spark with his stones and the fire caught quicker than he hoped. Kiehtan's aroma reached him and he moved his mouth to whisper, careful with each word and gentle as the morning wind: "You took the fingers of my hand. You took my daughter. You took my brother who was older than I. You took my friend, the great-warrior who bled in the sand. You took my brother who was younger than I. You have taken my niece. You have taken the greatest-man of Nahiganset. You have taken many of the people of the land. But I have tried to do your will. I ride with you. I wished to bring the iron to you, only to make it yours. I do not turn to Hobomok. I did not go to war until you spoke. Hear me now. The wise-man is coming to you. He will pretend to ask for your voice. But he will tell the people that you do not answer. Then he will go to Hobomok. Do not let Hobomok be loosed among the people of the whole land. For we cannot rebind him. The new people will be as slaves to him until he takes himself away, as babies on a board are slaves and helpless to birds that fly at their eyes. Answer the wise-man. I know you are stronger than Hobomok. I know you could even make Hobomok be as a servant to you, if you wanted. At Wachusett, speak loud to the whole people so we will be one people, so we will all hear you, we, Kiehtan's people. Speak to us in the first thunder. Let the rain clean the whole land for planting. Let us plant by the long river and have corn and beans again. Let us fish. Let us eat again, and live."

The blackness that had taken shape around him did not leave. It became as a fire gleaming on metal, as a gun pointed at him. The head above the gun was not pale and bearded. The hair of it was shaved and the face was painted: the skin was colored in the blue of Nahiganset, it was powdered with the pollen of Saghonnate, it was cut with the dotted patterns of Pocumptuck: the wolf hunched low in the hollow of its cheek and the owl sat over its eyes, which had no closing.

Dark of the last and thirteenth moon: the first moon strains to rise. At dusk, the great-man walks in his line through the woods before the base of Wachusett. He sees a black fox standing by its burrow. Over the head of the fox are arranged letters in a semicircle. He cannot read them, as they are like those in the Englishman's book. A voice speaks them aloud to him. The words say: Are you my murderer?

The great-man dragged himself on through swamp and mud. When the sun was down, the people neared the base of the mountain that even in darkness filled half the sky. A Nipmuck guard set in the woods signaled him and he paused.

"Have your men returned from the coast?" When Pometacom stopped walking, his legs trembled in the mud.

"Three days ago."

"Are the coastal towns burned?"

"No." The guard said nothing else.

"Not burned?"

"Not burned."

"Had you many losses?"

The guard did not reply.

The great-man set his legs moving forward, and when the people reached a good place beside the mountain, the line stopped and the men began to set up the poles that the women had been carrying. Pometacom shoved a sharpened pole into the earth: in war great-men set their own house poles. "Go find your husband," he said to his sister. "Send him to me. Then pass among the Nipmuck houses and ask for Weskautaug. Weskautaug must come to me now."

Soon Tuspaquin appeared before him, still blackened all over his body, but for the skin left round his eyes.

"Great-man, my brother-in-law!" Tuspaquin's sooted arms

embraced him. "Here, my friend, I bring you the ashes of Weymouth's houses from our journey south and the ashes of Scituate's barns from our way back. And silver and lead and powder from the walled house outside Plimouth! The woman and the baby there invite you to visit them, they found me so pleasant! Your brother's face on the pole in Plimouth forced me to make myself even more pleasant than usual!" Tuspaquin was as cheerful as his wife was grim.

"I have heard long ago of Weymouth, only eight houses were burned. And in Scituate, few more. Now I hear no towns are burned." Pometacom bent to fasten the last pole. "You ate shad more than you burned houses." He ceased from the heavy work.

His wife began to lay the mats.

"Why did you leave the nephew of Nashoba to himself so long?"

Tuspaquin reached for something at his belt. "Here, this came for you while I was in the southland."

It was his mother's best stone knife, in the shape of a half-moon. The great-man felt the sharpness of its edge.

"It's to be a present for your adopted son's wedding. Your mother is poor and hasn't any metal knife to send. But she's well."

"And your wife is well."

"She has greeted me."

"She must begin to greet me again!"

"She will. Only wait through the planting moon." The two men sat on the mats as soon as they were put down. "She will cease to mourn during the weeding moon, that's when her son died. It is the Englishman's way. The preacher taught her."

"There's another woman even more necessary to me in her greeting." Pometacom's eyes looked black in the light of the new fire his wife set.

"Saghonnate." Tuspaquin kept his voice low.

Pometacom nodded. "Where's her house?"

Tuspaquin pointed over his shoulder. "She and the slant-headed nephew speak frequently since we arrived. They are like two snakes at seed-time, standing on the path to mate."

"What does the nephew say?" Pometacom pulled his mantle around him.

"He screams for war but doesn't want war. He only wants to go against Boston now before the leaves are out and frighten them so he can make peace. So he can sit down when the fish come in. He'll never go to the south with us. He is forever counting his men."

"How many has he?"

"He lost a lot. He has fewer than six hundred."

"Fewer?" Pometacom let go of the mantle.

"So, it was good I left the Nipmuck alone at Marlborough, where he ate too much and lost so many!" Tuspaquin smiled.

The guards raised the doorway of Pometacom's new house and Weskautaug hurried inside.

Pometacom pretended he had not been asleep and motioned the wise-man to the fire, but did not welcome him.

"Great-man, I do you service." Weskautaug spoke first. "It was necessary I get to the mountain directly. And it's lucky that I did. For, difficult as it was, I have arranged everything. An odd one of the Nipmuck will dance with the southland."

Pometacom rubbed his bad hand with his good. "It's set, then. One from the south, one from the north."

Weskautaug stood across the fire, repeating the great-man's words with slight change and warming his hands: "One from the north, one from the south."

At daybreak Pometacom sent along the base of the mountain to the great-woman of Saghonnate and summoned her to pay him her respects. She did not arrive. He sent half a basket of beads, his last. She did not arrive. When the sun sat at the top of the sky, he sent Otan-nick to her. The young man should tell her this: if she doesn't come, Saghonnate will cease to be when we return to the southland. Her lands will become the place where the great-man would allow Englishmen to live in peace, paying him tribute.

She arrived.

"I do you service, great-woman." He stood high over the shrunken woman and spoke out of respect for her age.

"You have done me service enough." Her eyes were dark and glittery and her voice was still like the sound of shellfish walking on stone.

He indicated a bed on which she might sit.

"I am standing."

"I have done you no disservice, great-woman. Only your neighbor Benjamin Church has done you disservice." He did not wish to sit in her presence.

She said nothing.

"Did Benjamin Church keep his promise to you? Or did he forget to come with his soldiers to walk you to Plimouth when the war began? Is that why you let your forty men walk without you to Plimouth last summer? Not that they were entirely alone, having two hundred of Nahiganset behind them. Were you waiting for your man, your own Englishman?" He saw his hand strike the great-woman's face; but his hand had not moved.

No answer.

"Perhaps we kept Benjamin Church too busy. I'm so sorry you had to go to the swamp of the Nahiganset instead of to Plimouth. It was because Benjamin Church was busy, too busy." He stopped himself.

"I have been busy myself, great-man." Her hand was on her hip.

He ignored her. "You are dancing with the inland people here, great-woman? Though you would not dance at Montaup with your own people?"

"Yes. I dance at Wachusett." She gave an inexplicable smile. "When the thunder comes, I and my man will dance. The nephew of Nashoba and his woman will dance. All of us will dance. You will watch us dancing, great-man of Pokanocket, king of Kickamuit, which is no more than a village by a spring where an Englishman's stone fort stands!" She spat at his feet. "I hold you in my hand, like an ant."

It would be several days before the thunder; the sky was clear and the air not ready. He would give a feast without inviting Saghonnate. At the next daybreak Pometacom went into the woods. "It is for the new people," he said, smoothing the nose of his black stallion. He raised the club high. "The new people are a coat for us to wear against the cold." He brought the club down hard on the head of the stallion.

He sent others to cut the horse. The meat was a long time on the rack.

He delivered a bit of seed corn to each of the four great-men of the Nipmuck; to the great-man of the river he sent his mother's stone knife. He had the most men. They would give him their allegiance. He was their father. Saghonnate would belong nowhere.

When the sun was halfway down, Pometacom took a careful look at everything his women had prepared. It was not plentiful, but it was more than he had seen for some time. Then he heard an odd sound.

His wife looked up from the fire. "Is that the thunder?"

"It couldn't be. Not yet."

The rolling sound came again. Thunder always sounded odd when it has been so long absent from the ear.

"It is the thunder!" His wife looked toward him questioningly.

"I rest in Kiehtan," he said. "Save everything. Come to the mountain with the women. We will feast tomorrow." A calm settled in his arms and legs, his hands grew warm. In Kiehtan was a great quiet. Kiehtan would speak to the whole land.

He dressed in the three belts of the people.

"Tonight, dance only for the thunder," he told Weskautaug,

who came quickly when he was summoned. "And greet the whole people. Tomorrow night we will name the greatest and the wisest."

"I'm ready." Weskautaug left as quickly.

When the top of the mountain turned orange in the sunset, the people camping at its base began to climb. The path went up steeply over rock. Pometacom was grateful for the footsteps worn into the central groove. They made the climbing easier. Never before had this path to the Nipmuck dancing place strained his breath or tired his legs. He did not wish to appear winded at the top in front of so many.

Lying just below the peak of the mountain, the dancing place gave an almost circular view of the land below. He thought he caught the smallest glint of the great bay of the south, far off. The orange light of the setting sun and the many hundreds of torches brought a glow to the red paint on his palms and beneath his eyes. The light caused the black he had smeared upon himself to darken and it made brighter the white dots he had spattered on himself for rain.

His friend Kuttiomp was nowhere among the hundreds of faces marked with the wolf.

"Thirty-six." The number was spoken nearby. Everyone was talking.

The talking began to hush toward the center of the circle, lingering longest at the edges of the vast collection of people. At the center, a large space on the ground was left cleared. Weskautaug was walking into that center, followed by a small wise-man wearing the head of a bird and body feathers. There was something peculiar about the way this wise-man carried himself; or perhaps he was only waddling like a bird.

This must be the odd one of the Nipmuck beside whom he would dance tomorrow night. Pometacom adjusted the shoulder belt to hang evenly at his knees.

Slowly and with care, Weskautaug and the birdlike man

spread a deerskin on the ground. Weskautaug knelt on the skin and motioned the hundreds of standing men to kneel. Then he struck the ground with his hands and began to sing. The ground shook as the people beat upon it in high reply:

"*Ha! Hee no hoo. Wah! Hee no hay.*"

A third man loomed behind Weskautaug. This one wore a ruffled English shirt and carried a gun in his right hand. His face and body were painted black and red, and the great-man could not even tell from which people he came. He was neither so tall as the men of the river or of the daybreak nor so slight as the people of the point. He was broad, like the inland people. Weskautaug stood and, instead of the customary whine, a deep, loud voice issued from him and two thousand throats opened for air.

"*You say you are of the whole land.*
You say you want to fight the Englishmen.
You say you have spoken with Kiehtan.
So why have you come to me?"

Fear touched the great-man's lips. Weskautaug wasn't calling on a god to speak; he was speaking for the god, and it was Hobomok.

The broad, shirted man knelt on the deerskin before Weskautaug and sang out in reply:

"*I come to you because Kiehtan has not brought us victory.*"

The two thousand curved their shoulders to protect their necks as Hobomok answered:

"*Shirt-man, you love Englishmen!*
You took their pigs and chickens.
You dressed in their clothes.

You drank of their drink.
I, only I, hated the strangers from the start.
I, only I, have roared since their first approach."

The shirted man leaned forward to make his reply:

"At first, I welcomed them, my lord. Now I do not."

Weskautaug pointed a finger down at the shirted man:

"Shirt-man, I am told you joke with Englishmen.
You send them warnings and they flee.
True, you hold a gun in one hand.
But in the other? Does your other hand work?
Or is it broken?"

There was another intake of breath and Pometacom's tongue went cold. His hands pressed the beads of the great-belt against his thighs.

Weskautaug leaned farther over the kneeling man:

"Shirt-man, your warriors weaken and fly home to fields.
They see you have two hearts, and only one gun, one hand.
You would fight on and on, never winning.
But you were clever to come to me: I will help you."

Pometacom squinted to see more clearly as the wind began in the buds of the trees. The flutter collected itself around Weskautaug and the wise-man held something up in his hands. He pulled it back and forth, into a strip. Then he pushed it into a ball and pulled it out to greater length and made it shimmer. He spoke again, as he worked:

"Kiehtan is angry at you, people of the whole land,
because you love the Englishmen's god.

You do not wish to go to the southwest when you die,
you wish to be lifted straight up.
And you fear their god's sicknesses.
Kiehtan will not help you, people of the whole land.
He is jealous; he is quiet in his anger, sleeping.
Only I, Hobomok, will help you."

The wind came stronger and the men around Pometacom hid their faces in their arms. Named, Hobomok let himself loose among the whole people and was walking over stones. Only Pometacom kept his eyes open, staring at the odd, feathered wise-man who was rocking back and forth beside Weskautaug. There was something very peculiar about this odd one: it was a woman!

Far off from the west came the roll of thunder and then Pometacom knew the thunder was not of Kiehtan. The wise-man had arranged this thunder! Pometacom put his hands to his ears, but his fingers did not shut out the voice that came in the wind:

"Listen to me, people of the whole land.
Make haste to fight at Boston, then rest and fish.
Send this man with one gun from the people.
He poisons you with a long war that will never end.
Send him away from you.
Tell him to go! Tell him! Tell him!"

The kneeling man stood up on the deerskin and waited.

Pometacom watched as the other men took their arms from their faces and opened their eyes. Many turned toward Pometacom and the great-man took his hands from his ears.

"Go away! Go away!" A shout came from the throat of the bird-woman. Her voice was like the sound of shellfish on stone. It was she of Saghonnate. A great heat filled Pometacom's chest and arms.

A few shouts from old men in the inner ring joined hers. Not really enough to force the shirted man from the deerskin, but he did move off it, and vanished into the crowd.

The man in the shirt, then, was the odd one of the Nipmuck.

Pometacom felt his eyes and ears must protrude from his body, so much did he strain to catch what Weskautaug did now:

"I, Hobomok, will listen only when the whole people comes.
I never shut my ears to the whole land, nor cover them;
as a great fish hears in his body every noise,
I, Hobomok, hear the world. Now I hear a man with one gun,
he speaks. He says, 'I shall leave this body.
I shall seek Hobomok. He will aid me.'
So call this man back! Call him back!"

"Come back! Come back!" This time there were quite a few voices.

The shirted man stumbled out of the crowd and onto the deerskin. The outlines of his thick body suddenly took on a shape familiar to Pometacom. The head slanted quickly in above the eyebrows. The shirted man was the nephew of Nashoba.

Pometacom's throat grew tight. The wise-man placing himself before the whole people was Weskautaug: one from the south. And the nephew of Nashoba was also there: one from the north.

The jelly in Weskautaug's hands had taken on a long shape and ceased to be a transparent foaming substance. It became a gun. Weskautaug held the gun up, cocked it, raised it high over his head and shot it off. There came an orange flash and a flame that shot out of the barrel with a roar.

Then Weskautaug threw the gun to the shirted man, who caught it with a clap. The shirted man showed to the crowd first his right hand, which was perfect, and then his left, which was also perfect. "These are my hands," the slant-headed man called out. "I have two."

The slant-headed nephew would be greatest-man, if the whole people hailed him. Pometacom's head moved, his eyes searched out the faces of friends. Their foreheads were confused; their eyes unsure.

Weskautaug began a quiet song of the river people; he was using it somehow to make a promise to the Pocumptuck. When the song was over, Weskautaug spoke to the crowd in his normal voice, only louder: "Now let us test this man again to see if he is still divided. Send him away again, my friends."

"Go! Go!" Every man was shouting, except one. Pometacom kept his lips pressed tight.

The shirted man stumbled off the deerskin and vanished again into the crowd.

Once more the wind's voice came:

"The people of the whole land will break the strangers
only when they have melted into one people,
only when not a single man withholds himself.
Call him back, call back this man.
He is your greatest-man!"

"Come back to us!" The voice was as a single cry from two thousand mouths, except one. Pometacom remained silent and stood as if layers of himself were peeled off, as if he were skinned alive.

In the center, at the inner edge of the crowd, the shirted man reeled and wavered by the edge of the deerskin. He put one foot toward the skin, but, try as he did, he could not raise the other foot from the earth.

Then Pometacom felt a hand upon his shoulder. He turned to look into sorrowful eyes: Kuttiomp.

"Call out now," Kuttiomp whispered. "Or they will kill you."

"Our greatest-man cannot get back to us!" Weskautaug

sang out. "We must call him to us, one at a time. Begin there!" The wise-man pointed into the crowd, directly at the great-man of the river.

"Come back to us! Come back!" the young man of the river cried, clear and loud.

Slowly the circle of response made its way toward Pometacom. He opened his mouth as if to vomit: "Come back!" he called out.

A wild laugh rang from the beak of the bird-woman.

The shirted figure jumped easily onto the deerskin then, without waiting for any other voices. With both arms outstretched and with a gun in each hand, the slant-headed nephew stood with Weskautaug at the center of the people. The greatest-man and the wisest raised their hands together: sun, moon, the two eyes of the people.

Instead of leading into the dance of the two-headed snake, Weskautaug separated the people he had brought together by causing each to kneel and begin his own song. One by one, the men rose singing to run to the deerskin and shake a gun southwest toward the town called Sudbury, first in the final string that led directly to Boston. Each recited how he would burn, how suck, how strike at Sudbury. A continual song of welcome to Hobomok went on simultaneously and, as he knelt, Pometacom fitted the words of his own song into the chopping rhythm of his hands against the earth. "*Yo hah weh hee,*" he sang, pounding the earth. It did not matter what came from his lips. Behind his eyes he saw what he would do. He would send Kuttiomp to the wise-man's house to find the great stone tube. Through it he would have Otan-nick whisper under the mats of the wise-man's sleeping house: "There is only one god, wise-man. He made the sky, five thousand years ago and more. He made all things himself, out of nothing, thief! Nobody helped him, opener of traps! And unless you know the one god, to die is to perish always, always. Englishmen and Dutchmen know him and they do not perish! But you will drown in the deep, wise-man, where the one god throws you." Then he would cast

Weskautaug out of Pokanocket and give him the long knife. Yes, he, Pometacom, would become as several have before, both great and wise. That is what Kiehtan had been suggesting to him for so long; that is where the path led. And that is why Kiehtan had been darkening his vision. It was why he had seen the woman of the animals when he wintered; yes, now he recognized it all. The path behind was very clear. So was the path ahead: the people of the whole land was not his people.

Kuttiomp's villagers could not find him anywhere in the houses at the base of the mountain. Word finally came that he had run off before the dance. He had gone home.

Before the dance? Surely Kuttiomp's face was at the dance! Kuttiomp's voice. Or perhaps it was Kuttiomp's dreamer who had warned him? That was the way things would come to Pometacom now. "Track him," the great-man directed. "But return by midday. Every man is needed for Sudbury."

Until the attack on Sudbury was over, the southland would appear to be one with the whole land, so that the northland would suspect nothing. "We are not of these people. They are Hobomok's. There is no people of the whole land. We will go home; we are Kiehtan's." Naonanto's cousin agreed. Tuspaquin nodded. The great-man of the two coves said "*Hee.*" Weetamoo, also, and she gave them all tobacco.

"To them will be the northland. To us will be the southland." Naonanto's cousin raised up his tobacco.

"And she of Saghonnate will have no home at all!" Weetamoo shut her tobacco bag.

"Go for the tube," Pometacom told Otan-nick. "He who left us for others must be cast out."

The thirty-six warriors of Pokanocket and five young women, carrying carved wooden flintlocks that the nephew of Nashoba bid the women take, went off with Annawon to camp outside

Sudbury. The old men of Nipmuck built a great dancing house at the mountain. Here they would celebrate the victory and prepare to go to Boston. In a few days, thirty-four warriors of Pockanocket returned and all five of the women. Kuttiomp's daughter had outwitted Englishmen all by herself. Dropping her wooden gun in the marshes, she stood near the road that cuts through the flood plain at Sudbury. Twisting, turning, calling into the high grass of the meadow at the edge of the marsh, she was like a wolf that runs its tail over tall reeds, pretending to be a duck. "*Peeyaush netop*," she called softly. Oh, come here, my friend. I love you. I am lame. "*Nqunnuckquus*." Pometacom could see her pushing back her hair and motioning to the young Englishmen who were crossing Sudbury meadows with their guns on their shoulders: "*Peeyaush netop*," a soft voice calling to young men from a green marsh and a willowlike girl smiling, beckoning with her arms. The English boys ran into the reeds for her, their flintlocks uncocked and their long swords hanging at their belts. Then up rose Johettit's group, out of the reeds. "Lord Jesus!" Johettit shouted at the sky. "Deliver them from our hands!" But, as usual, nothing came out of the sky. Soon there were more English hands, more English heads. On the hill at Sudbury the nephew of Nashoba fought in the open again, as if he were an Englishman. "At daybreak," the fox whispered to his people, to all those who loved him.

Sounds of the dancing in the great house came to Pometacom as he dropped five painted stones into a bowl and shook them together. He sat on crusty ground, silver and shining in the moonlight. Around him stood his eight guards, but soon he would no longer need guards. The poison would be gone from Pokanocket, and the shame. The daybreak people and those of the point, who trust but themselves, would leave for the Connecticut, to collect their planters. Then, out of the northland forever. Exactly where his steps would take him, Pometacom did not know, except home.

Just before daybreak, when all the dancers had returned and gathered around him, the great-man who had become wise shook the bowl a last time and turned it upside down on the mat. He picked the bowl up: four black sides up and one white.

He picked up the fifth stone, with the white side still up, and laid it on one of Weskautaug's toes.

He threw a handful of reeds into the air. Fifty landed in a heap and one fell far from the others. He picked that one up and laid it on the toes of the other foot. The wise-man stood of his own will, without being bound to the pole.

There was a silence from those of the cleared land.

"One question, great-man." Weskautaug spoke calmly, as if he had come to pay a visit.

"Speak." Pometacom pulled the long knife from his belt.

"Was it not Hobomok who delivered the people of the whole land forty dead Englishmen on top of Sudbury hill?"

"It was my brother-in-law Tuspaquin, whose men fired the woods and made the Englishmen run out so that our men could shoot at them. I have a question for you. The wood in the wagon caught fire perfectly and the wagon ran in a straight line down Sudbury hill, flaming. Just as it got to the garrison house, it veered. Was that of Hobomok working against us? Or of the Englishmen's god working against us?"

There was no choice the wise-man could safely make, so he made none.

"I will tell you how to solve it. It was the way Kiehtan saw it, long ago. And Kiehtan the orderly would say that if a wagon veers, look for a disorderly stone. A troublesome stone. One that is different from the others. One that works against the others. Such a stone must be thrown out."

"Great-man, cast me out. I speak now for the last time. It is you, not I, who have become an Englishman."

"Come come come come!" The warriors lit sticks of pine and gave them out among the women and children under the trees. The children came forward to receive them, guarding the small flames from the wind with their hands.

Pometacom nodded and Weskautaug stretched out his hands, palms up.

The people advanced toward the wise-man with the tiny flames, hungry for flesh.

In the soft part of each wrist, the great-man made the first incisions, and Weskautaug with open eyes began his song. The people moved away. The great-man knelt to peel the skin back over the fingers; it did not pull easily, and he had to use his teeth.

13

Late in the afternoon during the dry heat of the moon of squash and beans, a thousand of them waded across Titicut where it is narrow. North of the river again, they were within reach of Taunton's horses and extensive cornfields and of smaller Bridgewater's farms. The towns of the south were not at all empty of Englishmen. The thousand followed the bank upriver toward Bridgewater for quite a long way, keeping under the trees. Branches and even trunks were still down from the great storm they had missed during the summer before. No one had cleaned the woods. After so much water from the heavy snows, it had turned surprisingly dry. The apple trees of the cleared land had withered; some leaves already fell from the maples. They traveled all their lands in darkness, pausing under trees in daylight. Except for Kickamuit neck, where they did not dare to go at all.

"Here." At the front of the long line, the great-man of the daybreak people indicated a spring earlier described to him by his brother-in-law Tuspaquin, who was walking at the end of the line.

"Keep the children quiet." The children had grown careless

in their own lands. Fires were made and kettles filled from a spring where very little water ran. The sky was clear; they did not set shelters. Smoke from the fires was spread about by the children so it would not rise and betray their location. It was good to be out of Tuspaquin's swampy island where they had rested and fed. At daybreak they would go against Bridgewater. If they could burn that town, they would try again to burn Taunton. His own try; this time he, too, would go into battle, and from now on, as everywhere they went was a trap. Let Taunton become again Cohannet–the pine place. Tuspaquin had killed a few men in the cornfields at Bridgewater on the way south during the planting moon, but had failed to burn the town. The great-man did not quite believe that he was home. It was as if the catch had been hauled in while he was elsewhere on the beach, looking for the others, for the spear point, for his hand. This was because he had not seen Kickamuit or climbed Montaup.

Was that the bark of a fox?

He listened. Yes, a real fox! Good. Come to help him in danger. Come to say, my great-man, my friend, my child, let me point to him who will kill you. It is—.

"Quiet!" Neimpauog's eyes moved in darting motions as he silenced a girl who was pounding corn too loud.

"It's time." The great-man motioned his adopted son to send the scouts out in the eight directions to gather news of the Englishmen's movements. Nomatuck had grown straighter and taller but there was as yet no bride to replace Kuttiomp's daughter. She had been found among the dead at the fishing falls on the long river, when the people had arrived there from the mountain; late in the planting moon.

"My brother." His sister came to his side. "There are berries by the river." She had withered to a brown wrinkled berry herself.

"Your eyes would be the eyes to find them! Do not go far off, my sister." The great-man's shoulders were rounded and he was glad he didn't have to hunt for anything but cows. To look a buck in the eyes, no; all his strength would be drawn into those open holes, those wounds, those doors.

The great-man's wife smeared raspberries into the pounded corn and the smell of them came into the air. Her eyes were hollow; she never slept, always ready to run. The first time the people camped in a new place, they were all less sure of daybreak, that there would be light.

Movement from the east. A whisper in his ear. "The Englishmen's captain Benjamin Church is on this side of the river. He has his many wagons filled with food. With him are his own soldiers and many of the warriors of Saghonnate. The men of the outlet walk in front of and beside and in back of the Englishmen, to protect them."

The great-woman of Saghonnate was camping with her women at the start of the narrow land. All her men now walked beside Benjamin Church. Benjamin Church gave them food. Benjamin Church promised not to sell them for slaves. Benjamin Church gave her men half the price he got when he sold the daybreak people for slaves, those that Benjamin Church took and who refused to smile at him. Others of the daybreak gave themselves to Benjamin Church and smiled. Oh, Pometacom knew Benjamin Church's way, as well as the Englishman now knew Pometacom's, and all his paths.

Very quietly then Pometacom spoke to each of his remaining great-men, walking into their separate areas by Titicut. He spoke first into the ear of Naonanto's cousin, the dead-eyed Nahiganset who wore bands of coins beneath his knees. He spoke to blackened Tuspaquin and to his broad uncle, Annawon. He spoke to those of the wet cove and the low cove, and to the great-woman of Pocasset, who had drawn her people as far as she could from the husband she disliked. "Benjamin Church is here. We cannot wade back over. It is too deep here. I will send men to cut a tree to lie across the river; we will go south to Mattapoiset by dark. Before the moon of squash and beans is full, we will come back here to go against Bridgewater."

The fires were put out and the bundles retied and lifted up. The pine fell as slowly and quietly as they could make it fall. The women were brought back from berrying. One by one the thousand started across the log. The Nahigansets went first, then the Pocassets, then the others, leaving Pokanocket the last on the far bank.

Captain Annawon stepped out onto the log. The women followed him, with their children. Then the other old men stepped out. Then uncle Unkompoin's slender form walked stiff-kneed onto the fallen tree.

Blast of a shot.

The old man wavered. To the left, to the right. He fell. Blood in the brown water, then nothing.

The people froze. The shot had come from downriver. There were no movements to be seen anywhere. And no more shots.

Sounds of English voices, not many. Sounds of Englishmen running off toward Bridgewater. They were too few. It could not be Benjamin Church and his men, but Benjamin Church would be here by dawn.

When a body falls into the water, my son, the people may not leave it. They must stay at the place until light comes. Pometacom ran along the log, searching the dark water for the form of his father's brother, the people's uncle. He saw nothing in the water.

He ran into the water. Soggy bottom, slow current. Others joined him to look, to feel with their feet, their hands, to touch the dead, under water. No one found anything but roots, branches, shadows of fish. A small river! Where could the body be?

Darkness, the squash moon small and young; the stars brilliant but not enough to show colors in the water. Uncle, my father's brother!

"Make camp." He told those still walking in the water. "Make it on the south side. We will stay beside him until the first light and then run south as day breaks. It is proper."

He took his gun and walked out to the log to sit.

Naonanto's cousin walked out on the log. He stood, balancing. He leaned down, he spoke: "It is foolish for us to stay here, great-man. This is not our uncle; it is yours."

Pometacom said nothing, his eyes resting on the coins at the slight man's knees.

"Nahiganset leaves you tonight by darkness. I do you no more service, my friend. It is over. The people of the point go west to their own lands. We are no longer safe together, anyway. We are too many to move rapidly, to hide securely."

"Your wife, Weetamoo?"

"She stays with you. She and I cease to be married."

Pometacom moved off the log and sat on its stub on the northern bank. The Nahiganset began to come over the log, to recross the river. Ten. Fifty. One hundred. Two hundred. Two hundred and sixty men. Then the women and the children. At Pometacom's feet, they turned to follow Titicut until it curved into the west. There they would leave the river, making their way through the woods to cross the Seekonk and walk to their home on the other side of the bay.

He watched their feet, silent on the log. The last ones raised their hands in farewell.

Pometacom was lost from the path; the way of it was not beneath his feet. In his stomach was a year he had swallowed but not digested, and he wandered. This way, the hair-wrapped feces of the wolf; that way the odor of the fox; and everywhere the hum of small mosquitoes. Yet he did not doubt the path existed or that it led forward to yet another swamp.

"Do not sing for the dead man," he told Otan-nick, who came to ask his will. "Rest. Sleep. I have both eyes; I will do what is necessary."

He sat alone.

In the two bags at his belt were the seeds and the bones of

the people. To the bone bag the great-man had added the piece he had taken from Weskautaug's thumb and two small rattlesnake teeth the wise-man had in his house. He wished to touch them now. He did not dare.

His strength was gone; he sought the face and the strong arm of Kiehtan, he opened his ears to the voice.

Was it laughter that he heard?

The wild giggle of Hobomok? No. It was a sound from the camp. A child crying.

Frogs. The crickets were heavy-voiced and old. The fireflies were green and weak. Part of his head seemed asleep. He took good breaths, breaths to fill himself. He rested the loaded gun more comfortably across his knees. In the bag around his neck there was powder for twenty or so more shots, a handful of slugs and one perfect bullet.

It was well. He had seen the cleared land again. The men of Rehoboth had scarcely planted their fields. The order of Englishmen was gone from the squares they had set on the plain, even though the round fields of Pokanocket were not yet to be seen replacing them. The dogs and cats that the Englishmen so loved to keep in their barns were running wild in the woods and over the fields. There were few sounds from the blackened heaps of houses of Rehoboth. The people of Rehoboth that he could make out by squinting through a reed looked sick and weak. They lived in lean-tos. A handful tended the corners left to their fields. Few Englishmen had returned to Swansea and no smoke rose at noon over the green fields there, though there had been wisps of it at Hezekiah Willett's house near the pig fence; the house was finished and the woman had been brought into it. This time they had not seen him, did not wave. Would never wave. On Mattapoiset a few Englishmen lingered in the forty houses. He had seen Hugh Cole's sons in the fields. It was acceptable that they be there. His friends need not leave, though they and he would never speak of anything. At Kickamuit–the spring, the moon lost itself in the hard stone of the Englishman's fort that blocked the path to the wading place.

The fort must be broken down. He must see to that before Weetamoo took her men and left. It was wise to move in smaller groups. But without Pocasset's men, he could no longer go against a town of Englishmen. He could not stand and fight with Thomas Leonard at Taunton. He could only elude Englishmen. A wolf cuts his tongue on a bone and bleeds to death.

So, Thomas Leonard, my friend. Are you well?

Off in the woods behind him he could sense the wagons of Benjamin Church, the baskets full of food and even the short, compact black-haired man who hunted him. With the squat warriors of Saghonnate gathered around him. With some of Pokanocket's men as well; perhaps Kuttiomp was among them.

All his lost ones. There were his fishermen who had been sleeping in the roar and boom of the big falls on Connecticut. When he'd reached the falls from Wachusett, they were scattered, dead. He heard the story from Unkompoin, one of the few found alive at the river's edge. The old men and women had been sleeping with full bellies, fat with salmon and with English milk which the captive Englishwomen had taken from some cows. Kuttiomp's daughter had been sleeping among them, resting from all she'd done at Sudbury and from making ready for her wedding. She had slept through it, one woman said. When the long barrel of a gun was shoved in at the edge of the sleeping mat and fired, Kuttiomp's daughter never woke. An orange flash, screams. So many killed. Bodies ripped by wolves found at the new forge, in the fields of new corn, washing up at the banks of the river.

Daybreak, the Englishmen had learned when to attack.

Mosquitoes landed on Pometacom's bare head and flew away. He longed to grow his hair. To pull it down on his forehead. To bind it in a band. To sleep.

His eyes shut, opened. Sound of the narrow river moving on. The red coat that had hung so long in the trees by his father's grave, it must be gone, all gone. Tattered over so many winters, had the air taken it entirely? Or had the Englishmen cut it down? There were good furs over his brother Wamsutta and over his brother Sunconewhew in the first swamp, without his head. Did the dreamer wander with or without its head? I had to leave you, my father, my brothers. I had to take the people to where it was safe. I became as those who see by day and night. Yet I cannot do it, though I feel you. Is it you who come to me?

No.

Will of Saghonnate?

No.

Kuttiomp?

That's who it was! Someone he knew was waking by Benjamin Church's wagon. Someone lay with a hand on Benjamin Church's bundles of food. Someone was coming to find him. Kuttiomp must have been caught by Benjamin Church's men. "We won't kill you, man of Pokanocket," Benjamin Church always said. "If you will join us, come and lead us to the great-man who began the war."

Oh, my friend Kuttiomp, who wins every gamble, does your shadow wind through the woods among the sleeping forms, looking for me, searching? And is it to aid me, or to bind me?

Palms, hands brushing his shoulders!

He did not move.

There is a place beyond which everything waits.

Dampness on the lightly pressing fingers.

Uncle.

Uncle, you come from water? Go to the other bank, Uncle. The southern bank. There the path begins. He tightened his hands on the gun.

The fingers of the other hands stroked his shoulders and slipped off.

He thought of the thumb bone in his bag, of the teeth; but he did not touch them. He had not mastered the ways of them and from the thumb bone alone could grow a shadbush large enough to smother him, if he were not careful.

After a while Pometacom began to breathe more deeply; the other man's dreamer was gone and so was the uncle's.

He began to be able to make out the mist. Light was touching the top of the trees. The voices of birds calling, answering. It was time to go. He must wake the people, yet he sat on, wanting to see into the water of the river.

"No! He's one of yours!"

He wheeled at the voice behind him and fired a slug into the woods at a shape in Englishman's clothes.

He ran out onto the log and, crouching low, got to the south bank. Calling, "Scatter! Scatter!"

He plunged into the woods to the right of the camp.

He could hear the people getting up and running many ways. "Scatter!" they called and then it was quiet.

The voice that had warned him had sounded familiar, but he had seen only the Englishman who had fired at him: short, compact, black-haired. Breathing more slowly now, he waited behind a tree.

Sounds of running. Nomatuck emerged from behind trees and hailed him with a hand. They waited silently and separately. Others passed them and signaled but all moved on to wait at a distance. He listened for sounds of trouble, screams. There was nothing. Everyone was safe.

There was the sound of English shoes on the log. Two shots, close together at the campsite. No shouts. Then there was the sound of English shoes recrossing the log. Then, far off, the sound of English wagons creaking.

They were safe!

They waited a little longer before they began to hoot and call, searching the woods. At camp, the few goods they had left were strewn about and the women began to collect them. But when the people were all gathered from the woods, there were only half of them. The others were gone. They had been stolen silently by Englishmen at gunpoint and led noiselessly over the log.

His wife did not appear. His sister did not appear. His son

did not appear. Something that was like a web inside the great-man undid itself and he could not stand up.

At last it was raining, a day-long rain. There had been clouds covering the full moon when they passed the pig fence and the hill of the dead. The rain had begun when they crept by the stone fort, though the smell of the sea that was in the rain made them at first believe it was only heavy mist. Twenty men and a handful of women and children walked quietly into the bad-smelling grove. The great-man's sister had led him here long ago: "This is what you do." She had crouched in her bright dress that flashed like birds in a berry bush and left her waste in its proper place. But then she had looked around, behind herself, afraid. Walking now in the darkness, the great-man who would have bound the whole land looked behind himself. Of what had his sister been afraid in those days? They came to the good-smelling cedars and followed the lowland to the western slope of Montaup which rose dark above them. They reached the swamp in a wet dawn. Light brought them the orange lilies and the green cabbages that smelled of the skunk, of his lost uncle. Here below Montaup he would shut his eyes; here sink into the damp ground. Here, Benjamin Church would find him.

"It looks different." Red-eyed Johettit spoke as they put together a lean-to on the lowest slope of the hill above a brown, muddy brook.

"This is Montaup, knife of Rehoboth, where we summer. This is where we dry our fish and put our corn on mats in the sun, or cover it in rain such as this. How is it different?"

"The rocks are more crumbled, different. It is not the same as when we left. It is . . . older."

"Older?"

"Yes."

"You were not here long enough to know the land!"

"I see the same thing, my nephew." The big voice of his

uncle Annawon had grown the stronger as the band of people grew weaker.

"You were not a child here either, my uncle. You are of Squannock–the green swamp. Montaup is the same to me as it always was."

Up on the hill they would dance the first corn, were they not become as men of the old time, without corn. He could hear the sea wild beneath the rain. Perhaps the day would bring a storm that bends trees. Good. He would die in a rage of waters, his canoe circling beyond his power to control it. Then the waters would quiet to carry him to the rim of the world. He would not have to walk. It would be restful. The sun rose higher behind the rain clouds, and they moved into the lean-to and slept.

Noon: oysters round and roasted. The smell of bass on the fire. Raining still. There was a time when the world was full of old men who were sure of everything.

"My nephew?" His uncle Annawon ate beside him in the shelter on the slope and quieted his voice to limit it to the great-man who had once mended the net of the daybreak people. "Last time I shot an Englishman, something odd happened. It was in the fight at the river, not long after they stole our people. My bullet landed in the left elbow of an Englishman. I saw it land. At dusk, just before we ceased fighting, I myself was grazed by a bullet." The uncle stopped.

"Yes?"

"It passed me near the left elbow, at exactly the same spot."

"Yes?"

"What significance do you find in that?"

Pometacom eyed the others, to see if they had heard. "Uncle." He lowered his voice. "Such thoughts have frozen the fingers of our men on the triggers of their guns since we left Wachusett–the mountain. We lost over a hundred people while we were picking berries on Pocasset, from just such thoughts.

No man of ours dared fire at Englishmen. I tell you, their god is no greater than ours."

Over a hundred people captured. The hundred glad, too, to have done with it. Glad to be penned into the horse pound at Bridgewater and fed chickens. Glad to be given rum to drink. So the scouts had reported after they had seen the hundred laughing and talking.

"But their god brings rain whenever they need it." Johettit spoke. He had been listening; Johettit was always listening.

The great-man did not answer Johettit. There was stubble on Pometacom's soot-streaked head as he rose to stand apart from the men. Outside, he stretched his arms north and south: "*Yo hah weh hee.*" He began his song at its new place. "*I have come home. I have fought the strangers and I am destroyed.*" He felt easier. He had to watch even his own men now, had to stand when his own lookouts stood, had to keep his hand upon his gun when any other man touched a weapon. The song always comforted him.

He called his adopted son to him. "You, my son, leave camp at daybreak." He reached into his bullet bag. "Go to Plimouth. Find out what's happening at the square house. If they are still alive. Get this to my son." He handed Nomatuck the second of his two perfect bullets. "Tell him that when he takes his name wintering, it might begin with this mark *P*. But if it does not, the bullet will still be his."

Nomatuck touched the mark with his finger and took the bullet.

"And if you do not find him, it is yours." Pometacom's eyes held those of his adopted son.

"Great-man, my father, I do your will." Nomatuck put the bullet into his own bag.

"And find out this. Where is Benjamin Church? And send word to the narrow land, to the shrunken great-woman who befriends Benjamin Church. Tell her that I spit upon her and all of her people Saghonnate." He led Nomatuck back to the shelter and watched the young man unroll a mat where it was driest.

Annawon spoke again: "My nephew, our guard has been too weak."

"Why do you say that?" Johettit turned quickly to address the captain.

This Johettit of Rehoboth and his brother Otan-nick survived every fight, outlived half the men of Pokanocket. There was significance in that.

"There would be a hundred more of us now if we had put more guards at Pocasset. We were too hungry. We grew careless when we saw the berries."

"I wasn't there." Like Englishmen, Johettit always spoke with thought for himself alone, not for the people. "I had gone to the neck village to kill the new horses."

"It is the people of the cleared land we speak of," the great-man of Pokanocket said to Johettit. Indeed, there was no more daybreak people. After the fight near Bridgewater, the great-man of the most eastern place, the low cove Agawam, had knelt. He bared his neck: "I have come a long way with you, great-man, but the journey ends. My son is now too sick for me to move each day on my shoulders. He will be safer in my own swamps at home. I go straightaway, unless you kill me." "Rise," Pometacom said, not even touching his long knife. "There is no more daybreak people. You are Agawam. I am Pokanocket. Go." Then the great-man of the wet cove had knelt and said, "I, too." And then Weetamoo had left, taking her warriors. She started toward Mattapoiset and Pocasset.

"How should we set more guards, my uncle?" Pometacom spoke respectfully to the captain. "There are only twenty of us. Benjamin Church must have ten of ours now. He knows all our movements. Our own warriors will be aiming guns with real bullets in them at us next time we fight. We will not fight the Englishmen again. We will only run from place to place within our lands. Coming here for shellfish and bass. Going into the woods past Cohannet for small game, beyond the forge, where we used to hunt. Picking into what the planters have left on Seekonk plain. That is our life, my uncle. We are rattlesnakes; we bite when they step on us. Guards are not needed for such a life."

"And for winter?"

"For winter?" Pometacom laughed.

There was a silence then, and the sound of pounding as a woman worked at the corn they had taken from Rehoboth's fields. His wife in the square house at Plimouth where the hanged three had sat would soon be unclean. The last traces of himself and the blood of the people left in her would be washed away. Pounding, resting. Pounding, resting. Soon they would be slaves, all of his few remaining warriors, pounding and resting for Englishmen.

"We need guards even on our own land, my nephew." Annawon licked his fingers clean of oysters.

"We could leave here, we could go to Uncas, cousin of the Pequots." Otan-nick spoke little now, being not wise-man nor, lately, letter writer, since there was no further need for letters.

"Uncas would send our heads to Plimouth before sunset." Annawon spoke for the great-man.

"Northward to the Pennacook, then?" The silver piece in Otan-nick's hair had survived hunger, ice and fire. So it was with metal.

"If refuge were possible among the Pennacook, the buzzard-eyed uncle of Nahiganset would have sent us word of his safety from there." Annawon did not mention the name of the uncle of Nahiganset; he and his two hundred men must be dead.

"I say we should go to the great-woman of Saghonnate." Johettit spoke with a clear voice.

"We do not speak her name, knife of Rehoboth! It is as if she were dead."

"The children? Why not send the youngest ones to her?" Otan-nick tried to soften his brother's misstep.

"You two chlidren of Rehoboth can go back to your father."

The brothers were silent then.

The bark of the fox was coming toward them from the cove.

Pometacom answered with a similar sound. Two of their men appeared with another striped bass to show.

Wonderful!

They handed the bass to the women. Oh, it was wonderful to eat again from the sea. Weetamoo had been caught by surprise while eating roasted clams at Mattapoiset. She, too, had grown too hungry to be careful. Eating clams, she had looked up into the holes that shoot the fire from guns. She ran off, pushing a raft into Titicut to save herself, the people. Falling off. Her body had filled itself with water as she drowned. The way Sassamon's had not filled. Weetamoo's hair snagged onto bushes near Hugh Cole's land. The Englishmen sliced off her head. Pometacom had seen the head last time he and his men circled Taunton. The hair hung twisted like black snakes down the pole on Taunton's green: Weetamoo–the married woman, my brother's wife, my wife's sister. The hair on the top of her head was white with the droppings of birds.

The two who had been fishing sat.

"We cannot go to the old queen." Johettit was more careful now at not naming people. But with so many dead, it was hard to know whom he meant.

"What talk is this?" one of the fishermen said as a woman brought him oysters. Few men had their own wives now, few women their own children.

"The old queen of Nahiganset beyond the point, would she hide us?"

"Pah! She went to Plimouth long ago."

"Let us look into something strange, great-man of Squannock." Johettit moved himself to sit closer to Annawon. "My captain, in the planting moon, after we found our people dead at the big falls on Connecticut, I went with Tuspaquin to burn Bridgewater. We had rags. We greased them. I held a burning rag in my head, ready to send it toward a house. The sky was blue. But thunder came and rain came and put the fire out."

"I was not there." Annawon kept on eating.

Pometacom spoke to Johettit. "This thing I know about their god: he wasn't here until they brought him here. He does not live where Kiehtan lives. He does not bring the dead to life in Kiehtan's places. My brother-in-law killed men in the corn-fields near Taunton and they stayed dead. You yourself called out for Lord Jesus to save the Englishmen in the meadow when she who was to be Nomatuck's wife sang to them: but they died and Lord Jesus did not save them. Nor did he reach out of the sky to pick up the yellow-haired man of Swansea you yourself killed at the pig fence, so eager were you for hair!"

"But their god speaks to them without their dancing. He's always with them. Last time, when we went against Bridge-water? During the hilling moon, when it began to get dry? We were outside the garrison before daybreak. But when the light came, there they were, running toward us with their guns loaded. How did the Englishmen know we were standing there?" Johettit had learned to wait his turn, if nothing else.

"They knew because you killed the yellow-haired man who lived near the pig fence. And stole his black man. Because you forgot that the yellow-haired man knows all our words and that he taught them to the black man. Because you did nothing when the black man escaped from us. Because the black man went straight to the Englishmen at Bridgewater and told them we were coming against their town. You forgot that a man should be suspicious when someone who was in camp is gone. And you never should have killed that yellow-haired man. He was my friend."

Hezekiah Willett, whom I may not name.

"But we did him honor, great-man! We gave him pain and we braided his hair with all the beads we had left!"

"His father was a friend of my father. I counted him among the people."

Silence came into the camp. Under the rain and behind it, the sound of the swamp brook grew stronger. The sound of the tide in the bay blew nearer with the wind, or farther. In the shelter Pometacom of the generation that rises and falls leaned against the rock ledge behind him. At the top of his ledge were others leaning into it, and a watchman sitting in a tree, drenched.

"My son, do you sleep?"

"No, my father."

"When you are in Plimouth, find out if the old man of Pakachoog at the start of the Nipmuck river was truly tied to a tree on the green at Boston and shot before the eyes of Englishmen. And was it the one-eyed uncle of Nashoba who caught him and tied him with rope and led him to Boston? Or was it the slant-headed nephew of Nashoba who wished so much to lead the people to his own peace that he bargained with a wise-man? And did the Englishmen let the uncle or the nephew live? Oh, is my friend of Pakachoog, who joined me when I was in Pocasset swamp and gave me hope by going against the town near him, truly dead? And—"

"We had all that from an honest friend. Neither the nephew nor the uncle took him in, yet they both were jerked from the ropes in Boston, afterward." The old captain ceased eating to speak out of turn; sometimes it is proper, even necessary.

Pokanocket was become dried corn, good only to be saved for seed.

Smell of darkness, of the reeds; smell of the cabbages that grew soft and green into the mud; smell of the cool northwest wind that blew the rain: darkness approaching. The great-man had already loaded his gun with a slug. Now he poured a little powder into the pan. There was enough powder for four shots, five.

"My great-man." Johettit raised himself onto his heels by the small fire. "I have been thinking a long time. I have not spoken what I think. Now I do. I ask you this, how can we live in hiding forever? I ask you if it would not be better to grow our hair and wear English trousers." His voice spread out in the dampness, echoing.

"They must hunt us." The great-man who had been born so much later than his older brother moved his fingers around the gun. Would it even fire, in this dampness? "We will erase every track. Like wildcats, we will be hunted. We will know every net. Their snares will not contain us. And we will not thirst."

"Great-man, you have made me one of the cleared land as my father was long ago and you have taught me when to speak and that my voice should be heard in turn. This is my turn to speak. I say we should ask for peace." Johettit kept himself on his heels, calm.

"You want Natick and its bleeding pigs?" The great-man rose in a casual manner, with the gun in his hand. Though he did not raise it to sight, it was pointed at Johettit. Annawon and Otan-nick sat alert.

He cocked the gun. "Kneel down, young man. You speak treason against the people."

Johettit's hand went for his gun.

The great-man fired and blew the slug into the chest of the other. Blood spurted onto the bushes of the shelter as Johettit fell over.

"May his soul wander! May he be barred from the house at the rim of the world!" The great-man whose hair was growing reached for another slug. He jammed it down the shaft of the gun. He did not want to dampen any more of his powder, but he poured a little into the pan.

Otan-nick made a small movement toward his fallen brother, then held himself motionless.

"Women, take him away and burn him. Throw his ashes in water."

The next morning, Otan-nick was gone.

Good, it would not be long before Otan-nick brought the Englishmen.

All day the drizzling rain and then the wind heightened and the trees began to creak. "After the coming of Awanagus–the stranger, the weather was very good for a number of years and then there came a storm that made the trees pliant as flowers, there was significance in that, my sons." Metacomet thought of his wife and son in the jail at Plimouth, in the square house. His sister had died there. My wife, do they whip you? Be brave, it is soon over. You are here beside me, a bride in a new cloak, full of soft feathers. My son Neimpauog, my thunderer, I hear you speak. Do you live, my son? Do you live?

Evening dimmed the woods and still the Englishmen had not come; the great-man's breathing grew quicker. Nothing could hurt him, he had been readying his hands all day. He would sing his song and remain riding southwest across the great plain on his black stallion, the horse he had eaten at the mountain of the Nipmuck. He would be free from bearded men's laws and their intent, he would step out to catch up with his wife and his son at the rim of the world, or to wait for them there.

"My uncle, my captain, do you think their god will give them dry powder in this rain?" He felt happy again, free.

"I do you service, great-man." Annawon said nothing more but rose and went to one of the other shelters. Then to another. Then Annawon went off with a handful of men and a fishing net.

Darkness, and there were still no Englishmen.

"We must have more guards. We must move camp every day." Annawon shook five stones in a bowl.

"I do not leave Montaup in summer; it is my house in

summer." He stared into the darkness, but his voice was not so strong as his uncle's.

Annawon picked up the bowl: four blacks and one white. "Tomorrow we will talk of it, shall we, my nephew?"

It was good that it would be Annawon. "Tomorrow will bring whatever it brings, my uncle. Only Kiehtan can see it."

Under the shelter, the great-man stripped off his wet leggings and sat in his small cloth. He took his almost empty powder horns from his neck. He opened a basket and took out the great belt of the daybreak people. Now that there was only Squannock–the green swamp and Pokanocket–the cleared land, he should give the belt to Annawon.

"I served your father well, my nephew." Annawon's deep voice came from the fire at the open side of the shelter and filled the darkness between them. "Send out the eight scouts now. Tomorrow we will move camp."

"Hey! Scouts!" The great-man sent them off recklessly, too loud. He ran his fingers over the beaded shoulder belt and saw it ripped into a hundred pieces and stuffed into a hundred Englishmen's pockets. See this? It's a piece of the belt of my friend who used to sit at the rum house in the big chair. No, he would not give this belt to Annawon yet; he refolded it.

"If we leave this land, my uncle, they will take Montaup and Kickamuit from us forever. It is the law. It is written on cloth." He undid the headbelt of the two clubs, the union of the cleared land and the lake. This he would give to Tuspaquin when next they met in the wandering track they shared. It might be under the apple trees of Pocasset or by the clam flats on Mattapoiset. Last, he unfolded the chest belt of Pokanocket and pressed its cool white star to his eyes, against his forehead. His oldest brother, the one who had died in the first sickness and whom he had never known, that brother had seen the star. That brother should have led the people. He refolded the headbelt with the soft side out and laid it over the others for a pillow. He wrapped the purple blanket around himself. *Pur-ple.*

Pis-tol. He placed the loaded gun with the powder already in the pan carefully beside him. The powder must not tilt out of the pan. He laid a bit of deer hide over the powder to keep it as dry as possible. If he died here, then the people would not have abandoned the land. The Englishmen could not take it. Metacomet stretched himself out. The eight scouts returned, with no reports.

He could give the shoulder belt to Annawon and let the people go, free of him. They could run to Benjamin Church. Or he who was never born to lead them and who was now contagion to them could go away from them. Creep out by darkness, while they slept. Crawl north to Frenchmen, so cold. Swim into the bay and find himself an island, even a friend.

No, he was the people. His head lay upon the five-pointed star. So long as he lived, Pokanocket lived. And when he died, it must be on this land. It would not be long from now. Metacomet rested his hand upon the gun. He would need it, to shoot at the great dog that stood by the door to the grandmother's lodge in the southwest. I did not kill too many deer. I killed as a warrior does, grandmother. I did not grow my hair during war; I did not live as a boy for Plimouth. It is well with me, grandmother. After the food, he would wake and climb the smooth, worn ladder up the cliff. There he would see the face of Kiehtan, who would take him into his own house, opening the door, holding it wide. He would laugh and play and run and leap; he would be Tasomacon, whole and free.

Run fast, my warriors, for the Englishmen will be upon us. This time the fox Wakwah does not bring you out by night, by water. His touch on the gun lessened; his breathing deepened. He was walking on a path and he heard a boy's voice call him from behind, but he did not turn around, it is not proper. He kept his face and his feet forward but he did call out behind him. He called: Neimpauog, my son, do you still live? Send your dreamer to look for me and I shall send mine to look for you. Do not be afraid. A great dog waits at the door. Only follow, follow me. I will show you how. I will show you everything.

Bullets thumping through the boughs overhead. He grabbed up his powder horns and his gun and plunged downhill through the pre-dawn dimness into the swamp. His bare feet oozed into the mud, faster; he forced his thighs to rise higher than they could and to move still faster. In the drizzle ahead, he saw two men standing near trees with guns pointed at him. One an Englishman, one not. He ran to the left, to the right. Movement ahead and the Englishman fired but there was only the outside flash. No roar of bullet.

He ran to the left again. A dull glint of something silver on the shaved head of the second man and he heard the roar of a bullet coming out of a barrel. But how strong he was! He did not die. How his chest collided with the bullet, how large he was, a bear, indestructible, a wildcat; again roar, again collision; how much larger . . . He fell into the muddy water and reared back, his neck stiffening.

"*Iootash! Iootash!*" A deep voice faded behind him. He could not move his head, so he flexed the fingers of his good hand, as much as they would go, toward the southwest. His left hand was caught under him, holding the gun. His chin was slipping into the mud. He did not hear the three huzzahs, nor feel himself dragged by the feet out of the water to the upland. Nor did he perceive the speech of the executioner, nor feel the axe that severed his head from his neck and split him roughly into four quarters. The breezes of Montaup blew against the four quarters hung on four trees; they were mild breezes during the corn moon when Naonanto's cousin was shot at Aquidneck and Muttuamp at Boston; they were cooler during the harvest moon when Tuspaquin and Annawon were shot at Plimouth; they were cold during the frost moon when Neimpauog and his mother were led aboard a slave ship. The skies of Plimouth would brighten and darken for a whole generation over the pole that held his head, and only when a black-hatted English preacher touched the dried bone of his jaw and pulled it off did he begin to sing.

14

"This indenture made the 14th day of September, One Thousand Six Hundred and Eighty . . . between Josiah Winslow of the Colony of New Plimouth and four merchants of Boston in consideration of the sum of eleven hundred pounds. All that tract of land situate within the Colony of New Plimouth commonly called and known by the name of Mount Hope Neck and Poppasquash Neck, with all the islands lying near, excepting only the lands formerly granted to the inhabitants of Swansea, at the northern end or entrance of the neck, providing the covenanters will, within the space of twelve months next, cause good and sufficient highways to be laid out from all the adjacent towns onto the said Mount Hope Neck. And further that when there shall be settled upon the neck the full number of sixty families that then it shall be a county and there shall be liberty granted unto them to keep a county court on the said neck. And all actions arising within the same to be tried there and that the town that shall be built on the said neck shall be the county or shire town . . . signed, sealed and delivered on the 29th day of September, 1680, at the General Court, Plimouth."

A Note on Sources

The best modern account of the Wampanoag war is Douglas Leach's *Flintlock and Tomahawk* (Norton, 1966). The war from Rehoboth's point of view is well represented in Richard Le Baron Bowen's *Early Rehoboth* (1946).

Among the most important contemporary sources are: John Easton's *A Relacion of the Indyan Warre* (1675), which appears in Charles Lincoln's *Narratives of the Indian Wars* (1913); William Hubbard's *A Narrative of the Troubles with the Indians in New-England* (1677), reprinted by Samuel Drake as *The History of the Indian Wars* (1864; rprt. ed., Franklin, 1971); Increase Mather's *A Relation of the Troubles Which have Hapned in New-England* (1677), reprinted by Samuel Drake in *Early History of New England* (1864); Mary Rowlandson's *Narrative of the Captivity of Mrs. Mary Rowlandson* (1682), reprinted in John C. Miller's *The Colonial Image* (Braziller, 1962); Benjamin Church's memoirs, as told in his son Thomas Church's *Entertaining Passages Relating to Philip's War* (1716), edited by Alan and Mary Simpson as *Diary of King Philip's War by Colonel Benjamin Church* (Pequot, 1975); *The Records of the Colony of New Plymouth in New England,* edited by Nathaniel B. Shurtleff and David Pulsifer, (1855–61; rprt. ed., AMS, 1968).

Invaluable earlier works include: *Mourt's Relation* (1622), reprinted as *A Journal of the Pilgrims at Plymouth,* edited by Dwight B. Heath (Corinth, 1963); William Wood's *New England's Prospect* (1634), reprinted in facsimile by Da Capo (1968); Daniel Gookin's *An Historical Account of the Doings and Sufferings of the Christian Indians of New England* (1638), *Archaeologia Americana: Transactions and Collections of the American Antiquarian Society,* Vol. 2 (1836), reprinted separately by Arno Press (1972); William Bradford's *Of Plymouth Plantation: 1620–1647,* edited by Samuel Eliot Morison (Knopf, 1952).

For names, see John C. Huden's *Indian Place Names of New England* (Museum of the American Indian, Heye Foundation, 1962).